Joker's Queen

Hunter Creek Archangel's Warriors MC Bk 10

Ciara St James

Copyright

Copyright 2023 Property of Ciara St James LLC. All rights reserved as this is the property of Ciara St James LLC. The characters and events portrayed in this book are fictitious. Any similarity to real persons, living or dead, is coincidental and not intended by the author.

No part of this book may be reproduced, or stored in a retrieval system, or transmitted in any form or by any means, electronic, mechanical, Photocopying, recording, or otherwise, without express written permission of the publisher, Ciara St James LLC. In addition, no part of this book may be used to create, feed, or refine artificial intelligence models, for any purpose without written permission of the author.

ISBN: 978-1-955751-53-7

Printed in the United States of America
Editing by Mary Kern @ Ms. K Edits
Book cover by Tracie Douglas @ Dark Waters Covers

Blurb

Joker is the life of his club. They don't know that his laughter and jokes hide the pain of never being able to have the woman he thinks could've been his. The woman who walked away years ago without a backward glance. So imagine his shock when he comes face-to-face with that woman again in his clubhouse.

Raina's life hasn't been without pain and sorrow. However, she's back in Hunters Creek because of family. And she's here facing Joker, although she knew she should stay away, because she has a warning for him, and his club. Once she delivers it, she won't have to see Joker again, and be reminded of her heartache.

Her warning is about a common enemy. In revealing it, she reveals so much more to Joker. Part of that revelation is the fact she didn't abandon him, and that she's a free woman now. One he can claim, if that's still his wish. He jumps at the opportunity to claim her, and her daughter, Belle.

As these two admit their love ten years or more in the making, Joker works to bring their past to a close, to eliminate the threat. Only, they have no idea there's another threat out there. One that reveals a whole twisted plot, and history that began for the Warriors over fifteen years ago. Along with more enemies, new friends are made, and there's no denying the claim to Joker's Queen.

Warning

This book is intended for adult readers. It contains foul language, adult situations, discusses events such as stalkers, assault, torture and murder that may trigger some readers. Sexual situations are graphic. There is no cheating, no cliffhangers and it has a HEA.

Dedication

This book is dedicated to my daughter, Kat. Your dad and I are so proud of the woman you've become and how you pursued your dream. Your time as a dispatcher and now as a police officer are wonderful things. Thank you for the stories from your dispatch days which I shamelessly used in this book. I couldn't help it and you were kind enough to let me. Love you!

Hunters Creek Members/ Old Ladies

Nicholas Williams (Bull) President w/ Jocelyn
Jenson Davis (Tank) Vice President w/ Brynlee
Wilder Breslin (Payne) Enforcer w/ Jayla
Kellan Knight (Ajax) w/ Jessica
Brooks O'Connor (Player) Secretary w/ TBD
Donovan Wood (Bear) Treasurer/Chaplain w/ Ilara
Luca Moretti (Demon) w/ Zara
Kai Blakely (Slash) w/ TBD
Aaron Fairbanks (Joker) w/ Raina
Ronan Alexander (Rebel) Road Captain w/ Madisen
Bryson Snyder (Ace) w/ Devyn
Slone Taylor (Maverick) w/ Rylan
Damian Cavallo (Outlaw) w/ Tarin
Jake Newman (Iceman) w/ TBD
Tate Da Silva (Renegade) w/ TBD
Alex Lane (Loki) w/ TBD
Bryce Kincaid (Vex) w/ TBD

Reading Order

For Dublin Falls Archangel's Warriors MC (DFAW), Hunters Creek Archangel's Warriors MC (HCAW), Iron Punishers MC (IPMC), Dark Patriots (DP), & Pagan Souls of Cherokee MC (PSCMC)

Terror's Temptress DFAW 1
Savage's Princess DFAW 2
Steel & Hammer's Hellcat DFAW 3
Menace's Siren DFAW 4
Ranger's Enchantress DFAW 5
Ghost's Beauty DFAW 6
Viper's Vixen DFAW 7
Devil Dog's Precious DFAW 8
Blaze's Spitfire DFAW 9
Smoke's Tigress DFAW 10
Hawk's Huntress DFAW 11
Bull's Duchess HCAW 1
Storm's Flame DFAW 12
Rebel's Firecracker HCAW 2
Ajax's Nymph HCAW 3
Razor's Wildcat DFAW 13
Capone's Wild Thing DFAW 14
Falcon's She Devil DFAW 15
Demon's Hellion HCAW 4
Torch's Tornado DFAW 16
Voodoo's Sorceress DFAW 17

Reaper's Banshee IPMC 1
Bear's Beloved HCAW 5
Outlaw's Jewel HVAW 6
Undertaker's Resurrection DP 1
Agony's Medicine Woman PSCMC 1
Ink's Whirlwind IP 2
Payne's Goddess HCAW 7
Maverick's Kitten HCAW 8
Tiger & Thorn's Tempest DFAW 18
Dare's Doll PSC 2
Maniac's Imp IP 3
Tank's Treasure HCAW 9
Blade's Boo DFAW 19
Law's Valkyrie DFAW 20
Gabriel's Retaliation DP 2
Knight's Bright Eyes PSC 3
Joker's Queen HCAW 10

For Ares Infidels MC

Sin's Enticement AIMC 1
Executioner's Enthrallment AIMC 2
Pitbull's Enslavement AIMC 3
Omen's Entrapment AIMC 4
Cuffs' Enchainment AIMC 5
Rampage's Enchantment AIMC 6
Wrecker's Ensnarement AIMC 7
Trident's Enjoyment AIMC 8
Fang's Enlightenment AIMC 9
Talon's Enamorment AIMC 10
Ares Infidels in NY AIMC 11
Phantom's Emblazonment AIMC 12
Saint's Enrapturement AIMC 13

For O'Sheerans Mafia

Darragh's Dilemma
Cian's Complication

Please follow Ciara on Facebook, For information on new releases & to catch up with Ciara, go to www.ciara-st-james.com or www.facebook.com/ciara.stjames.1 or www.facebook.com/groups/tenilloguardians or https://www.facebook.com/groups/1112302942958940

Joker: Chapter 1

My road name was Joker, so you'd expect me to be the one cracking the jokes, but no, instead I was on the receiving end of one. The joke was the fact that my club, my MC club, had made me the manager of our spa, Angel's Glamour. What the hell? Had they all been drunk or on acid when they did that? And was I unknowingly under the influence of a mind-altering substance when I agreed? The answer had to be hell yes to both questions, because that was the only way to explain this insanity I was living. And I didn't find it funny. Plus, who ever heard of a biker club owning and running a spa? Again, I was convinced that we'd all been tripping when we bought it.

Sure, I was lucky that my brother Maverick's old lady, Rylan, dealt with the day-to-day running of the spa, thank God. If I had to deal with scheduling, cancellations, squabbling employees, and angry customers all day, every day, I'd be in prison for murder. And prison clothes wouldn't be my best look or color. Nor would I make a good boyfriend for my cellmate, Nasty Boo Boo. I was one hundred and fifty percent heterosexual, so no cock for me, thank you very much. I was all about pussy.

At the time we discussed buying the spa, we all thought it would be a good way to diversify our businesses. It did that. The spa we bought had been doing a great deal of business. It had only increased since we took over, which made us happy on the money end. I just couldn't help but think that someone else would be better at managing it.

The main reason I thought I was the wrong person was because I couldn't sympathize with the customers. I thought it was ridiculous to lose your ever-loving mind over the fact you forgot to schedule a massage after your facial, or that we were booked and couldn't get you in until next week. Watching full grown women yell and burst into tears over that shit made me glad I was single. If they were an example of the available women in my world, forget it.

Of course, I knew it wasn't true. Look at the women my brothers had claimed. They were all wonderful, loving, strong women. They matched my brothers perfectly. Dare I say they were all soulmates. The problem with that was, they set the damn bar really high for us single guys, who wanted to have an old lady and family, if we were so fortunate.

Did I want that? If the perfect woman came along, yes, but my perfect woman was one who was independent, had her own mind, but willing to bend and compromise. She would have to be strong, and know that at times, I wouldn't always be there to do things, and she'd have to cope. If I was away on club business for any length of time, which happened upon occasion, she'd have to keep everything at home going, which, if we had kids, meant taking care of them, and anything that went wrong.

Sure, she'd have help if she needed it, from my club brothers and their old ladies, who would remain there too, but I wanted her not to have to depend on them. I would be fine if she had a job outside the home. After all, she had a right to fulfill her ambitions. As long as her job didn't take her away from her family all the time. I'd seen what having a wife who was a doctor did to Demon at first. Zara was always being called away to the hospital. However, that was now a thing of the past. When the clinic opened and she took over running it, she got a nine-to-five job, with only a rare emergency call. They were much happier now.

The reason I didn't want a woman with a job like that wasn't because I wanted her to be a wife, mother, employee, and homemaker while I sat on my ass and did nothing. I'd do my share too. It was because I didn't want to be an observer in my family. My mama hadn't raised me that way. If I ever acted like everything had to be done by my wife, she'd come whoop my ass even if I was thirty-four years old and stood a foot taller than her. No one messed with Abbie Fairbanks. She'd lay your ass out or chew you a new one. Shit, now that I thought about it, I was living up to the old adage. Guys wanted to marry a woman like their mothers. Dear God, maybe I should just hide and never leave the house.

Don't get me wrong, I love my mama dearly. She is a loving woman, and you can always count on her, but she can be a bit intense. When I was a kid, my dad somehow knew how to handle her. She'd go on a tirade about something, and he'd just smile, say something softly to her, and she'd settle down for him. That wasn't the case for the rest of us. And although her personality could be exasperating at times, she was independent, knew her own mind, but was willing to listen. She was strong and could take care of anything and everything if my dad wasn't there. See, she was a lot like my dream woman. I'd go to my death bed with that secret. If I told the guys this, they'd never let me hear the end of it.

You'd think in all the years I'd been on this earth, I might have met at least one woman who fit the bill. Well, you'd be half right. Sure, there had been a few who had some of those qualities. Unfortunately, they didn't have them all, or they were already taken by my brothers. The one woman I thought might have those qualities or grow to have them was the one I could never have. It had been a long time since I thought of her. However, thinking of her did me no good. I met her years ago, and she belonged to another. I would never be a man who took a woman away from her husband. She was long gone, and better forgotten.

A squeal of laughter got my attention. I glanced up from the beer I was enjoying in the common room of our clubhouse. It was eight o'clock at night on a Thursday. Not one of our standard party nights. The women and kids were here. I couldn't help but smile. The squealer had been Hope.

She looked so happy and healthy. It was hard to believe that almost two years ago, she had been diagnosed with leukemia. Bear and Ilara didn't know if she'd live. Fast forward to now, and she was in remission, and everything looked good that she'd stay this way. Of course, she would be monitored closely until the five-year mark after remission. That was when doctors would consider her actually cured. We were lucky she had great oncology doctors, and we had our own personal doctor in Zara. She kept a very close eye on Hope. All of us prayed for her to be cured, and for this nightmare to be behind all of them, and us.

She was three-and-a-half now. Her twin brothers, Ryker and River, were a little over a year old. The happiness I saw on Bear's face every time he looked at his kids, grandkid, and his wife made me feel a bit jealous. Just like I felt with the others. Bear had always wanted kids and a wife, but he thought he was sterile due to an evil bitch in his past. He got the shock of his life when he hooked up with Ilara.

Bear thought he found his family, which he had, only he got even more than he bargained for. He discovered he had an adult daughter, Tarin, who he didn't know about and then Ilara got pregnant with the boys. Now he had four kids ranging from twenty-seven to one-year-old. Add to it he had a granddaughter, Melody, who was only two months younger than his sons. We loved to tease him that he was a cradle robber. All he did was grin and nod when we said it.

Hope was laughing because Payne and Jayla's baby boy, Storm, who had been born three months ago, had gripped her finger in his tiny fist. Even though she had brothers at home, she loved all the babies, and wanted to hold and mother them. Well, she'd get even more here soon. Next month, Maverick and Rylan would be welcoming their second baby, another girl. Mav was pumped that this time he got to be here with Rylan for the pregnancy. With Amiah, he hadn't known about her until she was a year old. A misunderstanding and horrible situation was to blame for that mess.

Thankfully, Rylan came back to Hunters Creek and they reconnected.

In addition to their baby, two months after they were due, Tank and his wife, Brynlee, would be having a baby boy. He would join his seven-year-old brother, Easton. With those two added, that would bring our count up to fifteen kids. Sounded like a lot until you compared it to our Dublin Falls chapter. They had just over forty kids there. We told them to figure out what birth control was, and to start their own school.

Speaking of kids, we'd decided in church last week that it was time to start looking for a minibus, to haul them around as they got older. Dublin Falls had one and they swore by it. Jesus, to think, a bunch of tough bikers, who could and would kill if they had to, were worried about a minibus. It went along with the spa and let's not forget the bakery. We were your modern-day MC. Some might think we were weak, but they'd find out the hard way they were wrong, if they tested us. Loving our families didn't make us weak. It made us stronger and more determined. Even if I didn't have a wife and kids, I'd die to protect the ones we had here, and at our sister chapters, and even our friends' clubs. Nothing was more important than family.

I watched Hope give Storm a kiss on his little head, then she turned around and spotted me. Her smile got bigger as she ran toward me. I set down my bottle and opened my arms just in time to catch her, as she jumped literally up in the air and forward. I hugged her tight and growled, as I attacked her neck with my mouth, rubbing my short beard against her skin. She shrieked and laughed. She loved it when any of us did that. She said it tickled.

"Hey there Baby Cakes, what's shaking?"

"Just my bottom, Uncle Joker. What's shaking on you?" she said with a grin as she shook her butt.

"Just my heart from loving you."

This was our standard greeting. It started not long after she started talking. I asked her that question one day, and Bear had told her what to say. I'd come back with the heart comment, and she loved it. Since then, it was the way she greeted me. I secretly loved it.

"Uncle Joker, when I grow up, you'll be my husband, won't you?" she asked out of the blue.

I gave her a stunned look. This was a first. How did you tell her that the thirty-one-year age difference might be a bit much? Besides the fact her daddy would kill me. A realistic bear-like growl came from behind me. I swear I felt a hot breath on my neck, and the hairs stood up. My skin burned on my back as if it had been raked by claws.

"You're not marrying anyone, especially Uncle Joker. He's too old for you, plus you're gonna stay with Mama and me forever," Bear told her gruffly.

I glanced over my shoulder to meet his intense stare. "Hey, don't look at me like that. She said it. However, she does have excellent taste in men," I said back with a wink.

"Besides, by the time you're old enough to get married, Uncle Joker will be dead. I think he'll meet a bear in the woods and be eaten," he said back just as quickly. His meaning didn't escape her keen mind, even if she was only three.

"Daddy, you can't eat Uncle Joker. I'm telling Mama you're being mean again. She'll put you in a time out, and spank your bottom," she said indignantly, before she jumped out of my arms to go find her mama.

"God, I hope to hell she spanks my ass," he muttered.

"Shut up. I don't need to know what goes on in your bedroom with Ilara. Although, I never knew she was the Dom, and you the sub. Good to know," I said with a smirk.

"Shut up, asshole, and don't give my daughter any ideas. She's never marrying. Find yourself a woman before you're too old to please her, and Hope is old enough to think you and her are walking down the aisle," he told me as he gave me the middle finger.

"Man, if I could find the right one, I would, but it seems the good ones are taken by assholes like you and these other guys, as well as the guys over in Dublin Falls. Shit, now that I think of it, all our friends too! Where the hell are they hiding? Maybe if someone rounded them all up and we had one of those old-fashioned balls, like they did for debutantes, then we could meet them, and see if any are my match," I said, not really meaning it. I just liked to joke around.

He had a contemplative look on his face. Oh no, I should've kept my big mouth shut. "Bear, I was joking. Don't go getting any ideas," I warned him.

"I think it's a great idea. Not sure there's one out there who could stand you, but there are other brothers, and even friends who want to meet someone. They can deny it if they want to, but I know it's true. With the right woman, your life is a thousand times better."

"I know you're all crazy in love with Ilara and your family. That's great, and I'm happy as shit for you and the others who've found that, but not all of us are fated to find that. Some of us are better off single. Think of it this way. If I settled down, there would be so many women disappointed and crying. They do love themselves a piece of Joker," I said with a grin.

"I see things haven't changed in all these years. You're still full of yourself, aren't you, Aaron? Oops, I mean Joker," said a soft, sultry female voice behind me. I stiffened. It couldn't be. She was long gone. Slowly turning around, trying not to appear shocked, excited, or disappointed when I found out it wasn't her, I looked behind me.

Standing there, like something out of my memories or a dream, stood Raina. The woman I'd thought about way too many times over the years. The woman I'd had so many inappropriate thoughts and dreams about. The woman who I had no right to even think about as a friend. Let alone anything else. The woman who'd left Hunters Creek, and never looked back or called.

Obviously, she'd gotten older, although I didn't see any lines on her face. She was still the tiny sexy dynamo I remembered, much to my regret. Why?

Because my body was reacting to her, and that was a no-no. She was almost a foot shorter than my six foot two. Her body had filled out more, but it looked amazing on her. She had those wider hips and ample breasts I found attractive as hell.

She was a gorgeous woman. I quickly calculated that she would be around twenty-eight now. Ten years ago, that age difference had seemed bigger. Her hair was shorter than I remembered, although still long. It ended just below her shoulder blades. It was still that dark chocolate brown color with golden highlights in it. It was in a cascade of waves around her face. Her green eyes stood out on her lightly tanned face.

I shook off the trip down memory lane, found my voice and answered her. "Raina, what the hell are you doing here?" Not my finest comeback, but my brain was scrambling to believe she was here, and not a figment of my overactive imagination.

"Good to see you too, Joker. I hope I'm not interrupting your bragging session too much, but I need to talk to you. That guy, Gavin, over there, let me in and said you were in here," she said calmly, as she pointed to one of our prospects. He was watching us, or I should say Raina, avidly. Even from this distance, I saw the interest on his face.

He could just forget that. Raina wasn't for the likes of him. Besides, she was off limits anyway, and older than him. He was only twenty-two. He, and our other new prospect, Walker, had been with us only three months. They came aboard not long before we voted in Kian and Riggs, or Predator and Stalker, as they were known now, as members. He should know better than to let someone in the compound without clearing it with one of us. I'd have to educate him later.

"You're not interrupting any such thing. Bear and I were messing around. What brings you here? The last I heard, you left town ten years ago, and no one seemed to know where you went. Decided to come back and visit old friends?" I hoped the anger I was feeling didn't come through in my tone.

"Do you really want to revisit why I felt I had to leave? And do you want to stand here and subtly snipe at me for doing it? I don't have time for this, nor do I care to do it. I came to give you a warning, not because I wanted to see you or this club."

"It's good to see you again, Raina. It's been too long. How're you and Belle doing?" Bear asked her kindly, with a smile on his face. When he looked at me, his eyes were giving me a warning. It said, *shut the fuck up and find out why she is here.*

Her presence had gotten the attention of the other members. The ones who'd been here back then, which were more than half of us, would recognize her. The newer members, and their old ladies, wouldn't. As she stood there glaring at me, I saw Bull making his way over with Demon and Tank not far behind.

"Hello Bear, you're looking good. Belle and I are doing fine. Joker, can we go somewhere quiet, so I can tell you what I came to say? It won't take long, then I'll get out of your hair. I know you must be busy."

Bull, Demon, and Tank arrived just as she

finished. She nodded at them.

"Hello Raina, it's been a long time, sweetheart. I'm glad to see you. What brings you here to Hunters Creek? Are you home to see your granddaddy?" Bull asked her with a smile. Tank and Demon didn't say anything, but they did nod at her. They looked concerned.

"Hello, Bull, Tank, Demon, yeah, you could say it's something like that. Listen, I just need a few minutes of Joker's time, then I'll leave. It's important, and he needs to know it."

"Why don't we go into church? It's quieter in there and we can hear ourselves think," Bull suggested.

"Church? I thought no one but members were allowed in there?" she said, looking nervous. I guess she did remember some things from the past.

"True, but we do make exceptions. It's clear that you have something important to say. Or is it personal, only for Joker's ears?" Demon asked.

"It's not just for Joker's ears, no. Fine, if you want to hear it, then let's go. I need to get home soon," she said quickly.

"Right this way," Bear said, as he pointed toward the hallway which led to church. Bull and the others took the lead. I brought up the rear, with her right in front of me.

I'd like to say I ignored her, but I couldn't. Not only was I lost in memories, I was drowning in her. Her perfume and sexy appearance were teasing me. As she walked ahead of me, I could see her ass. It was plumper than I remembered, and it made me want to reach out and touch it. To see if it was as tight as it looked. Her ass was one an ass man like me could get lost in for hours. Caressing it, licking it, kissing it, biting it, and spanking it all came to mind as my cock tried to stiffen more. *Down boy, she's not for you*, I reminded him, but the stubborn fucker wouldn't listen. I only hoped no one else noticed it.

Entering church, the light came on automatically. We had it on one of those switches. Bull had complained that we left the light on one time too many times, so the next day, he changed it out. Bull went to the head of the table, as he should. Tank sat down on his left, as a VP should. Bear took his seat. Bull pointed to the chair, which would normally be Payne's on his right, and indicated Raina should take it. Demon was down the table on the left. I took my seat across from him. We all looked expectantly at her.

I was watching her so closely, I saw the slight shudder that went through her body and the nervous way she swallowed. What the hell was going on? Why was she in Hunters Creek and, more importantly, what would bring her to our clubhouse? Raina had wanted nothing to do with any of us ten years ago when she left. "Okay, we're here and listening. Tell us what was so important to get you to come here, sweetheart. If I recall correctly, you said you'd never come here again," Bull reminded her. He did it in a nice way, without any animosity in his voice.

Raina closed her eyes for a moment and sighed. A slight blush spread across her cheeks. When she opened her eyes, she met Bull's. I noticed even though I was right beside her, she was avoiding looking at me. I wasn't gonna have that. Bull might be the president of the club, but she specifically came to talk to me. To do that, she needed to face me. I reached over and took her hand. She swung her head around to look at me. I saw the surprise and something else in her eyes. She tugged on it, but I didn't let go. A tremor ran through her.

"You came to talk to me. Talk. What was so urgent you came here of all places, Raina? And when did you get into town? I thought you never came here anymore." I couldn't help but throw that in there. I was dying to know why she was here, and how long she expected to stay. Not that it should matter. She was off limits, I kept telling myself.

"I came because I thought it was only fair that I warn you and your club. It's the right thing to do."

"Warn us about what?" I asked. *What the hell could she know that would require her to feel like she had to warn us?*

"I need to explain something first for it to make sense. Over the past ten years, despite the fact he's in prison, I've remained in touch with Parker. I felt it was only right that he knew what was happening with Belle, since she's his daughter. Anyway, I only bring that up, so you understand how I know what I'm about to tell you."

I didn't know why she thought we needed her to say that. Of course, she would be in contact with Parker. He was her husband, and the father of her daughter. They had to be waiting anxiously for him to get out of prison. Thinking about it, he should be eligible for a parole hearing soon. His original sentence was for fifteen years and he had served two-thirds of it. Most of the time, the system would release you after you served that much time, as long as you behaved while you were in there. I was pulled from those thoughts by her next words.

"Parker is due to have a parole hearing in a month. He's hoping to get out," she paused.

"Honey, that's good. I hope when he does, the three of you get your lives back on track. Although, why would we need to be warned of it? Parker isn't a part of this club anymore. He was kicked out and not patched in, before he ever landed himself in the predicament that put him in prison," Bear reminded her.

"I know that. You don't need to remind me of that fact. It's burned in my brain forever. I'm telling you this, because when I got his letter explaining he was up for the hearing, he told me something else. Apparently, he blames the club and, even more specifically, you, Joker, for him going to prison. He's vowed that you'll pay for it when he gets out," she said in a rush.

When she stopped talking, we all looked at each other, stunned. What the fuck? What she said made no sense. We didn't do anything to get him sent to prison. That was all on him. And how was it our fault he got kicked out of the club when he was prospecting?

"Raina, that doesn't make a bit of sense. How are we responsible, and especially Joker? Yes, we did kick him out of the club, but he deserved it. Parker didn't follow the rules and he refused to change. He was deliberately defiant. We won't tolerate that from anyone, not even someone who was a member's blood family. As for why he went to prison, we had nothing to do with that. He did that all on his own," Bull said gruffly.

"I know and I agree. Parker's woes and mistakes were all his. He has no one to blame for what happened to him other than himself. However, he doesn't see it that way. He told me that if Joker had used his influence with the club, he wouldn't have been kicked out. He thinks other members and even Joker were threatened by his ideas and willingness to do whatever it took to make money for the club. He said Joker was the one to convince you guys to kick him out and not give him a patch."

"That's bullshit! Joker tried to help him. We all did. He wouldn't listen. Every one of us voted to oust him and it wasn't brought to the table by Joker. I was the one who did it," Demon told her.

She nodded her head. "I understand, I do. Please, let me finish. These are his words, not mine. Anyway, he said that if you hadn't kicked him out, he wouldn't have had to find other ways to support his family. He believes his turning to stealing was all your fault. His minor busts to his last one of aggravated armed robbery were all your fault. He truly believes that if you had let him patch in, that he wouldn't have ended up in prison. Because of that, he said when he gets out, he's gonna make you all pay."

Her expression was anxious when she said that

last part. I saw her face was almost white. Her fingers in mine had tightened in my hand. I rubbed my thumb over the back of her hand, hoping she would find it soothing. Her body was practically vibrating with her tension.

"Jesus Christ, is he insane?! Raina, I swear to God, the club had nothing to do with him turning to crime. We tried to warn him and even offered him help, after he was out of the club, and after that first time he got caught stealing. He refused. He's not thinking clearly. Surely, as his wife, you can make him understand that. If he gets out, he should concentrate on resuming a life with you and Belle, not getting revenge for something that never happened," Bull told her incredulously.

She looked up from the table where she had been staring for the past few seconds. "Bull, I'm not able to tell him anything. He's angry with me, too. I was shocked when he told me what he did. His letters are rarely fun to read, but I have to do it for Belle."

"Why would he be angry with you? You did nothing wrong. You're his damn wife. He should be sending nothing but love to you and Belle," Tank protested.

She burst out laughing, only it wasn't a humorous laugh. It was mocking. "He hates me almost as much as he hates you guys. In his mind, I betrayed him, too. If it wasn't for Belle, I'd never accept a letter or send him one again. I only wanted her to have some small piece of him that wasn't awful, if it existed, which it doesn't. It's been years since I read anything to her or even opened them. The only reason I read this one was in the hopes it might be nice for a change."

"What the hell does he think you did to betray him?" Demon asked. I wanted to know the same thing.

"Once he went to prison, I divorced him. That's why I left Hunters Creek. I knew staying here would be hard on Belle. She didn't need to grow up as the daughter of a thief. I only wish I'd divorced him sooner. I held off and it was a mistake."

Her revelation that she had wanted to divorce Parker before he ever went to prison and that she did after he went, stunned the hell out of me. My eyes went to her left hand, which I now noticed was bare. Sonofabitch, she wasn't married. I didn't know if she had a boyfriend, it was likely, but the knowledge that she was likely single brought my old, hidden feelings raging to the surface. All those forbidden feelings about her hit me like a truck.

That's when I realized that I still wanted her, my cousin's wife. I mean his ex-wife. *And there is nothing to stop you from pursuing her like you wanted all those years ago*, a little voice in the back of my mind said. I tried to block it out, but the next unbidden thought popped up. The only thing that stopped me then was knowing she was his wife. As long as she wasn't remarried, I had a second chance. The question was, would I take it?

Raina: Chapter 2

I couldn't believe that I was once again sitting in the Warriors' clubhouse. Or that I was in their sacred church. Never in a thousand years did I think either of those things would happen. Entering the compound this evening, it had looked familiar, yet very different from what I remembered. Looking at the guys who had been here ten years ago, I had dim memories of them. The only memories that weren't dim, that were in fact crystal clear, were the ones I had of Joker.

He was still exactly like I remembered him. Yeah, he'd gotten a bit older, and had a few lines on his face that he didn't have back then, but other than that, he was the same. A tall, brawny man who I'd secretly always found fascinating and, dare I say, attractive. Of course, when I met him, I was already married and pregnant with Belle.

Parker and I were both too young to be married and to be having a kid, but we had messed up. A broken condom one night had made sure of that. I had no business having sex at sixteen, but all the other girls were, and I thought I was in love. At the time, Parker seemed so mature at eighteen, compared to my sixteen. He talked like he was worldly and had his whole future mapped out. I fell for it hook, line, and sinker. By the time I started to realize I was wrong, and he wasn't the guy I thought he was, and that I had mistaken lust for love, it was too late. I was pregnant at sixteen and married at my parents' insistence.

You'd think in this day and age that would be a thing of the past. Nope, not with my parents. They had been extremely old-fashioned and were embarrassed that their teenage daughter had sex outside of marriage. In their minds, the only way to fix that was to have us marry. I met Joker for the first time at a family dinner at my in-laws' house, a few months after we got married. I was six months pregnant and feeling it. Imagine my surprise when Joker walked through the door.

He was smiling and joking with one of his other cousins. His height caught my attention first. He was a few inches over six feet tall, which was a good ten inches more than my five feet two. He had those wide shoulders that were full of muscle which gave him what I called a brawny look. His lower arms were tattooed. He was wearing a leather vest with a logo and writing on it. Later, I found out it was a cut and he belonged to the local MC, the Archangel's Warriors.

It was more than his height and build that caught my attention that day. It was his personality and looks, too. He was fun and loving with his family. He made everyone smile and appear happier. He lifted my depressed mood, even when he wasn't talking to me. Add to all that personality, the bonus, which was his looks. He wasn't what some might call classically handsome, but he was handsome to me.

His medium brown hair was kept cut shorter,

although not in a buzz cut. It was the opposite of Parker's buzzed look. He had a nicely trimmed mustache and beard the same color as his hair. His eyes were a dark brown. His face was kissed by the sun. I had found him captivating. He appeared several years older than me and Parker. I later found out he was six years older than me.

When Parker brought him over to be introduced to me, I was tongue-tied. He smiled and welcomed me to the family. I mumbled something back, I don't recall what it was. For the rest of the day, he made sure to talk to me and include me in discussions. He asked for my opinions and didn't belittle them. It was a breath of fresh air. Parker by then had started to tell me I was stupid. He never did it in front of people, but I heard enough of it in private. From then on out, any time I had an opportunity to be around Joker, I took it.

Which was why I was thrilled when Parker came home one day, soon after I had Belle, to say he was going to join the Warriors. He explained that he would have to prospect for a while. Joker had agreed to sponsor him. Parker was confident that he wouldn't have to wait a year to get patched in. He boasted to me that he'd be in within six months, and to give him a few years and he'd be running it. I thought he was full of crap, but I didn't tell him that.

At first, things were better. Even as a prospect, he did earn money. Not as much as the members did, but he made enough, so we were able to rent a place and keep food on the table and gas in the one car we had and his old bike. Although he often bitched about how much Belle cost us, she actually didn't. I didn't buy disposable diapers since they cost too much. Instead, she got the old-fashioned cloth ones that I had to wash constantly. Her clothes were either gifts from my parents, his family, or I got them second-hand. I breastfed her rather than use formula to save money. I did everything I knew how to do, to save us money, but he never acknowledged it.

He spent so much time at the clubhouse with what he said were his prospect duties, I rarely saw him. It wasn't until about three months into his prospecting, that I started to suspect he was cheating on me. By then, I knew women were at the club all the time, and some of them, the ones they called bunnies, were sort of on-call for the guys.

The rare times he did come home, he smelled of smoke, booze and perfume. I found lipstick on one of his shirts. I confronted him about it, and he laughed, and said I was crazy. He said he helped a drunk woman to her car, and she'd laid her head on his shoulder. Another thing that made me suspicious was he stopped having sex with me. As soon as Belle was born, that was it. Not that he did it that much while I was pregnant. He claimed the sight of my pregnant body made him sick when I got bigger.

I knew if he wasn't sleeping with me, he had to be sleeping with someone. However, the truly sad part of it was, I was glad he was leaving me alone. Sex had lost its appeal quickly for me. Even before we got married, Parker had never been able to make me have an orgasm. If I wanted one of those, I had to take care of myself.

As my discontent grew, I kept talking myself out

of divorcing him. How would that look? Eighteen and divorced with a baby to care for. How would I live? My parents wouldn't want me to move in with them. I would be an embarrassment again. My grandparents would let me live with them, but they were old, and to have a crying baby in the house would be hard on them, so I stayed with him, and tried to make the best of it.

It all went to pieces around the six-month mark when he had boasted they'd patch him in. He came home in a rage. It seemed the club had kicked him out, saying he wasn't the right fit for the club. He'd been livid, and for the first time, I was afraid of him. He ranted into the night about how sorry they were going to be, and how he was going to show them he didn't need their fucking club.

That was the beginning of the end. Soon, he was staying out all night and drinking. He had a new set of friends who gave me the creeps. New things like stereo equipment, a new television started to appear in our apartment. I knew that he wasn't working, despite me begging him to find a job. He said they were all beneath him, and he'd wait until he found one that was right for him. When I'd ask him where he got the money, he told me to mind my own business. I found out where he was getting it when he got arrested for petty theft. He should've gotten at least a year in jail for it, but the witness who identified him later recanted, and said they didn't know if he was the one or not.

I thought that might scare him enough to stop, and to get a real job. It didn't. The money kept coming until one day, the cops knocked on our door, and arrested him for aggravated armed robbery. He'd robbed a local gas station late at night, and it was one that did a lot of business. He was caught on tape. There was no getting out of it this time. When his case went to court, he was found guilty, and given a fifteen-year sentence. He went ballistic about that. I knew he was lucky not to get the max sentence, which was thirty years.

When they took him to prison, all I felt was relief. I didn't waste time filing for a divorce. I didn't even tell my parents or his family. Then I packed up Belle, and I got the hell out of town. Several hours away, I had a high school friend I'd stayed in touch with, despite Parker. She offered to let us stay with her until I found a job and a place of my own. I left, and I didn't look back, other than to make sure I stayed in touch with my grandparents and sent my forwarding address to both families. My grandparents begged me to come back and live with them, but I told them I didn't want Belle to grow up with the stigma of being Parker Pierson's daughter. Everyone in town was gossiping about him and me.

That was ten years ago. Now look at me, back here where it all started, warning the Warriors, finding out Joker was as attractive as ever, and I was watching them mutter to each other over what I had told them. Finally, Bull looked at me again. He gave me a smile.

"I'm sorry sweetheart, we didn't mean to be rude and ignore you. This is just a shock to us. We had no idea he felt like that or that you two were no longer together. Did you come all this way from wherever you live now, to tell us this? If so, thank you."

"It wasn't that far, Bull. I moved back to Hunters

Creek a couple of weeks ago. I just thought you ought to know. It looks likely he'll get parole according to his lawyer. If that happens, I hope he'll forget all this nonsense about revenge and stay away, but if he doesn't, you need to be ready. You need to have your security or whatever in place. Parker is a vindictive man," I warned them.

Joker hadn't said anything for a long time. He was looking at me with a furled brow. I wondered what he was thinking. Did he hate me more now that he knew I divorced his cousin? Not that it should make a difference, but I found I didn't like that idea. Finally, he spoke.

"Raina, you said he thinks you betrayed him by divorcing him and that he hates you, almost as much as he hates us, so what about you?"

"What about me?"

"If he threatened us, did he make any threats against you in that letter?"

The knot I'd been carrying around in my stomach since I read Parker's letter two days ago, clenched tighter. The urge to vomit grew. I had been trying not to think about what he said about me. All I'd concentrated on was finding the courage to come here and tell them what he said about the club. I planned to worry about my situation afterward.

"Raina, what did he say?" Bull asked. He still sounded nice, but there was now an edge to his tone. His brow was pulled down. Demon, Bear, and Tank, along with Joker, were looking at me the same way.

"Whatever he said or didn't say about me isn't the point. I just came to warn you. Now, since I've done that, I'll be on my way. Please, take him seriously. I see you have a lot of kids and women here now. I'd hate for anything to happen to any of you."

I stood up. It was time to get out of here. Only I couldn't leave, because Joker was still latched onto my arm and he wasn't letting go. His grip was firm, but he wasn't hurting me. His eyes were boring into mine. I felt like he could see into my soul, which was ridiculous. He stood up abruptly as he let go of my arm, but only to put both hands on my shoulders and press me back down in my chair. Once I was there, he sat back down.

"Answer the damn question, Raina. What did Parker say about you? I know he had to have said something and the way you're evading the question, it had to be bad. Let us help you."

"Why the hell would you help me? I'm nothing to you or this club. All I am is the ex-wife of a former prospect you kicked out. You have no obligation to me."

"Like hell I don't. You're family. It's my duty, even if it isn't the club's, to protect you and Belle," he said heatedly.

"No, it isn't! We're not your family. Did you miss the part where I said I divorced him? The day I did, I stopped being a part of the Pierson slash Fairbanks family. Sure, Belle is technically, but she doesn't even know any of you."

"I'm not gonna argue with you about this. You're

family, bottom line. I'm not gonna let you leave until you tell me what he goddamn said," he growled.

This was a different Joker. I'd always seen him smiling, happy, and quick with a joke or to tease. Now, he was angry and intense. My heart sped up. I didn't know if it was from alarm or something else. We stared at each other without saying a word. The others just sat there watching us. I saw Tank and Bear exchange what looked like amused glances. Finally, I'd had enough. It was getting late and I needed to get home. I'd left Belle alone with Granddaddy long enough.

"Fine, just so you'll stop, I'll tell you. Then I need to leave. Belle is at home with Granddaddy and I can't leave them for long. Yes, Parker made some threats toward me too. He said that I'd pay for betraying him and taking Belle away. He said that we'd all be back together soon, and I'd know that divorcing him was a mistake. He also said that I'd pay for breaking my wedding vows all these years, by being with other men. There. Are you happy?"

Joker's eyes started to blaze like there was a fire inside them. "You can't tell me you mean to ignore that. You just warned us to take him seriously. You have to do the same. You said Belle is with Byron. Are you staying with him or do you live somewhere else? What about your boyfriend or husband? Can he adequately protect the two of you?"

My mouth fell open at the absurd mention of a boyfriend or husband. As much as it galled me to tell him, I heard the words spill out of me, without me being able to stop them.

"We're living with Granddaddy. He needs help. And there's no boyfriend or husband. I don't need a man to protect me. I can do it myself. I've been taking care of us for the past ten years."

"Would he go after your former boyfriends then?" Demon asked, surprising me. He had this funny smirk on his face.

"I don't have any of those either. Listen, I've got to go. I told Granddaddy I'd be back by nine thirty. It's almost that now."

This time Joker let me stand and move away. As we all left church, I was acutely aware of him walking behind me. My skin felt like it was prickling all over. Ignoring those still in the clubhouse, I went straight to the front door. I pushed it open and stepped outside. It was the crunch of heavy footsteps on gravel that told me someone was still behind me. I knew it had to be Joker. When I got to my car and opened my door, he stopped me. I stared up at him. He made me feel so damn small and delicate. I wasn't like that. I was strong. I made sure I was.

"Raina, this isn't over. You said the hearing is in a month. That gives us a month to get everything in place. I'll be seeing you soon. Tell Byron I'll be by."

"What do you mean, you'll see me soon? There's no need for that. And why would I tell him that?"

A smile crept across his face, washing away his steely look from before. "Because we will most certainly be seeing each other again. And since you're living with

Byron, he'll be seeing me too. I can't wait to meet Belle, now that she's older. It's time she got to know her other side of the family. Tell her, her cousin, Joker, will be by."

"No, you're not coming by. She doesn't know Parker's side of the family, and I don't think she needs to know any of you now. You had your chance. No one gave a damn before."

"We had no goddamn idea where you went! You up and left," he said angrily.

"I did tell your family where we went! I told Parker's parents. They had my address. Don't tell me they didn't share that with you. Not a single one of you called, sent a card, or anything. Belle's been mine for ten years. I'll be damned if you can come into her life, acting all concerned and loving now," I yelled back.

Suddenly, his hands were on my upper arms and he had me pressed against the side of the car. I gasped. A bolt of fear shot through me. He growled this funny low sound.

"Please don't flinch away from me or look at me like that again, Raina. I would never hit you. I'd fucking cut off my hand if I did and my club would beat the hell out of me. I want you to focus on me, that's all, and I need to touch you. My aunt and uncle didn't tell anyone they had your address. They claimed that you moved, and they had no idea where you went. I swear that's the truth. We all asked them for it when we found out you were gone."

His admission surprised me and confused me. The surprise was, they had lied about having our address. The confusion was, why did he need to touch me? That was weird.

"I had no idea. Why would they lie about that? I couldn't live here. I didn't ever want to cut Belle off from having a family. I hoped she still would. Yeah, I left without telling anyone, but as soon as I got settled, I called them and my family and told them where we were. I offered to have them come anytime they wanted. It was after that, when no one came, other than Granddaddy and MeMe, that I realized they didn't want anything to do with us. And why do you have to be touching me to talk to me? That makes no sense."

"I'll find out why the fuck they lied. We asked again and again. I even asked your parents, and they claimed they had no idea and they asked me not to bother your grandparents, because they were devastated by your abandoning everyone. Jesus Christ, why would they all lie? As for why I need to touch you to talk to you, I don't need to. I want to, so I know you're real. After all this time, I can't believe you're back."

The look of wonder on his face confused me. I never imagined him missing Belle that much. She was barely over a year old when I left. I guess I didn't know him that well after all.

"Well, I am back. I really need to go, Joker. It's late."

He slowly let go of me. I felt cold when he did, which was ridiculous. I got in the driver's seat. He leaned down and over me as he hooked my seatbelt. I thought that was the sweetest thing a man had ever done for me. My breath was almost coming in pants. I had to get out of here before I made a fool of myself. His position put his mouth close to mine. My mind went off into la-la-land, as I tried to imagine what his lips would feel like pressed to mine. Jerking back, I put distance between us. He stood back up.

"Goodbye, Joker," I told him, as I shut the door.

Starting my engine, I didn't waste time getting to the gate. As it opened, I looked in the rearview mirror. He was still there, watching me leave. I tore my gaze away and shot out the gate once it was open far enough.

The drive to town wasn't that long. The whole drive, I thought of Joker and how he was still affecting me. I had to stay away from him. Nothing could ever be between us, and the last thing I wanted to do was make a fool out of myself and let him see I had this crush on him. Hell, I was twenty-eight years old. It was time to stop having crushes.

At the house, I parked in the garage and hurried inside. I breathed a sigh of relief when I found them both sitting in the living room watching a movie. Belle was curled up with my granddaddy in his big chair. He was smiling down at her. I ached seeing them like that. Over the years, he and MeMe had visited us several times. On top of that, I called them all the time and sent them pictures of Belle. They adored her. It had crushed all of us when MeMe died last year of a heart attack in her sleep.

Granddaddy hadn't been the same since losing her. Then a couple of months ago, I found out his

COPD was much worse than he let on. He was at what they called end-stage. He couldn't do anything without oxygen and even with it, he got short of breath and had to sit down. At times, his nail beds and lips got bluish in color. I'd been to the doctor's office with him and they said he was declining and didn't have that long to live. Maybe a year or more at the most. It could be less. It was that... the thought of losing the last family member who cared about us, that brought me back to Hunters Creek. I wouldn't let him die alone. My parents were in their own selfish world and never came by to see him. They were no help.

"Hey you two, it's bedtime." I said cheerfully.

I hadn't told Granddaddy about Parker's threats. If I did, he'd only worry. I asked him to watch Belle tonight so I could go out for a drink with an old school friend. He'd been more than happy to do it. I hated to lie to him, but if I told him I was going to see the Warriors, he would've demanded to know why. The same if I said I had to talk to Joker or anyone in Parker's family.

"Mommy," Belle said with a smile as she gave him a kiss, then got off his lap. Hugging her tight, I kissed her. She was my one true joy in life. She always made me smile. She was already bathed and in her pajamas.

"Hello Love Bug. Did you behave?"

She nodded her head. "Yes, I did. We had popcorn and watched movies. Did you have fun?"

"Good. Yes, I had a good time. Now, tell Granddaddy goodnight and then let's brush your teeth. It's late."

She did what I asked, but she grumbled about it. It took me a few minutes to get her into bed. After I did, I went to help him get ready for the night. He refused to let me help him bathe, but he had started to let me do things like run his bath, get out his clothes, do laundry and cooking. He gave me a kiss before he retired, then I was left alone with my thoughts. They weren't going to let me sleep much tonight, I was afraid.

Joker: Chapter 3

Two days, that's how long I lasted, before I knew I had to go see Raina again. It was two of the longest days of my life. Since she came to warn the club, I thought of nothing but her. Bull, Demon, Tank, Bear, and I had called the club together, and told them what she wanted the following day. For those who remembered Parker, they weren't all that surprised. For those who didn't know him, they couldn't believe someone would act like him. I wish I could say I was surprised.

All my life, Parker had always been something of a braggart, and a little asshole. He was four years younger than me and would often try to do everything I did. It was like he was in competition with me. Which was why I wasn't around him much as we got older and especially after I joined the Warriors.

When I found out that he had married his young girlfriend because she was pregnant, I didn't know what to expect, although I figured she'd be like him. Self-centered and out for what she could get. Imagine my utter shock when I met her. Raina bowled me over for several reasons.

One was the fact she was sweet, caring and a selfless person. All you had to do was talk to her for a few minutes to see that. Second, she was gorgeous.

I'd been instantly attracted to her, which was a fucking huge no. She was married to my cousin and pregnant with his baby. I wasn't gonna go there. However, as the months passed, and I got to know her more, it got harder and harder to ignore my attraction. I tried to drown it out by sleeping with women at the clubhouse, but it didn't help. Every time I saw her, she was more beautiful to me. Hell, being nine months pregnant, didn't detract at all from her beauty.

It was right after Belle was born, that I gave into Parker's pleas to sponsor him as a prospect. He said he wanted to be able to take care of his family, and to be a good husband and father. Despite my misgivings, I presented him to the club, and they agreed to give him a chance. I was upfront with them about my worries.

Fast forward to the six-month mark. He wasn't cutting it and in fact, got worse and worse. He wouldn't listen. He would disappear and we couldn't find him. He claimed he was home with Raina and Belle, but I found out that was a lie. Finally, church was held, and we decided to let him go. When we called him in and told him, he'd been livid and told us how sorry we all would be that we let someone like him go. He swore he'd be a success and we'd regret it.

As the months flew by, he got into more and more trouble. I heard rumors about the crowd he was with and tried to talk to him, but he told me to go to hell. The first petty theft charge, I hoped would wake him up, but it didn't. When he got arrested for aggravated armed robbery, I knew he'd do hard time. I prayed for his wife and daughters' sakes that it wouldn't be years and years. When he got fifteen years, I vowed our extended family would make sure they were cared for. I hoped that he'd smarten up on the inside and come out a better man for their sake.

When I found out Raina had packed up and left town without a forwarding address or phone number, it had hurt. I admit, I'd gotten mad and thought, fuck her. I did my best, after talking to her family, and finding out they didn't know where she was either, to forget her. She wanted to be on her own, that's what she'd get.

However, looking back now, knowing what I did today, I wanted to kick myself in the ass. Why didn't I go to her grandparents and ask? Why didn't I see if Outlaw could find her and Belle? And I was worried. Had they struggled much all these years? What had they gone without, while I had more than enough as well as my family? That ate at me.

The one thing I was happy about was her admission that she didn't have a boyfriend or husband, and she didn't appear to have any former ones. As hard as I found that to believe, I was ecstatic. This meant there would be no one in my way if I decided to pursue her. The question was, did I want to?

Flipping and flopping in my bed the past two nights had answered that question loud and clear. I did. I wanted to pursue it with my absolute best effort and see if there might be something there that we could build a relationship on. Maybe even have enough for it to be one of those once-in-a-lifetime relationships, like what my married brothers and parents had. The soulmates for life kind.

However, before I saw her, I had to go see someone first. I'd been holding off, trying to calm my anger. It was as good as it was going to get. The ride over to my aunt and uncle's place wasn't long. As I rode there, I tried to tell myself to keep my cool. Maybe there was a reasonable explanation for why they told the rest of the family they had no address or phone number for Raina. What that could be, I had no clue, but it was possible.

When I parked my bike in their driveway, I saw that my parents' car was there. Good. I'd asked them to stop by, and not to say anything about me coming by. They were told to act surprised when I arrived. They'd asked me why, and I told them I'd explain later. Of course, I knew once I was done with PJ and Bernie, they'd have no doubt why. The real reason why I wanted my parents here was to keep me from strangling one of them, if what Raina said was true, which I was suspecting it was. How they could be that callous to their only grandchild was beyond me.

As I approached the front door, it opened and PJ peeked out. He looked confused and dare I say, slightly worried. PJ was my dad's first cousin on his mom's side. That was why we had different last names. He had always been different from my dad, more standoffish, and less loving. Bernie, Bernadette, wasn't as bad as him, but she wasn't a ray of sunshine either. She tended to defer to PJ, and whatever he said, went.

"Hey, what brings you here, Joker?" he called out.

"I just thought I'd stop by. Haven't seen you guys in forever. I see it's a good day to visit. Dad and Mom are here. How are you PJ?"

In my family, we typically used the title cousin before their name, except with PJ and Bernie. They didn't like it and had told us not to do it.

"Oh, we're doing alright. Why don't you come in?" He held the door open.

As I passed him, I saw him checking me out. His upper lip curled a tiny bit. I knew he was doing it because I was wearing my cut. Despite the fact his own son tried to join us, he looked down on us. I think it started after we kicked Parker out, now that I thought about it.

Who the hell he thought he was to do that, I had no idea. I wanted to wipe that look off his face, by telling him I made more money, and had more in the bank than he did. Wouldn't that piss him off? I'd pay to have someone record it if I did. Once inside, he took me to the kitchen. Sitting around the kitchen table were my parents and Bernie. She gave me a startled look as well.

"H-hello, Joker. What brings you here?" she stuttered, as she exchanged a look with PJ.

"Oh, I thought I'd stop and we'd have a chat. How've you been Bernie? Hey Mom, Dad, how're you guys?"

I acted like I hadn't talked to or seen them in a while, when in fact, I saw them last weekend and talked to them earlier today to set this up. They both got up and gave me hugs. Mom gave me a kiss on the cheek once I bent down so she could reach me. I laughed at her. She knew it was because I was teasing her about her five-foot-two tiny self. She smacked me in the chest.

"Don't laugh at me, Aaron Fairbanks! I brought you into this world, I can take you out," she threatened. See, she was feisty, and an ass kicker.

"Whoa, control her, Dad. She's getting meaner," I teased.

I gave Bernie a peck on the cheek. I knew she didn't like it, but I didn't care. I made PJ shake my hand since he didn't offer his. Once that was out of the way and I was given a glass of iced tea, I sat down. PJ and Bernie looked uncomfortable as they sat there. Dad and Mom appeared to be relaxed, but I knew they were alert, and feeling the undercurrent in the room.

"So, what have you been up to, son?" Dad asked.

"You know, work and the club, the usual."

"Work? You mean you at that women's spa? You call that work?" PJ said with a sneer.

Who he thought he was to sneer at me, I had no idea. He worked behind a desk at the local insurance company. It wasn't like he had a glamorous job or anything. Bernie worked there too, as his secretary slash assistant or something. I stared at him until he started to squirm, then I answered him.

"Actually, I do call it work. As the club's manager, I do work. Thankfully, my brother, Maverick's old lady, Rylan, takes care of the stuff that would drive me insane. However, I make sure they get everything they need to do their jobs, pay the bills, balance the books, and report out to the club. If there are issues Rylan can't handle, then I take care of those. It keeps me busy, along with the other work I do for the club. What can I say, it keeps the cash coming in really nice too."

"It sure does. Did I tell you, he's having a house built? It should be done soon, shouldn't it, Joker?" Mom said excitedly. In general, my parents were good about using my club name. They knew what it meant to me. Only once in a while did they slip up.

"It is. Tank said it should be ready by the end of the month. That'll be five months since they started. They were able to begin working on it in March. The crew was slow to start since they had to finish building Tank and Brynlee's house first. It was ready in April. That made them very happy and way ahead of the baby coming in November."

"Why in the world do you need a house? You don't have a family. And all those kids your club keeps having. Don't they know what birth control is?" PJ asked with a slight roll of his eyes.

"Yes, they do know what birth control is, but they want to have families. They love their wives and want to have kids. We don't have half what they do in Dublin Falls, although we have enough to get a minibus, which we're doing. As for why I want a house when I'm single. That's easy. I don't plan to stay single. I'll need a house for my family," I said with a smile.

"A family? Who're you planning to settle down with? Is it anyone we know or is this a future woman you hope you meet?" Bernie asked.

I could hear a tad bit of interest in her voice. I knew she wanted to know, so she could go around town telling everyone, She was a horrible gossip. Never tell her anything you didn't want known to God and everyone.

"Actually, I do have someone in mind. I just need time to make her feel the same. We're more than compatible enough to make each other happy for the next forty or fifty years. However, even if I don't, it's time for a house. I'm tired of the noise, and not enough privacy at the clubhouse."

I saw my mom's face light up. She glanced at my dad. I didn't feel bad for getting their hopes up since I was telling the truth. It was my hope that Raina and I would be compatible, and end up in a committed, forever kind of relationship. Was I jumping the gun, maybe, but it was all to help play into my next moves. I planned to jolt them when I revealed who it was.

"Who?" Mom asked breathlessly.

"Why the hell would you care about noise and privacy? All you bikers do is drink, listen to music, and screw women," PJ snorted.

"PJ," my dad said warningly.

"What? It's true?" he protested.

"No, it's not. Although there is some drinking and music. As for the other, what consenting adults do isn't anyone's business. I hate to burst your bubble, but those aren't the only things we do. We own and manage a dozen businesses and are adding another one soon. All of them are very successful. That's not by chance and without work. How else do you explain all those really nice, big houses we have or that kick-ass compound we built?"

I gave him a satisfied smirk. His house was small, older, and beginning to show its age, since he didn't bother to do repairs or upkeep. The property was lucky to have the lawn mowed in the summer. It drove my dad crazy to see how little PJ cared about his home. Mom couldn't understand why Bernie didn't put her foot down and make him do it.

"I figured it was all the drugs and guns you run, oh, and the women," PJ snapped.

I was getting under his skin. Good. I wanted him off kilter when I asked the big questions. He was almost where I wanted him. Mom gasped in outrage. I held up my hand to stop her from tearing him a new asshole. Bernie might not say shit to him, but Mom would, and it was likely to include her fist.

"Now, PJ, you know damn well my club doesn't do any of that shit. We're a legit club, and all our revenue sources are as well. We make good money and have a financial wizard who invests our money for us. He gets returns you wouldn't believe. That's on our personal money, as well as the club's money. Bull is no fool. That man knows how to make and invest. Hell, your own son tried to join us. If we did all those things, why would you let him prospect with us?"

PJ scowled. He hated Bull. He knew that Bull was a man who had a huge amount of money. It bugged him.

None of us would tell him that Bull started out with it. He came from money. PJ really hated me mentioning Parker and his failed attempt to join the Warriors.

"Parker got smart and got out before it was too late," Bernie said piously.

"Oh yeah, and we see how well that worked out. He's doing fifteen years for being smart. It's been ten years. Any idea when he might get out, or is he gonna serve the whole sentence? They do that when you don't behave yourself. He hasn't had more time added, has he?" I shoved the next verbal knife in.

PJ came out of his chair. He glared at me. "Shut your mouth, Aaron. Parker would've never gone to prison if people in this town didn't have it out for him. He's due to get out any day now if you must know. His parole hearing is next month."

"So I heard. Think he and Raina will get back together? Belle is what, eleven now? I bet he misses them."

"How is he supposed to get back with her? She left, and no one knows where that ungrateful slut went. Not seeing her again will be the best thing to happen to him," Bernie said sharply.

"But she's his wife. I expect he might not see it that way," I added. I was enjoying this.

"She's not… he won't see it that way," PJ hurriedly said, after catching himself almost telling the truth. Now comes the fun part.

"When were you gonna tell the family that Raina

divorced his ass right after he went to prison? Or how about the fact you've known since she left exactly where they are, and could've seen or talked to your granddaughter any time you wanted? And why did you deny the rest of the family that connection to them, even if you didn't want it?" I slammed them verbally, as my voice got louder and meaner. My fury was slipping through.

Both of them went pale as ghosts and they exchanged panicked looks. Mom gasped and Dad snapped to attention. After taking several tense moments to get a hold of themselves, PJ tried to lie. "You don't know what you're talking about. Who told you those lies? Raina didn't divorce Parker and we have no idea where they went. We wanted to have a relationship with Belle, but her whore of a mother denied us that."

I slammed my fist down on the table, making the glasses rattle on it. I came to my feet. I bent forward and glared at PJ. He could see the desire to beat him on my face. My dad saw it too. He stayed in his seat. He knew I would never accuse someone of something like this, unless I knew what I was talking about. Slowly, I reached into my cut, and pulled out a piece of paper. I unfolded it, and laid it in the middle of the table, where everyone could see it. *Divorce Decree* was written in bold letters across the top. Further down it had the names *Parker Pierson* and *Raina Pierson*. It was dated six months after Parker went to prison.

"Then what the hell is this?"

"Where did you get that? It's a forgery." They tripped over each other to say. PJ was the one to ask where I got it.

"Like hell it is. I had my computer friend find it. It's a public record. As if that isn't enough, Raina told me herself that she divorced him."

Bernie whimpered and gave PJ a frightened look. "W-when did you talk to Raina? Where?"

"I talked to her two nights ago, when she came to the clubhouse to see me. She told me all about Parker's parole hearing, what happened after he went to prison. And imagine my surprise not only to find out they were divorced, but you knew where her and Belle were all this time. She gave her address and phone number to you and her parents. So, again, I ask. Why would you lie to your family and tell us she ran off with Belle and you had no idea where they were?"

Bernie came to her feet shakily. Both of them were eyeing me and my parents like we would bite. The look on my parents' faces said they were ready to do it. I wanted to strangle the two in front of me.

"You all need to leave," PJ ordered.

"I'll leave, but I will get my answers, PJ. Believe me, I will. And if you talk to your worthless son, let him know that we're ready for him, and if he comes near Belle and Raina, he'll regret it."

"You can't threaten our son!" Bernie yelled.

"I can do any damn thing I want when it comes to protecting my family," I told her coldly. My parents and I were walking toward the front door as I said it.

"She's not your family! She divorced your cousin. Honestly, I don't think Belle is Parker's daughter. Everyone knows that Raina was a slut. He wasn't the only guy she was sleeping with in high school," Bernie snapped.

I didn't believe that for a second. Parker had been a little manwhore. "Raina was no slut or whore. I have no doubt Belle is Parker's poor kid. At least she has one good parent. Well, at least she does for now, she'll soon have two."

"What does that mean?" PJ asked, as we paused on their front porch. Dad and Mom were down on the lawn already. I stopped and faced my angry and scared cousins. Smiling like I was the cat who ate the canary, I dropped my last two bombs.

"It means that Raina and Belle are back in Hunters Creek, and as soon as I convince Raina I'm the man for her, Belle will have a real daddy, not a worthless piece of shit. Have a nice day," I said as I walked down the steps. Their shouts and orders for me to come back went unanswered. Mom and Dad walked beside me.

"Son, is all that true?" Dad whispered.

"It sure is. I'll explain later. Right now, I need to go see my woman, and her daughter. I've gotta warn her about what I did, and to tell her what my intentions are. I'll stop by tonight and we'll talk, okay?"

He slapped me on the back and nodded, as he grinned at me. Mom gave me a quick hug, and then they got in their car. We pulled out one after the other once

I was on my bike and ready. Bernie and PJ were still on their porch staring at us in horror. A good start, I'd say, to finding out why the lies. I'd shake them up, make them sweat, then come back for the kill later.

Raina: Chapter 4

I love cleaning the bathroom. I love cleaning the bathroom. Maybe if I chanted that enough times, it would be true. Nope, it wouldn't. This was one thing I couldn't talk myself into believing. These weren't brussels sprouts. With those, if I chanted that they were good for me enough times, I could choke a couple down. After all, I had to set a good example for Belle. If she had to eat them, then so did I. No amount of choking down this bathroom would make it true. *I HATE CLEANING THE GODDAMN BATHROOM!* Where was my fairy godmother when I needed the bitch? Oh yeah, I forgot, I don't have one of those.

If I did, then my life would've been drastically different than it had been these past twelve years. I wouldn't go back and wish that I never had my daughter. She was my true and utter joy and I would never want to wish her away. I would try and see if I could've held off on being a mom for a few years. And if I could've had her father be a good man, who would love us, and do everything in his power to provide for us, I'd have done that in a heartbeat. I wasn't lazy. I would've done my part too. I would've been able to stay in my hometown, and close to my grandparents who I adored. I would've been here when MeMe passed.

I know... what was that old saying? If wishes

were horses, then beggars could ride or something like that. Granddaddy was always quoting it. It didn't do to wish your life away. And procrastinating wasn't going to get this bathroom clean, and me paroled to clean other parts of the house. The ones I didn't hate. I made myself do this first and used the carrot of the other parts to motivate myself. If I didn't, the bathroom might never get scrubbed, and that was gross.

Belle helped me a lot, but the bathroom she just never seemed to get as clean as I liked it. Of course, being my daughter, maybe she did that on purpose, so I had to do it. Hmm, I'd have to see if she was a sneaky shit or not. If she was, the bathroom might become her one and only duty. I'd do everything else if she would take this away.

Huffing and puffing as I practically stood on my head, I scrubbed the bottom of the tub. Damn, I know I scoured this thing last week. Didn't I? Yeah, I know I did. I'd been busy bringing everything in the house back to its usual level of cleanliness since I got to town. With MeMe gone, Granddaddy hadn't been able to keep up. And let's face it, he never cleaned when she was alive. Not because he wouldn't, she just thought of that as her thing. She loved to do it. God, why hadn't I inherited that gene? Instead, I inherited her height and body shape.

"Mommykins, come here!" A scream came floating down the hall from my daughter who was in the front of the house. I jumped and hit the top of my head off the faucet. My eyes watered, and I saw stars. Rubbing it lightly with my hand and muttering profanities under my breath, I dropped the brush, and stomped out of the bathroom. How many times did I need to tell her to come get me, not to yell like she was being killed or the house was on fire? One of these days, I'd ignore her, and there *would* be something wrong.

"Belle Eden Pierson, how many times do I have to tell you not to scream like that?" I asked loudly, as I walked into the living room. That was where she and Granddaddy were playing checkers the last time I saw them. I came to a screeching halt when I saw they weren't alone. Standing there looking larger than life and sexy as hell was Joker. He grinned at me and ran his eyes up and down me.

That's when I realized how I looked and was dressed. My hair was up in a messy bun on the top of my head. Wisps had escaped and were falling in my face. I had on zero makeup and I was sweaty. Knowing it would be hot and dirty work, I'd thrown on an old pair of cut-off denim shorts and a tank top. Thankfully, I did put on a bra. I was too top heavy to comfortably work without one. My hands were encased in those long yellow rubber kitchen gloves, you know, the really sexy kind that made men go wild for you. Not. *Why, Lord? Why did you let him come here today and see me like this?*

Well, fuck, there wasn't anything I could do about it now, so I'd have to muscle through it. Hopefully, the flush on my face he'd think was exertion. I nodded my head at him and tried to smile. "Hello, Joker. This is a surprise. What brings you here?"

"I told you I'd be by, and to tell Byron I would be. I didn't mean to disturb your cleaning though. Do you want me to come back later?"

I wanted to say yes, but I might as well get this over with, whatever it was. "No, that's okay. Won't you have a seat while I go get changed? Belle, get Mr. Joker something to drink."

"You don't need to change because of me, Raina. You look just fine to me."

"Actually, I need to get this bleach smell off me. I'll only be a few minutes. Stay and talk to Granddaddy. I know he'll enjoy it."

I glanced at my granddaddy to find he was watching me and Joker with a twinkle in his eye. Oh no, he didn't need to get any ideas. There was nothing going to happen romantically between us. He had been after me for years to find a man and settle down. Since I came back, he'd been relentless about it. He told me he wanted to see me happy and settled before he died. Every time I heard that, I almost cried. The thought of him gone hurt, just like it hurt every time I thought of MeMe.

"I can do that. Take your time. I don't have anywhere to be. Besides, I need to get to know this beautiful young lady. She's the spitting image of her mother. Belle, I haven't seen you since you were a year old. Tell me all about yourself. What do you like to do?"

His voice faded away, as I left them and nearly ran to my room. Shutting the door, I scrambled to get off my skimpy clothes and to sponge myself clean and into something that would cover me more. The way he had looked at me had made me feel naked. As I rushed to get cleaned up and changed, I wondered what he was really doing here.

Ever since the other night at the clubhouse, I'd been unable to stop thinking about him. My secret infatuation with him had gotten worse after seeing him one time. And I knew there was no hope of us becoming anything, even if I did secretly fantasize about it deep down. The reason was simple. Men like him—sexy, dangerous, biker men, had more women than they could ever want throwing themselves at them day and night, I expect. I wasn't in their league nor did I want to be. The last thing I needed was a man who I could never trust out of my sight. Parker's betrayal had been enough.

I didn't think all men were cheaters. There were some who could be loyal. Granddaddy was an example. I knew he never strayed in his life. He had looked at MeMe like she was the sun up until the end. Bikers on the other hand, I didn't think they were the breed to be faithful. Not when they had women on-call at their compound for the express purpose of sex. It made me wonder about the girlfriends and wives I'd seen the other night. Did they not care that their men cheated on them? Or maybe they thought the trade-off was worth it—protection, a home, and someone to care for them and their children. It would never be enough for me, but if it was for them, I wished them well.

If I ever took that leap again, it would only be with a man I loved without a shadow of a doubt, and who I knew loved me and Belle. He didn't need to be wealthy or even good-looking. There were more things to life than looks. Parker had been handsome and look how that turned out. Although, I wasn't sure I'd ever marry again, even if I did find a man I wanted to share my life with. Once had been enough, I think. That way if the unthinkable happened, it would be much easier and faster to walk away. Getting a divorce was messy, drawn out and expensive. To this day, I hated the fact that my grandparents had to be the ones to pay the lawyer to get me free of Parker. My parents sure wouldn't. They thought I should stand by him and wait for him, like a good wife, until he was out of prison.

The irony was, if I had loved him and he had been a good man, even with the terrible mistakes he had made, I would've waited. However, that wasn't the case, and I didn't reconsider my decision to divorce him like I had before. I wanted to be free and clear of Parker Pierson. Well, as free as I could be with us sharing a daughter. I only had to get her to eighteen, and then that was it. She had no love for him, and once she was a legal adult, she didn't have to have anything to do with him. I hoped if he got parole next month he'd stay away from us, but I doubted it. My only hope was he would soon tire of us and leave.

I sighed as I checked myself in the mirror. I was more covered by the leggings and t-shirt I had put on and my hair was neater. I'd brushed it up into a neat bun. Still no makeup, but I wasn't gonna do that. He didn't need to know that I cared what he thought of me or how I looked. Taking a deep breath to fortify myself, I opened my bedroom door and walked sedately back to the living room. As I got closer, I could hear voices muttering and giggling from my daughter. I popped around the corner and took in the scene.

Granddaddy was in his favorite chair watching Joker and Belle talk. He had a smile on his face. Belle had a huge smile on her face and was eagerly talking to Joker. As for Joker, he was paying close attention to her, and smiling like he was enjoying whatever she was telling him. My chest hurt seeing that. This was what I wanted for her. To have a father who looked at her like that, and who cared enough to want to hear everything she said, even if it was only silly stories about her favorite television show.

Clearing my throat to get their attention, I pasted on a smile. Joker turned and came to his feet. Again, he raked me from head to toe with those dark chocolate eyes of his. He came toward me and held out his hand. I automatically took it. He pulled me close and lowered his head to place a kiss just to the side of my mouth. My breath caught.

"You look just as gorgeous as you did a few minutes ago, Raina. There was no need to change. Come sit down and talk to me," he whispered softly.

I let him lead me by the hand over to the couch, where he'd been sitting with Belle. She scooted over so I could sit down. Joker sat down on the other side of me. I didn't know what to say or do. My brain was on the fritz.

"Mommykins, Joker was telling me that he met you when you were pregnant with me. Do you know he's in a motorcycle club? That's why he wears that leather thing. It's called a cut. Did you know that?" she asked excitedly.

Hadn't he told her the biggest thing? That he was her dad's cousin? If he had, wouldn't she have said that first? Even if she didn't admit it, I knew she was curious about that side of her family. She knew my parents weren't loving people, and that's why we had nothing to do with them. Luckily, she'd had my grandparents at least.

"Yes, I was pregnant with you when we met. And I do know he's in a motorcycle club, and that is called a cut. Did he tell you why we met to begin with?"

I looked at Joker as I asked her. He raised his brows as if to ask, *do you want her to know?* I didn't think we should hide it. Eventually, it would come out. I nodded.

"No, why?"

"Joker and your dad are cousins, honey. Actually, Joker is his older third cousin. We met at a family dinner at your grandparent's house when I was about three months pregnant I think."

She immediately looked shocked, then I saw her edge away. I never talked ugly about Parker to her. However, I was honest now that she was older. She knew what he did and why we got divorced. She would be dating sooner than I liked to think, and I didn't want her to mistake attraction for love like I did. She looked down at her hands.

"Hey, don't look like that, Belle. Yes, I am your dad's cousin, but I'm nothing like him. What he did and how he left you and your mom to fend for yourselves pisses me off to no end," Joker told her softly.

She looked up at him. She narrowed her eyes. Oh no, here it comes. She wasn't a shy child and speaking her mind wasn't anything she wasn't able to do. If she got too rude, I'd have to shut this down. She knew not to be rude, but there was no telling if she'd remember it. Finding a member of her dad's family in front of her might be too much for her. I should've thought of that before I told her.

"If you're nothing like my dad, then why is this the first time I've met you? Why did you and the rest of his family abandon me and Mommykins and never write, call, or visit us? She didn't do anything wrong, but she was treated like she was the criminal. The only people who still loved us were Granddaddy and MeMe," she snapped.

"Belle, don't..." I didn't get to say more because Joker stopped me with a hand on my leg.

"Raina, don't stop her. She has a right to say what she thinks and to ask for the truth. Both of you have every right to be angry and hurt. I feel the same. I should've done more. I never should've believed the answers I was given. I could've found you. I let my anger stop me. That's something I'll have to live with and ask you to forgive me for. Belle, you're right. You and your mom didn't deserve that. Let me tell you what happened."

"Joker, maybe this isn't such a good idea."

"I think it is. She's mature enough to know that adults screw up and to call us on it. What did you tell her?"

"She told me everyone was upset with her for divorcing my dad and when she moved, she gave them our address and phone number. No one except for MeMe and Granddaddy ever called or came to see us. We didn't come back here because there were too many people who didn't like her and she didn't want them saying mean things to me. She was protecting me," my daughter said boldly.

"Well, that's sort of true. See, your mom thought none of us liked her and was mad at her, but that's not true. We were lied to."

"How?"

"Your mom decided to get out of town after your dad went to prison, and she did it without telling any of us she was doing it first, well, maybe she told your Granddaddy and MeMe, but no one else. She thought we were all on your dad's side and would try to stop her. Once she was out of town, she contacted both sets of your grandparents and gave them the information on where you were. Only they never shared it with anyone. When I found out you were gone, I went to my cousins, your dad's parents, and asked them where you were. They lied to me. They said your mom didn't tell them. That she'd run off with you."

"And you believed them?" Belle asked, outraged.

"Not at first. So, I went to see your mom's parents. They told me the same thing."

Granddaddy sat forward in his chair. He had a thunderous expression on his face. I hadn't told him about seeing Joker or what he told me. "My son and daughter-in-law did what?" he growled.

Joker gave me a surprised look then answered him. The cat was out of the bag, no use trying to put it back in. "Yeah, Byron, I'm afraid they did. I never imagined they'd lie. I had no idea they were upset at Raina for leaving Parker and I didn't know she was divorcing him. I planned to ask you and your wife, but they asked me not to. Said you were too upset by what Raina did to talk about it. I stupidly listened. After that, I admit, I was angry at her and tried to forget I ever knew her. I told myself that if she wanted it that way, so be it."

"How did you find out the truth? And how did you know she was in town and staying here?" Granddaddy asked.

"I saw him the other night, when I told you I went to meet a friend for drinks. I had to speak to him and his club about something. It's something we'll have to talk about later. Anyway, he confronted me about leaving without a forwarding address or anything and I told him that wasn't true. What made you believe me?" I asked Joker.

"I didn't want to believe it, but your voice rang true when you told me, so I went to see PJ and Bernie before I came here. I wanted to see what they had to say."

I stiffened. My in-laws had never liked me. I could only imagine what they said. I looked at Belle. She was avidly listening to us. "Love Bug, I need you to go to your room for a little bit, so the adults can talk."

"Mom, no! I want to hear. I'm not little anymore,"

she protested.

"Yes. Do as I say, young lady. There are things I don't want you to hear. They're not nice things, Belle," I warned her.

Seeing that I wasn't going to budge, she jumped to her feet, and huffed out of the room. I heard the door slam shut to her room a few moments later. I'd talk to her about that later. We didn't slam doors.

"Shit, I'm sorry. I didn't mean to reveal secrets. I didn't know you hadn't told Byron about the other night. I assume that means he doesn't know what prompted you to come to the clubhouse?"

I shook my head. "No, I didn't."

"Why didn't you?" Granddaddy asked sternly.

"Because I knew you'd worry and you don't need the stress."

"Girly, I've lived with stress all my life. Those doctors telling you to eliminate it from my life will kill me quicker than this COPD will. I'm dying, Raina. There's no way around it. I don't want to die not knowing what is going on with you and Belle. Tell me," he ordered.

I knew better than to ignore that tone. The way Joker sat up straighter, I knew that announcement took him by surprise. I guess my granddaddy wasn't telling anyone about how advanced his disease was. I knew my parents wouldn't know. He hadn't spoken to them in ten years. When they cut us out of their lives, he and MeMe washed their hands of them.

I missed the pleasure of seeing them at MeMe's funeral because I was out of the country with Belle. We had taken our first vacation, and went to Niagara Falls, Canada. He called us after the funeral was arranged, and we couldn't get back in time. I think he did it on purpose, so I wouldn't have to see my parents. He knew how much it hurt me to this day the way they treated me and my daughter.

"I got a letter from Parker the other day. I decided to open it since I haven't opened them in ages. I hoped maybe this one might be nicer and he'd ask about Belle. I was wrong. He was just as hateful as ever. He still thinks I betrayed him by divorcing him. What made me go see Joker and the Warriors was what else he wrote in it. He's coming up next month for a parole hearing. It looks like he'll get it, from what his lawyer says. He's served two-thirds of his sentence. Anyway, he was ranting in that letter about how he was going to make Joker and the Warriors pay for him going to prison. That it was all their fault."

"How the hell does his warped ass brain think that? No one made that boy rob that gas station with a gun other than himself. He pistol whipped that employee and it was caught on tape. What is wrong with him?"

"He said if the club hadn't kicked him out and would've patched him in, he would've been able to take care of his family and not turn to stealing to do it. He's vowing revenge on them."

"He's insane. That's all there is to it. So you

warned them, and that's how Joker knew how to find you. Why're you here? To tell her your family backed up her story?"

"No, I'm here because I want to see her again. Also, we need to talk about security."

"Security? Why would she need to know about the security you plan to put in place for your club?"

"It's not the club's security, Byron. It's the security her, you, and Belle need. What she isn't saying is that Parker is threatening her too. He plans for them to get back together and for her to pay for leaving him and being with other men since the divorce. He's dangerous to all of us," Joker said as he narrowed his gaze on me.

"What!?" Granddaddy tried to get out of his chair quickly, but he fell back. He was huffing in air as he did it. I raced over to him falling to my knees. Joker was right behind me.

"Don't get upset! This is why I didn't tell you. I knew you'd get like this. Parker isn't going to touch me or Belle. He's feeling like a big man since he's been in prison. He thinks he's got street cred or something. You know how he always thought he was bigger and better than he ever was."

"Like hell he won't. If you believe he meant what he said about the Warriors, then you have to believe what he said about you. He never forgave you for the divorce. Although, why he cared when he was cheating on you anyway, I don't know."

"He was what?" Joker's icy question sent a shiver

down my spine.

    I gulped. His face looked livid, although why, I had no idea. Surely, he knew about Parker cheating. He would've done it at the clubhouse.

Joker: Chapter 5

Almost twenty-four hours later, and I was still reeling from the latest revelation. When I went to visit Raina yesterday, I thought I knew everything. Boy, was I wrong. Finding out she hadn't told Byron about the letter, or the visit to the club was one thing. But to find out that Parker had cheated on Raina while they were married had been a punch in the gut to me. As stupid as he was, I never thought he'd do that.

She'd tried not to tell me about it, but I refused to let it go. In the end, she admitted Parker was cheating on her when he was a prospect, and that she assumed we knew it, as in the club. I made sure she knew that wasn't the case, and if we'd known about it, he'd have been given the beating of his life, and kicked out sooner.

When I left later, after informing them we would be ensuring security for all three of them, despite her ongoing protests it wasn't needed, I'd gone for a ride to try and clear my head. It hadn't helped. Nor did my awful night of sleep. I tossed and turned for hours. When I did sleep, I dreamed of her.

Here I was still trying to understand it. How in the hell could Parker have a woman like her, and cheat on her? Even as a teenager, there was something so mesmerizing about her, and the way she was with people. If she'd been my wife and mother of my child, I would've never looked twice at anyone else, let alone cheated on her.

That second meeting after all these years hadn't put a damper on my thoughts of seeing if we could have a future together. It only strengthened it, except I might have a harder time convincing her than I thought. The way she looked at me a few times told me she wasn't immune to me. However, Parker's betrayal and the fact she hadn't had a man in her life since then, told me she didn't trust men. Who could blame her? But I had to find a way to show her she could trust me, I just didn't know how. It would take more than words, that was for sure.

"What's got you all caught up in your head over here?" Rylan asked softly from behind me.

I turned to face her and smiled. I liked all the old ladies, but she was the one I was closest to. We spent more time together because of the spa. I needed a female's perspective on this. She might be able to help me.

"Do you have time to talk?"

"As long as we can sit down and I can park this boulder I'm carrying, then yes. Maverick has Amiah out on the swings."

As I nodded, she waddled over to one of the couches in the common room. I thought she looked cute as hell. Although I was smart enough not to mention she waddled, or it was cute. I knew better. I didn't want to die. Pregnant women were sensitive about what they looked like. I didn't know why. They all looked just as attractive as they did when they weren't pregnant, and some even more, like Raina had. Rylan sighed as she sat down. Her hands came to rest on her stomach.

"Okay, hit me. What can I help you with?"

"What makes you think I need help?"

She laughed. "Men get this look when they need help but don't want you to know it. You have that look. Is it the spa? Did something happen that I don't know about?" I heard a touch of anxiety in her voice. She was working less these days the closer she got to having the baby.

"No, it's not the spa. I have a question. What can a man do to prove to a woman that he won't cheat on her? I know words alone won't do the trick. Is there something he can do to prove it?"

Her mouth rounded as she stared at me. I could tell I surprised her. She didn't say anything for several moments, then the avalanche of questions started pouring out of her.

"Joker, where is this coming from? Are you seeing someone we don't know about? Does she think you cheated on her? Why would she think that? When can we meet her? Do I know her? How long have you been seeing her?"

I finally had to hold up my hand to stop her. She was figuratively vibrating with excitement. I didn't want her dropping that baby a month early. Maverick would kill me if she did.

"Whoa, hold on there, crazy woman. Can I get a

word in edgewise, or do you just want to stack up the questions until you run out of air or that baby is born?" I teased her.

She pushed on my arm, trying to shove me, but all it did was barely rock me. "Great, you're a boulder just like Maverick. Okay, smarty pants, I've stopped. Tell me before I tell my man you're picking on me and he beats your ass."

"You're an evil little shit, aren't you? Damn, I thought you were sweet. Mav needs to reconsider who he loves. I thought he had better taste," I pretended to mutter sadly.

This got her smacking me repeatedly, threatening more dire consequences, which made me laugh harder. The others in the common room were grinning at us. I stopped so I could get my answers. Soon the masses would descend on us if she kept it up.

"No, I haven't been seeing anyone that you don't know about. Even if I had been, I would never cheat. She's been cheated on in the past. She's divorced. You don't know her, but you've seen her. As for meeting her, only if you behave and help me."

She gasped and her eyes widened. "Is it the woman who came in here the other night to see you and then you took her into church? What's her name? Raina?"

"It is Raina. Did Maverick tell you who she is or why she came here?"

"He said she was someone from the past and she

came to warn the club. I tried to get him to tell me more, but he said not yet, damn man. He knows I've been dying to know, and so are the other old ladies. Apparently, none of the guys are talking. Why not?"

"Raina is from not just the club's past, but my past. About eleven years ago, Raina was married to someone who ended up prospecting for us. We had our doubts about him making it, but we let him try."

"Eleven years ago? She had to have been a baby. She can't be older than me," she said in surprise.

"She was sixteen when she got married, and seventeen when she had her daughter. She was eighteen when I last saw her. The man she was married to was my cousin, Parker."

"Your cousin? Is he still around town? I don't recall any of you mentioning a Parker or meeting one."

"He's not. Despite my doubts, I sponsored him. I knew he needed to take care of his family. Anyway, he didn't make the full prospecting period before we kicked him out. He wasn't a fit, not even close. After we did he started to steal. One night he robbed a gas station and assaulted the employee inside. He had a gun. That got him sent away for fifteen years. Raina and her daughter, Belle, left town. No one knew where they went. Or that's what we were told."

"Now she's back and you found out that's not the truth? What did she want to warn you about and what does it have to do with you convincing her that not all men cheat?"

I quickly told her the rest, except the part about me having been attracted to Raina since the first time I saw her. When I was done, she studied me.

"Your cousin is a dickhead, Joker. To do that to his family, and now he's making threats and you found out he cheated on her. I think it's great you want her to know not all men cheat, but why is that your job?" She was smirking as she said it. Damn woman knew why, but she was going to make me say it.

"You know why. I want her to see me as a man she can be with. In order to do that, she has to know I won't cheat. According to something she said, I know she hasn't had a boyfriend since she got a divorce. Can you help me or not?"

"I can do my best. For one thing, I think she needs to come here and get to know the club. She knew it back when there were no old ladies. She needs to know it now. She'll see how the men here treat their wives and children. That way we can talk you up to her and tell her what a good guy you are, but I'll only do it if you can promise me one thing."

"What? Anything."

"That this is more than you being bored and looking for excitement."

"Fuck no, it's not boredom or me looking for excitement! If I want to get laid, I can do that anytime. It's more than that. Shit, I can't believe I'm going to admit this. Here it goes. I met her after Parker married her and was instantly attracted to her. It didn't change as I got to know her, but she was his wife. Breaking up a marriage isn't me. I would never do that to anyone. However, knowing they're not married now, and she's not involved with anyone, I've got to try. This might be my only chance to find out if we could have something significant and lasting together."

"Are you in love with her?"

"Maybe, I don't know, but I'm sure I can be, and it wouldn't take a lot."

"What about her daughter? You know kids take effort, especially if they aren't yours."

"Belle is my family, no matter what. If people hadn't lied, she would've been a part of my life all along. I want both of them in my life, even if we can only be friends." I said it, but it wasn't what I wanted.

"Do you think Raina is attracted to you like you are to her?"

"I do. She's looked at me a couple times in a way that says she's not immune and she's reacted to my touch."

She clapped her hands and got a huge grin on her face. Oh damn, I was in trouble. I tried to get up to run, but she was quick, especially for a pregger. She latched onto my arm and hauled me back. "Stay here and let me get the girls. We have a battle to plan."

"Rylan, don't. If you tell the others, it'll be like a circus. I want to attract Raina, not terrify her, and have her leave town again," I protested.

"Hush, we'll be perfectly nice to her. Hey ladies, get your butts over here. Joker needs our help to get his woman," the little shit hollered. It was like waving steak in front of a bunch of hungry dogs. They came running and baying for my blood. I knew what a fox felt like when the bloodhounds were let loose to hunt it.

"Help! Keep your women back," I yelled to my brothers.

Those traitorous bastards just laughed and came with the women. I'd find a way to make them pay. We were brothers. They were supposed to have my back no matter what. They all gathered around me and stared avidly at me. I didn't have to say a word. Rylan eagerly told them everything I'd told her. When she was done, the ladies were all enthusiastically talking about what they could do. My brothers were smirking.

"I knew it. I knew the way you looked and acted the other night when she came, that you had a thing for her. Why didn't you say anything?" Demon asked.

"Because I knew it would turn into this. God, if you all scare her off, I'll kill you. Plus, it's humiliating to admit I lusted after someone's wife."

"Joker, you did, but you didn't do anything about it, and that's what counts. I never understood what she saw in Parker to be honest," Bull said.

"I'm not sure. She was young. All I know is she's not his now, and I have to find out if there's a chance for us. And we need to figure out, before his ass gets out, what we're going to do not only to protect the club but her, Belle, and Byron."

"I've been thinking about it. I've got ideas. We have time to prepare. Did you talk to his dad and mom about why they lied?" Bull asked.

"I did. Yesterday before I went to see her. They lied and said they didn't. So, I showed them the divorce decree Outlaw found and as I walked out with my parents, I might have hinted that she and I were already together."

The guys laughed. I didn't feel a bit remorseful. I was about to tell them about Byron's health when the alarm I set on my phone went off. Damn, time to go. "Hey, we'll have to finish this later. I gotta go. I promised the folks I'd come see them and explain what yesterday was about. I was supposed to do it last night, but I came back here instead. I had to swear I would today, or they threatened to come here."

"Well, get your ass over there, although we love to see them. We'll work on the game plan while you're gone," Rylan said.

"That's what terrifies me. Please, rein them in if you can," I pleaded to my brothers.

None of them promised, I noticed. Getting up, I waved at them as I headed out to get on my bike. Slipping on my helmet and sunglasses, I took off. My parents lived outside of town, the opposite from the compound. It was about a thirty-minute ride. I enjoyed it. The sun was out, and it was hot and humid. The breeze felt wonderful.

When I arrived, as I was parking my bike, they came out to greet me. I barely had time to get off my bike before I was almost knocked down by my dynamo mom. "Aaron, tell me what that was about yesterday at PJ and Bernie's house?"

"Mom, give me a chance. Can I at least come in the house?"

She rolled her eyes and huffed. Dad winked at me. After I got inside and was given a cold glass of lemonade, I told them everything, from the divorce to the lies and the fact he was making threats when he got out. When I was done, they were irate.

"I can't believe they'd be like that. I mean, if they didn't like Raina, there was still Belle. She's their grandchild," Mom shrieked in outrage.

"PJ has always been somewhat of an asshole, but this is a whole new low. Bernie goes along with whatever he says, so that's not a shock. What about Raina's parents? Why did they lie?" Dad asked.

"I haven't talked to them yet. I went to see her and Belle. They're at Byron's. Did you know he has COPD, and it's end-stage? He said something about dying soon."

"No, we had no idea. Oh, that poor man. He never got over losing Mabel, now this. He just got Raina and Belle back," Mom moaned sadly.

"Son, what do you plan to do? The rest of the family needs to know what PJ and Bernie did. We've all been angry at Raina for leaving without a word. We need to get them back in the fold. Plus, they need to be protected from Parker. I figure your club can take care of themselves. Are they willing to help protect them? We can pay. Your security agency does this kind of stuff," Dad mused aloud.

"Dad, I agree we should tell the rest of the family as soon as possible, although they'll need to let her come to them. Too many at once will overwhelm them, I think. As for their protection, the club is going to handle it. It's not going to cost a dime."

"It's nice of them to want to do it for free, but we can pay," he insisted.

"They won't accept. She's family, and they know what she means to me."

"What does she mean to you? What does that exactly mean? I know what you told Bernie and PJ, but I know it was just to rile them up. They deserved it for being heartless shitheads," Mom muttered.

"It was more than that. I've had a thing for Raina since the day I met her. I never said anything since she was married, but now she's not. I'd like to see if we could be a thing."

The squeal my mom gave almost ruptured my eardrums. She threw herself in my arms and squeezed me hard. Dad had to pry her off me. I swear it was like being crushed in the tentacles of an octopus.

"I knew it! I knew it. I told your dad you did even way back then. He told me I was crazy. Oh God, how I wish she'd married you instead of Parker and that Belle was your daughter," she babbled.

"Mom, if she had, I would've gone to prison for having sex with a minor. Remember, I'm six years older than her. What they would overlook in an eighteen-year-old they wouldn't have in a twenty-two-year-old."

She waved off my comment. "We need to get them over here for dinner. What about tomorrow night? I'll fix my homemade chicken, mashed potatoes, and noodles."

"Mom, slow down. Raina needs to get used to us again. We have to show her that the rest of our family isn't like her ex-in-laws. And she has no idea that I'm interested in her. I can't have you telling her or scaring her away. First, I'm gonna work on showing her she can trust me. Parker cheated on her. She has no reason to trust a man."

This set my mom off. It took both my dad and me to settle her down. She wanted to go to the prison and beat the shit out of Parker. I would've let her just for the fun of it, if I thought she wouldn't end up there too.

After she calmed down, we sat and talked about what to do, and how to approach bringing her into the family again, getting her to admit whether she would give me a chance, and how to make sure they were safe. It was dark by the time I rode back to the compound. Confronting her parents would have to wait until tomorrow after work. I wouldn't rest until I found out why they lied too.

Work had dragged along today. I knew it was

mainly because I was counting the hours until I could leave and go talk to Raina's dad and mom. Rudy and Gwen had never been the nicest or warmest people. In fact, when I met them, I wondered how they could be Raina's parents. Or how Rudy could be Byron and Mabel's son. All of them were warm and loving. I'd have to ask if Byron was sure he hadn't been mixed up at the hospital when he was born.

They lived in town on a quiet street. There were several older houses on that block, however, unlike PJ and Bernie's house, they at least kept it up. The house was freshly repaired and painted. The grass was perfectly mowed and flowers bloomed in the flowerbeds. They at least took pride in their home.

Rudy worked at the lumber mill. Our town still had an active one. It didn't do as much business as it did years ago, but they still cut down trees to make lumber and locally sold it. It was the same mill Byron had worked at until the day he retired. AW Construction got lumber from them when we could. We preferred to buy local and support the small businesses first. If they didn't have what we needed or not enough, then we went to the bigger retail giants. Some of their lumber was in my house. I loved knowing local trees would live on in my home.

I parked my bike in the driveway, then made my way up to the front door. I had to knock twice before it was answered. Gwen peered up at me with an uneasy look on her face when she opened the door. I hadn't been here in ten years. If I ran into them in town, I'd say hello or wave, but that was the extent of our conversations. She had to be remembering the last time

I came by to talk. "Hi, Gwen."

"Hi Joker, what're you doing here?"

"Is Rudy home? I need to talk to the two of you. It's important."

She looked like she was going to say no, then changed her mind. "He's here. Why don't you come inside?" She held open the door. That's when I saw Rudy standing off to the side. Coward. He sent his wife to the door. Stepping inside, I followed them to the kitchen.

"Why don't you two go out on the back porch, and relax? I'll be out with something cool to drink in a minute," she said. Southern hospitality ensured she made the offer, even though I knew she didn't want to.

"That would be nice. Thanks."

I might want to tear both of them a new ass, but I had been raised to be polite, until it was time not to be polite. Rudy opened the slider to the back. As he did, I noticed his hand was shaking. I kept my smile to myself. He gestured to one of the deck chairs at the table they had out there. I took it, and he sat in one of the other ones. He was staring at me like he didn't know what to say.

"How's work been at the mill? Tank said he keeps buying what he can from there. In fact, some of it is in my new house." I said to try and get him at ease.

"Your house? I didn't know you were having one built. Yeah, Tank and the construction guys come in a lot. We've been doing okay. At least it keeps me working. I'm too old to leave and work somewhere else.

Everything been good for you? Where do you work these days?"

As I went to answer him, Gwen came out with a tray. On it was a pitcher of iced tea and three glasses of ice. I got up and took it from her then sat it on the table.

"Thank you," she said softly. Her husband hadn't bothered to get up. She sat down next to him after I pulled out her chair for her.

"Yeah, I had AW start on it about five months ago. It's at the compound with the other houses. I need my own space. As for where I work, mainly I oversee Angel's Glamour from the business side for the club."

"Angel's Glamour? Isn't that the spa?" Gwen asked.

"It is. It's doing a ton of business. Thankfully, my brother, Maverick's wife, Rylan, does the day-to-day stuff."

"Oh, isn't she the one who came back to town with a baby?" Gwen said with a disdainful sniff.

"She is. Amiah is a doll. Maverick loves her as much as he loves Rylan. They're having another girl next month. I tease him that he's probably destined to have all girls."

They gave me a weak smile, but I knew they really didn't care. I took a sip of the tea. Usually, I like iced tea, but I had to work not to spit this out. It was pure sugar. I sat the glass down.

"So, what brings you here, Joker? I don't think you

came to talk about the mill or your club," Rudy said after another awkward pause.

"You're right, I didn't. I actually came to talk to you about Raina."

The way they reacted, you would've thought I hit them with an electric cattle prod. They sat up straight and Gwen's hand fluttered up to her neck. Rudy swallowed hard. I saw his Adam's apple bob. His eyes shifted left then right, before he met mine again. I guess PJ and Bernie hadn't bothered to warn them. "Raina? What about her? We haven't heard from her in years," he said nervously.

"I know. And who could blame her for not talking to you or coming to visit when she got back into town? After what she's been put through, I can't blame her."

"Back in town? Put her through? We don't know what you're talking about," he said hastily.

"You didn't know she moved back to take care of your dad? She's here with Belle and I think they plan to stay. Imagine my shock when I talked to her and found out she didn't just up and leave without telling anyone where she was all those years ago. Or that she'd divorced Parker. Mind telling me why when I asked you about her all those years ago you told me she left no forwarding address or phone number?"

Rudy looked like I had slapped him, while Gwen turned white and clutched her hands together. She looked at him.

"Tell me," I snapped. I was over being nice. I

wanted fucking answers and my patience was gone. First my cousins and now them. It made no sense why they would do it.

"I-you don't understand, Joker. It was for the best. You need to go. Stay away from Raina and let the past go," he finally said.

"I have no intention of staying away from her and Belle. And the past won't stay forgotten. I know PJ and Bernie lied. Why did you? You're her parents, for God's sake. You've had no contact with her for ten years! Don't make me force it out of you," I snarled.

"Because PJ said if we kept our mouths shut and didn't tell anyone where she went, then when Parker got out of prison, he'd give us a cut of the money he stole from the various places he robbed. I'd finally be able to retire from the damn mill," he almost shouted, as he literally shook in fear.

I stared at them in shock. It was true the cops never recovered the money he stole and there had been other things we knew he'd stolen, but it never amounted to that much. "What the fuck? Anything he stole before the gas station was long gone and there wasn't that much stolen from there. Not enough to make it worth betraying your daughter like that!" I snarled.

"Yes, there is! Rudy told me. He said when Parker robbed those houses, he got a lot of valuable stuff—jewelry, bonds, money and more. The people he stole from never told the cops everything that was taken."

I had to get up and pace, so I wouldn't grab him

by the neck and snap it like a twig. It took me a couple of minutes to calm down enough to speak again. "Rudy, he lied. There was no jewelry, large amounts of money or bonds stolen. He took some electronics he could hock and get cash for. There was a little bit of money too, but again, he spent it. There's no secret stash somewhere. They lied and you believed them. You sold out your flesh and blood for nothing. You make me sick. I can't believe you're her parents. I only have one more thing to say before I leave, because if I don't leave, I'll strangle you. Stay the fuck away from Raina, Belle, and Byron. If you don't, I'll make sure I ruin you in this town. I'll tell everyone what you did and why. You never deserved them, but that's okay, I'll take care of them from now on."

I took the back steps two at a time to get away from them as they sputtered and begged me not to tell anyone. I went around the house and got on my bike as fast as I could. I had to get out of there before I did something that landed my ass in jail. As I sped off, I tried to decide if I should tell Raina and Byron or keep it to myself. They deserved to know, but the pain would likely kill Byron, and Raina didn't need any more. I just didn't know if I could lie to them. There had been too many damn lies told in this town as it was.

Raina: Chapter 6

I hadn't seen or heard a word out of Joker in six days. After he'd stopped by and talked to us, I thought he'd be back. When he left, he indicated he would. Instead, it was radio silence. In an effort to keep my mind off obsessing over why, I stayed busy.

A big help in doing that was I started working at the local police station as a dispatcher. When I moved away, I had nothing but a high school diploma and no job experience. It made the jobs I could get scarce. Or at least any I could get that would pay enough money to allow me to keep a roof over our heads and food in our stomachs. I got lucky somehow. I saw an ad for nine-one-one dispatchers needed. It said no experience was needed, that they would train you, so I applied.

I was stunned when I got the job. Sure, it was tough to work and raise Belle, but I had my friend, Eva. She helped out as much as she could and put me in contact with others I could trust. It was all because of them that I did as well as I did. It got easier when Belle started school. I worked the morning shift, which meant I only had to have someone get her off to school, pick her up, and keep her for less than an hour after school during the week. On the weekends, she stayed with those friends all day.

When we decided to move back here, I looked for jobs online. I still had to work. Imagine my surprise when I saw they needed dispatchers here. It seemed like fate. I immediately applied, and they asked me to come and interview. It took a couple of interviews with different levels of management before I was offered a position. They were excited that I had experience. I was excited to get a job in town and do what I knew.

Really, all I had to learn was their policies and procedures and the call codes they used over the radio. Those differed from police department to police department. They were nice enough to give me time to get settled before starting. While I did, I studied their codes so I could hit the ground running, I hoped. I'd still have someone training me, but I hoped they wouldn't have to do it for long.

It was because of my new job and the desire to keep my mind occupied that I was out tonight. My primary trainer, Connie, had asked me to go out with her, and a few of the others who worked in dispatch and had the night off. She and I were already on our way to becoming fast friends. The others I didn't know well yet, but I thought we could be friends too.

They were going to have a few drinks and listen to live music. At first, I thanked them and said no, but when I told Granddaddy about it, he insisted I go. He asked me when was the last time I went out to relax and have fun. When I couldn't tell him, he ordered me to accept. My daughter turned traitor and ganged up on me too. Which is how I found myself trying to have a good time while fighting not to think about Joker.

They brought me to the most popular bar in Hunters Creek called the Dark Angel. I recalled seeing it in passing years ago, but since I wasn't old enough to drink then, I had never gone inside. Now, it was a bar slash restaurant, they told me. I had to admit it was busy. The music was starting and more and more people kept coming through the door. Connie, Hana, Tessa, Cray, and Leif were turning out to be a fun group. They found us a table, and we settled in early. They warned me if we waited until later, it would be impossible to get seats.

The band who was warming up was called Disciples of Mischief. From the sounds of the music, they were mainly old rock n roll, which was fine by me. As I relaxed, I got out of my head and into what they were saying. I was laughing at one of Cray's jokes when I felt a tap on my left shoulder. I turned to see who it was. I was startled to see a woman I didn't know, and a man I did. The man was Demon from the Warriors.

"Oh, hi Demon," I said. I didn't know what else to say. After confessing all I had that night at the club to him, Joker, Bull, Bear and Tank, I felt a bit weird.

"Hey, Raina. It's good to see you again. I want to introduce you to my wife, Zara. Hellion, this is Raina."

His wife immediately stuck out her hand and shook mine. She was smiling and looked happy to meet me. "It's great to officially meet you, Raina."

"It's nice to meet you too. Should I call you Zara or Hellion?" I asked with a grin. I thought it was funny to hear him call her such a name.

She laughed. "Either, although Demon is the one who usually calls me that. If I'm really bad, the other Warriors will do it to get a rise out of me. We came over not just so I could meet you, but to see if you and your friends might want to join our group. We have the best seats in the house," she pointed toward the back.

The spot she pointed to was an area I thought was off limits when I saw it earlier. It was empty when we came in. Now, I saw it had several men in cuts and women sitting there. A quick look told me Joker wasn't one of them. He probably had a date tonight or was back at the clubhouse with one of those bunnies, I thought acidly. I guess going out was for married couples only.

"Oh, that's so sweet of you, but we're fine here. We don't want to intrude on your night. We won't be staying long, I don't think," I quickly said.

Zara gave me a disappointed look, while Demon stared hard at me. "Well, if you change your mind, please come join us. We plan to be here most of the night. It's our night out without the kids."

"Then you need to enjoy it. I know what it's like to get one of those. Belle and Granddaddy shoved me out the door and threatened me if I didn't go out," I said, laughing.

"I can see Byron doing that. How's he doing?" Demon asked.

"He has his good and bad days. Today was a good one. I left Belle in charge, which he grumbled about. He said he didn't need an eleven-year-old telling him what to do."

"No doubt, but then again, our year-and-a-half-old son tries to boss us around," Zara said with a chuckle.

"Oh, that's such a sweet age. I didn't know you had a son, Demon. Congratulations."

He grinned as he took his phone out of his cut and fiddled with it. Less than a minute later, I was looking at pictures of an adorable little boy who looked a lot like his daddy.

"He's gorgeous. What's his name?"

"It's Alessandro, but we call him Alex. Had to go for the Italian names with Demon being Italian, you know. Do you have any pictures of Belle?" Zara asked.

My companions listened to us and the ones with kids smiled. Connie and Hana had kids, but the others didn't. They were single, although they were used to us talking about ours and showing pictures. While I got out my phone to show my pictures, Demon and Zara quickly introduced themselves to my new friends and shook their hands. Finally, I handed over my phone. Demon whistled.

"Damn, Raina, she looks like a carbon copy of you. When she starts dating, it's gonna be hell. We'll have to stock up on more guns."

"She's beautiful, and Demon's right," Zara said at the same time.

"Thank you. Stock up on guns? Why would you

need to do that?" I asked, puzzled. I might need to do that, but they wouldn't. Maybe that's what he meant.

"Because we take care of family, and she's family," he said enigmatically.

"Uh, okay, if you say so. Hey, we don't want to keep you from your group. Maybe we can talk later," I said to end this odd conversation. They nodded and said goodbye to us before going back to their friends. As soon as they were out of earshot, Tessa started talking excitedly.

"I didn't know you knew any of the Warriors! Wow, I've seen them around town, but I've never talked to one before. Demon is a hunk. Too bad he's married. Do you think you could introduce me to any of his single club members?"

"I knew them years ago when I lived here. As for introducing you to the single ones, I don't know who is or isn't single, and I don't know them well enough to do that. When I knew them, none were married. And FYI, they call each other brothers, not members."

Leif scooted his chair closer to mine. I leaned as far away as I could. He'd been acting oddly since we got here earlier. At work, he had always been nice and maybe a tad flirty, but I thought it was just his personality. Now, I wondered. He wasn't doing it to Tessa, and she was on the other side of him. I hoped he wasn't getting any ideas. I wasn't looking for a man or anything else.

"What about you? Did you ever date any of the Warriors?" he asked.

"No, I never dated any of them." He didn't need to know I had been married to someone who wanted to be one of them. My past wasn't something I talked about with them. They knew I grew up here, but that was it.

He was interrupted from asking anything else by the arrival of more Warriors and their wives. Payne introduced me to his wife, Jayla. After him, it was Rebel and Madisen. The fourth couple I didn't know either of them. He introduced himself as Ace and his wife as Devyn. She explained she was Bull's stepdaughter. That was news to me. I had no idea Bull had remarried. When I knew him, he'd been a widower for years and had a daughter, Harlow, older than me. I wondered where she was these days. All of them were sweet and talked to my friends and extended the invitation to join them again. I declined a second time. When they walked off, I looked at Connie, Tessa, and Hana.

"Are you ready to dance? I think I need to move. It's been ages since I've danced."

They nodded eagerly and stood up. Hana asked the guys if they were coming, but they shook their heads no. It was a relief. I didn't want Leif dancing up close to me. The music was pounding, and it was hard to hear. Just what I wanted. We found a spot and let the music take us. Hana danced very stiffly. Connie was looser and had some sense of rhythm. Sadly, Tessa was enthusiastic but had not an ounce of rhythm. As for me, I always thought I danced rather well, but who knew, maybe I didn't. I didn't care. I found it fun and that's all that mattered.

We were dancing to a second fast song when Zara, Jayla, Devyn, and Madisen joined us. We welcomed them and tried to talk over the music as we danced. The second song became a third one. As the third song came to an end, a slow one started up. I turned to head back to the table to take a breather as the Warriors' old ladies left, only I was stopped. Leif was standing there looking expectantly at me. From the look on his face, he knew this was going to be a slow song before it even started to get to the floor that fast. He must've asked the band to play one. "Come on, Raina, dance with me," he said with a smile and a wink.

"I need a break, Leif, but I'm sure one of the others would love to." I said, as I stepped away from him.

He caught me unaware, and I was twirled back toward him as he tugged me into his arms. He was laughing and telling me not to go. I knew he didn't mean anything by it, but I didn't think it was funny. I didn't want to dance with him. I hated to be manhandled. I pushed against his chest. "Leif, I said no. Let go," I ordered him.

"Don't be such a Debbie Downer. It won't hurt you to slow dance with me."

"It might not hurt her, but it'll hurt you if you make me use this Debbie and this Downer," I heard gruffly said behind me. I knew that voice even over the music. Slowly turning around, I laid eyes on the man who had been occupying my mind to no end. The one I was here to forget.

Joker was standing there. He was holding up both

fists, so I knew who Debbie and Downer were. Even upset, like he obviously was, he could still throw in a joke. Although, if he got truly angry would he? Lord, what a thing to be thinking about at a time like this? I must be off my rocker. What I should be doing was diffusing this tense moment before it got out of hand. I gave it a try. "Joker, I didn't see you come in. This is Leif. He's one of my coworkers. He didn't mean any harm. He was just messing around."

"That's not what it looked like to me. It looked like he wasn't listening to you and had his hands on you. Besides, it's not his turn to dance with you, it's mine. Come take a whirl around the floor with me, Raina. I want to see if you can still dance."

Rather than ignore him and let the two of them possibly fight, I nodded and held out my hands to him. Leif had dropped his hold on me when Joker threatened him and stepped back. He was scowling, but he didn't say anything as I was whisked away.

Being taken into Joker's arms and danced across the floor flooded my mind with memories. This wasn't the first time we'd danced together. The first time was at a holiday party and we were all at Joker's parents' house. Someone had turned on music and Joker started to dance. First, he danced with his mom, Abbie. She laughed the whole time. Not because he couldn't dance, but because he was teasing her. You could tell he was a wonderful dancer. From there he moved onto other ladies in the family.

I wasn't expecting him to plant himself in front of me and insist he had to dance with me too. He refused to move until I said yes. When I did and he took me in his arms, it was all I could do not to moan. By then I knew I didn't truly love Parker and Joker had become my secret crush. It was like dancing on a cloud with him. To this day, it was the single best dance of my life. Afterward, Parker had sneered and muttered in my ear that Joker was an idiot for making a fool out of himself like that. I thought he showed he was a real man. He wasn't afraid to show he had a softer side or that he could dance.

"Are you going to talk to me or am I to get the cold shoulder for interrupting that charming request to dance? If you want to dance with him instead, I'll take you to him," he said with a frown. He came to a halt in the middle of the floor.

"Don't be silly. I didn't want to dance with him. Dance, we look stupid just standing here. Besides, he probably would be one of those guys who just stands in one spot and sways or he'd step all over my toes. At least with you, I know neither will happen."

"Ahh, you remember then?"

"Remember what?"

"That I'm Fred Astaire. Which makes you Ginger."

I couldn't help but laugh as he wiggled his eyebrows at me as he said it, then he swung me back into a waltz of all things. Not the kind of dance this music called for. People moved out of our way. He didn't stop.

"You might be Fred, but I'm no Ginger. Yes, I

remember. I never asked. Is Abbie the reason you know how to dance so well?"

"Nope. My dad is. His mom made him take all kinds of dance lessons when he was growing up. She said it would get him the ladies. When I was a kid, he told me the same thing when he put me in those same lessons. So, is he right? Will it get me the lady?"

"I doubt you need me to answer that for you, Joker. Your dance moves have surely gotten you more than one lady in your time."

"There's only one lady I want to get. She's dancing with me right now," he said.

I gaped at him. He was no longer smiling or sounding like he was joking. He had a very serious look on his face. "Joker…" I didn't know what to say. I was too scared to imagine he was meaning what I thought. Why would he want anything to do with me?

"You think about it while we dance. Then when we're done, you come sit with me and the rest of the club."

"I can't. I mean, I can dance this dance with you, but not sit with you. I'm here with a group of coworkers. I can't just abandon them."

"You mean there are more Leifs here I'll have to run off?"

"No, there are no more Leifs, although Cray is with us too. It's us three ladies and two guys."

"If the guys behave, they can join us too. Now,

shh, I need to concentrate and count my steps or I'll mess up and step on your toes."

Again, I laughed, because he was back to giving me a silly grin. I shut up and let him whirl me around and around the floor. By now, most people had stopped dancing and stood there watching us. It's not every day you see a biker waltzing in a bar. When the music came to an end, there was thunderous applause. He bowed, then with a sway of his hand, he indicated me. I gave a tiny bow. As we were leaving the dance floor, Tessa came bounding up to us with Connie and Hana not far behind. A bit behind them was Leif and Cray. Cray was smiling, but Leif was looking pissed off.

"That was awesome. I had no idea you knew how to dance like that," Tessa said, as she almost devoured Joker with her hungry gaze. Instantly, I wanted to scratch her eyes out.

"Only with him. He's the real dancer, and he makes whoever dances with him look good."

"Well, then he'll have to dance with me then," she cooed.

"Sorry, I only dance with family, my closest friends and special people," he quickly said.

"Which is Raina?" she asked with a frown.

"Family, a close friend, and one hundred percent special." His arm wrapped around my waist and tugged me against him. The look he gave me was tender.

"Really? Do tell," Connie said.

"I will. Why don't you all join us in our section? I wanna chat with Raina, and she said she was here with coworkers. I didn't realize she had a job yet. Please, join us."

"Yes, let's do it. The others in his club already asked, and you said no, but you can't say no this time. I think it'll be fun," Hana added.

Knowing I was outnumbered, I gave in. "Okay, is there anything at our table we need to get?"

They all shook their heads. I knew better than to bring a purse. Everything I needed was in my jean pockets—a car key, my ID, and my debit card. The only one not looking thrilled at the prospect of joining the Warriors was Leif. As we headed to their section, Joker held me close. His hand on my hip felt like it was burning through my clothes. I was hyper aware of him and the reaction my body was having to him.

My skin felt like there were tiny jolts of electricity zapping along my nerve endings. My nipples were hard nubs and my vajayjay was tingling and feeling slightly damp. Oh my God, I was turned on in the middle of the bar. Thank goodness no one knew but me. I had to work not to fan myself.

Everyone greeted us loudly and enthusiastically when we got to their tables. They indicated open spots for everyone. Joker held onto me as he pulled out a chair. When I sat down, he pushed it closer to the table then sat in the empty one beside me. On my other side was a guy I didn't recognize. He smiled broadly and held out his hand.

"Hi, I'm Predator. It's a pleasure to meet you. I saw you at the clubhouse the night you came to see Joker."

"Hi. Sorry, there were so many people there that I didn't know. I'm Raina. You're new to the club since I lived here last. How long have you been a member?"

"I was just voted in along with another brother, Stalker, a few months ago. I hear you haven't been back in Hunters Creek in a long time."

"I haven't."

I was kept from saying more by Joker interrupting us to introduce two other men I didn't recognize. They were Iceman and Renegade. There was a fourth who had joined them that I did know. It was Slash.

"Hello Slash, it's nice to see you again." I held my hand over the table to him. He leaned across and took it. I thought he would shake it, but instead, he kissed my fingers and winked at me.

"The pleasure is all mine, lovely Raina. You've gotten even more beautiful than the other night, and I didn't think that was possible."

"She is more beautiful and I expect she'll continue to grow even more so, although you might not see it. It's hard to do that if your eyes have been plucked out," Iceman said, as he chuckled and glanced at Joker.

I did the same and saw he was staring intently at Slash with his eyes narrowed. He wasn't smiling. Slowly, all he did was nod. Slash threw back his head and laughed his ass off, which got the others laughing. Lord, what was wrong with them? Had they been drinking that much already?

Joker reached over and took my hand out of Slash's grip and laid it down on his thigh. He pressed it down. The feel of his rock-hard muscle did nothing to cool my heated state. I tried to move it, but he held it there.

"So, tell us where you all work? I didn't know Raina had started working. You've only been back what, a month?" Joker said.

"Just about. I started this week. I'm working for the police department as a dispatcher," I explained.

While I told them this, a waitress came to the table. She had refills for their drinks. She gave us expectant looks. Joker leaned toward her and whispered something in her ear. She nodded and wrote it down then she moved on to the others. I guess I'd wait to see what I got. It should be interesting.

"Sorry about that. So, how long will it take for you to be trained? There has to be a lot to learn. I had no idea they took on people who have no experience," Joker continued.

"They don't, but then again, I'm experienced. I've been doing nine-one-one dispatch for almost ten years. I got lucky when I left town and found someone willing to train me. All I really need to do is learn their call codes, policies, and procedures here. It'll probably take me a couple of months."

"She's being modest. She's already killing it. They've never seen anyone catch on like her. She came into work on Monday already knowing a ton of our call codes. She studied the past couple of weeks while she waited to start. She's putting the rest of us to shame," Connie told them with a smile.

"Better watch out. She's wicked smart. She'll be running the place in six months," Joker said.

"How do you know whether I'm smart or not?"

"I know more than you think, Raina," came his reply.

"Well, she better not. I'm up for the supervisor position when it opens up," Hana said. She smiled as she said it, but I heard an uneasy tone underlying her voice.

"You don't have to worry about that. Even if they did offer it to me, which they won't, I couldn't accept it. I have Belle to take care of. Granddaddy does fine as an adult presence for her, but she needs someone to help her with her homework, plan school events, do the PTA stuff, etcetera. When it comes to those things, I'm her only option. The supervisor spot would mean overtime."

"Babe, you're not alone anymore. You have the whole club, me and my parents now. If you ever get offered the job and you want to take it, then do it. Belle will be more than cared for," Joker said.

I could tell he was totally serious. I was stunned at the offer. It was generous but not anything I would ever do. I hated to impose on people. "Thank you, but I couldn't. So, tell me what all of you do for work?"

This got them telling us about their jobs, which got the focus off me like I wanted, although Joker kept giving me what looked like contemplative looks. When my drink arrived, I had to laugh when I took a tentative sip. It was a Shirley Temple. When I joined the family, I was too young to drink, so at one of the family get-togethers, Joker had made me one of these, so I wouldn't feel left out. Even though I was more than old enough to drink, I didn't do it often and never when I would be driving like I was tonight. Tessa and the others had kept trying to get me to drink something alcoholic all night, but I stuck to soda.

"You remembered," I told him.

"I never forget anything when it comes to you, Raina," he uttered softly. His intense stare made me want to squirm. Instead of asking him what he meant, I took another sip. As the night wore on, I fought more and more to ignore how much he was affecting me.

Joker: Chapter 7

Staying away from Raina had gone on long enough. I'd tried my hardest, wanting to give her time to settle back into life here, and me time to work on plans for her protection when Parker got out. However, after getting the text last night from Demon telling me she was at the Dark Angel, and with a man, I'd ridden like hell to get there, and put a stop to it.

There was no way in hell I was going to let another man worm his way into her life and heart. All those past six days of torture had done was more than solidify in my mind and heart that I would do everything in my power to win her heart. If in the end, she told me she had no feelings for me, then I'd know I did my best. It would still hurt like a motherfucker to let the dream go, but I would. I'd never try to force her to feel something she didn't. I wanted her to be happy, not miserable.

Sitting at the table, after having her in my arms, had been a pleasure mixed with hell. The hell part was not being able to hold her or kiss her like I wanted. That brief dance and then holding her hand wasn't nearly enough to curb my appetite for her company and touch. In addition, I had to watch her coworker stare holes into me when she wasn't looking. Leif had the hots for her and he didn't like any competition. Too bad for him, but

I wasn't leaving her to him. I could tell the way she acted toward him she only saw him as a friend. He needed to get the memo.

When the night came to an end, I followed her home to make sure she got there safely, even though she told me not to. Again, Leif offered to make sure she did, but she said no. Like he was safe to do anything. The idiot had a few too many drinks, in my opinion, to be behind the wheel. We tried to get him to let someone call him a ride, but he refused. Iceman and Renegade ended up following him. The ladies with her had all ridden together, and they weren't close to the legal limit. Watching that garage door close behind her and not being able to go inside had been awful.

Which was why I was here bright and early this morning. I knew it was probably too early for a Sunday, but I wanted to make sure they didn't eat breakfast. I was going to take all of them out for it. Byron would enjoy the outing, and it would give me time with Raina, and an opportunity to get to know Belle better. I knocked on the door and waited to see if anyone would answer it. A minute or so later, the door swung open, and I saw the smiling face of Belle. "Good morning, Belle. Do you remember me?"

"Sure, I remember you, Joker. Good morning. Are you here to see my mom?"

She looked adorable with her messy hair and pajamas with kittens on them. Since it was summer, it was a tank and short set. Damn, she was the spitting image of her mom. "Actually, I'm here to see all of you. Are your mom and granddaddy awake?"

"They are. Mom is in her room and Granddaddy is in his chair. Come in." She held the door open wider.

As I followed her inside, I shut the door. Walking into the living room, I saw Byron in his recliner. He was drinking a cup of coffee. He nodded. Belle hurried down the hallway. She must be going to tell her mom I was here.

"Mornin', Joker. What brings you here so early on a Sunday? Shouldn't you be sleeping off a night of partying?" he asked with a grin.

"I did go out last night, but I didn't need to sleep it off. Didn't Raina tell you? She went to the Dark Angel last night with her coworkers and ended up spending it with me and some of the club. I went to bed after I made sure she got home alright."

"I was in bed when she got home. That was nice of you to do. Do you two have a date or something this morning?" he asked this with a twinkle in his eyes.

"I was hoping I'd get here in time to take the three of you out to breakfast."

"Now, how can that be a date if you take me and Belle with you?" he asked innocently.

"She won't go without you, and I have to take my time easing her into the dating idea. So, can I assume you're okay with us dating?" I asked boldly. I might as well know his stance from the start.

"Boy, as long as you don't hurt her, or force her to do anything she doesn't want, then I'm more than okay with it. You're nothing like your worthless cousin. I never liked that boy. I hated when she married him. I tried to tell her just because she was pregnant, she didn't need to marry the fool, but her damn parents insisted on it, and wouldn't let up until she did. They convinced her if she didn't, she'd be called a whore, and shunned by the whole town."

His admission filled me with even more anger toward Rudy and Gwen. I'd been fighting this past week not to go pay them another visit and beat the hell out of Rudy. I wouldn't hit a woman, so Gwen was safe. Their betrayal of Raina was something I'd never forgive or understand.

"I'd never do that to her, Byron. You and I need to have a long talk. There are some things you should know, but that can wait. I think I hear the ladies joining us."

We both glanced toward the hallway. When she came into sight, I wanted to groan. She wasn't in her pajamas, too bad. I would've loved to see what she wore to bed. Or better yet, what she might not. Was it too much to hope she slept naked like I did? She had her hair up in a ponytail. Unlike last night, she had on no makeup. I preferred her like this. Although with it, she was still stunning. She had on a short summer dress that hit mid-thigh. It was lilac with tiny dark purple flowers on it. I saw that Belle had changed into a dress similar to her mom's, only it was pink, and had fixed her hair the same.

Raina gave me a shy smile. "Good morning, Joker. Belle said you came to see all of us. Can I get you a cup of coffee?"

"Morning, love. Thanks for the offer, but I can wait. I did come to see all of you. I'm taking the three of you out to breakfast."

"Oh, you don't need to do that. If you're hungry, I can fix something here."

"I already told him yes, so go get your shoes and purse. We'll be leaving as soon as you get back. I'm hungry and I haven't been out to breakfast in ages. Are we going to Sadie's Place?" Byron asked as he came to his feet slowly.

I had to fight the urge to help him. He was a proud man and wouldn't like it. He had his oxygen on, which I knew now he had to use all the time. I hoped this wouldn't be too much for him. I'd have to keep an eye on him to make sure he didn't overdo it. "Is there any place else to have breakfast? I think it's the best in town," I replied.

"Agreed. All I need to do is get my shoes on, then I'm ready. Shoo, go get your stuff or we'll leave without you," he told his granddaughters.

Belle laughed. "You know you won't do that. If you did, I'd cry, and you'd feel terrible. Come on, Mommykins, let's go get our shoes. I'm hungry." As she took off for her room, she dragged Raina along with her.

"Thanks for the help," I told him, as he hobbled over to sit on the bench by the door where the shoes were.

He worked them on. Luckily, he had one of those

small oxygen machines which fit in a pack and you could carry it on your shoulder or across your chest. He had his angled diagonally across him. By the time he had his shoes on, the ladies were back. Raina went to pick up the car keys on the table by the door. I stopped her.

"No need for you to drive. I've got us covered."

She gave me a puzzled look as we went out the door. I closed it and waited for her to lock it, before taking her hand and walking her down the stairs. Belle had gone ahead with Byron. Sitting in the driveway was my Ford Bronco. I'd had it for a few years. I usually only drove it when I needed to haul something, or the weather was too cold and icy to ride my bike.

"I think Byron should sit in the front. It'll be easier for him to get in and out," I suggested to Raina. If he wasn't with us, I'd have her right beside me.

"I agree. I don't mind sitting in the back with Belle. I had no idea you had anything other than your bike," she said as I opened the passenger door for Byron then the back one for her and Belle.

Belle jumped in first. I kept a hand ready to help Byron in case he needed it, but he got in alright, if slowly. "It comes in handy to haul things and when the weather is too bad to ride safely or comfortably."

When Byron was settled, I closed his door then hers. Walking around to the driver's side, I opened my door then paused to take off my cut, and lay it over the seat before I got in.

"Joker, why did you take off your vest?" Belle asked curiously.

"Honey, it's called a cut not a vest," Raina quickly reminded her.

"Your mom is right. As for why I took it off, if you ride in a cage, which is anything not a bike in biker speak, you take it off, and then put it back on when you get out. It's discourteous to wear it in a vehicle. Just one of those weird biker things. You'll find there's a few of them, but you'll learn."

She didn't say anything, just smiled. "Have you been to Sadie's Place yet?" I asked Belle, although I was watching Raina in the rearview mirror as we got on the road.

"No, we haven't, I'm ashamed to say. We've been so busy getting into a new routine and going out tends to tire out Granddaddy, so I've been cooking. This will be a nice treat. Thank you for inviting us. Who else is going to be there from the club?" Raina asked.

"No one. This isn't a club event. Although, there's a chance someone might come in. Next weekend, we'll have you come out to the compound. The old ladies often cook on the weekend or we have a party. With the heat, you can enjoy a nice day in the pool."

"Ooh, that'll be fun. Please say we can go, Mom," Belle squealed.

"We'll see. It's nice of you to invite us, but we don't want to intrude."

"Raina, you'll soon learn that you'll never be intruding on anything we do. Like I told you, you're family. Mom and Dad will be there. They're dying to see you and Belle."

She gave me a nervous look. "Who else will be there?"

"Not them," was all I said, since little ears were listening.

I wasn't sure if Raina had told Belle about how her in-laws and parents had lied about her. After what they did, there was no damn way they'd ever be invited to any family events that we'd go to. They gave up their right to be part of their lives when they turned their backs on them.

"Oh, you mean my grandparents. I don't want to see them. They're mean and they lie. Granddaddy and MeMe are the only nice ones," she said blithely. Well, I guess that answered my question.

"I agree, but my parents aren't like them. Nor is the rest of the Fairbanks. Your dad's side, the Piersons, are a bit standoffish. Luckily, there aren't that many of them."

"Do you have brothers and sisters?"

"I have a younger brother. His name is Andrew. He lives in Nevada. He's a lawyer. We don't see much of him. He comes home maybe once a year. Dad and Mom go see him once a year at least. I told him as soon as he gets married and starts having kids, he'll have to come back more often or move home. No way my parents will be able to live far away from their grandkids."

"You'll have to give them some too, boy," Byron said out of the blue. As I glanced over at him, he winked.

"I'm working on it, Byron. Believe me, I'm working on it." A peek at Raina and I saw her stiffen and look slightly upset. She had no clue I was referring to her and Belle. I'd have to clue her in soon. Maybe next weekend if I could hold out that long.

Further talk was cut short by us arriving at Sadie's Place. It was just after eight but the place was already more than two-thirds packed. Hopefully, we wouldn't have to wait long to get a table. It would get worse as the morning wore on and people got out of church.

Finding a parking spot, I took it, then helped them out of the Bronco after I put my cut back on. Walking in with Raina on my arm felt right. Belle was holding onto Byron and they were ahead of us. People were standing and sitting around the hostess stand. I recognized the hostess. It was Sadie's daughter, Angela. She had been working here since high school. She was close to my age.

"Well, long time no see, Joker. Where have you been hiding yourself? I thought I'd see you at the Dark Angel again, but I haven't. You still owe me a drink," she said with a smile.

I wanted to groan. Angela had gotten a divorce last year, and she'd been running kind of wild since then. She would often go out drinking, and more than one guy in town had found a companion for the night.

I thought she should stay at home more with her two kids. She and I had never hooked up, but she sure tried. The drink comment was because the last time I saw her, she wanted me to buy her drinks, and I told her I was leaving.

"I'll let the bartender know to put one on my tab the next time you come in, since I've never bought you any. How long is the wait to get a table for four?"

Angela barely paid any attention to Byron since she knew him. Belle got a cursory glance. Raina on the other hand, stared at her intently. "Well, if it isn't Raina Pierson. What brings you back to town? Last I heard, you ran off, and no one knew where you went. Isn't her husband your cousin, Joker? I would've thought you'd be the last one to be with her. Poor PJ, Gwen, Rudy, and Bernie were left high and dry, just like you were, Mr. Anderson," she said sweetly to Byron after cutting down Raina.

I wasn't gonna stand for anyone doing that to Raina. I opened my mouth to put Angela in her place, but Belle beat me to it. "My mom didn't run off and leave anyone high and dry. She left town so people like you wouldn't have more rude things to say about her. My grandparents knew where we were. They chose not to visit, unlike Granddaddy and MeMe did."

If looks could kill, Belle would've incinerated her. Angela's mouth fell open in shock. It was all I could do to muffle my laughter. Byron was grinning and Raina was trying to look unfazed by either remark.

"Down tiger there's no need to get upset. You're

right. She didn't leave without telling anyone. The problem is that those she did tell lied to the rest of us. Our table?" I asked again.

"I-well, umm, it'll probably be at least twenty minutes," Angela muttered. Her cheeks were red from embarrassment or anger. I wasn't sure which one.

"Will that do or do you wanna try somewhere else? We can go to Cookeville if you prefer." I offered Raina. If she changed her mind about eating here, I'd take her elsewhere.

"I'm fine to wait if you guys are," Raina said.

Byron nodded. Belle was too busy staring at Angela to indicate one way or the other, but I figured if she didn't want to stay, she would've said so. "Then put us on the list. Outside will be fine too. It's a really nice day and the heat hasn't gotten too bad yet."

As we moved off to find a place to wait, we were the center of attention. I knew a lot of them remembered who Raina was and wondered why she was back. Others heard what Belle said and added to it. I didn't want them to be uncomfortable, but again, if they were going to stay in Hunters Creek, and I was going to do my damndest to make it happen, then they would have to get used to it. I drew Raina aside. "Babe, we can go somewhere else if this is too much?"

"We don't need to. Ten years ago I was young and scared. I didn't want Belle to be exposed to ugly talk and rumors. She's old enough now to handle it, in case you didn't figure it out just now," she said with a grin.

"Hell, she made me want to run and hide. She's a feisty little thing, isn't she? I wonder where she gets it from?" I teased her.

"Oh, that's all Granddaddy there. I'm as sweet as a church lady."

I burst out laughing. Her words were at total odds with the wicked grin she got on her face when she said it. "Uh huh, sure you are. And if I believe that, you have an oasis to sell me in the middle of the desert."

"Exactly!"

Still laughing, we rejoined Belle and Byron. As we waited for our table, we chatted. It was some about her work and the rest was Belle telling me about her friends she left behind. She missed them, but she was thrilled to be in Hunters Creek. I'd have to see about finding some kids her age that she could make friends with. When school started next month, she'd find some.

It was more like fifteen minutes rather than twenty before we were called to the hostess stand. Angela didn't bother to talk. She merely showed us to our table, which was outside, and dropped the menus and silverware on the table before she walked off.

As we looked over the menu, Raina leaned over to whisper in my ear. "I hope Belle didn't upset your lady friend too much. I'll have a talk with her about her attitude. If you think it'll help, I'll apologize to Angela before we leave. I don't want you to suffer because of my daughter."

"Raina, Angela's remark about owing her a drink

was because the last time I ran into her, she kept pushing for me to buy her one and I didn't. She's not my lady friend. Belle nor you owe her an apology. What she said was rude."

"Oh, well I thought she might be the woman you were referring to earlier. When Granddaddy mentioned kids and you said you were working on some for your parents."

"Sweetheart, I'll tell you all about who I had in mind later, when there aren't so many ears around."

"You don't have to. I wasn't trying to be nosy, just wanted to make sure Belle didn't cause you problems," was her quick response.

"I know you're not, but you should know. Later."

She gave me a puzzled look but didn't say more as she went back to her menu. When our waitress came to get our drink order, I smiled. It was Sadie. Unlike her daughter, she was sweet as pie.

"Well, look at who the cat dragged in. Joker, you haven't been in to see me in at least a month. And Byron, it's so good to see you out and about. Raina, it's good to see you, honey. You're as beautiful as ever. And this little miss has to be Belle. You are your mama's twin. How long are you in town for? I hope it's a long visit."

"Hi, Sadie, it's good to be back. We've actually moved back and we're staying with Granddaddy," Raina told her with a genuine smile.

"Well, hallelujah, this calls for pie after breakfast. Let me get your drinks then I'll be back for your orders."

From that point on, we enjoyed our breakfast. The place maintained a steady business, and every table was full almost the entire time, both inside and out. We did get more looks, but no one had enough guts to come over and speak to us. By the time we were done, we were stuffed. Sadie insisted on sending us home with a slice of pie for each of us. The only minor disagreement came when we went to pay. Raina tried to pay for the three of them. I wasn't having it. I invited them, I'd pay. She gave in once I explained and refused to back down.

Back in the car, I asked if they wanted to take a drive. All three of them seemed more than fine with the suggestion, so I headed through town. As we passed various places, I pointed out the ones the club owned. There were a bunch more than when she lived here.

"It's so amazing what you guys have done, Joker. Bull must be so proud of how the club has grown. And some of them aren't what I would think an MC would own."

"What? You mean a spa, a bakery, a shelter, and a bookstore don't scream dangerous bikers, beware?"

She chuckled and shook her head no. "No, they don't, which means I'm being stereotypical, aren't I? Sorry."

"Nothing to be sorry about. We never imagined it either. The bakery came along by chance and that's how Rebel met Madisen. She's the chief baker and owns a percentage of the bakery. Warriors' Haven was due to the number of women and kids who we have helped out of terrible situations. Demon runs it with help. The spa we bought out when the last owner put it up for sale. The old ladies went there and loved it. They convinced us it would be a great investment. For some weird reason, the club thought it would be funny to put me in charge of it. Thank God, Maverick's Rylan manages the day-to-day with the customers. Payne's Jayla worked in the bookstore and after they got together, her boss sold it and we bought it. Do you want to see what we're adding next?"

"Sure, although I can't imagine what it could be?"

Smiling, I drove them over to the apartment building we were finalizing the sale on with Mr. Maguire, Rylan's old landlord. It was the place Rylan lived in when she first moved to Hunters Creek. As I pointed it out, I explained why we were buying it. "Rylan lived here when she first came to Hunters Creek. Mr. Maguire owned it. You remember him."

"That mean old man who ran the farmers' market and would scowl at people and throw tomatoes at the kids who irritated him?" Raina asked in shock.

"Yep, that's him. Surprise, surprise, he wasn't any better as a landlord. If you needed something fixed, he'd argue and complain about it to make you feel bad for asking him to do something about it. Well, he finally got an offer he couldn't refuse, and we bought it. It's a decent place, and we'll make money. There's gonna be some repairs done to bring it up to our standards, which Tank and his guys at the construction company can handle. We're renaming it Warriors' Abodes. That was Loki's idea. Since he came up with it, he'll be the one in charge of managing it."

"I love how you relate the names back in some way, if you can, to the club and put at least one member in charge. Other than having more responsibility, does it mean anything else for the ones who manage them?" she asked.

"All of us get a cut of all the businesses, but the one in charge gets a slightly larger cut."

"That sounds more than fair," Byron said.

After showing them the businesses, we went for a long ride in the country. We showed Belle several of our haunts growing up. By the time we were done and I dropped them off at home, I didn't want to leave, but I had some things I had to do before work tomorrow. As I left, I got them to promise they'd come to the compound next weekend. Well, more like I said what time I would pick them up and not to tell me no, because the club wouldn't take no for an answer. Byron was the one to assure me they would go. Riding away, I made my plans for next weekend.

Raina: Chapter 8

I was so glad to see my shift coming to an end. This week has been stressful at work for a variety of reasons. For one, Leif had been acting cold toward me. I knew it had to do with Saturday night at the bar, and how I had said no to dancing with him. Since then, I watched him when he wasn't aware, and I saw how he acted with other women. Yeah, he'd been acting flirty with me, and I had taken it as only being friendly. Knowing that he was hoping for something more, made me tone down my cheerfulness around him. I was still polite, but no more sitting with him on break unless others were with us, and never with me sitting next to him.

He was an attractive man, and I knew a lot of women would be thrilled to have him pay attention to them. He just wasn't for me. The only man who I thought about romantically was the one I couldn't have. Why? Number one reason was I wasn't his type. I saw him being with really outgoing, sexy, and daring women. I wasn't like that. Number two, he'd said he had someone in mind, so that meant he was taken or on the verge of it. Number three reason was even if he could've seen me as a potential girlfriend, I was his cousin's ex-wife. That would make things way too awkward for him and his family. The Piersons and Fairbanks associated with each other during all the holidays. I remembered that distinctly.

However, since he was making an effort to be friendly, I was going to spend time with him. I wanted Belle to have at least one person from her dad's family who she could call a friend and rely on if she ever needed help. Lord knows other than Granddaddy she wasn't getting anyone from my side. I hadn't bothered to call or stop by to tell my parents we were in town. Ten years of silence built up a wall of resentment in me against them. If I never saw them again, it would be fine by me.

Another thing to stress me was the thought of the countdown to Parker's likely parole getting shorter and shorter. His hearing was in just over two weeks. If they granted it, he would be out a few days later, I think. So at best, I had three weeks before I found out if his threats were real, or just a bunch of hot air. Unbeknownst to anyone, even Granddaddy, I'd been going to the local indoor shooting range. I took one of his handguns to practice with. I hadn't kept up my shooting skills over the years, much to my shame. It was time to brush up on them. If Parker came after us, I'd have a surprise for him. He wasn't going to hurt me, our daughter, or Granddaddy.

Work in general was stressful, We had a lot of calls and it seemed people were going loco in the hot, humid Tennessee summer. I was thankful I didn't work the night shift. It was worse. I had only an hour until I was off, then I had the entire weekend to unwind.

"Hey Raina, come here. There's someone I want

you to meet," Connie called to me from her station.

It was quiet enough that I could do it, so I got up and walked over. Standing there was a police officer. Since I started last week, I'd met several of them as they came into headquarters for various reasons. All so far had seemed very nice. I wondered which one this was, and if I'd talked to him on the radio or not yet. He straightened as I got to them. He was tall. He was maybe six feet. He was stocky. I would guess him to be in his early thirties. He had dark blond hair and a mustache. He smiled.

"Zev, this is Raina Pierson. Raina, this is Zev, or Officer Oberlin as you've probably heard on the radio. She's the newest voice you've been hearing on the radio. He's Darius's best friend."

Darius was Connie's husband, and he was an officer in Hunters Creek too. I'd met him and liked him a lot. I immediately held out my hand. "It's nice to meet you, Officer Oberlin. We've spoken on the radio a few times."

He shook my hand slowly. "Hello, Raina, it's a pleasure to meet you. Please, call me Zev. I've heard Darius and Connie singing your praises. I had to come see who this angel was. Your voice on the radio sounds like a siren. I can see the voice doesn't lie. Connie swears you'll be as knowledgeable as her on everything here by the end of the month. I hope you'll be staying in Hunters Creek and not leaving us."

I laughed. He had one of those friendly, sort of flirty but in a fun way charm about him. He wasn't like Leif, who I noticed was staring at us from across the room. "I don't know if that's true, and I'm no siren unless you meant the horn kind on your squad car."

All three of us laughed. He shook his head. "No, I meant the female kind. Dare I say you could be one of those phone sex operators and make a fortune."

I blushed. "No one has ever said that before, but I guess if they decide to fire me, I have something I might be able to fall back on. Are you here just to give Connie a hard time, and make me blush or did you have to come in today for something else? I know most of the guys stay out of here unless they absolutely have to be here."

"I came to drop off paperwork and thought I should drop in and meet you. Connie says you're originally from here. It's a great place. I only moved here five years ago after I got out of the Army. I was stationed at Fort Campbell for my last tour."

"Let me guess, you were an MP, right?"

"Got it in one. Guilty as charged."

"Guess who she's friends with, Zev?" Connie said excitedly.

"Who?"

"The Archangel's Warriors. We went out Saturday night, and they asked us to sit with them at their reserved seating in the Dark Angel. I told Darius about it, but he forgets to tell you stuff I want you to know."

"Really? Are they old family friends?"

"You could say that. My ex-husband's cousin is a

member."

I didn't go into details. He didn't need to know all my history, not that it would be hard to find out in this town. For some reason, it felt odd to be talking to a cop about the Warriors even though they were not an outlaw gang like some MCs were. I'd seen those before in my old jobs.

"No shit, wow. I see them riding around all the time, and I've seen their compound out in the country. It looks like an interesting place. I bet it's even better from the inside. Where did you move back from? Have you been gone for a long time?"

I hadn't talked too much to my new coworkers about where I was or why. I knew it would come up soon and there was no use hiding it. "I've been gone for ten years. My daughter and I lived in Albany, Georgia. I had a friend from high school who moved there when we graduated. She knew I needed a break."

"Break?" he asked.

"I left when my husband went to prison and I divorced him. Being in a small town at that time was too much for me."

They both looked startled. I knew this would likely spread like fire around here. Honestly, I was surprised no one had said something the first week. Hunters Creek wasn't that big of a town. Most people had lived here all their lives and for generations.

"Shit, sorry, I didn't know," he muttered, looking uncomfortable.

"Don't be, it's not your fault. I'm shocked no one said anything yet. Parker deserved what he got time for. Now that my daughter is older and my granddaddy is older, we came back to take care of him."

"How old is your daughter?"

"Belle is eleven. Do you have any kids?"

He nodded. "I do. My son is twelve, I was twenty-one when he was born. His mother and I got married too young, and we grew apart. Being an Army wife was tough. They live in Dickson. Two hours isn't bad and I get him every other weekend and one week a month. We split the major holidays."

"I don't think I could stand it if I couldn't have Belle with me all the time. You're much stronger than I am."

"Oh, I wouldn't say..."

"Hey Raina, are you done talking, or do you want me to keep covering your calls?" came the slightly acid question from Tessa.

Her attitude surprised me. Usually, she was one of the ones who took every opportunity to chat to people and take smoke breaks. What crawled up her ass? "The phones aren't ringing off the hook, Tessa. I'm sorry you can't keep up. I don't want you to feel overworked. Since I didn't get my ten-minute break earlier, I was taking it now," I told her breezily.

She dropped back into her chair with a petulant look on her face. It wasn't a good look on her. She had no right to say anything to me. She took more breaks and chatted twenty times more than I did. Turning back to Connie and Zev, I told them goodbye.

"It was nice to meet you, Zev. I need to get back to work. I have to get out of here on time. My daughter and I have plans. Stay safe out there."

"It was great to meet you too. Hopefully, we'll meet again soon and can talk more without the conversation Nazi yelling at us."

This made me laugh. He stuck around another minute or so talking to Connie as I retook my seat and checked my monitors. The rest of the hour passed quietly. When it struck three o'clock, I was ready with my purse. I walked out as I waved and called out happy weekend to the others. Most of them returned the wish except for Leif and Tessa. They were standing with their heads together. Seeing them like that, I thought they made the perfect couple.

Forgetting them and their weird behavior, I headed out. A quick stop at the store to grab a few things I needed to make dinner tonight was the first order of business. Granddaddy and Belle both had requested I make fried chicken with mashed potatoes and gravy. They said the vegetable could be my choice, but the other two were non-negotiable. I should bring home fish sticks and see what they'd say. The look on their faces would be priceless, I bet.

In order to make the chicken, I needed breading mix, a few herbs we didn't have at the house and to pick up more potatoes. With those in the cart, I went to the produce area to figure out what vegetables to make. Standing there debating between asparagus, broccoli, and corn on the cob, I was startled when I heard a swift inhale, and my name spoken in a shocked tone behind me.

Swinging around, I froze. Standing there were my parents. As I let the shock move through me, I had inane thoughts about them. The first was how old they looked. When I left, they barely had any gray hair. Now, both of them had heads full of gray hair. Both had a ton of lines, and their skin looked old and dry. What shook me from my unkind thoughts was their remark.

"Why did you come back here? You should've stayed away," my mom hissed.

"Why shouldn't I come back? It's my home and Granddaddy is here. He needs help. Not that you would know that. You don't bother to check on him or anything. I've been here over a month and not one call." I said it, knowing that Granddaddy wouldn't speak to them.

"It's none of your business how often we talk to or see my dad," my dad huffed, although he looked a bit ashamed. It was probably due to the number of people around us. I wasn't bothering to keep my voice down. If they wanted to confront me in a public store, then they had to accept the consequences. Mom was darting worried looks around us. There were people who had stopped and were gawking.

"Sure it is. He's my grandfather and my daughter's great-grandfather. Unlike you, he hasn't forgotten he has a granddaughter. Belle is doing wonderful, in case you give a damn, which I know you don't. If you did, you would've called or come to see us in the last ten years. I heard you told people I left without a forwarding address or number. I knew you were less than warm and fuzzy, but I didn't know you were liars."

The color drained out of their faces. I saw my dad clench his hands into fists. He had never been physically violent. He was more the verbal abuse kind of man. He'd been very vocal when I was at home about how I disappointed him and had to do better. In the past, I never talked back or made any kind of scenes. Which is how I ended up married at sixteen.

"You need to leave and take your daughter with you. Everything was great until you came back here. You have no shame. You divorced your husband while he was in prison. I bet you were the one who drove him to steal in the first place," Dad hissed.

"I didn't drive him to anything. He was the one who was too proud, or maybe he was too lazy to work to take care of his family. I wasn't the one spending the money he got from his ill-gotten gains. And I sure didn't have any to raise his daughter with these last ten years, however you should be happy. He's getting out soon, I hear. You three can form a support group along with his parents. From what I know, he's not any more mature than he was then."

"What were you doing, siccing Joker on us?" Mom whispered.

"Joker? I didn't sic him on you. When did you talk

to him?"

Instantly, they both clammed up, and walked off as if the hounds of hell were after them. The people standing around us stared at me with their mouths open.

"You can't pick your family, can you? Have a great day," I said as sweetly as I could, while my brain was going a hundred miles an hour thinking about Joker. When had he seen them, and what had he said? I knew when I got home, I'd see if I could find his number and call him. I had to know.

Grabbing several ears of corn, I put them in my cart and headed for the checkout. Not wanting to talk to anyone, I used one of those self-checkout ones, which I hated. It always told me to put my stuff in the bag when I'd already done it. I usually wanted to kick the machines, but today, it was the least of my worries. Driving home after I got in the car was done in a daze. I didn't realize I'd driven the whole distance until the car shut off, and I looked around to find myself in the garage. That was a dangerous way to drive. I knew better.

Climbing out, I grabbed my bags and purse, then hurried to the door which connected the garage to the house. I found it locked, which was good. I'd been lecturing both of them not to leave it unlocked. They thought as long as the main garage door was shut, they were safe. I wasn't that convinced. Fishing out my house key, I put it in the lock and unlocked it. Opening the door, I got a shock. A loud beeping started buzzing. Frantically looking around to figure out what was doing that, I saw a small box next to the door. *What in the world? Granddaddy didn't have an alarm system.*

Belle came running into the washroom. "Here, let me show you, Mommy," she said excitedly, as she punched in numbers then it went quiet.

"Since when do we have an alarm?" I asked, as I handed her a bag to carry. We walked toward the kitchen.

"Since today," she said unhelpfully.

"I know that, Love Bug," I said sarcastically. She grinned at me.

Granddaddy had almost put in an alarm system several years ago. He got as far as having the wires run to the mudroom, then he decided it wasn't needed and they were left there. It had driven MeMe crazy when she had to look at these wires peeking out of the wall every time she went to the garage or did laundry. She'd threatened to rewire him one day. He would always laugh and kiss her when she said that, and she'd melt. I'd heard and witnessed it several times over the years. I found him sitting at the kitchen table drinking a cup of coffee.

"Mind telling me how we have an alarm system since this morning and why? I thought you said it wasn't necessary."

"It wasn't, but with the two of you here and because of other factors, it is now. Joker agreed."

"Joker? What does he have to do with this?"

"He got the guys and gals from Salvation Security to come and install it for us. Remember, the Warriors own a security business now and they do this kind of stuff and more."

"I do remember, but I don't remember you and him talking about it, or you telling me you were going to do it. How much did it cost? You have to let me pay half. It's for our security too." I knew with Parker getting out and the threats he made, it was smart. That had to be why Granddaddy was doing it now.

He shook his head. "No, you're not. This was needed, and anyway, the bill has been taken care of."

"You paid it already? Well, I can still give you the money. Tell me how much it was." I insisted as I unpacked the groceries. Belle had left us alone and gone to her room.

"It didn't cost me anything, so there's nothing for you to repay."

"Come on, I'm not stupid. This wasn't cheap, even if you did have the wiring already done. How much?"

"I have no idea. They wouldn't tell me and refused my money. Said it had already been taken care of."

A niggling suspicion entered my mind. "Who took care of it?"

"They said Joker did. I called him to find out, and he refused to tell me, and said he wouldn't take our money."

"Granddaddy! That's too much. We can't just

accept it. We have to get him to see reason."

"Well, you can try. Why don't we invite him over for dinner tonight so we can talk to him?"

It wasn't a bad idea. I wanted to talk to him anyway about my parents. This way I could get answers to both issues. "Okay, let's do that. Call or text him and see if he is available. He might have other plans." I wanted to ask him when he got Joker's number, but I stayed quiet.

I got a sly smile in return as he took out his phone. "If he does, he'll change them. There's no way he'd miss coming to see…us." He tapped away slowly on the phone.

Every time I saw him with a cell phone or a computer, I had to smile. It took some convincing years ago to get him to have either. After he and MeMe learned how to use them, they loved them. They texted, emailed, and FaceTimed me and Belle all the time. It had really been a blessing, and the way we kept close despite the six-hour distance between us. They knew why I refused to come back to Hunters Creek. They never complained and would come to see us several times a year. Sometimes, I'd meet them somewhere in the middle, and we'd have a family holiday. While he texted, I went to change into some comfy clothes before starting to cook. When I got back, he was smiling.

"He said he'd love to come to dinner. He'll be here at six."

"Damn, it won't be ready until probably closer to seven o'clock," I muttered, as I pulled out the trash can, and started to shuck the husks and silk off the corn. He got up to help.

"I got this. You sit and relax. Tell me what the two of you did today, other than let people in to install an alarm."

"Well, we asked them a lot of questions. They were really patient with Belle. She had a ton of them. I think she's gonna grow up to be some kind of tech person. She has the mind and knack. They even let her help, which she thought was cool. In between, we went to the park. She had fun there with some dogs other people brought to walk and swung on the swings. I took her to lunch at the Dairy Queen, then we spent time playing checkers. Oh, and I started to show her how to play chess."

"Chess? Lord, really. Well, hopefully she'll be a better player than I ever was. I could never beat you." I gave him a mock frown.

He laughed. "I know. I think she will. She apparently got my gaming brain, not yours."

I playfully stuck out my tongue which got him to teasing me that he'd make me lick a bar of soap. When I was young and stuck out my tongue, that was their punishment. God, I could still taste that Irish Springs soap. Yuck!

As soon as I was done with the corn, I prepared my mix to make the breading for the steak. I was in the middle of coating them and putting them aside until I was ready to cook them, when I heard the roar of a motorcycle. I tensed up. It had to be him. Since my hands were covered in goo and seasonings, Granddaddy went to get the door. The sound of Joker's deep voice talking sent shivers through me. I had to tell myself to settle the hell down.

Belle came wandering into the kitchen. As Granddaddy and Joker came into the kitchen, her face lit up and she surprised me by running over to Joker and hugging him. He seemed startled for a moment, then he hugged her back and kissed her hair. "Hey there, Bells. How're you doing? Are you helping your mom cook dinner?"

"Nope, I'm a disaster in the kitchen. I'm hopeless. Give me something mechanical or something I can put together and I'm great. Cooking makes no sense to me," she told him candidly and truthfully.

He glanced over at me. I gave him what I hoped was a casual smile. "Hi Joker. I hope you like fried chicken, mashed potatoes, and corn on the cob."

"I love all those. Thank you for the invite. Is she telling the truth about her kitchen abilities? Surely, she inherited them from you or Mabel."

I shook my head. "Sorry, but she's telling the gospel. She can burn water, I swear."

He grinned at me then looked down at her. She was watching him. "Girly, we'll have to see if Ms. Marie over in Dublin Falls and the ladies at the club can help. If you want to learn that is, or if you don't, then don't worry about it. You do you."

"I really don't care if I learn or not. I'm living with

Mommykins forever anyway. She likes to cook," she said mischievously. This was an old debate of ours.

"Young lady, you're not living with me forever! You'll grow up, get a job, get married, have kids, and make me happy,"

"No, I'm gonna lie on the couch, and play video games and watch movies while you work, cook and clean."

Joker's face was comical. He looked shocked and affronted all at the same time. We couldn't keep going. Both of us burst out laughing, which clued him in that we were being silly.

"Damn, you had me going there for a minute. I thought I was gonna have to stage an intervention or something. Don't do that to me. My ticker might give," he said as he clutched his chest and staggered like he was having a heart attack. Belle giggled and grabbed his arm.

"Hurry, Mommy, he needs CPR," she yelled.

Instantly, my cheeks grew warm as I imagined putting my mouth on his. I cursed silently and tried to make it stop. I knew my cheeks were red. Based on the smirk spreading across Joker's face, he saw it and knew what I was thinking. He winked at me.

"Yeah Raina, hurry. I need mouth-to-mouth. I think this is the big one, so you might have to do it for a long time to revive me." His voice sounded growly as he said it.

I heard Granddaddy snort, and he put his hand up

to hide his smile. I was going to kill all three of them. Thinking fast, I held up my messy hands. "You don't need mouth-to-mouth. I bet hand-to-mouth with lots of chicken goo will do the trick." I stepped toward him. He faked a horrified look and grabbed Belle, putting her in front of him.

"Save me, Bells," he said in a quivery voice. She dissolved in laughter.

"Joker, you're on your own. Chicken goo is my worst nightmare." She wiggled out of his grip and took off for the living room.

Granddaddy looked at him. "You're on your own, boy," he said then he too went to the living room.

Joker sighed. "Left to fight my own battles. The shame of it. Are you sure you won't give me traditional CPR, babe?"

My heart leaped at him calling me babe. I knew it didn't mean anything, and he'd called me that a few times, but it still affected me. "Nope, you'll have to either call an ambulance or suffer the goo."

"Well shit, okay I guess my heart is fine. Can I help you with anything?"

He came over to stand beside me. His closeness made my body come alive. I fought it back. There was no reason to get all hot and bothered by Joker. He was Belle's cousin. I had to find a way to accept that and stop with this nonsense. Maybe this was a sign. It was time to think about finding someone. I hadn't had the desire to do it before, but maybe now was the time.

"No, I think I have it all under control. However, I do have a couple of things I want to talk to you about."

"I bet I know what one of them is. Hang on and we'll talk after dinner if that's alright with you. We can take a walk or something."

I wasn't sure it was a good idea for me to go anywhere with him alone, but if that was what it took to get answers, then I'd do it. I nodded. "Okay, after dinner. Why don't you go talk to Granddaddy and Belle? I'm about to start the fried chicken. The potatoes are already cooking and they shouldn't have too long left. You can help Belle set the table if you want. She can do that without it becoming a disaster," I said with a grin.

His smile warmed me. I used my wrist to flip on the water to wash my hands as I told him that. I got another shock. While I was washing them, he leaned down and placed a gentle, barely there kiss on my lips. I inhaled harshly. I knew my eyes got big. I didn't know what to say.

"I'll do that. Holler if you need help. I'm not a disaster in the kitchen and I'll gladly help, beautiful." I watched as he casually sauntered out of the kitchen. *What the hell? Joker had kissed me. What was he thinking?*

It took me a minute or so to shake it off and remember what I was doing. Shutting off the water, I dried my hands, and got my mind back on the task at hand. Dissecting why he kissed me would have to wait until I was alone. For now, I had dinner to make without ruining it.

Joker: Chapter 9

It was hard to act casual and sit talking then eat dinner, when all I wanted to do was be alone with Raina and kiss her again. Only this time, it wouldn't be a peck. It would be a full-blown kiss hopefully with tongue. I wanted to know what she tasted like and it wasn't just the taste of her mouth. My desire for her was raging. I wanted to taste her skin and the most intimate part of her, her pussy. Shit, the dreams I'd been having about her were pornographic. I was beating off a few times a day to the images of her in my mind.

I could've gone to any number of women, including the bunnies. They would've gladly helped me to work off some frustration, but it wasn't them I wanted, and I wasn't willing to accept a pale substitute. Yeah, I'd fucked them in the past, but not anymore. With Raina back in my life, I only wanted her, and I didn't see that changing. *Jesus, please, let her come to feel the same. I'll take it as slow as she wants, even if it kills me, just as long as she'll have me.* I sent up my new daily prayer.

Dinner was great and I enjoyed every bite, but I wanted to get to our private talk. I insisted on doing the dishes with Belle since Raina had cooked. She thanked me with a smile that made my heart skip a beat. While we handled the dishes, she sat talking to Byron.

While she was cooking, I talked to him. Belle had been engrossed in a television show. He warned me she was going to insist on paying for half the alarm installation.

"Byron, she can insist all she wants, but she's not paying and neither are you. You need security here, especially with Parker getting out. I wouldn't put anything past him. You had the wiring done, which was the hard part. Installing the cameras and the keypad was nothing. Outlaw said he wished all jobs were this easy."

"I appreciate it more than you know, but you have to let me repay you somehow if you won't take money."

I leaned closer to him, so Belle wouldn't accidentally hear me. "You can get your beautiful granddaughter to see me as someone other than her ex-husband's cousin. Get her to see I'm a man and I want her, that would be more than enough repayment."

"Joker, I don't think you have to worry about that. She sees you as a man, she just doesn't know how to handle it. Men have not been a part of her life. Hell, other than Parker, I don't even know if she's kissed another man or not. She's skittish and has reason to be. Boy, I'll help you, as long as you can swear on your club and cut of yours that you only have honorable intentions. If this is just a fling for you or a way to get back at Parker, then hell no. I'll do everything I can to get her to stay as far away from you as I can if that's the case. And I'll pay for the damn security alarm to make sure you can't hold that over us," his expression had grown fierce. I didn't doubt a word he was saying.

"I can swear not only on my club and cut, but on

my own mother's head that I'm not just fooling around or trying to get revenge on Parker. I've wanted Raina since the day I met her. That's hard for me to admit, when it means I wanted another man's wife and not just any man, my own cousin's wife. I never said or did anything then because that wouldn't be right. But now, she's not his and is free to be with me. I only hope I can convince her of it and to give me a chance."

He didn't say anything for a minute or so. I squirmed inwardly. Finally, he nodded his head. "Then I'll do whatever I can to help. Don't make me regret this, Joker. If you do, I will find a way to make you pay."

"You won't ever regret it, I promise, Byron." I held out my hand and we shook on it.

Fast forward to two hours later, and I was walking in the warm evening air with the woman I craved. Maybe this wasn't such a good idea. We were still in a neighborhood, but there were places I could drag her off to, to devour her. I felt sort of like a wild beast when it came to her. She seemed to be uneasy. I had to do something about that. "So, what was it you wanted to talk to me about? I assume it's about the security system."

She glanced at me. We stopped on the sidewalk in front of a small stand of trees. "I do. Let's go sit over here. There's a tree that makes a nice seat. Bella and I found it last week when we were exploring." she waved toward the trees.

I let her take the lead. She was right, not far into the trees, there was a downed one which was perfect for sitting. Before she sat down, I brushed it with my hand, to make sure there wasn't anything that might hurt her ass. She gave me a confused look. "I don't want you to sit on something that hurts. Go ahead, sit." As soon as she sat down, I sat beside her and took her hand in mine.

I left a little bit of space between us, but not too much. The wind was blowing gently and her perfume and what I thought was just her unique scent was swamping my nose. I inhaled deeply to take it into my lungs. I never wanted to forget those smells. I was happy she didn't let go of my hand. Instead, she clasped her other one around our joined hands.

"Granddaddy said that it was the club's company who installed the alarm system. I know the wiring was already done, but there was still equipment and the labor involved. They told him it was taken care of when he asked for the bill. Joker, we can't accept that. You have to let us pay for it. It's wonderful you want to do that, but it's not necessary. We can pay for it. I know you did it because of Parker."

"Before I answer that, there's something I need from you."

"What?"

"Joker is my club name and I love it, and it's one I answer to with pride. Using it when we're around the club, other clubs and even regular people is a sign of respect in my world."

She interrupted me. "I know. I remember it from when Parker was prospecting. He was excited to get one when he patched in. That's why I use it."

"And I love that you do, but when it's just us, I want you to call me Aaron, not Joker."

Her eyes widened. I'd stunned her. She didn't say anything for several moments. When she did, she sounded kind of scared. "I can't do that. Using your real name is something you should only allow your immediate family or someone special to you to do. I remember that too. And what if I mess up and call you Aaron in front of people or even Belle? Then she might start to call you that too. I think I should stick to Joker but thank you for asking me. It makes me happy you consider me family enough to use it."

I lifted our joined hands and placed a kiss on her soft hand. She had such small, delicate hands. I saw her shiver. Her pupils dilated slightly. That's what I needed to see. Proof that she wasn't immune to me. She felt the pull between us, just like I did.

"Baby, it's not because I think of you as family. It's because you're fucking special to me, and I want to hear you say my name. As for Belle, if she wants to call me that when it's just us and Byron, then I'm fine with it. My family has gotten in the habit of using Joker, so they don't mess up, although Mom does call me Aaron from time to time. Usually, when she wants to get my attention and be serious. If you happen to mess up, it won't be the end of the world. However, not having you use it might be the end. Please, I need this." I let her hear the plea in my voice.

She took a deep breath then let it out and nodded her head. Relief flooded me. "Okay, if that's what you want and you're fine with me possibly messing up, then I'll do it. Aaron, you have to let us pay for the alarm," she said with a twinkle in her eyes.

"Thank you. And the answer is still no, but nice try. Now, I have a special name I want to use for you. It's one I think is perfect for you."

"Really? What name?"

"Queen."

She blinked at me in amazement, I think. "Queen? Why in the world would you think to call me that? I'm far from royalty, believe me."

"Your name means queen, but it's more than that. To me you're a damn queen. Anyone who thinks differently, needs to talk to me."

"Well, I-I don't know what to say. It's beautiful and nothing I ever expected. Although, it might raise some eyebrows, if you call me that in front of people. They'll wonder what's going on between us," she said as if warning me.

"Let them. Now, is there anything else you want to talk about, other than the alarm and that's been put to bed."

"There is, but the alarm isn't put to bed as you say. We don't expect you or the club to do that. It's great you want us to be safe. However, you don't need to do it."

"That's the least we're going to do. Parker is getting out most likely, and it's just over two weeks away. He'll come here, I know it. You, Belle, and Byron need to be safe. If I had my way, you'd all move to the compound, so we could watch you twenty-four seven. We have townhomes now. They're for guests. You'd have your privacy but be guarded. The fence is monitored with cameras. The gate will be manned at all times. We have guns."

"Jesus, don't you think that's a bit much? You make it sound like you do this all the time and you're going to war. I can assure you, we have guns too and me and Granddaddy know how to use them. With the alarm we'll be fine. Again, I appreciate your offer and worry, but we'll be fine."

"I can't help it. If anything happens to you three, I'll never be able to forgive myself. The alarm was because you should have it, regardless. And you can't go without guards. You go to work and the store. Belle and Byron go to the park and other places. Yeah, you might carry a gun, but if he surprises you, he could hurt you. That's why, if you don't agree to come stay with us, you'll have bikers and other men hanging around your house and work all the time."

"Hanging around? Why? Who?"

"The club and those who work for us at Salvation. They'll be your bodyguards. That's when I can't do it myself." I told her bluntly.

"Jo— I mean Aaron, you can't do that! Think of the wasted time and those men will be losing their pay from their jobs. No, you will not do that. We don't need bodyguards, for God's sake. You're acting like Parker is coming for us with an army and an arsenal. It's ridiculous. He's just one man."

In a flash, I had a hold of her upper arms. I didn't squeeze hard enough to bruise her, but I did grip her tightly. She gave me a startled look. I stared hard at her, so she could see how sincere I was about to be.

"It's not a waste if it keeps you safe. Those from Salvation will be compensated. As for my brothers and I, we have people who can cover for us at our businesses. We won't lose any money. And even if we did, we don't care. Yeah, we've done this more than a few times. The old ladies here and at our other chapters and our friends' clubs rarely come to us without danger. As for Parker, we have no idea who he might know. He's been in prison for ten years. I can guarantee you, he's made friends and they might be the kind with connections who will help him. Your safety and that of Belle and Byron is very important. The club knows how I feel about you."

"Feels about us? What does that mean? You're not making sense, Aaron."

To hear her say my name and the way she said it made me harden. Fuck, what I wouldn't give to have her saying my name, as I thrust in and out of her delicious body and at the point of her tipping over the edge, into a full-blown orgasm. By God, I'd hear that one day, her screaming my name as she came on my cock. I could feel myself growing harder and lengthening in my jeans. I should hide it, but maybe this would show her what she did to me and it was time to confess I wanted her to be mine. It had been in the making for over eleven years.

I pulled her to me then lowered my head to claim her mouth the way I'd been dying to. She froze for a second or two, then as I pressed harder and moved my lips against hers, she kissed me back hesitantly. This spurred me to kiss her more hungrily. As she gasped, I thrust my tongue inside her mouth to taste her more and to tease her tongue with mine. Exploring the wet cavern of her mouth made me fully harden.

I groaned as her tongue tentatively touched mine. Flicking mine back and forth, her tongue grew bolder. Her lips were kissing mine harder. Reluctantly, I withdrew my tongue, but it was only so I could nibble on her lower lip with my teeth. I latched onto it and pulled gently on it, then licked to soothe where I'd bitten. She moaned. Her hands were now on my shoulders, and she was pulling me closer. I don't think she realized she was even doing it.

Letting go of her arms, I gripped her waist and picked her up. She yelped in alarm, but I kept kissing her, as I moved her until she was straddling my lap. That put her pussy closer to my aching cock. I wanted to grind into her, but that might scare her to death. I kept telling myself to slow down, but it was impossible. Her response and the moans and whimpers coming from her spurred me on. Her hands came up and gripped the back of my short hair.

She tore her mouth away from mine, which made me growl in displeasure. I tried to yank her back, but she resisted. I opened my eyes to stare at her. Her face was flushed pink, and she was breathing hard like I was.

"Aaron, we have to stop. This is crazy," she panted.

Her mouth said that, but her eyes and her body were screaming at me to continue. Her pupils were dilated fully. She had an almost painful expression on her face. Her hands were tugging on my hair and her body was rising and falling. She was like a snake sensuously enticing me. I hauled her closer to my chest and the bulge in my jeans, then I took my hands off her waist, and slid them up to cup her breasts. They were encased in a bra, which I hated, but I gave them a tender squeeze, then I started to knead them. Her moan was loud and long. Her eyelids closed.

"Look at me," I ordered a little harshly. Her eyelids flew open.

"If wanting you more than my next breath, wanting to know what you taste like, and what brings you pleasure are crazy, then this is crazy. Fuck woman, haven't you figured it out yet? I want you. I need you. I ache for you so much it's about to kill me. Tell me this isn't one-sided. If it is, I'll fucking die," I groaned out between clenched teeth.

I wanted to touch her bare breasts, suck on her nipples, and then spread her out naked, and eat her pussy and ass until she came a few times, then sink my cock into her and fuck her until we both came like a volcano. Something told me she would be the best sex of my life.

"Aaron, God, don't. If it was just me, then I'd say the hell with it, and have the first fling or hookup, or whatever this is, with you. Something I never thought of doing, but it's not just me. I have Belle to think about. I can't do that to her. She's already becoming attached to you. If we did this, when it was over, it would hurt her not to see you anymore. I can't. I'm sorry. I hope you can understand and still remain my friend, her friend." She gnawed on her bottom lip with her teeth when she got done.

The worry on her face killed me. She had no clue what this was. I had to tell her. Coming here tonight, I planned to spend time with her and get her to be more comfortable with me. I didn't plan to kiss her or do any of this. I planned to work on my long game. That went out the window with that kiss.

"My Queen, beautiful Raina, you have no idea what I want from you. I can tell you, it's not a fling or a hookup. It's not an affair for a few weeks or months then we're done. No, what I want, no, what I need, is for you to be mine in every way. I want you in my life, in my bed, hell, in my house. I'll never hurt you or Belle by leaving you. And I know she's a part of you. I want her too. I'd love for her to come to see me as more than her cousin. One day, if she was comfortable with it, I would want her to think of me as her dad."

The shock on her face was enough to make me want to laugh then cry. How had no man ever won her heart and made her his? There had to be men who wanted her. It was impossible that none had seen what I did. It was more than her physical beauty which consumed me. She was beautiful and full of light on the inside. Poetic shit kept coming to my mind when I thought of her.

"Aaron, are you alright? Did you take something before we came out for this walk?"

"Jesus Christ, you can't think the only way a man wants you is if he's drugged or drunk? Don't you look in the mirror? Have men never asked you out, told you that you're beautiful and they want you?" I asked in disgust. This wasn't how I pictured this going. In my dreams, when this time came, she was going to throw herself in my arms and declare her undying love for me.

If she couldn't believe I wanted her, then how in the hell would I ever convince her that I loved her? Yeah, love. I'd been half there with her years ago. I lied to Rylan when I denied it. Having her return had only pushed me into full-blown love. It was fast and probably insane, but it was true. I'd always been dumbfounded at how fast Bull and my other brothers, as well as the Dublin Falls guys and our friends fell in love so quickly. It was like they looked at a woman, and pow, it was blindingly obvious to them. For me, it had taken years, although if she had never left Hunters Creek, I knew I'd have fallen completely for her in no time. If only she'd divorced Parker and stayed, then we could've been together for years, had more kids, and be enjoying a family of our very own right now.

"Sure, guys have asked me out, and I went on a few dates, but they were only interested in getting me in bed. They moved on as soon as I made it clear I wasn't into playing the happy divorcée and wanted only something if it was going to be long term. Surely that's not what you want. You're a very attractive man, Aaron. You can have any woman, and I know there's been a lot. You have them on-call for God's sake at the clubhouse. I know about the bunnies and the women who come from town to have sex with you and the guys. Parker was very vocal about them and I have no doubt they were some of the women he cheated on me with. You won't want to give that up and I won't be with someone who doesn't. Being cheated on hurts so much and I'm not going to go into something knowing it's a given. I'm sorry, but I can't, no matter how much I want you," the last bit was barely above a whisper. She looked devastated.

"Parker cheating on you tells me he didn't love you. He didn't want his wife and daughter. For that alone, he's a fucking idiot. Sure, there are men and women who cheat. I've been with those women you mentioned, but I wasn't involved with anyone. There hasn't been a serious girlfriend in my life since I was a teenager. But that doesn't mean if I had, that I would've cheated on her. Loyalty is everything to men like us and I don't just expect it from you. I expect it from myself and so would the club."

"So, if you cheated, they'd call you out on it?"

"Call me out, beat my ass, help my woman leave me, and probably strip my patch. However, that's not gonna happen. My parents have been together for forty years, and I can guarantee you, neither of them has cheated. When you love someone, you won't cheat."

She sucked in a harsh breath as she stared at me. "Love someone?"

I laid my forehead on hers and nodded. "Yes, love.

I love you Raina. I started to fall for you the day I met you all those years ago. I hated the fact you belonged to Parker. It ate at me and the fact there was nothing I could do about it pissed me off. It killed me to find out you left. However, since you came back, I've continued to fall. I love you. I don't expect you to feel the same for me, but I hope with time, you will. I want you as mine, my Queen. I want you as my old lady." As I finished confessing my deepest secret, I kissed her again.

This time it was wild and out of control. She plastered herself against me, ran her hands up and down my chest, as she pressed her pussy down on my hard cock. Both of us moaned, as streaks of pleasure flashed through us. At least I hoped it was pleasure for her because it was for me. I'd never been this acutely turned on and ready to explode. It wouldn't take much for me to come. She rubbed back and forth on my erection. I had to tear my mouth away from hers. "Baby, stop. Please. I'm gonna come if you don't."

Abruptly, she stood up. I missed her immediately. As I reached to bring her close again, she dropped to her knees. Her hands went to my belt and started to undo it. I grabbed her hands. "Raina, what the hell? No, not like this."

"Yes, like this. No one can see us. We're far enough back here that no one can see us from the street. You saw the way we came in. No one comes back here. Let me taste you, Aaron."

She sounded frantic. I didn't want to stop her, but I had to. Our first intimate moment wasn't going to be in the woods where anyone could see us. If we were at the compound, then I wouldn't care. None of them would say anything. "Baby, listen to me. I won't have our first time where strangers can find us. As much as I want you to put your hands and mouth on my cock, I can't."

I saw her start to withdraw into herself. She thought I was rejecting her, not the situation. I slid my hands under her armpits and hoisted her back up to straddle me. I gave her a hard look. "This isn't me rejecting you. It's me saying hell no to the place. If you want me, then you'll come to the compound tomorrow for the party I told you about."

"But that was supposed to be for all of us."

"It is. And as much as it'll drive me wild, I still want you all there, but when it's time, I want you to send Belle home with Byron, and you stay. I want you to spend the night with me. I'm not saying we have to do more than kiss and maybe pleasure each other if you still want that, but I need you in my arms. Give me that."

"Aaron, what will Granddaddy say to that? He'll know what we're gonna do."

"He already knows, babe. I told him I want you and I intend to win your heart. He gave me his approval as long as I never hurt you. I swore to him and I'm swearing to you, I won't. Please say yes. Become mine, Raina."

Her answer was to give me a passionate kiss as she mumbled, "Yes." I took it and got a little lost in her kiss, but not too lost. There would be time for that tomorrow. All I had to do was survive tonight, and part of tomorrow without losing my mind. I hoped I was strong enough to do it.

Raina: Chapter 10

I was so nervous, I felt like I might faint, as we pulled through the gate at the Warriors' compound. The last time I was here, other than the brief visit a couple of weeks ago, was for a family day when Parker was a prospect. The club had insisted he bring me. He hadn't been happy. Looking around, I saw a lot of things had changed. The clubhouse was still a two-story mini mansion that they had converted to their clubhouse years ago. It looked like they were keeping it up.

The gate was a more substantial one than I remembered. The fence around it had been changed to cement walls which were twelve feet tall and had sharp wire at the top. What the hell? No wonder Joker wanted us to stay here. It looked like a fortress. A prospect opened the gate after we told him who we were. I knew he was a prospect since it was on his cut. He told us where to park, which was up by the clubhouse. I passed a long line of bikes to find a spot.

As I pulled in to park, I saw the houses. It was dark the other night, and I hadn't been able to see them. There were about a dozen of them. They all had different styles to them, but they were all homey-looking from here. Not far away there was what looked like townhomes. There were four of them. This must be where Joker had wanted us to stay. They looked brand new. Coming to a stop, I sat in the car. Granddaddy looked at me. "Are you alright, Raina?"

"I think so. It's all so unreal. Tell me I'm not making a mistake," I pleaded.

I'd told him last night what Joker wanted, as far as me staying tonight after they went home. He wasn't stupid. He knew that meant we would likely be making out or possibly having sex. I told him about Joker's confession of love. It had stunned the hell out of me. So much so, I had forgotten to tell him how I felt. I'd have to correct that today or tonight. That is if I didn't run first.

He patted my arm reassuringly. "Honey, it's never a mistake to enjoy your life, to have true intimacy and hopefully, love. I believe what he said. You can trust him." He couldn't say more with Belle in the car.

"Okay, let's do this. If I faint, just get me to the car and take me home so I can hide in shame."

He laughed. His laughter was interrupted by my door flying open. I gasped then smiled. Standing there looking beyond yummy was Joker. He was gazing at me like I was his next meal. Before I could say a word, he reached in, and undid my seatbelt, then he hauled me out of the car. His mouth came crashing down on mine, as he kissed me like a starving man. I gave into his urgency. Everything and everyone faded, including my daughter and grandfather. I heard whistles and people's voices saying something. It was my daughter who got through my befuddled mind.

"Wow, do you see that? He's kissing Mommykins. Can he do that? I thought he was our cousin."

I tried to get away from Joker's amazing mouth to explain, but he refused to stop kissing me, and held me tighter. I heard an amused laugh, then Bull's voice of all people. "Sweetheart, he's your cousin on your dad's side, not your mom's. He can kiss her all he wants. I think you should get used to it. Do you mind?"

"Oh no, I don't mind! I like Joker. I just never saw Mommy kiss anyone other than me, Granddaddy and MeMe. Does this mean they're getting married and we'll live here?"

I could hear what sounded like excitement in her voice. This time, when I tried to pull away, he let me. He gave me an amused look and winked before he turned to my daughter. "Bells, I'd like to talk to you about you and your mom. Why don't we give you a quick tour and get Byron settled, then I'll tell you what I want, and we'll see if you want the same thing?"

"Sure, we can do that. Do you have a house?"

He wrapped an arm around me, which was a good thing, since my legs were weak. "I do. It's almost finished. Just a couple of weeks at the most and it's done. I'll show you and you can tell me how to decorate it. I have no idea. If it's left to me, it'll be all white inside."

She groaned and shook her head. "You can't do that. Your house has to have personality. I can help you with that, and so can Mommy. We love to paint and decorate, don't we?" This was her first attempt to include me.

"Yes, we do, although our taste might not be

Joker's," I warned her. My voice came out all croaky sounding.

"Wow, you must really know how to kiss, Joker, to make Mommy sound like that."

Everyone who was standing around, which felt like the whole club laughed, even Granddaddy did, the traitor. I blushed and tried to ignore them. Joker grinned.

"You and Byron stay with us. Tell me if you need to take a break or anything, Byron. We can look at everything in stages. The clubhouse is first, but before we do that, I want to make sure you know everyone."

This led to a long introduction. I knew most of the guys, but the women, new guys and the kids were making my head spin. How would I remember all of them? Belle was overjoyed to see the little kids and babies. None were her age, but she liked to be a mother hen. She did it with the smaller kids back in Albany, at the places she'd stayed while I worked.

Once the introductions were out of the way, he took us to see the clubhouse. For me it was familiar, but this was the first time Granddaddy had been here. He was very interested in their setup and asked a lot of questions. Belle found the pool tables and dart boards fascinating. I could see Joker and the guys might need to teach her how to play if we were around much. She had a gleam in her eyes.

The women were so welcoming. They chatted away as the men talked. The few I'd met started first, then the rest gradually joined in. The babies and toddlers were a riot to watch. The oldest was a little girl named Hope. She belonged to Bear and his wife, Ilara. Belle took to her immediately.

Like Bull, Bear had been one of the older guys in the club. I was a little taken aback that he had started a family at his age, but you could see he adored his wife and kids. When I was told Tarin was his adult daughter who he never knew he had, which made him a grandfather with kids barely older than his grandkids, I had to laugh. Bull was in the same boat.

We were served drinks and given time to slowly explore. I knew Joker was taking it slow because of Granddaddy. Even with his oxygen, he got short of breath very easily. Once we were done at the clubhouse, I was further surprised. When we came outside, there was a golf cart sitting there.

"You can ride on this," Bull said.

"Thank you. Which one of you plays golf?" I asked.

I heard laughter then Slash yelled. "Yeah Bull, tell her why you have a golf cart and how you play golf every weekend."

"Slash, you can wake up dead, you know," Bull growled at him then he grinned.

"None of us play golf, sweetheart. I got that because my tired old bones sometimes get tired of walking all over the compound and taking my bike isn't the best thing."

"You're not old. Stop saying that," his wife,

Jocelyn, admonished him. The look they gave each other heated up the already hot, humid summer day. He gave her a kiss.

"Thanks, Bull, we'll take it. I'll bring them back after I show them the other stuff," Joker promised.

Granddaddy got up front with Joker and I sat in the second row with Belle. I was surprised at the speed it could go. "Wow, I had no idea golf carts go this fast," I told Joker as he came to a stop.

He grinned. "They don't usually, but this one has been modified. Your top speed for a regular one is twelve to fourteen miles an hour. This one can do twenty-five. Bull doesn't like to waste time. So, here is the playground and the pool. Belle, you brought your bathing suit, didn't you? We'll be out here later." She nodded enthusiastically. She'd been so happy to hear they had a pool. Joker told us last night before he left to bring our suits.

Once we were done admiring those two things, our next stop was the townhomes. He told us about them and even took us inside to see one. I knew from the looks he kept giving me, he wanted me to say yes to coming here. After that, he took us by the various houses and told us which belonged to whom. The last one he stopped at was his.

I stood outside admiring it. I loved the little house Granddaddy had, since it was my childhood sanctuary. Back in Albany, we'd lived in an apartment. When I was married to Parker, it had been a cheap apartment. My mom and dad's house was okay, but it hadn't ever felt like a home. It lacked warmth due to them, I guess. Just looking at the outside of Joker's, I knew this could be a very warm and welcoming family home.

"What made you pick this house and this size? Were you planning to settle down and have a family even before we came back?" I asked him, slightly worried that maybe he had been thinking of someone else when he built this. I wasn't sure, if we actually got together, and I moved in with him, that I'd be able to live in a house he had built for someone else. It would feel weird. Although he said he hadn't had a girlfriend since he was a teenager.

He knew what I was meaning by the look he gave me. It was a frown. "It wasn't because I had some woman in mind to live in it with me. I always had a slight hope that maybe one day, I might find someone I could love and build a life with. I wasn't willing to wait for a day that might never come. Living all these years in the clubhouse was okay, but I'm older and I want privacy. Loud music and partying at all hours of the night aren't my thing anymore. That's why I asked Tank to build me a house. If I'd known you would be back in my life, I would've waited for you."

He paused then continued. "It's almost done. I want you and Belle to live here with me, babe. And before you say it, I know that Byron can't be alone. He's more than welcome too. I have the room. Now, if there's anything you don't like, we'll change it, short of tearing the whole house down and starting all over. I don't think I could stand to stay in the clubhouse for another five or six months."

"It's beautiful. I love this style." It had a Victorian look to it, but with a more modern twist. It was painted a medium forest green color, I would call it. The trim and front door was a crisp, bright white which made it pop. It had a long porch across most of the front and on the second floor what looked like a small turret.

"Let's go check out your future home," he whispered to me. I took his hand and let him lead us inside. Belle was behind us telling Granddaddy how much she loved the turret.

The inside didn't disappoint. Entering the foyer, we went left, and we wound our way through the downstairs. It had a three-car garage, a guest bedroom, and a full bath along with a utility room. There was a den and then you entered a rotunda area before you found the family room, nook, kitchen, dining room and living room. In the back, off the family room was a covered porch.

Upstairs was three more bedrooms and two full bathrooms, a bonus room and loft before you got to the master suite. It had a bathroom, a walk-in closet, and a sitting area. I felt my mouth hanging open the whole time he gave us the tour. When we were done, we left the other two admiring the loft area. He took me into the master and shut the door. This was the one room that already had furniture in it. It had a bedroom suite which included a king-sized bed. I tried not to imagine us on it.

"Aaron, what in the world were you thinking? If you never found someone to settle down with, you'd be rattling around in this monster alone. You could house a couple of families in this place. As it is, you could get lost in here."

"I don't know. I saw the house and the floor plan and it was like it was talking to me. There wasn't another one I wanted like this one. I tried to go smaller but every time I looked at those plans, I kept coming back to this one. Finally, I said fuck it and told them to build it. I guess someone upstairs knew I was going to find you again. What do you think? Do you like it? Could you see all of you living here one day?"

"Aaron, I love this house and of course it would be a dream to live here, but I think you're jumping the gun. We don't know what'll happen or how fast. Although, there is something I need to tell you. I forgot last night. I hope you'll forgive me."

I saw his body stiffen. He thought it was going to be bad news. Pulling his head down, so I could reach him, I got close enough he could feel my breath on his mouth. "I happen to love you too. Just in case you were wondering. I'm as guilty as you for having feelings for someone I shouldn't have all those years ago," I whispered, right before I kissed him.

The groan that came tearing out of him sounded animalistic, and as if he was in pain. However, his kiss was anything but painful. He ravaged my mouth while I tried to do the same to his. Our teeth nipped at each other's lips and tongue. He sucked my tongue hard before tugging my head back by my ponytail and deepening the kiss. I don't know what would've happened if there wasn't a knock at the door then my granddaddy hollered at us.

"Hey, I'm taking Belle outside to look at the backyard. We'll see you out there, soon I hope." I could hear the amusement and teasing in his voice. I swear as he walked away, he even chuckled softly. It was enough to make us stop and give each other sheepish smiles.

"I don't know whether to thank him or to go kick his ass and that's plain wrong to do to a man his age. I think we'd better rejoin them, my Queen, before we get ourselves into trouble. There'll be time for this later," he said right before he gave me a quick peck on the mouth and stepped back.

I didn't want to agree, but he was right. I held out my hand for him to take. As we began to walk to the bedroom door, I noticed he was walking funny. Glancing down, I saw why. He had what looked like a raging hard-on. When I'd been rubbing on it last evening, it felt really big, but I didn't look. Now, seeing it even like this, I thought he had to be huge. Oh God, could I handle it? Equal parts apprehension and exhilaration filled me. I guess I'd find out which one when the time came.

We took it slow getting outside, which allowed his excitement to calm down. I gave him a wicked smile and wink when I saw it had gone down. He pulled me close and growled in my ear. "You'll pay later for that, Raina."

"I hope so," I whispered back, which made his nostrils flare, and his eyes heat again.

"Behave," he said just as we reached them, which

stopped me from smarting off again. I was starting to enjoy this freedom to say whatever I wanted. With Parker, I hadn't been able to do it. I found out quickly he was moody and easily upset. He would yell, then storm out. Fortunately, he had never gotten physical with me. Even as young as I was at the time, if he had, I'd have left him immediately. We got back in the cart and headed back toward the clubhouse. I pointed to the open land and woods that spread out further beyond the houses.

"What's back there?"

"Mainly land, trees and an old crematorium."

"Did you say crematorium?" I asked, thinking I'd heard him wrong. His nod confirmed I didn't need a hearing check.

"Yep. This mansion was owned by a family who had a funeral home in town. They had their crematorium out here at the house for some odd reason."

"I remember them. I didn't know this is where they cremated the bodies though. They were decent folks if a bit odd," Granddaddy added.

"But it's not operational, right?" I hurried to verify. I didn't think it could be and be sold.

"It is very much still working. We keep it locked up. Right now, the kids aren't big enough to go out there, but when they get older, they will. Plus, even though we have the walls, we don't want to chance anyone getting in and wandering in there. Why? Do you wanna see it?"

"Oh no, not me. I was scared for the kids. Although, the thought is kind of creepy," I told him with a shiver.

"Cool. Are there ghosts around here from all the dead bodies?" Belle asked excitedly.

"Belle, hush, don't you dare say that. If there are ghosts, I'm out of here," I admonished her.

Joker laughed. "I haven't seen any, but I guess it could be possible. Maybe one of these nights, we'll go looking for them, Belle. We'll leave your mom at the house."

"You can leave me in the next town, thank you very much. I now know where she gets her paranormal love. It's from your side of the family, not mine."

"I've had a few run-ins that made me think there could be ghosts. If I was a bit younger, I'd go with you two," Granddaddy said out of the blue.

"God, you're all crazy. I hope there's more sane people at the clubhouse or I'm gonna have to run and hide at home."

"Oh, no, I'm not gonna let you run, babe. You can stay with some of the others. I can promise you, not many of them probably want to ghost hunt either," Joker assured me.

My mind stayed on the ghosts until we got back and parked the cart. Then my mind was back in the here and now mode. I was looking forward to today, but nervous about later, in a good way. I only hoped I didn't chicken out when the time came.

Joker:

Today with Raina, Belle and even Byron was incredible. They had gotten to know everyone and vice versa and they relaxed and soon felt like they had always been part of our club family. There was plenty of laughter, eating and fun activities. One of those had almost killed me though.

It was the end of August, which in Tennessee guaranteed the weather would be hot and very humid. Being able to escape into a pool was almost a must. Ever since we'd added one, we'd been kicking ourselves for not doing it sooner. Of course, we all ended up out there and in the water today. That's what almost killed me.

When I saw Raina in her bathing suit, I didn't think I'd be able to cope. For one, she looked so damn sexy I wasn't liking the idea of my single brothers checking her out, even though I knew they wouldn't do anything. Finding out I was possessive was news to me. Secondly, my erection came back, and I was afraid I'd die from sexual frustration. Not knowing what else to do, I herded her into the water as fast as I could. My brothers, the fuckers, all knew what I was doing and smirked at me.

Her bathing suit matched the one Belle had on. It wasn't even a two piece. It was an overall modest navy-blue suit. It was cut high on the legs and dipped pretty low in the back. However, on Belle it looked like an innocent kid's suit. On Raina, it was a whole different story. She had hips, a perfect ass and those breasts which were way more than a handful. Hell, she didn't even have much cleavage showing, but it was enough.

Somehow, I don't honestly know how I survived the experience. I did worry that my cock might fall off from being filled with blood for so long. When men took those blue pills, didn't they warn you to seek medical attention, if you have an erection for longer than four hours? I hadn't gone seeking it, which made me worry I'd done irreversible damage. However, later it went down, and when I got excited again and it rose to the occasion, I had hope.

It was now after dark. Walker had driven Belle and Byron back home in my Bronco. Belle had wanted to stay, but Byron convinced her they would have a fun horror movie night. Apparently, Raina didn't do those and Belle loved them. I could tell the two of us would have fun together watching those while Raina was otherwise busy.

I could tell Raina's nerves were worsening after they left. I tried to help her relax. I told her that nothing had to happen tonight. All I wanted was for her to stay and let me hold her. Sure, I wanted more, but I wasn't going to rush her. Cold showers hadn't killed me yet.

Presently, we were outside gathered around the firepits. Not that we needed the warmth, but they gave us light, and the night had cooled off enough to be bearable. Some of the couples had gone in with the kids.

Others had been able to leave their kids with the retiring couples, so they could stay longer. That was one of the good things about our club. Everyone was willing to help out each other and return the favor. Raina noticed it and remarked on it. "Do they always end up doing this? Some staying and the others watching their kids so they can?"

"They do. Or sometimes we have outside help from people we know and trust who come and watch them. In fact, we've recently found a couple of ladies who we trust to do that. They're not here tonight, but Lolly and Kamila are women who we helped out a while back at Warriors' Haven. They decided to settle here and have gotten their lives back on track. They share an apartment and each have jobs. To earn extra money, they offered to watch the kids anytime someone needed them. They're single but love kids. You saw the room inside the clubhouse. There are times we put them down there for the night and have them watched over, while their parents have fun."

"That wasn't here when Belle was a baby, was it? If it was, I don't remember it being here the one time I came to the family event."

"No, we didn't have it then. It came after the kids started multiplying in Dublin Falls. Bull had his house built first on the compound. He had one in town that he raised Harlow in, but when she had kids, he wanted them safer and behind the walls. They started that in Dublin Falls too and Bull loved the idea. It's kind of the trend for all our chapters and those of our friends."

"Tell me about your friends. They're all MCs,

right?"

"Not all of them, One is just a group of people who run a security slash rescue, slash military contractor type of company. They're called the Dark Patriots. They're up in Virginia. The rest are MCs with the same kind of philosophy as us. They might have been into less legal things years ago, but not anymore. None ever dealt drugs or in flesh. There's two other chapters of Warriors, although we're not as close to them as we are the other groups. There's one in Louisville, Kentucky and another in Gastonia, North Carolina. That's actually where Tiger and Falcon came from as well as Thorn and Teagan, before they were part of Dublin Falls.

"There are a few Pagan Souls clubs, but we're close to the one in Cherokee, North Carolina and the one in Lake Oconee, Georgia. The closest to us is a group in Knoxville called the Ruthless Marauders. Up in Bristol, Virginia, is another club, the Iron Punishers. Their president, Reaper, is the brother of Harper. She's Viper's wife over in Dublin Falls. The final one is the Horsemen of Wrath down in Florida. Their president is the father of one of our brothers in Dublin Falls, Torch's wife, Brooklyn. She's how we got involved with them."

"Wow, and all these have been ones you've befriended in the last ten years since I left?"

"Yeah, they are. Most we owe to Terror in Dublin Falls. His settling down brought more allies to us, most by accident. We've all helped each other out in various ways over the years, and we've become what we like to call an extended MC family."

"I think this is amazing. I never expected anything like this. And seeing how the club is now, I see how it's grown into a very close-knit family. Years ago, you were all close, but nothing like this. Do all of them have wives and kids and a similar setup to here?"

"Dublin Falls has only a few single guys left. It's very much like us. Cherokee has started to finally settle down. They have two old ladies. No one in Lake Oconee has claimed an old lady yet, well officially anyway, but that's another story. The same goes for the Horsemen and the Marauders. The Iron Punishers and the Dark Patriots have all started as well, but only have a few couples."

"That is crazy. What about Brooklyn's dad in Florida? I would've thought he would be because he has her. Is he divorced?"

"He was married when Brooklyn was a baby. His wife was murdered when Brooklyn was small and he never claimed another woman. She's hoping he'll be like Bull and get a second chance at love. He's still young, only in his late forties, I think."

She gasped. "Oh my God, how terrible! I can't imagine how badly that had to hurt. Do you know what happened to her? Did they catch her murderer?"

I didn't really want to tell her that, since it might make her fear being in a club. Although those days were much more dangerous than they were now. Still, we couldn't guarantee we'd never attract enemies or that they wouldn't come after us. Most were by association, and due to our women. I hurried to figure out how to say this. When I didn't answer her right away, she patted my hand after several moments.

"It's okay if you'd rather not tell me. I know there are things you guys consider club business and it can't be shared with anyone not a member. I'm recalling more stuff than I thought I would about this life. Parker didn't tell me a lot, but he did tell me the rules. I'm just not sure if they were all club rules or his. Tell me if I get them wrong or if you've added more. I'd hate to cause trouble by not knowing them."

"Baby, it's my job to make sure you know them and I will. So far, you've been right on the nose. In this case, it's not club business to know what happened to Diablo's wife. I'm trying to think of how to tell you then explain the rest."

"Just tell me. And if it's something you can't tell me, then say that."

"Alright then. There was a rival MC in those days. At the time, the Horsemen were into some illegal stuff and this other club wanted what they had which included one of them wanting Diablo's wife. Of course she loved Diablo and wouldn't ever leave him. The man became obsessed and when he tried to take her by force, he ended up killing her. It happened where Brooklyn saw it, although her mom had hidden her. To this day, she can still be triggered. After that, Diablo became obsessed with protecting her, not that you can blame him. He did find the man and he was taken care of."

"You mean he was killed."

"Yes, he was. You have to understand, we live by a

few different rules than regular society. It's much more of one where we take care of our own. That doesn't mean we never turn people over to the law. We do, but at times, when we know they won't get the punishment they deserve, or their victims the justice they deserve, we take care of it personally. You can never tell anyone this, Raina. If you do, we'll all face the rest of our lives in prison."

I knew she would know this, but I wanted to emphasize it. I hoped it wasn't something she couldn't live with, because it was one thing I couldn't and wouldn't change. "We never hurt innocent people. We see ourselves as protectors of them."

"Joker, I'd never narc on any of you, unless I found out you were hurting innocent people, then I'd have no choice. I'm not so naïve that I don't know the world isn't always black and white, or that our legal system can always mete out justice. Heck, look at how many people get off on technicalities or get very short sentences for terrible crimes. The idea of Parker getting out after only ten years is ridiculous. I thought he should do more than the fifteen he was sentenced to in the first place. He beat that gas station attendant so badly, he was in the hospital for weeks and had to go to rehab for months. He almost killed him."

"I agree, and after this many years on the inside, I don't have a lot of hope that he's reformed or feels remorse. It's more likely he's gotten worse," I warned her. I had to prepare her that if he came after her, Belle, Byron, or any of us for real, I'd have no choice but to put him down permanently.

"You think he's gonna do it and when he does, he'll really hurt or even kill some of us, don't you?"

I nodded. She added, "And in order to stop him, you and the club will do whatever it takes to protect us." Again, I nodded.

"I have a gun and I've been practicing with it. If he comes after us, I will protect myself and my family, Joker. And I was taught by Granddaddy to shoot to kill, not to wound. I'd hate to kill Belle's father, but I'll do it. I'd rather have him be dead than anyone else," she warned me.

Relief filled me. Along with it came the realization that it was time to call it a night and leave the socializing and serious talk for another time. I needed to have alone time with her. I stood up and held out my hand. "Let's go. I think it's time we said goodnight."

She blushed but she didn't protest. She took my hand and stood up. I didn't waste time in telling everyone goodnight. They told us the same, but I could see the smiles on their faces. They knew I wanted alone time with her. They didn't know that sex was very unlikely, or at least full-on sex. If I was lucky, we might fool around a bit.

As I walked her to my house, I realized I was nervous. This would be the first time I stayed in the house. I'd bought the bedroom suite in anticipation of the move and was grateful I did now that she was staying with me. No way I would want to have our first night together in my room at the clubhouse. I didn't want to do anything to push her away from me. Whatever we did, we would christen the bed and house. I wanted this to be the beginning of the rest of our lives together.

Joker: Chapter 11

I could tell she was getting more and more nervous as we walked to the house, then entered it. I wanted to put her at ease. Maybe I should've started out in my room at the clubhouse in case she wanted to sit and talk or something. Here, all we could do was shower, and sit on the bed. There wasn't a television in there yet to watch movies on. Damn, I should've thought this through better. I halted in the foyer.

"Baby, I think we should go back to my room at the clubhouse. I didn't think this through. There's no place to sit other than the bed and no TV, in case you just want to talk or watch a movie or something. I can tell you're nervous. You don't have to be. Nothing has to happen, I told you that. All I want is to spend time with you. I thought of doing it here because we'd have privacy. Let me grab your bag out of my room and we can go back." As I went to walk away, she caught a hold of my arm. I stopped to see what she wanted. I'd brought her overnight bag to the house earlier.

"I don't want to go to the clubhouse. I don't want to watch TV. I do want us to talk, but we can do that sitting on your bed. I'm nervous, I won't lie. You can see it. However, it's because I don't know what to do."

"What do you mean, you don't know what to do?"

"I mean, I don't know how to really flirt or how to initiate anything between us. I told the truth. I haven't really dated anyone nor have I been with anyone since my divorce. And truth be told, God, I can't believe I'm gonna tell you this," she groaned as she covered her face with her hands.

I removed them. "Raina, you can tell me anything. Don't ever be embarrassed around me. Say it."

"My experiences with Parker were terrible. We were both young and had no idea what we were doing. He'd been with others, I knew that, before and after. However, he didn't do much. Or at least he didn't do any of the stuff I saw in movies, read in books, or saw in other things. I thought that was because those were make believe, but then some women I met talked and they seemed to have experienced those things. Am I making sense?"

"Let me see if I have it straight. There was no real foreplay or intimacy between you other than the sexual act itself?" As I got done stating that, she nodded. Her face was adorably pink. "You've read about other things and wonder what is real and what you might like. Have you ever watched porn?"

"I have. I was curious," she said softly, getting even pinker.

"Babe, there's no need to blush. I think most adults have seen at least one. Hell knows, I've seen my fair share. And there are things they show that a lot of people do and enjoy, although there's more too. Can I ask you a few questions?" I asked, as we walked slowly toward the stairs to go upstairs. If she wanted to stay then that was what we'd do. We'd taken off our shoes when we entered the house before I thought better of it.

"Sure, what?"

"First, have you ever had an orgasm? If so, was it self-induced or with him?"

God, I hated talking about her having sex with Parker, but I needed to know. I wanted our sex life to be as satisfying for her as it was for me. I had no doubts from her prior comments that I'd be teaching her new things and we'd have to explore her boundaries. Now, I was revising that a bit. If she didn't even know what an orgasm felt like, it would be one of the first things I had to address when the time came.

"I never had one with him. I've had them since, but I'll be honest, they weren't anything huge. Some women act like they're these huge deals. I've never found that to be true. Maybe I'm just not wired like them."

"Did you use your fingers or toys to do it?"

"Aaron, I can't tell you that!"

"Yes, you can. I'm gonna tell you what I like and show you how I like it best. Which was it?"

"I tried both. I have this vibrator thing."

"See, that wasn't that hard. You said there wasn't foreplay. Does that mean nothing other than kissing on the mouth or was there touching, kissing, and tasting other parts of your bodies, including here?"

As I said that, I placed my hand between her legs. We'd made it to the second floor and were outside the bedroom. She jumped. I gently rubbed back and forth. I wanted her to be able to relax and let me touch her. The only way I knew how was to just try it and see. If I was rushing her, I knew I'd be able to tell. She shuddered but didn't pull away or tell me to stop. In fact, she pressed closer.

"There was hardly any of that. Mainly kissing on the mouth, and he would fondle my breasts then it was on to the main event."

"And did he ever have you do any of those things to him? What about oral sex? Blow jobs? Hand jobs?"

"No, the one time I tried to give him a blow job, he pushed me away and said not to do that. Jesus, Aaron. This is humiliating. I know less about sex than a fourteen-year-old does! There's no way I can satisfy you. I think I'd better go home."

She tried to leave and head back down the stairs, but I stopped her by scooping her up in my arms and walking into the bedroom. I didn't stop until I sat her down on the bed. She stared up at me looking slightly stunned. I leaned in and took her mouth. As she responded, I leaned closer and closer until she tipped back and was flat on her back. Crawling up, I straddled her.

Her hands came up to paw at my back. Seeing the issue, I wiggled out of my cut and laid it on the foot of the bed without breaking contact with her hot, sweet mouth. As soon as it was out of the way, her hands ran up and down my back. I ran mine from her chin to her heaving breasts. I kneaded them over and over, while I wished I could see them and touch her bare skin. I wanted to suck and nibble on her nipples. I wondered if I could make her come just by doing that.

Her confession of knowing next to nothing didn't turn me off a bit. It excited the hell out of me because it meant I'd form those memories with her. She would have even less reason to remember him. How I wished we'd met first, and I was closer to her age. Then I would've been able to claim her one hundred percent. These thoughts were new and went along with my newly discovered possessive nature.

Suddenly, her hands were tugging on the bottom of my shirt, pulling it out of my pants. I helped her get it free. As soon as it was, her hands slid up my back along my bare skin. Her touch made me shiver and ache more. My cock was hard as a post already. Hoping she might be willing now, I ran my hands down to the bottom of her tank. I paused and parted our mouths long enough to ask, "Can I?"

"God, yes, please," she whispered back, panting.

Unable to wait or take it slow now that I had her permission, I pushed up her tank and exposed her bra. I kneaded her breasts over and over through her bra until I couldn't take it, then I unsnapped it. She had on a front closure one and the bra fell away to expose her breasts. When that happened, I stopped kissing her and sat back a bit to admire her. She laid there with her arms at her sides, but I could tell she wanted to cover herself.

I moaned. "God yes, those are even more beautiful than I imagined. Look at those pretty nipples. So pink. I've gotta taste them, baby. Is that alright?"

She nodded. Quickly lowering my head, I sucked the first one into my mouth, as I teased the other one with my fingers. She cried out and her hips came up off the bed, driving her shorts-covered pussy into my aching cock. I groaned long and hard and pressed back, as I increased the suction and tweaked the other one harder.

Her nipples were tight buds and responded perfectly to every touch. She wiggled and moaned. Yeah, I was more than positive I could get her off just by doing this. The pressure of her pussy against me was making me hornier. I could feel the precum coating the head of my cock in my jeans. I bit down on her nipple as I squeezed the other one hard between my thumb and finger. She stiffened then cried out louder as she shook and shook. Jesus, she was coming. I kept going as I watched her face. When she finally started to relax, I let go.

"That was one of the sexist things I've ever seen, Raina. You look so fucking beautiful when you come. And as much as I'd love to do this again and again, I think we should take a break. Maybe take our showers before bed. I'm getting a little too wound up."

My cock was hurting with the need to come, but I wasn't going to ask her to touch me or even better, suck it. I was going slow. I kept telling myself that so I wouldn't forget. If I had my way, she'd already be naked.

I'd be feasting on her pussy and she'd be touching my cock, maybe even sucking it too. Once we had enough, then I'd be inside her, claiming what was mine.

She shook her head. "No, I don't want to take a break. I want more."

"My Queen, we can't yet. Let me calm down, then I'll get you off again like that."

"Yes, we can. I want us both to take off our clothes and give each other more. I want to see your cock and taste it, Aaron."

I closed my eyes and moaned in pain. She was killing me. "Raina, please, baby, I can't. If we do that, I'll have to be inside you. I won't be able to resist. I swore I wouldn't push you too far or too fast. I don't want to break my promise. If you regretted it later, it would gut me."

Her hands came down and she tugged at my belt. It was like in the woods last night. Fuck! "You promised me last night I could see and touch you. I'm not letting you get away again. Unless you don't want me, then I want us to continue. As for you being inside of me, God, I hope so. I need to know what it's like to be with a man and feel actual sexual gratification. I'm nervous, but I want you inside me, Aaron. I want you to fuck me."

My heart tripped over itself as it sped up. Sending up a prayer that she wouldn't regret this, I made one thing clear before we went any further. "It won't be just fucking. With us, fucking will always include love, Raina. I love you and no matter what, I will always make love to you, no matter how hard and fast we go or what we do."

She gave a breathy sob and tugged on my belt. This time I helped her to get it undone then to lower my zipper. As soon as that was done, I undid the button and zipper on her denim shorts. Knowing I needed room to get her undressed, I stood up at the side of the bed. She reached for me like she thought I was leaving her. It would take a hundred men to make me do that now. "I need to get these clothes off us. Hold on."

Not wasting a moment, as she sat up and took off her tank and her bra, I worked her shorts down her hips and legs. Underneath, she had on a pair of hot pink bikini panties. The crotch was darker pink from her wetness. I buried my face, nose-first into them and inhaled deeply. Her scent made me wilder. It was this tantalizing musk with a floral scent. I growled, which vibrated against her clit. She shuddered and whimpered as she pressed herself against me harder. Pulling away, I yanked them down and off as I confessed. "I'm gonna eat your pussy until you can't come anymore. You smell like fucking heaven."

"Not until you take your clothes off. Hurry," she panted back.

Her hands were now busy tugging off my shirt. Working together, although we fumbled a bit, I finally was naked. I stood there to give her time to look her fill. She did run her eyes all over my chest and arms then down my stomach. When she got to my cock, she paused and groaned. "Oh God, it's bigger than I thought. It's beautiful. I never knew a man's cock could be that."

I chuckled. "I don't know about that, but I'm glad you think so. As for the size, it'll fit, I promise." I fisted myself and stroked my hand up and down. I was hoping that might help the urge to come. It didn't. As I stood there, fighting for better control, she surprised me. Suddenly she swung around and lunged at me. The next thing I knew, her hand was gripping me tightly and her tongue licked across the weeping head of my cock. Shock waves went through me. "Fuck," I cried out.

Looking up at me with her big, gorgeous green eyes, she slowly sucked me inside her hot, wet mouth. I saw stars. "Jesus, if you do that, I'm gonna come, babe. I don't think you're ready for that yet," I warned her. It wouldn't take a lot to have me shooting a load of cum in her mouth. She tightened her grip at the base and sucked harder. Giving up on talking her out of it, I let her play. As she did, I gave her instructions on what I liked.

"That's it. Suck harder." "Tighten your hand just a bit more, you won't hurt me." "Fuck, that feels so good. Play with my balls." While her movements and mouth might be untutored, her enthusiasm and enjoyment made up for it. I could tell by the way she acted and the expressions on her face, that she was enjoying it. As I got closer, I couldn't help but grip her ponytail and push her just a tad further down on me. I was trying not to make her gag, but she did anyway. I quickly pulled her back and let go. However, she apparently wanted more, because she took me deeper, and fought against her gag reflex.

"Baby, you don't have to go deeper. What you're

doing is great. Although, in a minute, you'll need to stop before I come."

She let go of me with a pop. Her eyes were on fire. "I'm not stopping. I never knew sucking cock would be like this. I'm wet just from this. I want to taste you like you plan to taste me."

"Are you sure? A lot of women don't like the taste of cum."

"I'm not other women and I won't know if I do or not until I try. Come in my mouth, Aaron," she said before engulfing me again. This time she threw it all at me. A harder grip, teasing my balls, sucking me hard, hollowing her cheeks to do it and taking me deeper. When I hit the back of her throat, she pushed me deeper despite gagging. Groaning. I grabbed her hair again and began to fuck her mouth the way I longed to do although not as deep as I could and would go one day if she liked it. It didn't take much watching her bobbing up and down on me and feeling all those sensations for me to be there.

"I'm coming," I warned her, then a few seconds later I let loose. I expected her to get one taste and pull away. She shocked me by swallowing it all and humming as she did it. I came so much, I almost felt it in my knees. When I was finally drained and going limp, she let go. She placed a kiss on the head then looked up at me as she licked her swollen, red lips.

"How did I do?"

I answered her by taking her down on the mattress and kissing the hell out of her. The taste of my own cum didn't deter me. In the past, I'd never kissed a woman after I got off in her mouth. The thought had turned me off. In Raina's case, it turned me on. We hungrily kissed each other until we had to take a breather. Breaking apart, I told her how good it was and made her an offer.

"You did fucking fantastic. I can't ever recall coming that hard before. How was your first taste of cum? Are you willing to suck me off again like that? It's okay if you decide not to. I expect you'd like to go rinse your mouth even if you like it."

"It tasted different than I imagined. It wasn't bitter. I didn't hate it, so I think you can count on me doing it again. However, I do think a rinse might be good. I'll be back." As she got out of bed, I watched her ass all the way to her bag then into the bathroom. Watching it jiggle made my cock twitch. Fuck, maybe it wouldn't take me long to recover after all. I laid there enjoying the glow as she ran water. She was gone so long, I was about to go see if she was alright, when it shut off and she came back out. I gestured for her to come to me. As she reached the bed, I stood up, hoisted her up and lay her down on her back.

"Now, it's my turn. I want you to come all over my face and in my mouth, Raina. I know I'm gonna love the taste of your cum."

She moaned as I pulled her legs apart to make room for my upper body. I was a big guy and needed lots of room. Pushing them out then up, I spread her wide. I took a moment to admire her up close. She was covered in fine, closely cropped hair that matched the hair on her head. Running my finger down her folds, I collected her honey. I sucked my finger clean and moaned. She tasted even better than I imagined.

Letting go of my finger, I swiped my tongue from her hole to her clit where I sucked for a moment, causing her to jerk and cry out, then back to her entrance and passed it to her asshole. I rimmed it which caused her to tense a moment then she relaxed, then I went back up to her clit.

As I ate her, I wondered if she'd one day let me do more than tongue her ass. Which was crazy. As experienced as I was at sex, the one thing that never had interested me was anal. I never wanted to put my cock in some woman's ass. However, with Raina, the thought came to mind and was teasing me. With her, I'd be willing to try anything once, as long as she was willing. I wondered how tight it would feel around me. I knew a lot of my brothers and friends swore by it.

I worked her good. Along with licking and sucking, I used my teeth on her folds and her clit, which made her sob and beg me not to stop. I had no plans to do that until after she came at least a couple of times. Eventually, I used my fingers to fuck her tight as hell pussy. Jesus, she was gonna squeeze my cock in half as tight as she was.

The more I played the more honey she spilled. I lapped it up like a starving man. I'd always enjoyed going down on a woman, but none of them tasted like this. Suddenly, her thighs closed around my head and she came. As she did, she wailed and shook. I didn't stop tonguing her until she went limp. Then I only paused for a couple of seconds and started again.

"Aaron, no! You can't," she sobbed.

"Oh, yes I can and I am. Come again for me, my Queen. I need more of your sweet honey," I told her gruffly.

This time, I did all the same things I did last time, only this time, I teased her asshole with my tongue and finger. I didn't breach her, but I was tempted. It only took maybe five minutes for her to topple over the edge and come. I swear she came even harder and longer than the first time. This time, when she relaxed, I did stop and sat up on my knees. Eating her pussy had gotten me hard again, but I didn't want to assume she was ready for more, despite what she said when we started. This was way more than I ever hoped to get tonight.

"Kiss me," she whispered, holding out her arms.

"You'll taste your honey if I do. Are you okay with that?"

"I want to know what I taste like. Kiss me."

I gave her what she wanted. As we kissed and it got hotter and wilder, I had my answer. She wasn't turned off by smelling or tasting herself on me. It was hard to stop, but we needed to clean up. I eased back.

"Where are you going?"

"I thought we could go get cleaned up and then we can either sleep or talk if you want."

She frowned. "You don't want to have sex with

me?" As she said it, I saw the fear on her face. She thought I changed my mind.

"I want to be inside of you more than you know, but this was way more than I thought we'd do tonight. I don't want us to go too fast."

She glanced down at my erect cock which was pointing at her like an arrow. She smirked. "I think something wants it and thinks you should shut up."

I laughed because she was right. If my cock had a mouth, it would be telling me to *shut the fuck up, dumbass*. "He hates me right now," I admitted. There was no denying it. It was dark red, and the veins were standing up down my length. Precum was oozing out the slit again just at the thought of feeling her snug pussy around it.

"Then don't disappoint it or me. I don't want to stop, Aaron. I want to know what it feels like to have you inside of me." She moaned as she said it and cupped her breasts as if they ached. I reached up and tweaked her nipples. She moaned louder.

"Your wish is my command, but before we do that, we need to discuss contraception. I have condoms, but I don't want to use them. You're not by any chance on birth control, are you? If you are, what would you say to us going bare? I've never done that but I want to have nothing between us if it's not necessary."

"I am actually protected, but shouldn't we get tested first? I know you say you never, but a faulty condom is how I got Belle. Things can happen."

"You're right, they can, which is why I've always gotten tested regularly. As soon as you came back, even though I didn't know if this would happen, I got tested and I can assure you, there hasn't been anyone since. You're the only one I want, baby. I'm clean if you want to go bare." I was praying she'd say yes. I'd never lie about something like this. To endanger her health was against my code.

"I got tested after I figured out he was cheating and I was fine, thank God. There's been no need to test again. If you're sure then I do want that. I've never experienced it either."

I was shocked. Before I could think better of it, I blurted out, "You mean you guys used condoms even when you were pregnant? Why?"

She blushed then sighed. "He only touched me a couple of times early on and he wore one. After I started to get bigger, he said my body turned him off. Listen, no more talk about him. I just want to concentrate on us."

"Okay, I totally love that idea. Only one last comment then I'm done. He was a jackass and fool." With that out there and the contraceptive route agreed upon, I didn't delay. I wanted to be sure she was ready, and that I didn't hurt her, so I did play with her pussy, as I teased her breasts with my mouth. It didn't take long for her to be flooding my fingers with her honey again. I worked up to three fingers into her before I thought it was enough. Removing them, I laid down on the bed. She gave me a puzzled look.

"I want you to control how fast and deep we go. I

don't want to hurt you. Straddle me and ride me, baby." I urged her.

She sat up slowly then straddled me with a little help from me. Once she was poised over me, I held my cock up and notched it to her entrance, but that was it. I was determined to let her set the pace. A loud moan was torn out of me when she started to press down and the head pierced her. She was tighter and hotter than I imagined. Her slickness was helping me to get inside, but it was going to be a tight fit. Gripping her hips, I whispered to her. "Move up and down. Work me inside a little at a time. I'll help. If you need to rest, tell me. It's not a race. I'm not gonna enjoy this if I hurt you."

Nodding her head, she lifted up and then pressed down. This time she took a little more of me. Working together we eased my cock deeper and deeper. I wanted to howl with how fucking good it felt and pound into her until we both came screaming, but I couldn't. Finally, when I thought I might break, she seated herself fully on me. We both groaned. "Jesus, you feel like fucking heaven, Raina. That's it, my Queen. Ride me as fast and hard as you want. Make us come," I pleaded brokenly.

"You feel amazing, Aaron. I don't know how long I can last," she said back right before she blew up my world. She started out slow for only a couple of thrusts then she began to ride me harder and faster. Soon she was almost slamming herself down on me and I was using my feet to thrust up inside of her. It was hot, gritty, intense, and so goddamn glorious, I knew I wasn't gonna last.

Gritting my teeth, I rolled her over on her back. Pinning her legs back to her chest, I rode her hard and fast making sure to sink my cock as deep as possible. She was moaning and crying out, encouraging me to fuck her harder. Sweat slid down my spine as I pistoned in and out of her. After more time than I thought possible to hold out, my balls drew up and my teeth ached from clenching them.

I was about to beg her to come before I did, when she tightened around me even more, and she screamed. As she did, I felt her flood my cock with more honey and she began to rhythmically clench and unclench around me. It was all I needed. I gave one more hard thrust then held still as I jerked and filled her with my cum. A scream literally tore out of me, it was that intense and felt that amazing.

I didn't stop thrusting until my cock was limp and spent. Then I slowly withdrew and fell down next to her, breathing like I'd just run a race. She was lying there with her eyes closed and breathing raggedly. I touched her face. She opened her eyes and looked at me. She appeared dazed but she did smile. "That was utterly insane," she whispered.

"Yes, it fucking was," I moaned. We both closed our eyes.

Raina: Chapter 12

If anyone had ever told me that I could be this happy, I would've told them they were crazy. Connecting with Joker again after all these years was amazing, but the way everything had clicked and escalated even more since last weekend when I stayed with him and we made love for the first time, was unbelievable. We'd made love several times, until I was sore, before he ended up taking me home late on Sunday. He wasn't thrilled about it. He wanted me to stay with him, but I had Belle and Granddaddy to worry about. He seemed to understand, and he didn't make me feel bad about it.

Every night since, he'd come over for dinner and spend time with us. After Belle would go to bed, we'd sneak off to be together at his house for a few hours then he'd bring me home. The only nights we didn't were the last two. He'd stayed until she went to bed then we went to my room. I had felt weird at first, but he told me he'd asked permission first, so he could be sure it wouldn't be disrespectful. Granddaddy would just smile and tell us to go when we asked him if he was alright to watch Belle the nights I left with him. I knew this couldn't go on forever. We'd have to figure out a better plan. All I knew was neither of us wanted to be apart.

Joker insisted he had a plan. He was adamant

we move into his house at the compound, including Granddaddy. I was hard pressed not to agree, even if it seemed insanely fast, but I didn't want to take him away from his home. He'd lived here for the past fifty years. Joker kept reminding me it wasn't fast. We'd been falling in love with each other for close to twelve years. When I thought of it like that, we were way behind.

Tonight after work was the start of the weekend. We had plans to talk about the whole living arrangements. Speaking of work, I'd floated through the week with a smile on my face. Connie and Hana asked me what put it on my face and if Joker was the cause. All I did was smile harder. Even Cray had asked and grinned when I wouldn't say. The only ones who didn't were Leif and Tessa. They were still acting squirrelly. I ignored them. I guess they weren't my friends after all. It was their loss.

The plan was tonight I was going to hang at the clubhouse and stay the night, then tomorrow we'd bring Belle and Granddaddy over to spend time with us. One of the things we'd done this week was go furniture shopping together. Joker insisted I had to help choose what would go in our house. Every time he said that, it made me warm and happy.

And it wasn't just me who went shopping. He insisted Belle had to come too, so she could pick out her bedroom furniture. This raised a lot of questions from her, which I had a hard time dodging. In the end we told her the truth, that we hoped to become a permanent couple and if it happened, or when as Joker insisted, we'd live with him. She'd been so thrilled I could barely contain her. It was all I could do to keep her from going home and packing her stuff, especially when he told her he wanted Granddaddy to move in too.

Finishing my notes in the system and seeing it was already three o'clock, I hurried to get my things and head for home. He was coming to the house to get me at five. I wanted time to shower, dress in comfy clothes, and make sure they were set for the night. I'd put on a stew this morning before work for them to have for dinner.

I was so occupied with what I had to do at home that I wasn't paying much attention when I went to my car. That's why I didn't see Tessa standing there until I almost ran into her. When I did see her, I wanted to groan. The expressions on her face told me I wouldn't like what she planned to say to me.

"Excuse me, I need to get into my car. I'm sorry but I don't have time to talk today," I said, hoping it might win me a reprieve. No such luck.

"You think you're something, don't you? With your biker lover and his club, but we know all about you," Tessa snapped at me.

I stopped to stare hard at her. If she wanted to do this, then we'd do it. "What is it you think you know about me, Tessa?"

"Besides you're a slut? Your ex-husband is a thief. You left this town in shame, so why didn't you stay gone? And we know that Joker is his cousin. Don't get used to him. He's just getting a piece of ass and then he'll move on. You should be ashamed and think of your daughter. It's disgusting that you're sleeping with her cousin. Child services should take her away from you before you make her like you. You were a slut when you were a teenager. I know how you trapped her poor dad," she said.

Fury tore through me. *Who the fuck did she think she was?* I rushed at her. She stepped back until her back was pressed against my car. "Listen very closely to me, Tessa. I don't know what made you such an ugly human being and I don't care. Just like I don't care what you think of me, although I think it's pretty funny that you're calling me a slut. I've heard the stories about how many of the cops, male dispatchers, and firemen you've slept with. You give new meaning to the term badge bunny. However, if you say one more word about Joker or my daughter, I'll put your ass on the ground. No one threatens to take my daughter away. And for your information, Joker and I are moving in together, so not so temporary, is it?"

She gasped then tried to act like she was tough. She shoved me away from her. "Bitch, I'll say or do whatever I want. There's nothing you can do about it. I think I'll call CPS myself and tell them they need to check your home out."

I knew false claims were made all the time and sometimes the poor parents had nothing but grief because of it. I didn't want that to happen, but I wasn't going to let her think she could threaten me.

"Go ahead and see what happens to you. I can promise you, it won't end well for you. What's the matter? Jealous that Leif likes me and not you? I've seen how you've been chatting with him, but he doesn't appear to be interested in more than a gossip buddy. Too bad, you've been friend-zoned," I said with a smirk.

She shrieked and like a viper her hand came up and she slapped me. It stung and instantly I was ready to beat her ass into the pavement. However, instead of slapping her, I pulled my fist back to punch her. I was prevented by a hand grabbing mine. I swung around to see who was attacking me from behind. I froze when I saw Zev. He looked angry. "What the hell is going on here, Raina? Why did she slap you?"

"Oh, yeah, ask her, you're just like all the rest, sucked in by her Ms. Innocent act. She's a slut and you all think she's a saint," Tessa screamed at him. His eyes widened.

"She was waiting for me at my car and attacked me verbally about my ex, my current boyfriend and even threatened to call CPS and lie to them that I'm a terrible mom. I told her a hard truth, so she slapped me."

He stared at me for a few moments then looked at her. "Tessa, mind telling me why you waited out here for Raina and got confrontational? I saw you slap her, so don't lie and say that didn't happen."

Tears filled her eyes. I knew they were fake, but would he? "She's been hateful and I wanted to make her stop. I didn't say anything about her kid. As for her boyfriend I said he would soon figure out what she was and leave her. She's been flirting with every guy in dispatch. Leif was mine and now he's all about her."

"That's a lie. You said my ex was a thief, that you'd call CPS, that Joker will leave me when he realizes what

I am, and you said I conned my ex into marrying me. I'm not flirting with anyone in dispatch. Leif seems to have a thing for me and she's mad about it, but I didn't encourage him."

"I think you two should just avoid each other. It's obvious you're not going to go back to being friends."

"I have no problem with that, believe me. I don't need supposed friends like her. I'll ignore her as long as she doesn't slander my name or make a false report to CPS."

"Tessa, I could arrest you for assault and you could spend up to a year in jail. With a cop as a witness, you'd have no way to deny it. I'll forget what I saw if you promise not to call CPS and stay away from Raina." She sulked then finally nodded jerkily before she stomped off. When she left, I wanted to cry as the tension left me.

"Are you alright? Do you need me to call someone to drive you home? Your boyfriend, maybe?" The way he said boyfriend told me he was curious.

"No, I can drive. Joker is coming over to the house in a bit anyway. Thank you. I thought we were friends, and then she turned on me. I wasn't lying about Leif. She does like him and he kind of acts like he likes me. I think it made her angry. The two of them have been whispering to each other for the past two weeks and glaring at me."

"I'm glad I could help and I can't blame Leif for being interested. I was kind of hoping to ask you out myself, but I guess I'm too late. Is it serious with this Joker guy?"

I felt awful having to tell him yes, since he was such a nice guy, but I didn't want anyone to have false hope. "It's very serious. I'm sorry. You seem like a great guy and if I wasn't with him, I might've said yes. I hope you understand and won't hold it against me. I'd like for us to be friends. As you can tell, I need those."

"I'm disappointed but not surprised. A woman like you isn't likely to be single long. I'd like to be your friend too," he said with a smile.

"Thank you. I hate to run out on you after you helped me, but I really do have things to do before he comes over."

"That's okay, I've got to head out to get my son anyway. Based on the name, I assume Joker is part of the local MC."

"He is. They're a great group of guys," I said tersely.

"Hey, I'm not implying anything. My boss, Chief Scarelli, and the club's president seem to be good friends. He tells us all the time they aren't the enemy. Drive safe and I'll see you next week, maybe. If you have any more trouble with Tessa, let me know. Her reputation precedes her. No one is going to believe her about you."

Laughing in relief, I agreed to do that before I got in the car. The drive home was short, thankfully. I was almost a half hour behind schedule. After greeting my family, I hurried to take my shower and get changed. Once I was done, I came out to the kitchen so I could visit with them and work on putting the finishing touches on the stew. I didn't mention my run-in. They didn't need to know it or be stressed about it.

Before I knew it, I heard a motorcycle coming. I ran to the door in excitement and had it open and waiting when he walked up. I threw myself in his arms then we kissed. It was the same every time we saw each other. When we finally stopped, I led him inside. Belle was standing there grinning.

"You couldn't even wait until he got inside? Mommykins, for shame. What will the neighbors think?" she teased.

I burst out laughing as Joker gave a loud roar and took off after her. She ran, screaming from him, but he caught her easily in the living room. I walked in to watch him get her down on the couch, and tickle her until she begged for mercy. When he stopped, he gave her a kiss on the cheek. "There you go. I knew all that talk was because you're jealous. I can't pass up the opportunity to kiss your mom, but I'll always have one for you too, okay?"

"Okay, if that's the case, then you can kiss her anywhere you want."

She didn't see the look he gave me, nor knew that her words had double meaning. He raked his eyes up and down me and licked his lips. I widened my eyes in warning, but he didn't say anything. The amused look on Granddaddy's face said he hadn't missed out on what she said, and what we were thinking. Lord, they all could make me blush, damn it.

I kept fussing over them until Granddaddy looked at Joker. "Get her out of here. We can survive dinner, and the night without her. I'm still able to wipe my own ass too," he grumbled good-naturedly.

"Granddaddy!!" Belle gasped in shock. He chuckled until he had tears in his eyes. Joker was grinning.

I gave my outrageous granddaddy a kiss. "Behave. I'll see you tomorrow."

"No guarantees on the behaving part, and don't make it too early. I plan to sleep in," he said with a wink.

"Love you," I told Belle, as she hugged me. When she let go of me, she gave Joker a hug and kiss on the cheek, which I saw pleased him.

"Later, Love Bug," he said, using my nickname for her. She beamed with joy.

Walking outside with my overnight bag, I came to a screeching halt. I'd totally forgotten he rode his bike to the house. "I need to get my car," I said, as I turned to go back inside and out through the garage.

He grabbed my arm and shook his head. "There's no need for that. Your bag will fit in one of the saddle bags."

"I don't have a helmet," I tried to argue. How could I tell him I was afraid to ride it?

"I have a helmet for you." When I didn't step closer to the bike, he studied me. After almost a minute of uncomfortable silence he broke it.

"Babe, are you afraid of riding? Did you have a bad experience when you rode with Parker? I promise, I'm safe and won't scare you."

"I never rode with Parker. I've not been on a bike."

He gave me an incredulous look. "I can understand not riding when you were pregnant, but what about before? He got a bike as soon as he turned sixteen."

"He never wanted me on it. He said it was his thing, and I would only ruin it."

"Goddamn motherfucking idiot. I swear, the more I find out the less I think he can be kin, and the more I want to beat his stupid ass into the ground. Sweetheart, I'd love nothing more than to have you on the back of my bike. It's your place. I've never let a woman ride with me other than my mom. And the only other females I'll allow on here are our daughters, but if you want to wait, I understand."

Hearing him say he wanted me there, and it was my place as well as saying "our daughters'", which told me he wanted kids, made me excited to try. That excitement drowned out the fear, although there was still a bit there. "No, I think I want to try. Just take it slow. I've always thought they look so cool and fun. I was disappointed I never got to ride, but now I'm not. I only want to ride with you, Aaron."

His smile made me happy I chose to try. He gave me a quick kiss then took my bag and purse. He put them in the saddlebags after taking out another helmet.

His was sitting on his seat. He helped me to get it on and latched it, then he put his on before he swung his leg over the seat. Then he looked down at my feet. Thankfully, rather than wearing shorts, I'd slipped on a pair of jeans and tennis shoes.

"Babe, do you have a pair of boots you can wear?"

"No, not here, I have them packed away in storage. Why?"

"I don't like you in those shoes but they'll do. Before you ride again, we'll go get you a proper pair of riding boots. Something that goes up over your ankle and is made of tough leather. The jeans are good though. No bare feet or legs on the bike. People who ride like that are asking for trouble. No matter how good of a rider you are, you could still go down. Boots and jeans can save your skin and hopefully more. Here, put on my jacket." He twisted around and got in the saddle bag. When he shut it, he held out a leather jacket that had the same logo and wording on it as his cut.

"What about your arms?"

"Mine are fine. They're not as delicate or soft as yours are. Now, ready to do this?"

I nodded. He turned back, then held out his hand and gave me step-by-step instructions on how to get on, where to place my feet and how to hold him. He warned me about the pipes, which could burn. After he was satisfied I had it down, then he told me how to lean with him and the bike. I was thankful for him taking the time to go over it all, because I didn't know any of it, other than I knew I had to hold on to him around the waist.

Finally, when he was ready. I jumped when he started it. The throaty growl sound was even louder this close. The rumbling vibration underneath me took me by surprise. If I was honest, it was kind of sexy. It made tiny tingles flutter through my pussy. He looked over his shoulder and gave me a smirk which told me he knew what it was doing to me. I smacked his hard stomach with my hand. He took it slow and easy. It was a slow ride to the end of the street. From there, he picked up speed, as we made our way through the neighborhood streets to the main road that ran through town. There we ran into a lot of cars and trucks, which made me nervous. I kept jumping every time someone would come up alongside us. At a red light he patted my leg and hollered back to me. "Relax, babe, I see them. It'll be better once we get outside of town."

Nodding my head so he knew I heard him, I saw him blow me a kiss then we were off. Gradually, as the cars thinned out and I got used to how he would lean, I relaxed more and more. I knew it would take several more rides to make me feel relaxed completely, but I was right. This was fun. I enjoyed the wind on my face and was glad I had put on my sunglasses before we left the house.

The ride out to the compound wasn't a long one, but for my first try, I thought it was long enough. Gavin was manning the gate when we came through it. He waved and we waved back. He gave me a thumbs up when he saw I was riding. I grinned back and gave him one. Instead of stopping at the clubhouse, which is what I thought Joker would do, he kept going until we were at his house. Parking in the garage, I waited for him to shut off his bike.

"Here, let me get off first. That'll make it easier for you," he said as he easily swung off.

He held out his hand so I had something to grasp as I got off. I was far from smooth like he was. In fact, I felt like a colt standing for the first time. He was sweet enough not to laugh at me. We stowed his jacket and our helmets in the bags after he removed my stuff. Hand-in-hand we went inside. Our shoes and boots came off in the mudroom. No tracking anything on his pristine new floors.

When we came out of it, I stopped in awe. Somehow, I don't know how he did it, but there was the furniture we'd picked out for the living room. At the store, they claimed it would take them a week or more to get it delivered. "How?"

"I called and talked to the manager. I explained why I needed it and he said he'd do what he could to make it happen. They delivered all of it yesterday."

"I love it. It looks perfect in here."

"You need to see the rest."

As he led me through the house, my astonishment grew. We'd picked out stuff for the living room, the nook, barstools for the kitchen, and Belle's room. It was all here. The rest I told him could wait. If we ended up moving in here, there were things I had in storage we should check out first. He had nothing, since he lived in the clubhouse all these years, other than a television, bath towels and washcloths, clothing, and stereo equipment.

By the time we made it to the master bedroom, I was so excited I couldn't contain it. He dropped my overnight bag as I launched myself at him. He wrapped me up tight against him. I gave him an intense kiss. When I let go, I had to tell him how much I loved it all.

"Aaron, the furniture looks even better in the house than it did in the store. Belle is going to die when she sees that room. What's left to do in the house? Most of the rooms are even painted the colors we talked about. How? It's only been two days since I've been here."

"Well, the other bedrooms and stuff will get done next week, but I had the prospects and my brothers who had time, working on the common areas, our room and Belle's first. They even have Byron's room done too. All we need to do is move his stuff from his house and he's good to go. As for Belle, I hope she loves it. The old ladies insisted they do it up and got her the curtains, bedding, and stuff for it. If she doesn't like something, we'll get her different stuff."

Her room had been done in the prettiest lilac I'd ever seen on three walls and then there was an accent wall of the palest, almost silvery gray. The bedding was cream, lilac, and gray. Her curtains were a gauzy cream color with purple butterflies on them. A rug of the same three colors was by the bed. He didn't just get her the bed, dresser, and nightstand either. No, he'd gone back and added the desk and chair that went with the set along with a bookshelf. They were like her other furniture—cream with gold edging. It was a room fit for a princess. Probably the sweetest surprise and one she'd love was the calligraphy sign of her name with *Love Bug* under it.

"You can't spoil her like that, Aaron. She's never had everything she wants, and I don't think she should. She's used to having a single mom, and we never had tons of extra money. Just having a new bed and dresser will thrill her. You didn't need to go get her the other pieces too."

"She deserves everything new and she'll need them. I know she's a reader like you and she needs a place to do her homework and study. You can argue but you won't win."

"I'll have to find a way to win then, won't I?" I said with a smirk. "Thank you, it's gorgeous and she won't want to change a single thing. I can't wait to tell the ladies thank you. Where did you get that sign made? It's so precious."

"Payne did it. He's the artist in the bunch. He does tattoos all the time and they often have words to them. He picked out a font he thought would look girly and then asked what I wanted it to say. I thought both her names were perfect."

"It is. God, I think I'm going to cry," I sniffed, as tears started to fill my eyes.

"Don't cry. What's wrong?"

"Nothing is wrong. It's just you've done more for her than Parker ever did. He never picked out anything for her, not even a onesie. He said that shit was women's work. She wasn't a boy, so he was disappointed."

"Sonofabitch. Babe, I'm so damn sorry and I hate that you both struggled all these years. How I wish I'd known you were divorcing him. We would've been together years ago."

"Me too. If we had, would we have had more kids, do you think?"

"Absolutely, as long as you wanted more. Do you want more?"

"Well, I'm still young enough to have them and I always wondered what it would be like to have more than one. Belle has wanted a sister and brother since she could talk. I'm not opposed to it, if you still want some." I told him shyly. Talking about babies made me want them again, like I had years ago.

"Hell yeah, I'd love some. Belle will always be considered by me to be mine, however, adding even one more would be awesome. Two or more would be even better, but that's up to you. I'm not the one who has to carry them for nine months. Was it rough for you when you were pregnant with her? I didn't see you much, so I don't remember it being, but what do I know?"

"Actually, I was fortunate, she was an easy pregnancy. I had some nausea but no vomiting. I've heard horror stories and I pity those women. It was because I didn't have many symptoms that I didn't know at first I was pregnant with her. I thought I'd skipped a period."

"Well, it sounds like we have some work ahead of

us when you're ready."

"Hold on there, big man, no babies until we've had time together, actually moved in together and figured out all the other things going on, like whether you know who is going to really come after us or not."

"I didn't hear the word wedding in there. You forgot one."

I froze. Despite all the things we'd been saying, I hadn't thought of us getting married. I swore after Parker I'd probably never get married again. Seeing his smile fade away, I knew I had to say something. "Aaron, I honestly never thought I'd get married again after I divorced him, even if I did meet someone. The fear of it going bad too and having to go through all the hoops to get a divorce made me say never again."

"Do you still feel like that? Because I'll be honest, I'd love nothing more than to make you my wife one day. However, if you're opposed to it, I'll settle for you being my old lady and me being your old man. In the biker world, it means more to some than a wedding." Although his words said one thing, I could tell he wanted both.

"Why don't we wait and see where we are in six months or a year? I'm not saying no. If there would be anyone I'd ever want to marry, it would be you. It's a long-seated worry that will take me time to shake if I can. Besides, we have time."

His smile came back and he nodded. "I can do that. Okay, do you want to do anything before we head over to the clubhouse? If you do, do it now, because they want us to hang with them tonight. I know what I'd love to do, but if we do that, we won't be going anywhere tonight." His sexy look told me he was thinking what I was.

"In that case, let's go. If I stay here alone with you, I won't be able to keep my hands off you."

His growl made me laugh then I took off for the stairs. It was going to be a fun night. I couldn't wait to have fun with the club then come back here to have our own special fun.

Joker: Chapter 13

Watching Raina's face as she saw the work done on the house and the furniture we'd picked out together had filled me with so much happiness, I wanted to yell about it at the top of my lungs. It had been a push to get this much done in a couple of days, but it was so worth it.

While I was thankful I'd been able to spend the evenings and part of the night with her for the past week, it wasn't nearly enough. I wanted her with me at all times. Hell, if I could have her at the spa, it would be wonderful. Having her here tonight was doubly special. Not only would she be furthering her friendship with the club, but she would be seeing and renewing her relationship with my parents.

They had been bugging me about her. Asking how she was, if I saw her or talked to her, Asking what Belle was like. They were still as pissed off as I was at PJ and Bernie for what they did. We couldn't understand why they would cut their only grandchild out of their lives. Even if they hated Raina, which they had no reason to, despite her divorcing Parker, they should've stayed in contact with Belle.

I told them what her parents said about them doing it so they would get a cut of the money from the things Parker stole. They'd been stunned, then irate. Like me, they knew whatever he stole he'd hocked and spent the money. There was no hidden stash somewhere just waiting for his stupid ass to get out of prison. That conversation was easier to have with my parents than it was to have with Byron and Raina. We had sat down after Belle went to bed the other night and I told them. I'd waited long enough.

"I forgot to tell you that I had a conversation with your parents right after you came back, babe."

"You did? Why? Where? What did they say? I saw them in the grocery store and they said some odd things to me then practically ran off. Is that because of you? I forgot to tell you."

"It most likely was. I went to their house and pretty much confronted them about you being back in town, which they claimed they didn't know. I told them you were staying with Byron and that his health isn't the greatest, but they would know that if they bothered to check on him or make sure he was alright. After some denial and attempts to get me off the subject, they finally told me why they lied like Parker's parents did. It all came down to money."

"Money? What money?" Byron asked.

"Apparently, they were convinced by PJ and Bernie that the stealing Parker did resulted in him having a lot of money hidden and they were promised when he got out of prison, they would get a cut that was worth their while. All they had to do was tell everyone Raina had disappeared without telling anyone where she was going and without a

way to contact her. I admit, it was all I could do not to plant my fist in your dad's face, Raina."

The look of utter devastation on her face was too much for me. I reached out and snagged her so I could hold her tightly. I murmured words of comfort as she sniffed back tears. While she was trying not to soak my shirt with her tears, I asked Byron the question that had been burning in my mind for a while.

"Byron, there's something I have to ask you about Rudy."

"Go ahead, what about that dumbass?" he growled. It was hard to remember most of the time Rudy was his son. They were as different as night and day.

"Well, I know Mable would've never cheated on you. She loved you too much, and she was an honorable woman. However, are you absolutely certain, I mean one hundred percent certain, that he wasn't mixed up at the hospital and you got the wrong baby?"

It took a moment or two for what I asked to sink in. When it did, Byron and Raina both burst out laughing. Well at least it made her stop wanting to cry. After they got themselves under control, Byron answered me.

"I wish I could say there was a chance, Joker, but there's not. Rudy was born at home. There were no babies close that he could've been mixed up with. I've often wondered if he was a changeling, like the fairies used to leave to trick humans into taking their babies."

"I don't know about changelings, but if he wasn't switched, then the only possible answer is you repeatedly *and viciously dropped him on his head. Or Mabel did when no one was looking. He could test the patience of a saint, so no judgment on either of you for doing it. I only wish you dropped him more to correct the problem."*

That had sent them off into peals of laughter again. We finished our talk then I took Raina back to the house with me for a few hours.

As we entered the clubhouse, the noise from conversations and the music someone had playing hit our ears. It wasn't as loud as it could be. I figured they had tamed it down because my parents were here, as well as the old ladies and the kids. They wouldn't be here long then they were headed for bed. Lolly and Kamila had been asked to come and watch over them in the kids' room. Thank God it was soundproof.

Besides reintroducing her to my parents, I was eager to have her meet Kamila and Lolly. I wanted her to be comfortable asking them to watch Belle whenever she needed a sitter. Or I guess I should say, when we did, not that Belle took much. She was almost old enough to stay alone. Just a couple more years and she would be old enough to babysit the other kids. She would make a fortune on the compound alone if she did that.

I barely had Raina clear of the door, and halfway to the bar to get us both something to drink, when we were waylaid by my parents. When Raina saw them, she froze and stared like she didn't know what to do. That's when I recalled one of the reasons I dearly loved my folks.

Mom opened her arms and gave her a hug while

saying, "Sweetheart, it's so good to see you. We've missed you and are so happy that you're home. We can't wait to see Belle. Joker told us she's so grown up now."

As Raina struggled to find words, Mom let go and passed her off to Dad, who gave her a bear hug. "It is damn good to see you. And PJ and Bernie are fucking morons for what they did. The rest of the family, at least on the Fairbanks' side, have disowned their stupid asses. I told the other Piersons they should do the same."

"Asa, such language. Poor Raina will think you're an uncouth barbarian," Mom chided him.

He rolled his eyes. "Abbie, she's with our son. I can guarantee you he says those words and worse around her. We're not uncouth, just unusually good with words."

This made Raina laugh, then she relaxed enough to talk to them. "Thank you, Mr. and Mrs. Fairbanks. It's good to be back and to see you again. I'm sure we can arrange for you to see Belle soon. She is very grown up and will pass me soon in height."

"Now, none of this Mr. and Mrs. stuff. Call us Asa and Abbie or if you prefer, Dad and Mom," Dad told her gruffly. Her cheeks turned pink, but it was from pleasure, I think, not embarrassment. See, I did luck out when it came to getting the best parents.

"Okay, thank you. I didn't know you were going to be here tonight. I thought it was the club only. Have you been to see Joker's house?"

Dad had finally let go of her when I pried her out of his arms. He gave her a wink when she went back to me.

"I wanted them to be a surprise. If you knew they were going to be here, you would've been nervous, wouldn't you?"

"Yeah, I would. You got me there."

"As a matter of fact, we did see it. He showed it to us before he went to get you after work. I love the colors you picked for the walls and the furniture. Thank God, you helped him or I hate to think what he might have put in there," Mom shuddered.

"Hey, I have taste. Don't go making her think I would've made it a bachelor pad. It wouldn't be," I protested.

"Sure, you do. I remember how you wanted to decorate your room when you were at home," was her comeback.

"I was fourteen for God's sake. That was twenty years ago. My taste has changed and improved drastically. I think neon green walls and orange circles on the walls and hot pink dildoes would've looked fantastic in our new house," I added with a grin.

All of them moaned, as if I'd hurt them, and they teased me more. I did it to get Raina even more comfortable with them. In no time she was chatting away with Mom and a few of the other old ladies. Dad pulled me aside.

"Son, she looks just like I remember her, gorgeous. And she's just as sweet. I hope the fact you had her help with that house and I see a little girl's room in it, that you mean to snatch her up and keep her. A woman like that is hard to find."

"I'm ahead of you, Dad. I'm working to get both of them and Byron moved to the house as soon as possible. Now that it's essentially done, other than some paint on the walls in the other rooms, we can move in."

"Byron? He'll be moving in too?"

"He can't be alone. His COPD is really bad. In fact, don't tell anyone, but it's really end-stage. I don't think he has more than a couple years left in him at the most. He's on oxygen all the time and he can't walk much or do other physical stuff for long before he's short of breath and has to take a long break. Raina and I both wouldn't feel at ease leaving him alone. The bedroom downstairs is going to be set up for him."

He slapped me on the back and squeezed my shoulder. He had a proud look on his face. "Son, I'm so damn proud of you. I can see Raina and Belle are what you need to make your life complete. I've been worried about you and so has your mom. For the past ten years, you've been acting like everything is a joke, which is part of your personality, but we could see the sadness underneath. That's gone now. You said the club was enough, but we knew it wasn't."

"I was sad because she was gone. I was half in love with her when she left. That killed me and made me doubt I'd ever find someone I could call mine. Having her back is an answer to a prayer I never dared make."

"Well, grab her with both hands and don't let her go. Now, enough talking to you. I want to get to know my future daughter-in-law more. She was always so quiet when she was young and they rarely came to the family get-togethers."

I patted him on the back and nodded then let him go talk to Raina. I went to finally get us those drinks. As Walker filled my order, Slash came up to me.

"Brother, I just wanted to tell you that you've got a good woman there. You seem to have the luck of the devil like Bull, Bear and the others do when it comes to finding someone." Something in his voice told me he wasn't joking. He was down about it.

"Slash, do you want to settle down and have a family? Or are you content to be single? Answer me truthfully."

He didn't say anything for a minute. I thought he was going to blow me off. However, he did say something eventually.

"I do. Years ago I would've told you hell no, being single was the bomb. You can drink and fuck anytime you want and anyone you want. There was no one to care if you came home or what time you did, but as the years have passed and I've watched what happened on Dublin Falls and now here, I came to realize that's lonely as fuck. Will I be that lucky, I don't know. So far no one has caught my eye and I'm creeping closer to forty. I'm thirty-seven, man."

"Look at Bull and Bear. They were in their early fifties and late forties when they found Jocelyn and Ilara. I hope it comes sooner than that, but don't give up. You have to keep your eyes open. I'm convinced your woman is out there and will appear when you least expect it. I never thought I'd see Raina again."

"And you get a daughter outta the gate. You know what you're gonna have to do and it better be soon?"

"What?"

"Get more guns. She looks like her momma and that means she's beautiful. She's eleven. She could start her period any day and that means all those physical changes that attract boys. I give you no longer than two years before you'll have to start killing boys, but don't worry. We'll have your back and pick off those little horny fuckers from the top of the walls. I've got a new scope for my AR-15."

"Slash, you're not over here inciting Joker to kill, are you?" Player said loudly, so others were sure to hear him.

Suddenly, we were mobbed by people who all wanted to know what we were talking about. When Slash told them, most laughed, but those with daughters, even if they were still young, nodded in agreement. Raina just stood there shaking her head like she didn't know what to do with me. Hell, Slash was right. Belle was on the cusp of womanhood. God, fuck my life. I wouldn't be able to work. I'd have to guard her at all times along with her momma.

"Hey, Bull!"

"Yeah?"

"I can't work at the spa anymore. You're gonna have to get someone to take my place."

He frowned. "Why the hell do I need to do that?"

"Because I'll have to work full time and then some, keeping the boys away from Belle and men away from Raina. I can't hold down a job on top of that." I gave him a shit-eating grin after I said it.

He gave me the middle finger, the unsympathetic bastard. "You'll have to suffer like the rest of us. I raised Harlow and still worked, and she turned out fine."

"You call becoming a Marine sniper, then the old lady to an MC president fine? She was ruined from the start. If you'd watched her closer, she'd still be here, not over there," I joked.

"I dare you to call Terror and tell him that. He'll be on his way here to beat your ass in a second," Demon yelled.

Demon was the one who was closest to Harlow. We all loved her and thought of her as a sister, but he really did. Terror had to get his approval to go after Harlow just like he did Bull's. It was hard to believe that was nine years ago. I pretended to dial my phone then started talking.

"Hey, Terror, you sister stealing asshole. We've decided that Harlow is much better off here, in Hunters Creek with her brothers and the others, than over there in Dublin Falls with you and your ugly crew. We want you to pack her and the kids up and send them here. If you're really nice, we might give you visitation rights," I said loudly.

When I quit talking, before the others could get too loud with their snickering, I heard a booming voice come from somewhere. It was like God speaking from above.

"Listen here, Joker, you fucker. If you make one step toward Dublin Falls, you'll find yourself disappearing as if you never existed. No one, and I mean no one, takes my Temptress or my kids away. Am I gonna have to come over there and teach you a lesson?"

I admit, I was stunned. As I looked around to figure out who called him, I saw Bull smirk then take his hand out from behind his back. That dirty bastard!

"Terror, I was just playing. There's no need to get homicidal. No one will take her. There are no give backs. You wanted her, you got her," I replied quickly.

"No give backs! I'll come there and shoot your ass myself," I heard Harlow yelling.

In a flash, it became a comedy show. When it was finally over a good five minutes or more later, there wasn't a dry eye in the place and Raina was back with me. She shook her head. Terror and Harlow had signed off as they laughed themselves silly.

"Is this what I have to look forward to for the rest of my life?"

"It sure is, baby."

"Good," she said right before she gave me one helluva kiss.

It wasn't long after that, when the kids were all down for the night and the adults were free to have fun, when the music got louder, Games of darts, poker and pool were started. Conversations around the various tables flowed along with the drinks. It was a relaxing night with my family.

I blame the alcohol, and how happy I was watching her have a good time, as the reason I forgot that bunnies, and hang arounds, would show up eventually. When the door opened, and some came strolling in, I wanted to groan. Mom and Dad had been around them before. It wasn't ever for long, and they hadn't necessarily approved of them, but they were polite. With Raina's past, and her reasonable assumption that Parker cheated on her and it was likely with women like them, I knew she would find it hard to be around them.

I glanced to my right and found her staring at them. I couldn't figure out what she was thinking by the look on her face. I took her hand in mine and kissed it, so she'd look at me.

"My Queen, are you ready to head home for the night? Mom and Dad will be leaving." I pointed to my parents, so she could see them starting to say goodbye to people.

She surprised me when she shook her head no. "No, I'm not ready to leave. I need to get used to seeing them, right? They're gonna be here for the foreseeable future. Or at least someone like them will be. How long do they last here? And why do they do it, I wonder?" she mused aloud.

She said it louder than she thought, and it caught the attention of one of the bunnies, Kayla, who was standing close to us. We only had three, and Kayla had been here a long time. Vida and Clover were newer. They came last year. Most came when they were in their early twenties, partied for a few years, then moved on to do other things in life. For some reason, Kayla wasn't one of them.

She was in her late twenties, I think. However, I wasn't sure. Our past encounters were about sex, not conversation or getting to know each other. It made me sound like a total hound dog, but it was true and typical of the MC life. It had been a while since she and I hooked up. In fact, before Raina came back, I'd been celibate for six months, because none of them interested me. My brothers had no idea. I pretended to be getting action away from the clubhouse.

"You wanna know why I do what? Who the hell are you? I haven't seen you around here before. We don't really need another bunny," Kayla said brusquely.

That was another reason she and I hadn't been hooking up in a while. Her attitude, which used to be fun, quiet, and even nice to others, had disappeared. She snapped at hang arounds and random people who came to the compound, just not to the members. She knew we'd kick her ass out if she talked to us like that. But now I was wondering had she been giving an attitude to the old ladies like this?

I was about to put her in her place and warn her to watch how she talked to Raina, but she beat me to it. My Queen had learned to be more vocal over the years, I was learning. She stood up for herself.

"I was just wondering what would attract a woman to be a bunny or even a hang around. Do you really enjoy sex that much, that you don't care who you have it with, or that they don't care for you, other than as a way to get their rocks off? I think that would be the most depressing life. I believe some of you might enjoy the sex while others have self-esteem issues. I'm not a bunny or a hang around. I'm with Joker." She said it calmly and with no attitude. It sounded like she was genuinely curious.

Kayla's eyes widened as she took in what Raina said. Vida and Clover had come up behind her and overheard the conversation. Shit, this could get ugly quick. I glanced around to be sure I had enough guys nearby to stop a cat fight, if one broke out. This was the last thing I wanted tonight or any other night. And to have it happen with my folks here too, Jesus.

"My self-esteem is just fine, thank you very much. I happen to like sex and the guys like me. I give them what they need. Just ask Joker. And since we're getting things out in the open, you're with Joker as what, his newest toy or as a new cum dumpster, like us," she sneered.

"That's enough, Kayla," Bull snapped at her before I could.

Instead of Raina getting upset, she shrugged.

"Well, as long as you're happy. Although, I hope you know to keep your hands and the rest of your body away from the married men. As for what I am to Joker, why don't you ask him? I know what he likes and wants. As for being a cum dumpster, I find that to be a degrading term. I feel so bad you see yourself like that. When he and I have sex, there is cum involved, but I'm hardly a dumpster."

Her reply stunned a lot of people, including me. I sat there waiting to see what else would happen and was ready to jump in, if I had to, but it was looking more and more like I wouldn't, or at least not much. I did tell Kayla who Raina was to me. It was past time the bunnies and hang arounds knew my hiatus was permanent. Raina was the only woman I'd be having sex with.

"Kayla, you asked who she is. Her name is Raina, or as I call her, my Queen. She's the only woman I've ever loved, and it's taken me over ten years to find her again. She's my old lady and one day, she might honor me and become my wife. She's the only woman I'll have sex with until the day I die. She's not a toy or a dumpster like you implied. Now, I'd appreciate it if you'd tone down your attitude. It's been too much for a while. She wasn't rude when she asked. You've had women ask you stuff like this in the past. I've heard them, and you've never been as snippy as you are now."

She stared at me in silence. The angry look on her face faded a bit but not all the way. The place had gotten quiet except for the music. After a long drawn-out silence, she answered.

"I'm tired of women like her looking down on women like me just because I don't live the way they think I should. Who gave them the right to judge me?"

"Kayla, I'm not judging you. I'm trying to understand. You do something I can't imagine doing. And my ex-husband I'm sure cheated on me several times with bunnies and hang arounds who came to this club years ago, before your time. I want to understand why women would help a man cheat. And I need to know the attraction men have to a woman like you, because I don't want to find myself in that terrible situation again. I divorced my ex. If Joker ever cheated, it would kill me."

"Fuck, baby, you never have to worry about me doing that. I fucking love you and would never do anything to hurt you or lose you. I need you to believe that."

By then I was out of my chair and kneeling on one knee at her feet. It looked like I was proposing. How I wish I was. I had her hands gripped in mine. I prayed she would see I was telling the truth.

I breathed a sigh of relief as she leaned toward me and right before she kissed me, she said clearly, so they all could hear. "I know you won't. I was just making a point. I don't want to judge them or feel like I can't comfortably have you come here without me. Does that make sense? I love you, Joker."

I had to nod to answer her because she was kissing the hell out of me. I'd fought my arousal all night. No getting a boner in front of the parents or the guys. However, with her declaration and that kiss, my control was over. It was time to take her home and make love to her. She'd be in no doubt of what I liked or how much I loved her.

Finally I stood up and broke the kiss. She didn't look happy, but that changed the instant I scooped her up out of her chair. There were several hoots and hollers. I smiled. My parents were smiling like crazy and waved at me as they mouthed, *goodnight*.

"We'll see you all later. Have a good night. My Queen and I need to have a private conversation."

There were a few lewd comments, but the rest were all shouts of encouragement and to have a good time. My last look at Kayla showed me a very unhappy woman. There had to be more going on than what she shared. This attitude was a one-hundred-and-eighty-degree difference. Hopefully, she'd get over whatever was causing it soon, or move along. No one wanted that in their face, even for sex.

Raina: Chapter 14

My worries that I did something wrong or went too far in questioning Kayla after she heard my remark were eased, when Joker swept me up and announced he was taking his queen home to have a private talk. My whole body came alive with anticipation. I knew whatever happened, the end result would be me having the best orgasms of my life.

When we entered the house, he paused long enough to take off his boots. He had to sit me down, which gave me the chance to take off my tennis shoes. As soon as they were both off, he picked me back up and headed for the stairs.

"Aaron, baby, you don't need to carry me all the way up those stairs and to the bedroom. I can walk. You'll throw out your back or something," I warned him out of concern.

I wasn't a terribly heavy woman, but I did weigh over a hundred pounds. I carried my extra weight in my hips and breasts.

He laughed at me. The man laughed in my face and shook his head as he kept walking. "Jesus, Raina, if I can't carry you at least that far, then I need to get to the gym more. Babe, I lift weights in the gym and boxes of supplies at the spa and most of them weigh more than you do by a long shot. My back is safe. I love the feel of you in my arms. It makes me feel like I'm taking care of you," he confessed.

"You do take care of me. You make me feel like the queen you call me. I can't believe you told everyone at the clubhouse that I'm your queen."

"Why wouldn't I? It's what you are and they would know it soon anyway. I want to always treat you like a queen and Belle like a princess. One day, if we're blessed with more kids, they'll be treated the same."

"Hurry up and help me get rid of all of our clothes. I need to feast my eyes on your naked wonder of a body then I need you to make love with me," I said hoarsely.

His gaze grew even more heated and his tongue peeked out to wet his lips. He took the stairs like they were nothing and practically ran to the back of the house to the master bedroom. The door was gently kicked shut, and in a blink I found myself standing beside the bed. The comforter and sheet was already pulled down. He'd prepared for us. On the nightstands and the dresser were a series of candles in glass jars. I hadn't noticed them earlier.

"Stay right there for just a minute," he said, before he rushed to the nightstand and picked up a lighter. He quickly went around the room lighting the candles. The last thing he did was put on music. It was slow and romantic, which kind of took me by surprise. Not what you would expect a biker to listen to, although he was teaching me my ideas about bikers were mainly way off the mark. As he came back to me, he took off his shirt and dropped it on the floor before reaching down to undo his belt and jeans. He was close enough when he did that, I could grab his hands.

"That's my job. Let me admire your tats for a minute. You have so many. How long did it take to get all these?" I ran a finger around one of them then another. His muscles flexed.

"I got my first one at eighteen. I add them when something catches my interest. I need to go get a couple more now. You can come with me when I do if you want. Payne won't mind. Hell, he'll try to talk you into getting one. He loves to ink virgin skin."

As I ran my fingers all over his chest and arms, I asked, "Why do you need a couple more? And I'd love to watch you get them. I keep forgetting Payne is a tattoo artist. If he did all yours, he's really talented. As for me getting one, we'll see."

"He did most of them. The reason I have to get more is because of you and Belle."

"Me and Belle? What do we have to do with it?"

As we were talking and I was admiring, he somehow got my tank and bra off. Now both of us were bare on the top.

"Your names, baby. I want them on me, so everyone knows you're mine. And if we have more kids, their names will be added too. Actually, I want Belle's name and date of birth. Yours will be different."

I was beyond touched that he wanted us permanently on his body. He had no names on him now.

I shivered as he ran his fingers lightly down my neck and across one of my nipples. My response just made him do it again, only this time to the opposite one.

"Where will you get them? Your chest and arms are pretty full. There's space on your back."

"No, not my back. Belle and other children will be on my thighs. Here, let me show you," he said, as he finished undoing his belt and zipper then he dropped his jeans.

I was too mesmerized by the huge bulge tenting his underwear to pay attention to him stepping out of his pants. He was a man who wore tight briefs, not boxers and they outlined his erection perfectly. I couldn't hold back the low moan I made. He smiled at me, the horrible man. He tapped his thigh.

"Eyes here, babe, not up there. We're having a serious talk right now."

I could hear the teasing in his voice. I had to whine, which was rather unbecoming, but I couldn't help it. "We can talk later. I see something I want."

"And I see two things I want and there's more under your clothes, but we have to finish this first. Trust me, the wait will be worth it. Now, I want to run Belle's name and birthdate down the length of my thigh right here." He pointed to his outer thigh. The area bulged with even more muscles than the rest. To punish him for making me wait, I ran my fingers up and down the spot he pointed out.

"I think this is a very good place to put it. And if

we have more? Where will you put them?"

He pointed to the same spot on his opposite thigh then to his inner thigh on both legs.

"Well, I think those will be great. Good thing there's only room for four total," I teased him with a wink and another caress. This one ran up his inner thigh until it was a scant inch from his balls. I saw him take a deep breath.

"Oh, if we want more, I still have the fronts and back of my legs. I think we could get twelve of them easily with plenty of room in between so they don't look crowded."

"You're crazy if you think I'm having twelve kids, Aaron Fairbanks. If that's what you want, forget it. The baby making factory has been shut down."

He laughed at me. "Babe, I'm just messing with you. I'll happily take whatever you give me, even if it's just Belle. Now, do you want to know where your tattoo is going?"

I nodded my head. I did actually want to know. He pointed to his stomach. It was one place he had no tats, and I thought that was because he didn't want them there. He ran his fingers across that taut, defined eight pack of his.

"Your name is going right here. I have to talk to Payne about how I want it designed, so that's a surprise. It is the only thing that will ever be on my stomach. Even if my heart wasn't already covered, I wouldn't put it there, because you own all of me to the core. To my absolute soul and this is as close as I can get to it."

His words were so damn sweet and romantic to me that I couldn't help it. I threw myself in his arms and attacked his mouth with mine. As the kiss grew more and more heated, our hands were busy. I got that evil underwear of his off. He somehow stepped on the toes of his socks and got them off, before he stripped off the rest of my clothes. As soon as we were naked, I was airborne and landing on the bed with a thump. He came down on top of me.

His mouth hungrily kissed and nibbled its way from my mouth to my breasts then to my stomach until he finally got to where I was literally weeping for him. He teased me lightly with just the tips of his fingers. It wasn't enough.

"Aaron, more," I cried.

"Do you know what I was thinking?"

"No more talk," I ordered, as I grabbed his head and tried to force it down to my aching pussy. Of course he easily resisted. He had the nerve to chuckle.

"Just a little more. You'll like this. Have you ever had your pussy totally bare?"

I stopped pushing on his head. "No, why?"

"Because I want to see what yours looks like naked. And because it will bring you more pleasure. You'll have nothing between it and my beard and mouth. You'll feel every single tiny sensation."

"Do you prefer it like that? Is that what most

women you've been with have been like and enjoy?" Even as I asked, I started to cool off. Finding myself compared to others he had been with didn't settle well with me. In an instant he was up and staring me in the face.

"I don't fucking care or remember what other women I've been with had and I sure never gave a fuck if they were enjoying it more or not. I'll say this again. Those women were just a fuck. I had zero feelings for them. As long as I got off and they enjoyed it enough, then I was happy. Call me an asshole if you want, but that's the truth. I only asked because I was reading something which said being bare would increase a woman's enjoyment. You could have a goddamn jungle down there and I'd still want you more than anyone else in the world, Raina. Understood?"

Seeing how sincere and upset he was, I caressed his face. "I do understand and I'm sorry. I'll try harder not to let things like that come to mind. It's just hard for me to still understand why, out of all the women in the world, you want me, or love me. I'm nothing special."

"The fact you can't see it, doesn't make it untrue. You're special to me and that's only part of why I love you. Now, let's forget my questions and move on to more pleasurable things." As he went to lower himself down again, I stopped him.

"No, I haven't tried it, although I know a lot of women who swear they only ever went that way. I'm willing to try it, but if we do and we like it, then I'd have to go have it waxed to keep it that way. Having prickly, itchy hair down there wouldn't do. My luck, I'd scratch in public and people would think I have an STD."

The laugh that got out of him made me laugh. I loved to hear him chuckle like he did. It was one of the most carefree things I ever heard. It made others instantly smile, laugh, and feel happier. When he stopped, he nodded.

"Okay, a deal. We'll talk about this more later. For now, I can't wait any longer. I have to taste you," he finished on a growl, then he lowered himself down and took his first swipe of my pussy with that magical tongue of his. That thing should be insured. I moaned and was instantly lost.

I had no idea how long he ate me or how many times he made me come before I couldn't take it anymore and I begged him to stop. When he did, he came right back to my mouth and kissed me, sharing my taste with me. He told me more than once that nothing tasted as good as my pussy. I was glad he thought so. For me, it was okay. I didn't hate it when he did this, but I thought his cock and cum tasted better.

As we kissed, he nudged my thighs wider apart. I gasped as I felt the head of his cock press into me. Since I was now used to him, even if he was still big, he was able to push inside much faster and harder than the first time. We both moaned at the feel of it. He paused for a moment to savor it before he sat up and lifted my ass off the bed with his hands. This allowed him to set a harsh and fast pace.

The slap of his pelvis against me made me tremble. My fingers clawed at his back. I knew I was leaving nail marks. The first time I did it, I was appalled and apologized profusely to him. He shrugged me off and said having my marks on him made him proud. It said he'd satisfied his woman. So now, as long as I didn't make him bleed like a tiger had clawed him, I didn't worry about it. His hiss and look of joy told me he was into it. I was just climbing toward my orgasm when he stopped and pulled out.

"Aaron, what's wrong?"

"Nothing. I want to try something else. Roll on your stomach and scoot over until your legs are dangling off the bed."

I was too horny to argue or ask questions. I just did what he asked, so he would go back to getting us off. While I did that, he took a step toward the nightstand and opened the drawer. He took something out, but I couldn't see what it was. His body hid it. I watched as he moved back to me. He had that hand behind his back. My curiosity now piqued, I asked him.

"Honey, what's behind your back?"

"Close your eyes and wait. You'll see. I want your honest response. Give it a chance before you tell me whether to stop or not."

Now I was almost as interested in what he had in mind as I was in having another orgasm. I did as he asked. Although I wanted to peek, I didn't. I heard him rustling a bit then he stepped between my spread legs. He and I had done doggie style more than a few times. He was slowly introducing me to other positions we could make love in. All of them so far got a thumbs up.

He knew without me having to tell him that I'd only ever had missionary-style sex with Parker.

As I felt him enter me again, I sighed. I didn't know why, but he always felt bigger and like he went deeper this way. He told me he did go deeper. As he fully sank in, I jumped when I felt something cool and wet touch my asshole. My head whipped to the side so I could look down my back. He was watching me. One hand was on my hip and the other was between my ass cheeks. A wiggling movement around and over my back hole told me it was his finger. I started to tense up, but his smack on my hip stopped me.

"Stop. Relax and feel. If you absolutely hate it and it's not just because it's different or you think it's forbidden, then I'll stop. I won't use force. I want you to enjoy this."

"Aaron, I've never…"

"I know. Would it surprise you if I told you that I've only done this and ran my tongue across an asshole? Playing inside a woman's ass has never been my thing."

"Really?"

I found it hard to believe. He was very sexually experienced. I knew he hadn't even started to show me the things we could do and share. He said there was time to introduce me to all those when I asked. I didn't want him to get bored having plain old sex with me. And I was curious to learn more. I might have only ever been with Parker before this, but over the past ten years I'd done a lot of reading and wondering.

"Yes, really. I know a lot of guys who swear it's amazing and they say it gets women off even more and they love it. I never cared to find out. However, since you came back, I've been wondering and I want to find out for myself as well, but only if you're willing. Do you wanna find out, my Queen? Do you want to know if this can get you off even harder? Do you think it'll make you hotter? Scream louder?"

The more he talked, the more I noticed his color getting darker on his skin. He had this almost dazed look in his eyes. That was what told me he was turned on by the thought. Well, that, and the fact he'd sped up his thrusts inside of me and his finger teasing my asshole had sped up and was pressing harder against me. He wanted to penetrate my ass. Taking a deep breath, I forced myself to relax as I gave him my answer. I'd be lying if I said I never wondered about it.

"I do want to find out, my love. I'm afraid but still curious. Dare I confess, I've wondered if it does feel good or just hurts. I've read it's both but the pain soon fades. Go ahead and put your finger in my ass and we'll see if you can make us both come harder." I taunted, as I wiggled my ass and clenched my inner pussy muscles around him.

He groaned and closed his eyes for a moment. When they snapped open, I saw the blaze in them. I didn't look away as he slowed his thrusts and gently pushed the tip of his slick finger inside. It burned and hurt, I'll admit. If this was what it was like the whole time, no way would we be doing this again. Shit, how did women, or men, for that matter, stand someone to put a cock in them? They wouldn't be able to sit for a week and going to the bathroom had to hurt like hell.

He paused and started thrusting his cock in and out a tiny bit faster. As I got caught up in that, I paid less attention to my ass. Suddenly, his finger inched deeper. I hissed as it pushed through a tight constriction and stopped to slowly thrust back and forth, not going any deeper.

"Are you alright, baby? Do you want me to stop?"

It wasn't burning as much once I got used to him going deeper. I didn't want to say no yet. We both needed to give this a fair chance.

"No, continue, just do it slowly. I'll be honest, I don't see the appeal, but I want to give it a fair try."

"Okay, then I'll keep going. I don't see it either."

That's when he started to sync the two thrusts up. As he did, I started to feel something else. It was this tingling, slightly nicer sensation. His finger on each thrust was going deeper, until he stopped advancing, which told me his finger was all the way in. When that happened he really sped up those coordinated thrusts. Then like magic, the burning and discomfort was mostly gone or maybe just forgotten, as that tingling radiated intensely throughout my ass. I swear it even reached my vagina. I moaned long and loudly.

"What is it? Am I hurting you?" he asked in a pant. He started to slow down.

"No! Don't stop. Keep going. More," I pleaded.

He did as I asked and that's when I finally knew what the hype was all about. A massive wave of pure heavenly fire exploded inside of me. It caused me to orgasm. Clenching down on his cock and finger hard, I cried his name and came harder than ever before. I was mindlessly thrusting myself back on his cock and finger, as I gushed my honey as he called it, down my thighs.

As I milked him, he froze and let out a guttural groan that was deeper than any I'd ever heard him make, then I felt him jerking inside of me as warmth spread inside my pussy. "Fuuuck," he moaned. His eyes were closed and a look of utter bliss was on his face.

As my orgasm finally ended, I closed my eyes. A few moments later, he laid down on my back. He was panting. His lips found my ear and he kissed it. "Jesus, I think I just had an out-of-body experience. Please tell me you enjoyed that."

"If you don't do that again and again, I'll kill you. That was freaking unbelievable once you get past the discomfort and burning. I came harder than I ever had."

"I felt it. You almost broke my finger and cock. Goddamn, that's going in the playbook."

"Playbook?"

"Yeah, I keep a list of things we've done and what you like in my head for us to do again. I also have one filled with things for us to try. This one was one I wasn't too sure about, but I thought what the hell. The worst you could do was say hell no. I was skeptical, honestly, of the guys who say it's the fucking bomb."

"While I'm happy you listened and got me to try it, I don't want to know who said they love it. I would never be able to look them in the face again."

He laughed which caused tiny jolts of pleasure to race through me. That made me clench down again. We both moaned. I wasn't sure we'd ever be able to move from this spot. What a way to be found when someone came looking for us.

An annoying sound jarred me out of the best sleep I'd had in ages. I didn't want to wake up. After hours of mind-blowing sex with Joker, we'd finally fallen to sleep. I felt the bed move.

"Baby, it's your phone. Do you want me to answer it?"

"Yeah," I mumbled. It was probably work calling to beg me to come in for a shift, since someone called off. It happened a lot. He could tell them "no" for me.

"Hey, what's up? She's asleep," I heard him say. His voice was gravelly sounding.

"What the hell?! We'll be there, just hold on. Make sure you're not left alone. Tell them to wait until we get there." The urgency in his voice, along with his words, had me coming awake instantly and sitting up to stare at him. He hung up and was already getting out of bed.

"Aaron, what happened? Who was that?"

"It was Byron. Don't panic, they're alright but we

need to get to his house."

I almost fell jumping out of bed. As we scrambled to find and put on clothes, he explained why Granddaddy was calling in the middle of the night. Although I knew if he was, it had to be bad.

"Someone tried to break into the house. He was woken up by the alarm going off. When he went to check it out, he found the window next to the back door had been broken. It appears they were scared away by the alarm. The alarm monitoring business alerted the cops. He sounded a bit shaken up but I could hear Belle in the background. She was asking for you and crying. The cops are there, so they're safe. I told him to not let them leave until we get there."

As he explained, he was tapping away on his phone. I felt sick. I'd left them alone, and now my child needed me. What kind of mother was I to go have sex all night with her boyfriend while her child and sick grandfather were left alone? A terrible one, was the answer. If Tessa ever learned of this, she'd for sure call CPS on me.

My hands shook so hard, I could barely get my clothes on. Suddenly, he was there helping me. "Babe, calm down, they're fine."

"But they might not have been. What if whoever it was didn't run and he kept coming in? They could be hurt or dead while I was here with you. I should've never left them alone."

"Hey, none of that. You're not at fault for having time away from them. Stop thinking that bullshit.

Come on. The guys will meet us there," he said, as he took my hand and led me to the bedroom door.

"The guys? Is that why you were on the phone? They don't need to come. It's the middle of the night."

"They do need to come. Not all of them, but a few. When something happens like this, if I didn't tell them right away, they'd have my ass, especially Bull. The man earned his name for more than his huge appearance, babe."

I nodded and then let him take the lead. I was too busy with the images in my head to pay attention. All I wanted was to get to my family and make sure they were alright.

Joker: Chapter 15

As we sped to Byron's house on my bike, going as fast as was safe in the dark, I kept wondering who had tried to get into his house. My mind went straight to Parker, but his parole hearing was still five days away. Unless it unexpectedly got moved forward, and I'd have Outlaw check to make sure it hadn't, I had no clue who would target them. If it wasn't Parker, it had to be merely coincidence.

Hunters Creek wasn't the most dangerous or unlawful town by any means, but we did have crime. Robberies and fights were the most common. There were domestic calls of course. Most of our drug-related problems were due to people being high and getting into trouble. Dealing itself was something we worked hard to keep out of town. We couldn't prevent people from ruining their life with drugs, but they'd have to go somewhere else to buy them. The same was true of illegal guns. Prostitution was harder to police. If they decided to do it on their own, that was on them. We watched for pimps and others forcing women into that profession along with signs of human trafficking.

A roar as we got closer to town caught my attention. Glancing in my mirrors, I saw lights coming up behind me. I tensed until they caught up to us and I saw it was some of my brothers. They gave me a chin lift or raised hand. I gave them one back. I figured some would come. They'd never leave a brother to deal with something like this alone.

It was four in the morning, so there was no traffic on the road other than us. When we entered town, there were only a few random cars on the road. Zooming onto Byron's street, I had a momentary thought that his neighbors would be shitting themselves. There were cop cars with lights flashing there and now a bunch of bikes. I pulled up in front of the house. Raina almost fell as she scrambled off the bike.

"Babe, slow down before you hurt yourself. Here, take off your helmet." I got off the bike and helped her with her helmet then took off mine. As we were finishing up, a cop came ambling over to us. He was frowning.

"You folks need to move off. There's nothing here to see."

"This is my house," she told him loudly.

"This house belongs to—" he was cut off by another cop coming up.

"She lives here, Gonzalez. Why don't you go and make sure the neighborhood search hasn't turned up anything? I'll take care of them."

Gonzalez gave us a pissy look before he did as the other cop said. I was about to thank him and ask how he knew Raina lived here, when she smiled and spoke to him.

"Thanks, Zev, so that's Gonzalez. I haven't met

him, but he always sounds like a dick on the radio. I see he lives up to his voice."

Zev laughed. "He sure does. He's a decent cop, but he's too full of himself and thinks everyone is a criminal. Seeing you ride up on bikes was proof enough for him. Hell, if he knew I rode, he'd probably think I was one too."

"He's an idiot. I'm glad to see you're here, but why? You don't work nights and I thought you had your son this weekend?"

"I do, but someone called out with the flu. He's asleep anyway and my mom is with him, so I said I'd help. Damn, we're being rude. Hi, I'm Zev Oberlin. I work with Raina. You must be her boyfriend, Joker," he said suddenly as he turned to me and held out his hand. I took it automatically. As I shook it, my club brothers joined us.

"I'm sorry. I'm not thinking clearly. Yes, this is Joker and these are some of his club brothers. This is Slash, Player, Loki, Predator, and Stalker," she said, as she pointed to each one. They all shook Zev's hand as he offered it to them. "This is Officer Zev Oberlin. We work together obviously."

"Nice to meet you, Officer Oberlin. Can you tell us where Byron and Belle are, before Raina loses her mind?" I asked. She was almost vibrating as she scanned the area out front of the house.

"Sure can. They're in the house in the living room. Why don't you go inside? We'll be right behind you," Zev told her.

She didn't bother to say anything. She did give me a quick kiss before she took off running. Thankfully, no one else tried to stop her. If they had, I figured she might deck them. As she disappeared inside, I got back to her friend. I noted he was a good-looking man, who was tall and ripped with muscles. I should be jealous of her working with someone like him, but I wasn't. I knew I had nothing to worry about.

"Please, call me Zev. Officer Oberlin sounds so damn stuffy. I wanted you alone to let you know that whoever tried to break in hasn't been spotted. We're canvassing the neighborhoods around here in case there's a suspicious car or person on foot. Her grandfather said to check into her ex, Parker Pierson. That he's supposedly getting out on parole soon and he has a grudge against her."

"He does. His hearing was set for the fourth of next month, but it could've gotten changed, I guess. He blames her for him going to prison," I explained. I didn't bother to mention he blamed the club too. If it came down to him disappearing, the fewer fingers pointing at us the better.

"Did she have anything to do with it? Did she testify against him?"

"No, nothing like that. He thinks his choosing to steal was her fault since he had to take care of her and their daughter. Listen, my cousin isn't right in the head, Zev. He's an idiot, actually."

"He's your cousin? And now you're her boyfriend. Does he know you two are together?"

"Not unless his parents told him. Why?"

"I just imagine that would rub his ass raw, that's all. Okay, why don't I let you go and I'll check into his parole hearing. I'll let her know if I find out anything about him or if we find a suspect."

"I'd appreciate it if you'd call me. She has enough on her plate as it is."

He agreed and after we exchanged numbers, we bid him goodbye and went into the house. I had to check that my other family was doing okay. I didn't want to be away from them a moment longer.

I found them in the living room. Byron was sitting calmly in his favorite chair. Belle was curled up on the couch with her mom. I could tell she had been crying and so had Raina. When Belle saw me, she shot up off the couch and came running to me. I wrapped her in my arms and gave her a kiss on the top of her head.

"It was so scary, Joker," she sobbed.

"Hey, I know it was, but you and Granddaddy are safe and that's what matters."

"I don't want to stay here. What if they come back and this time they do get in?"

I looked at Raina. This wasn't the way I wanted to get them in my house, but I'd take it. Although, I'd offer them another choice, even if I didn't want them to take it.

"I don't think whoever it was will be dumb enough to come back and try again. They know the house has an alarm and the police are alerted when it goes off. However, if you're that scared, you have a couple of options that we should talk to your mom and granddaddy about. One, I can stay here with you at night. Two, the three of you can move to my house at the compound. Your room is ready and all we'd have to do to get Byron's ready is to move his bedroom furniture in. It would take no time to do that. I'd love for you all three to live with me, but it's up to Mommy and Granddaddy to decide."

"I wanna go to your house!" she immediately said.

Raina gave me a lost look. Byron sat there looking calm. It was him who answered. "I appreciate the offer, I really do. And I want Raina and Belle to be where it's the safest. Why don't you take them to stay at your house and I can stay here?"

"No! Granddaddy, if you stay then I stay. I'm not leaving you here alone with… a possible burglar on the loose who might come back," As she paused before saying burglar, I knew she was thinking what I was, that Parker had somehow gotten parole early and he was the one who tried to break in.

Hating to wake him up this early, especially if it woke up Tarin and Melody, but knowing he might find out sooner than Zev, I stepped away, took out my phone and called Outlaw. He answered on the first ring. Jesus, didn't he ever fucking sleep?

"Hey, I'm already searching and so far, everything I found shows that Parker's parole hearing is still set for the fourth. It couldn't be him, however, just in case their fucking paperwork isn't up to date, I have someone who can check on the inside to make sure he's still in his cell. Give me an hour, maybe two tops and I'll know for sure."

"Thanks, Outlaw. Sorry you got up this early. I guess my club-wide text woke you. Shit, I need to create one to only go out to the single guys, unless it's an all-hands-on-deck situation."

"If you do that, be prepared for Bull to kick your ass into next Sunday and back. We're brothers and we all want to stay in the loop no matter what it is. Besides, it didn't wake me. Melody has been up most of the night teething. Tarin went to bed at two and I took over."

"How's she doing now? I don't hear her."

"She finally conked out. Don't tell Tarin or she'll kill me, but I rubbed a bit of whiskey on her gums and she went out like a light," he whispered like he was afraid Tarin would hear him. I laughed.

"Hey, don't knock it. You wait until you have one and they've been screaming for days. You'll do it too. Besides, my granny used to do that to me when I was little and I turned out just fine," he grumbled.

"That's up for debate," I shot back.

"Fuck you, man. You'll come back begging for my forgiveness one day soon. I know it. Anyway, how's Belle and Byron? Hell, how's Raina? She must be flipping out."

"Raina is still shaken. She thinks it was Parker too and not just some random burglary. Belle is freaked out and doesn't want to stay here. I offered to stay at night or have them come to my house. Belle wants that but Byron says he'll stay here. That's not gonna happen, so we're at a stalemate at the moment. Maybe if I can convince him and Raina it wasn't Parker, they might change their mind."

"Well, you go do that and leave me to this. I'll text once I know something for sure. If you need anything else, let me know."

"I will. Thanks, Outlaw."

"Not a problem. Bye."

Hanging up, I went back to the three of them. They were arguing. Belle for them to all move, Raina for them to calm down and Byron was insisting he had to stay here. Whistling to get their attention, I issued orders.

"Let's all calm down. According to my source, it was just someone random. Those kinds of guys don't come back once they know the house has an alarm. Raina, babe, why don't you take Belle to her room and get her to lie down? It's still the middle of the night and she has to be tired. I'll come get you in a bit."

I was hoping she wouldn't argue and take my hint it wasn't Parker and that I needed to talk to Byron alone. Thankfully, she did. Belle tried to say she wasn't tired, but she yawned in the middle of saying it. It took a couple of tries before she went with her mom, but only after I promised not to leave, as if I would do that. As soon as they were out of sight, I turned to Byron. He was sitting in his chair like he didn't have a worry in the world. He had a blanket over his legs. He gave me an innocent look.

"You can cut the crap, Byron. I want to know why you're insisting on staying here if the girls aren't. Don't tell me it's because it's your home. You would do anything for them, even move I think, so spill it."

"I don't know what you mean?" He said with an air of innocence I wasn't buying. Reaching out, I yanked the blanket off his legs. Just as I thought. He had a handgun underneath it. All the times I'd come over here, I never saw him with anything over his legs. I pointed to it.

"And that's what, to kill flies with?"

"Maybe."

"Byron, it wasn't Parker. Outlaw checked and his parole hearing hasn't been moved up. He's double checking to be positive. It was just bad luck."

"Even if it wasn't him, he'll be coming and when he does, he'll come here to find her. He wants revenge for what in his mind is her betrayal. I don't have much life left, Joker. I'm dying, even if Raina doesn't want to admit that. The doctors gave me six months, maybe a year. My lungs are shot. All those years working at the mill and not wearing masks did them in. No one knew then it could be dangerous to inhale the dust and there are fungi that grow in those trees. It causes COPD, asthma, and lung cancer. I've learned a lot over the last few years about it. There's no getting new lungs."

"You've been sick longer than she thinks, haven't you?"

He sighed then nodded. "I got it bad about five years ago. I was able to hide it whenever we went to see them in Albany, but a year ago, right after Mabel died, it got significantly worse. The doctors say it was the trauma of her death or some shit. If I hadn't fucked up and let it slip I was on oxygen, she would've never come home."

"Well, if you hadn't, I wouldn't have met her again and gotten the chance to have the woman I love, so I thank you from the bottom of my heart for fucking up. And if you're thinking that if she wasn't here, he wouldn't go after her, you're wrong. Don't forget, he has been sending letters to her address in Albany for years. He knew where to find her. It would be worse if she wasn't here. She'd be there alone without protection. Now, are you gonna come to the compound and stay or do I need to go home and get a bag and move my ass over here? Those are your options."

I gave him credit. The old man made me wait for an answer. It was a good ten minutes of us staring at each other and arguing before he gave me the answer I wanted.

"Alright, stop looking at me like that. You're making my trigger finger itch. I'll do whatever the girls want to do. So, let's see if we can get Raina back out here and find out. Hopefully, she got Belle to go back to sleep. God, she was shaking so hard right after it happened, I thought her teeth would rattle out of her head. That alarm is loud as hell. Scared the shit out of me when it went off. I don't know how it didn't wake up the whole neighborhood. Does it have to be that loud?"

"You need it to be loud to make sure you wake up and to scare people away. It did its job, along with alerting the cops."

"Speaking of alerting the cops, I know that having it monitored means a monthly fee. Who's doing that and when will the bill be coming? I want to set it up to auto pay," he stated.

"There isn't a bill."

"Which means you're covering it. I let you do the install without fighting you, but you're not paying for the monitoring too."

"Byron, we have a part of Salvation that does monitoring. It's not as big as well-known companies, but we have it. For our businesses and homes, there are no bills. Since my woman lives here, this is a family home and it won't either. You can fight it if you want, but no one will agree with you or send you a damn bill."

He huffed and would've argued more, but we were interrupted by the guys coming into the house.

"Everything is handled outside. The last of the officers came back and there have been no sightings of anyone suspicious. Zev said to tell you he'll be in touch. He seems like a decent guy. How's Raina and Belle? How're you holding up, Byron?" Player asked, as he came to stand by me.

When he saw the gun on Byron's lap, he smiled. "I knew it. You owe me ten bucks," he said to Stalker, who rolled his eyes and got out his wallet. The others laughed.

"So you were betting on him having a gun?"

"I was. Stalker said he wouldn't have one visible or even in the house around Belle. I told him like hell he wouldn't. If it wasn't visible, we'd easily find it."

"Stalker, not only would he have one in the house, so does Raina. You should know better." I chastised him.

"I know, I know. Any woman willing to put up with our asses has to be a pistol packin' momma and that includes her extended family. God, what if one of us falls for a woman who's afraid of guns?" he asked in sudden horror.

"Then she's a no go and can't be an old lady," Slash told him instantly.

"What?! That's not fair. You can't control who you fall for," Stalker protested.

"Yes, you can. First, any woman you think might have potential, you give her the questionnaire and see how she answers it. Some of the questions are asterisked and if they answer them wrong, they're automatically disqualified and you can't pursue that one," Player told him with a straight face.

"That's bullshit. And what questionnaire? I didn't know there was one."

"You didn't? Man, where the hell were you when we had that orientation talk with Predator about the rules now that you're members?" Slash asked him while frowning at him.

"What orientation? No one told me to be

anywhere for anything like that! Predator, did you really go to one?"

Predator nodded his head. Stalker looked as if he was getting upset and worried. I have no idea how long they would've kept the gag going, if it hadn't been for Slash bursting out laughing.

"You guys are a bunch of fuckers! You had me going. Honest to God, I can't trust you guys. From now on, I'm going to have to double check everything you tell me with Bull or Tank," Stalker snapped.

"Hell, they'd have been going along with it if they were here. You're too much fun to get going, Stalker," Slash told him.

"Well, maybe you should remember that I got the name Stalker for a reason. I can get into any of your places and be on top of you before you even know I'm there. Remember that, assholes," he said menacingly. This did give us all pause. He was one sneaky bastard that was true. He smiled when he saw our faces.

"Are you guys done torturing poor Stalker or do I need to put you all in time out until you can learn to play nice?" Raina asked from behind them. As they parted, she came through them to me. I hugged her to my side.

"It depends, will you be wearing a sexy school teacher outfit and have a ruler in your hand when you put us there? Because if you do, then I'm not done," Slash said to her as he wiggled his eyebrows.

"It won't matter, because you'll be dead before

you can enjoy it," I growled.

"Aww, come on. You know you all have a sexy teacher fantasy. Why can't Raina help fulfill mine? It's not like I'm gonna touch her or anything. I have eyes and I can't help it. She's a sexy woman."

"Because if Joker doesn't kill you, I will," Byron piped up to tell him. He patted his gun.

This got the rest of us laughing while Slash made a zipping motion with one hand, pretended to flick the key away then held both of them in the air like he was surrendering.

"Granddaddy, mind telling me why you have a gun on your lap?"

"It's for home protection."

"You have Joker and five other guys here for that, plus several officers outside. Please tell me that thing is registered."

"This one is. And the police are leaving. And as for these six, well I might need it for them. You heard Slash."

This made us all smile, even her.

"Babe, is Belle asleep?"

"She is. It took me reading to her and rubbing her back to get her there. She's really scared, Joker."

"I know. You understood what I said earlier. Outlaw says nothing shows an early parole. I was just talking to Byron about the move before these guys came in. He said he'd do whatever you and Belle want. So, do I need to go get clothes or do we need to pack your things and get some guys over here to move his bedroom set?"

"Wait. I don't want you to move my bedroom then just have to move it back in a few weeks," Byron protested.

"If you move in, it's to stay. You need to stay close, so you can have as much time with your girls as you can. They came here for you. No use in them running back and forth between here and there. Will you be able to leave this house?"

He got my meaning about spending time with his girls. If he was dying like he said, then his time was short. And he would be getting worse, not better. He'd need help, and I thought he'd rather it be from his family than strangers coming in. Although, if he ended up needing medical help, we'd bring them in too.

"I've lived in this house for a million years. It was the first place me and Mabel could afford to buy rather than rent. It has a lot of memories, but since she died, those memories hurt too. If you're absolutely sure you want an old crotchety man in your house and Raina is good with it too, then I say let's move. Even if this wasn't Parker, I'd feel better having them behind those walls."

Both of us nodded. So that was what got a truck to his house a couple of hours later and packing boxes brought. We'd work on what to do with the rest of his stuff later. Right now, we just needed his personal items, bedroom set and the personal belongings of Belle and Raina boxed and loaded then taken over to my house.

For such a sucky beginning, the day was turning out to be a good one after all. No more nights running between our houses and only having a few hours with her in my arms.

Belle when she woke up later and found out what we were planning to do was excited. She helped to pack up her room in a flurry of clothes and toys. As we worked, I got word from Outlaw that it was confirmed. Parker was still sitting in his cell at the State Penitentiary in West Tennessee. For some unknown reason, he wasn't sent to the big one in Nashville. I liked there were more miles between us and him even if he was inside.

It was late morning by the time we were loaded and headed to the compound. We sure got a lot of looks from the neighbors as we loaded their stuff then left. They didn't know what to think of all those bikers coming in and spiriting Byron away. I could only imagine what the grapevine would be saying. Probably that he'd been kidnapped by a gang of bikers. If only they knew.

Raina: Chapter 16

I was still amazed that we were able to get Granddaddy to agree to move to Joker's house so easily. I thought it would take a miracle to convince him to leave. I asked Joker what he said to him to get him to say yes, and he said he just stated the facts and Granddaddy saw the truth of them. I wasn't sure if that was all he said, but I'd accept it for now.

Once we got our stuff to the compound, it was unloaded and set up in no time. There were more hands willing to help than we'd ever need. It warmed my heart to see everyone not only welcoming me and Belle but Granddaddy too. They were all so welcoming to him that he had a smile on his face the whole time.

After we were settled, we ended up spending the rest of the day and evening together, just the four of us. That first night it had been incredible to know my whole family was under one roof. Joker made sure to show how happy he was by making love to me and making me beg for more when we went to bed. He was beyond thrilled to have us there.

On Sunday, it was a slow, lazy day which we spent part of hanging at the clubhouse with whoever was there. Granddaddy got to see all the kids and what the club was like even more as a family. He told me he'd never imagined it to be that close-knit. In the evening, the whole club ordered pizza and we ate together.

I was sad to see today come and have to go into work. However, we both had to work today. I only hoped it would go by fast. Joker told me not to take any shit off Tessa or Leif. I'd finally told him about my run-in with her and how Zev interceded. He wasn't happy that I waited to tell him, but with everything else going on, it didn't seem important. A jealous woman was the least of my worries.

I was growing increasingly nervous. Parker's hearing was in three days. If he got parole and even Outlaw had told Joker all things pointed to it happening, then I wondered how long we'd have to wait for him to come looking for us for his revenge. His prison was only four hours away. I wondered if he'd come to Hunters Creek and live with his parents. Knowing them, they were gonna go back to babying him as soon as he got out.

I'd had a lot of time to think about him and how he ended up being in the situation he was. And my short time with him and being around his parents had told me a lot. Parker was a classic case of an only child whose parents spoiled him rotten and thought he could do no wrong. In their minds, anything he did that wasn't right, was to be blamed on other people or circumstances. Any time he got in trouble when he was younger, they found ways to get him out of it. Too bad for them, they couldn't do that when he savagely beat that man at the gas station on his last robbery. There was no way out of it.

I loved Belle, but if she did wrong, she'd have to suffer the consequences. I wasn't proving my love for her by looking the other way, making lame excuses or by getting her out of it. I wanted her to grow up to be decent and a contributing to her community kind of person, not worthless space like her dad.

There was one thing I was totally looking forward to doing today. After I was off work, she and I were going school shopping. It started in a couple of weeks and she needed her supplies and new clothes. She'd grown over the summer. At first, Joker wanted us to wait until he could go with us, but I explained we had a ritual we liked to do and it would also give us "girl time" together. Something we hadn't had recently. Once he knew that, he was fine with us going alone. We wanted to do it now so we could go without anyone. After Parker got out, we'd have to go with guards, which wouldn't be as much fun. Since Joker had to work, Gavin was going to drop her off at my work at three o'clock so we could go from there. I couldn't wait.

I settled at my monitors and right out of the gate, I had a call. From there, it was a steady day of calls. Most were stupid ones that made me want to yell into the phone at the callers. I was an emergency dispatcher. We had a non-emergency line that people could call for those kinds of things. It never ceased to amaze me what people thought was an emergency.

I was tempted so many times to have them fined for calling in non-emergency things on the emergency line. We had the right to do it, but I didn't want to tie up our precious officers any more by having them have to go do that. The worst part was, despite how stupid it might be, we usually had to dispatch an officer to respond to the complaint.

Today, I had three of them in a row, a new personal record. The first one was a woman calling to report that her neighbor had been leaving their porch light on day and night for three days. She wanted the police to go over and tell them to turn it off. And if they didn't, to arrest them for disturbing the peace. How exactly was it disturbing the peace? I asked. She said it shined in her living room window and bugged her if she didn't close her blinds at night. And she didn't like to close her blinds, because then she couldn't see out to see what was going on in her neighborhood. That was code for I'm a nibshit and spy on my neighbors.

Call two was a man reporting a cat was up in the tree across the street and it was meowing. He couldn't get it down and wanted us to have a policeman or the fire department come out to get it out of the tree. Has anyone ever heard of calling animal control? I was less upset at him because he was trying to be a good person.

The third one was a doozy and when I was done with that call, I had to say a prayer to keep myself from going to the woman's house and choking her. She was what we called a frequent flier. She called in all the time with the same complaint and when we wouldn't do anything about it, she threatened our jobs and to call the mayor or some other authority figure to have us fired.

Her issue was she had an ongoing dispute with her one neighbor. There was a row of trees planted between them. They were thick and blocked her view from her house. More like it blocked her view from spying on them. She wanted them cut down and didn't understand why we couldn't make her neighbor do it. All of us had explained that they were on his property and he was allowed to plant whatever he wanted on his property. She'd tried to have the homeowner's association make him do it initially, but they told her no, so she thought the police would and should do it. We got a call once a week sometimes more from her insisting we come out and take care of this.

"Mrs. Blake, as we've told you before, we can't make your neighbor cut down his trees just because you feel they block your view. An officer isn't going to be dispatched to talk to them. The fire department can't come out and chop down the trees either. Even if we could do something about it, this is an emergency line. Those trees aren't an emergency." I explained, for the tenth time since I'd started here.

"What's your name?" she asked angrily. I knew what was coming, but I gave it to her. Sometimes I wished all our calls weren't monitored so I could tell her what I really wanted to say.

"It's Raina."

"Raina what?"

"Raina will do. I'm the only Raina who works here."

"Well, Raina, I'm calling the chief of police and the mayor. You'll be looking for a new job by the end of the day, if you don't do as I say," she said acidly. She was lucky I couldn't reach her through the phone. If I could, I'd have punched her in the face for the tone she had taken. Bitch.

"Ma'am, I don't work for the chief of police or the mayor. And even if I did, they wouldn't fire me for doing my job. Please, stop calling and tying up our lines for non-emergency issues and your personal quarrel. People who really need us can't get through when you're doing that." It was as nasty as I'd gotten with her.

"How dare you talk to me that way?! I should come down there and teach you manners."

"If you come down here, you'll be the one to learn manners. Good day ma'am." I hung up on her. If I got in trouble for saying what I said, oh well.

"So Mrs. Blake strikes again. I thought you handled her well. The times I've wanted to call her an old biddy bitch are in the dozens. Maybe she'll have a heart attack because you talked back and die. Wouldn't that be a relief?" Connie asked from behind me.

I turned around and laughed. "Don't make me wish for it. You're so bad. How's your day been so far?"

"The usual Monday stuff. People who don't know what an emergency line is for, although they are nothing like Mrs. Blake. How about you? Ready for a break?"

"God yes, let's go."

All of us took turns taking a break. We tried to stick to some sort of schedule, but it wasn't always possible. By the looks of it, everyone else was in their seats and the phones weren't ringing off the hook, so we'd better run for it. As we hurried out to go to the breakroom, we passed Tessa's desk. She sneered at me. I ignored her ass.

When we got into the breakroom, Connie pounced. "What the hell is up with Tessa? She's been a bitch for weeks, but that look she just gave you could almost kill."

As we got a soda out of the vending machine, I told her about the confrontation we had in the parking lot last week. She was aghast.

"I can't believe her. I mean, I kinda thought she liked Leif before you came. She's been through almost everyone else who's single and some who aren't. He was bound to get in her sights sometime, but for her to be so jealous of you is nuts. You have Joker. Why would you give Leif the time of day? And even if you did, it's not your fault he likes you and not her."

"I don't understand it either. I'm upset that I thought I was making another friend here, and she turned out to be this way."

"I'm sorry. And if you were to split with Joker, then Zev is much more your type anyway. Too bad he didn't see you first," she sighed.

"Connie, don't even think that! Zev is great, but Joker is the man for me. And we're not going to split up. I just moved into his house with my family over the weekend."

She squealed when I said that. The rest of our

break was spent with her grilling me about his house and what it was like to live with the Warriors. It was kind of nice to get back to work when it was time. I loved her but she did ask a lot of questions. An hour later I wished I was back in the break room talking to her. I wanted to be anywhere but there.

Sometimes as a dispatcher you get calls that are life and death. You're trained to handle them, but they still hit you hard. The worst was when it involved a child. As I answered the call, I soon found out it was one of those.

"Nine-one-one, Raina speaking. What's your emergency?"

"Help! Please help. Oh my God, my baby isn't breathing. Help," a sobbing woman screamed into the phone.

She was crying so hard it was hard to understand her. As soon as I figured out what the call was about, I started typing in the message on our system, so an officer would dispatch, along with the paramedics at the fire station. My heartbeat sped up, and I switched into serious dispatcher mode.

"Ma'am, try to calm down. I'm sending help. Tell me where the baby is right now. How old is he?"

"He's in his crib. He's six months old. Hurry!"

"I have police and an ambulance on the way. Stay on the phone with me. We're gonna do everything we can to help your baby. I need you to take him out of the crib and lie him on the floor or somewhere hard."

"But…"

"Do it. Tell me when you have him there." I ordered her, knowing she'd respond better to a calm voice telling her what to do.

There were rustling sounds. I prayed she'd hurry. As I waited, I read the notes coming in and kept up a soothing chatter with her. A squad car had responded and was on its way, ETA, five minutes. The fire department was dispatched as well.

"He's on the counter," came her sobbing reply.

"Good. I need you to check if he's breathing. Put your face down next to his nose and mouth then listen and feel for air movement. Do that and tell me what you find."

The next several minutes lasted forever for me and tore out my heart. The baby wasn't breathing and was blue. I walked her through performing CPR, but she couldn't get him to breathe. I kept her breathing for him. Luckily, the officer arrived and right behind him, the paramedics on the fire engine. I had to hang up once they got there, although I didn't want to. I waited on the edge of my seat to find out the outcome. It was Zev who reported it an hour later. He called me directly.

"Hi Zev, what can I do for you?" I asked, recognizing his number.

"I thought you might want to know what happened with the baby who wasn't breathing," came his soft response. He'd been the officer dispatched.

"Thank you, I have been wondering. Please tell me you got him breathing, and he's alright."

"Fuck, I'm sorry, Raina, but he didn't make it. It looks like he was dead for a while, likely SIDS. Maybe I shouldn't have told you, but I figured you'd be worrying about it." I could hear the remorse in his voice.

I sniffed to hold back the tears. "That's not your fault. You're right, I was worrying. Thank you, Zev. Are you alright?"

"I hate fucking calls like this. They make me think of my son. I'm gonna need a drink after work today," was his gruff reply.

"I hear you, me too. They're the worst and I always think of Belle too." I told him. He was about to say more when the lines lit up with calls. "Damn, I hate to go, but we have several calls lighting up the lines, Zev. I have to answer one. I hope you have a peaceful remainder of the day. Stay safe."

"And I hope you and I have no more calls like that. Later, Raina."

As soon as he hung up, I answered the next call. It was one after the other after that. It was over an hour later before I could get away to take a break. Instead of going to the breakroom, I went outside. Once I was clear of the windows, I sat down on the ground and started to cry.

I was so lost in my misery, and the thoughts of what it would do to me if that was Belle, that I didn't notice anyone had walked up, until I felt a hand on my shoulder. Looking up, I was surprised to see Zev standing there. He sat down beside me and put an arm around my shoulders.

"Hey, enough of that. No more tears. I know it sucks, but you're gonna make yourself sick and me cry."

"Zev, what're you doing here?"

"I knew you would be cycling about this, so I stopped to check on you. I saw you sitting here. Here, wipe your eyes," he handed me a hankie from his pocket. I took it and wiped as I apologized.

"Thank you. Sorry you had to see me like this. I must look like a raccoon. I'll have to go clean up before I go back to the office and scare people. How're you doing? It had to hit you just as hard. You'd think after all these years doing this, I'd be used to calls like that one."

"If you get used to those kinds of calls, then it's time to quit. We're human and we have to be able to vent sometimes. It did hit hard. I can remember my son at that age. It never gets better even at his age. We just have additional worries to add to the list. I live in dread of him starting to drive in a few years," he shuddered and looked slightly ill.

"God, don't remind me! Belle is only a year behind him. Knowing her, she'll come home and want to get a bike like Joker has."

"Jesus, I hadn't thought of that. I ride and Junior loves to ride with me. Shit." He looked horrified at the thought.

"Junior, so he's a Zev too?"

"He is. His mother insisted. I tried to tell her no, but she got her hands on the paperwork for the birth certificate first. Lucky for me, he doesn't seem to hate it, so I might not be killed in my sleep," he joked.

I was laughing at his remark and the look on his face when I heard the roar of a bike. Looking up to see which officer was a rider, I was caught off guard to see Joker pulling into the parking lot. I went to stand up and Zev took my hand to help me. The look on Joker's face as he parked and stalked toward us wasn't good. He looked upset. Surely, he didn't think there was something between me and Zev? I hurried toward him to try and prevent a fight.

"Joker, it's not what you think. What're you doing here in the middle of the day?"

He enveloped me in his arms and held me close. I was tense, waiting for him to start in on Zev. Instead, he shocked me.

"Hey, thanks man, for the call. I appreciate it. That had to be rough. I've got her now. You doing okay?" he asked Zev calmly.

"No problem. I figured she wouldn't call you. I'm getting there. It was a tough one. Hey, I gotta run, but take care of her. Raina, I'll see you later."

"Bye, stay safe," I called out to him as he walked off to get in his squad car. When he was in it, I glanced up at Joker. He was staring down at me with a stern look on his face.

"Why're you looking at me like that?"

"Because I had to get a call from Zev, to tell me my woman was upset and needed me. You should've called me, Raina."

"I didn't think of it. Aaron, I'm not used to having someone to lean on. When this shit happens, I've always had to deal on my own. I didn't call Zev either. He found me sitting here."

"I get that, but you need to start remembering you're not on your own with Belle anymore. You have me, Byron, and the whole Warrior family plus my parents to help. I want you to promise, if something like this happens again, you'll call me. I don't want you crying alone."

"I promise, but I hate to disturb you and take you away from work to come baby me."

"It's not babying you. It's comforting. And there's nothing at the spa that's more important than you." As he finished telling me that, he gave me a kiss. It was like a shot of sunshine and instantly I felt better. I don't know how long we would've kissed if we hadn't been interrupted. When we were, it was by the last person I wanted to see or speak to.

"Jesus, can't you go eight hours without sucking his face off and throwing yourself at him?"

I glanced around to find Tessa standing close by, with a cigarette in her hand scowling at us. She was obviously on her dozenth smoke break.

"Can't you go an hour without being a jealous bitch?" I said back without thinking.

She gasped. "Look who is calling someone a bitch. Do you know that when you're not around she's flirting with Leif and Zev, one of the officers? She's cheating on you and I've seen her flirt with others too," she told Joker with a smirk.

"She's not flirting with anyone, let alone cheating on me. I know Zev, and he's a friend. As for Leif, it's in his wet dreams that she flirts with him. What's the matter, Tessa? Ran through all the available men here at the police station and the fire department? Or is it they finally realized you're a slut and not to give you the time of day? I've heard all about how you go through them like water and play them against each other," he told her with a smile.

Her shocked expression and gasp were priceless. I didn't feel a bit of remorse for what he or I said as she stomped off. I even giggled. I know, I'm terrible. He chuckled too.

"I think my job here is done. If I don't go now, I'll be dragging you home and I don't think your boss will like that. What time do you think you and Belle will be home from your shopping spree?"

"Assuming I get out of here on time, I say we should be home by eight at the latest. I planned to take her out to dinner, if that's okay? Will you and Granddaddy be able to fend for yourselves?"

"Don't worry about us. I can fix us something. Call when you're on your way. If it's gonna be later than eight, let me know, so I don't worry."

"It won't be. If we need longer, we'll go another day. Alright, I have to get back to work. Thank you for coming over here. I do feel better. Love you."

"Love you too," he said.

He gave me one more kiss, although this one was short, then he walked me to the office door before he headed to his bike. I entered feeling a thousand times better. It was wonderful to have people to rely on. I forgot what that felt like over the years.

Lucky for me, the rest of the day didn't have any more terrible calls like the baby. However, I did have another one that wasn't an emergency and made me laugh hysterically when I got off the phone and told the rest of the dispatchers about it. Honestly, I couldn't make this shit up.

A call came through from a man. He apparently took a woman from the bar with him to a hotel. At first, I wanted to ask him how they could be drunk at one o'clock in the afternoon, but I decided not to ask. I wish I had because it would've saved me longer from the reason for his call.

He informed me that when he got her to the hotel, he took Viagra. After it went into effect, he was ready to go, but the woman in question decided she wasn't interested in having sex after all and refused to do it, not even a blow job he explained in disgust. I wanted to hang up, but I didn't. He informed me the reason he was calling nine-one-one was to ask for a police officer to come to the hotel and bring him some dirty magazines or whatever they carried in their cars for that to help him get rid of his problem.

"Sir, the officers do not carry dirty magazines in their cars. It's not part of their job to provide those to people. If you have an erection that won't go away and it's been more than four hours, then you need to seek medical attention. I can send an ambulance to take you to the emergency room," I told him while I wanted to tell him to hang the hell up.

"I don't want to go to the hospital. Are you sure none of them carry those with them?"

"Sir, I'm positive they don't." As we were talking, I had to input in the system everything he was saying to me. God, I couldn't wait for the officers and other dispatchers to read it. I'd have a ton of calls about it. They'd tease me to death for being the lucky one to get it.

"Well, they should."

"Well, they don't. Can I send an ambulance or not? I don't know what else I can do to help you."

"I do. Why don't you stay on the line? Um, yeah, your voice seems to be helping." As he said that, I heard what could only be sounds of him jacking off and him panting.

"That's not in my job description. I hope everything turns out okay, Goodbye," I said hastily.

"Wait, just a couple more minutes, I'm close. Fuck! your voice is sexy," he cried, as I disconnected the call.

That was the talk of the center for the rest of the day. I was relieved when Gavin dropped Belle off at the office so they had to stop. I felt like I needed a shower. Thank God, I was able to leave on time. Well, I did as soon as I introduced her to my coworkers. I saw some of them checking Gavin out when he came in with her. He didn't just drop her off at the door. No, he made sure she was escorted to me. He waved off my thanks and said he was only doing his job.

Outside, we got in my car. She was excited since she loved to shop. "Where to first?" she asked.

"I thought we'd head to the big store here in town. If we need more options, we'll have to go another day either to Cookeville or even Nashville. Maybe we can go this weekend. Right now, let's see what we can get here in town."

With that as our first destination, I headed out. The hours flew by as we shopped and chatted. She was so happy we'd moved here and that we were living with Joker. She really seemed to like him. After we shopped for hours, we took time to relax and grab dinner. I laughed the whole time as we ate and caught up. I hoped we'd always be able to have fun like this. I'd heard the teen years were hell, especially when you had a daughter. I hoped that wasn't going to be the case with her. Being a single mom had made us very close, and I needed that.

I texted Joker while we were at dinner, to let him know we would be home on time. At seven o'clock, we left Cookeville to head home. Wow, I was already thinking of the compound as home. It wasn't a long drive, so we'd be there well before eight. We were driving down the 111 toward home. It wasn't completely dark yet, but there didn't seem to be many people on the road. We were coming up on a short string of buildings. There was a warehouse-looking place, a small strip mall building, another warehouse-type place then a gas station on the left. I'd passed them many times over the years when I lived here before and we had been to Cookeville.

Right as we were passing the first warehouse, bright lights flicked on. It was a car that was sitting in the deserted parking lot. Someone was working late, was my thought, however, I was wrong. Suddenly, the vehicle came screaming out of the parking lot onto the main road. I slowed down to let them pass, since they seemed to be in such a hurry. That was my fatal mistake. Instead of passing us, they swerved and rammed into my side of the car. I heard Belle scream as I did. My head hit the side window making a loud thunk noise. Things started to go hazy right after it did. I struggled to stay awake and to check on Belle. I reached toward her and then that was it, utter darkness.

Joker: Chapter 17

Byron and I spent a very enjoyable evening together after I got home from the spa. I fixed us steaks on the grill and baked potatoes. What man didn't love those? Along with them, just to make sure it would meet the dietary requirements of Raina, if she asked, and I knew she would, we had steamed asparagus. We thoroughly enjoyed every bite. For dessert we had a slice of chocolate pie Raina and Belle made the night before.

With our dessert, I had a glass of brandy with him. I hadn't had one of those in a long time. He told me about his life and how he met his wife. I told him how I felt the first time I met Raina all those years ago and how it had killed me knowing she was Parker's wife and I had no chance with her. On top of those kinds of conversations, we bitched about his son and talked about what we'd be doing to protect all of us once Parker made parole, if he was dumb enough to come after us.

I was kinds of hoping he'd fuck up and do something terrible and they'd yank his parole hearing, but I didn't think we'd get that lucky. If he had found a way to keep his nose clean for ten years, he wouldn't be dumb enough to mess it up now, although how he'd stayed alive for that long I had no idea. Keeping his big mouth shut had never been one of his abilities. I lost count of the number of times he got his ass kicked as a kid and teenager for mouthing off to someone. Byron loved my stories about those times.

Now, we were watching a cowboy movie on the television. It was an old black and white western that we had discovered we both loved. Even if I had seen it a hundred times at least, it never got old. I was so into it, I didn't notice the time until I got up to refill our drinks. That's when I saw it was after eight o'clock.

The last text I had from Raina was when they were sitting down to dinner and she promised they'd be home by no later than eight o'clock. Why the hell weren't they here? Taking out my cell phone, I called her number. It rang and rang before going to voicemail. Maybe it died on her. I looked up Belle's number and called her phone with the same result. An uneasy feeling curled in my stomach. Not wanting to alarm Byron, I took his refill to him then I stepped outside. I called Outlaw.

As usual, he answered right away. "Hello, brother, what's up?"

"I hate to bug you, but I need you to see if you can locate Belle or Raina's phone? They're not answering. It goes to voicemail, and they were due home at eight."

"Sure, give me their numbers and a few minutes to see what I can find. It might not give me more than where their last call came from, but I'll try. Do you wanna get a few guys together and ride out?"

"I might, but first, see what you find. She'd hate it if I rallied the troops only to find out they were late due to dinner going over and their phones dying."

He laughed, "I hear ya. Be back to you as soon as I can. Now, give me those numbers."

I rattled them off before I hung up. I paced the yard waiting for his call back. I didn't want to go inside only to have to leave again. That would raise Byron's suspicions. The sound of the back door shutting behind me had me turning around. He was standing there giving me the look.

"What's going on and don't lie and say nothing. I know that look. And I saw the time. They're late and by the way you're pacing, they didn't answer their phones."

"Byron, you need to stay calm. It might be nothing other than dinner ran over and their phones died."

"Or they could have broken down or worse somewhere. Who did you call?"

"I called Outlaw. He's gonna see where their phones last pinged a cell tower. He'll call back in a few."

He sat down on the porch on a chair. I knew there was no way I'd get him to go back inside until he knew more. Just in case we did need to go search for them, I sent out a heads-up message to the guys telling them what was up. All of them responded within a minute or so, saying they would be ready if I needed them.

It was almost ten minutes by the time Outlaw called me back. I was about to go out of my mind. "What the hell took you so long?" I snapped.

"I called Smoke to see if he could pinpoint their phones better. He couldn't. The last place they were located at was the restaurant in Cookeville. That was two hours ago. We should go looking. I bet they had car trouble. There's a lot of roadway without houses along the 111. Businesses would be closed by now. I'm sure they're fine," he tried to convince us both, I think.

"I hope so. I'm getting the guys rounded up. Please stay here and see if you can find out anything else. Call the hospitals too, will you?"

"I'll make some calls. Just don't borrow trouble, Joker," he cautioned me.

I was on my phone sending a new text as soon as he hung up. After sending it off, I turned to Byron. "I've got to go find them. Stay here in case they come back. Some of the guys will be going with me. If you need anything, call Bull or one of the prospects." I'd made sure the other day that he had everyone's number in case of an emergency.

"I'd like to say take me with you, but I'll only slow you down. Bring them home, son."

"I will."

Not bothering to waste more time, I ran to the garage to get my bike. By the time I got it and was headed toward the gate, several of my brothers were pulling out of their driveways or the clubhouse to meet me. I stopped to give them the plan.

"Thanks guys. They would've taken the 111 home. They were in Cookeville. I don't think we need everyone."

"We'll go and if we find out it was all for nothing, then we'll come back. It's a nice night for a ride," Tank informed me. I hated the fact he was leaving his pregnant wife and son at home, but I knew since Bull wasn't going, he would.

"Thanks, it means a lot," I told them. They all nodded and gestured for me to go ahead. I took the lead and the others fell in behind me.

It didn't take us long to find her car. It was along the road with the driver's side smashed in. I almost forgot to shut off my bike when I came to a stop behind it. Running toward the car, I couldn't tell if they were inside or not. I screamed their names, but no one answered. I tried to open the driver's door, but it was jammed shut from being smashed. Peering inside with a flashlight, I saw the car was empty. The front passenger door was hanging open. Tank was on that side of the car.

Looking around into the dark and the trees not far from the road, I shouted, "Where the fuck are they?"

"We'll start looking. Maybe they walked to find help or they're resting at one of these buildings. You stay here and call the cops. We'll start searching," Tank ordered me.

As he rode off with some of the guys, a few started searching the trees near me. I called the law, but not the main line. I called Zev. I prayed he'd be home and could come. If not, then I'd call the others. I trusted him. I was so relieved when he answered. I told him it was me.

"Hey, Joker, to what do I owe the pleasure of your call?" he asked nicely after he knew who was calling him.

"I need your help. Zev."

"Sure, what is it?"

"Raina and Belle didn't make it home tonight. They were shopping in Cookeville. We just found her car along the 111, about halfway between there and Hunters Creek. It's down from that gas station. The whole side is smashed in. We're looking for them, but I think we might need the law. I thought of you first. I don't know the others well at the station other than Chief Scarelli and I know Bull will likely call him. Would you be available to help us look? Or do you have your boy with you?" I knew about his son from Raina. I had no idea if this was his day or week to have him.

"No, Junior is with his mom. Sure, I can help. I know where you're at. I should be there in about fifteen minutes."

"Thanks. Man. I appreciate it. I know you're off duty."

"Not a problem."

With that out of the way, I called Bull even though it was likely Tank might have already alerted him. I gave him a quick rundown and then joined the others searching. As each guy came back saying he didn't find them, my stomach knotted more and more. I was about to go to the gas station and the small store up the road again, when a bike pulled up. It was Zev. He got off and came over to me.

"Tell me where you've looked," he got right to the point, which I liked. I quickly told him. When I was done, he went to look at the car. He was running his flashlight all over it. He called me over.

"See that mark there," he said, pointing to a dark scraped spot along the seam on the driver's door.

"Yeah, what about it?"

"Come look at this one," he rounded the car and showed me an almost identical one on Belle's door. "Someone tried to pry the door open on Raina's side and they couldn't, so they did it on this one. See the skid marks on the passenger side panels and doors. It hit that tree back there and then slid past it, which crushed her door, just not as badly as Raina's. Someone got them out of the car."

"I have Outlaw calling the hospitals. Let me check with him. Maybe someone took them to get checked."

My hands shook as I called Outlaw, only to be disappointed when he told me no one matching their descriptions had been brought to the ER at any hospital within fifty miles of us. I got off the phone and told Zev.

He swore. "Fuck, okay, then we have to assume since they haven't arrived at your clubhouse, that they've been taken elsewhere. There's no reason I can think of for someone to do that and not let them call you. I hate to say it, but could this be related to Parker? I know his hearing isn't for a few more days, but could he have friends? Anyone willing to help him get his hands on her before he gets out?"

Swearing, I called Outlaw back. I didn't bother with niceties. "I need you to get in contact with whoever verified Parker was still in prison. I need to know who he's been hanging out with or befriending while he's been inside who would be willing to help him on the outside. Did a cellmate or buddy recently get out? That kind of stuff. It looks like they were taken, Outlaw. There's no reason why they haven't called unless they're not allowed to call."

"Motherfucker, okay, let me find out. Hang in there. You know we'll find them."

"I hope so."

An hour later and we'd exhausted the area. No one found them nor had anyone at the gas station remembered seeing them, even after being shown a picture and Zev had flashed his badge at them. Knowing we weren't going to accomplish anything else here, we headed back to the compound. Zev followed us. We called for one of the tow trucks to come pick up her car. Initially, Zev wanted to call it in, but we convinced him the cops couldn't do anything more than he was. He reluctantly didn't push it.

We went straight to the clubhouse when we got there. I'd have one of the prospects go get Byron at the house. We needed to be where we could coordinate and meet. Before that happened though, I needed to introduce Zev to the rest of the guys and Bull. After I did that, I'd find out if Outlaw had any success, although if he had, I knew he would've called me already. Bull was waiting in the common room when we came walking in. He came straight to me and gave me a man hug.

"We've got everyone on alert. Smoke and Everly are working with Outlaw to see if they can find anything that'll help. He's still working to get information out of the prison. I just talked to him. He's in his office here. Terror has his guys on standby if we need them. I had Walker bring Byron here. He's in the kitchen with Jocelyn right now."

"Thank you, Pres. You don't know how much this helps and means."

"Yes, I do. If you recall, I've been in your shoes."

He was right. He did know. When Jocelyn had been attacked in her home and called him in fear, it had killed him not knowing what he'd find when we arrived at her house. Her issue had been taken care of in a permanent way once we found out who it was.

"Yeah, you were. Hey, I want to introduce all of you to someone." I gestured to Zev to come over. He was standing talking to Tank and the ones who went with me. As he approached, the others came to gather around us. He didn't act afraid, but he was alert. I gave him credit. I didn't know a lot of cops who'd walk into a room full of bikers alone and not worry.

"Bull, guys this is Zev Oberlin. He's an officer with Hunters Creek PD. He's a friend of Raina's. Zev, this is Bull, he's our club president."

"Hello, it's nice to meet you. I've seen you with Chief Scarelli before." He shook Bull's hand.

"I've seen you too. Thanks for helping out. Joe is on his way."

From there I introduced my other brothers, and they all shook his hand. Afterward, they sat down to wait. Bull didn't want to plan more before Scarelli got here. I went to check on Byron. When I entered the kitchen, he was sitting at the counter watching Jocelyn working on something. He came to his feet when he saw me. I saw the hope on his face.

"I'm sorry, we haven't found them yet. How're you doing?"

"Don't worry about me. You just worry about finding our girls. Jocelyn is keeping an eye on me and doing a great job of pretending she wasn't told to babysit me," he said, as he puffed out a breath. Even not exerting himself, he was short of breath. It worried me. I noticed it a few times since he moved in.

"I wasn't told to babysit you. I was told to keep you out of trouble and if you tried to run off on your own, to tackle you," she said with a smile. This got a chuckle out of him.

"Well, I wouldn't complain if a beautiful young thing like you tackled me. Maybe I'll go for it just to get that," he teased her back. She winked at him as she laughed.

"Hey, there better be less flirting in here," came the growl from the doorway. It was Bull and he was grinning.

They bantered back and forth for a couple of

minutes as I filled Byron in on what was happening and that we'd be going into church soon. He promised he'd stick with Jocelyn. I left them to rejoin the others. Bull joined us a minute later, which was only seconds before Gavin came through the front door with Scarelli. He eyed Zev as he came up to us.

"I didn't know you'd be here, Oberlin. What brings you here? And how do you know the Warriors?"

"Relax Joe, he's here to help. He's friends with Raina and he was helping Joker and a few of the guys look for her and Belle. I told you they found her car. There's no sign of them anywhere near there or at any of the hospitals. We had the car towed to the garage. I don't want to bring anyone else official into this unless it becomes absolutely necessary. That means I need you both to swear you'll keep this between us."

"I don't understand. Wouldn't it be better to have everyone possible out looking for them? We could issue a BOLO and even get other officers in the towns around here watching for them?" Zev said, looking confused.

"Zev, if you're gonna be friends with the club, you'll need to learn fast that there are things which fall under club business and it's not always best to put everything down in an official way. That way, if decisions have to be made later, there's no fallout," Scarelli told him.

"You mean if they kill someone and don't want to go to prison?"

"There's a lot of gray in this world. As much as I'd like to say we can always catch the bad guys and make them pay for their crimes, we can't. Even when we do catch them, we can't always put them behind bars, since they can get off due to technicalities and shit."

"And you're alright with that happening?" Zev shot back.

"I don't agree with the world not allowing us to do our jobs. What I can live with is the fact that I know that if Bull and his guys have to do something technically illegal, it'll never involve hurting innocents and it's always going to be in them to protect this town and the people in it. You have no idea the things they keep out of Hunters Creek. So yeah, I can sleep at night just fine," Scarelli shot back at him. We all stood there silently, waiting to see if this was where Zev would leave or not.

After what felt like forever, Zev nodded. "I can live with that. Tell me what you want me to do."

"Just to be clear, if you go behind our backs and try to have us arrested, or some other shit later, you won't get a second chance to do it. Don't make yourself an enemy. You'll be treated just like those who hurt our loved ones," I warned him. I wanted him to know we would kill him without coming out and saying it. He was still an unknown entity.

"I'm not stupid. I understand."

"Good. So, how about we get this show on the road? Everyone, head to church. I'm gonna get Outlaw," Bull ordered.

Down the hall we went, then we filed into church,

taking our regular seats. I pointed to a couple of chairs against the wall. Scarelli and Zev took those. It was only a minute or so later before Outlaw and Bull joined us. Bull slammed his gavel on the table and the meeting started. I gave Outlaw a hopeful look.

He met my intense look and nodded. Good. He had something. I'd take anything at the moment.

"I was finally able to get to my contact at the prison in Henning. He said he has guys on the inside who could get the information we want on who has shared a cell with Parker and who he was friends with during his stay. He's not sure how fast they can get back to him. He's not going through normal communication channels. After they get those names and he gives them to me, I'll have to start working on them to see if they have kin, contacts, whatever around here or within the state. It won't be quick, I'm sorry. But when we have those, I've got every hacker and computer expert in all the clubs ready to help me divide and conquer. Did you find their phones by any chance?"

I held them up. They were on the floor in the car and one of the guys picked them up.

"Damn, I was kind of hoping they still have them and they'd come back on. Okay, that's alright," he muttered.

"What about someone paying a visit to Parker and leaning on him for information? This other shit could take too much time. Time that they might not have," I asked, despite thinking it made me sick.

"That was going to be my next suggestion. I can

have my guy go in and do it, or do you want to do it?" Outlaw asked as he stared hard at me.

"Fuck, I wanna do it more than you know, but that's four hours away. What if you find them or have a lead here? I don't want to be gone if that happens." I was torn.

"Why don't you stay here and I'll go? I'm sure he'll talk," Payne said. As our enforcer and a man who loved to inflict pain on those who deserved it, he would be ideal.

"Thanks, how soon can you head out there? And how fast can your man get him in to see Parker?" I asked Outlaw.

"I can go as soon as Outlaw says we're good," Payne answered.

"I'll call him. He should be able to get us in today. If not, tomorrow at the latest. He knows this is urgent. He won't wait," Outlaw promised.

"Set it up. While they're working Parker, and Outlaw is waiting to work any leads, we're kind of at a standstill. Without knowing a vehicle description or anything, we can't go around riding the area looking for a sighting. As much as it pains me, we'll have it hang here," Bull said, as he watched me.

I wanted to protest, but he was right. All that would do is waste gas.

"Why the fuck didn't I have her get the tracker sooner? I was gonna have Outlaw do it Wednesday. Sonofabitch!" I snarled. I was pissed at myself. If I had gone ahead and done it, we'd have a way to find them right now.

"You had no way of knowing this would happen. Parker is still in prison. You were having it placed before he got out. How were you to know?" Tank asked.

"A tracker wouldn't do you any good on the car or their phones, so what kind of tracker are you talking about?" Zev asked, looking puzzled.

"We have access to one you can inject. All of us and our old ladies have them. Older kids too," Outlaw explained.

"How the hell do you have access to something like that? I didn't even know that was possible. Sure, there's been some developments but they have short range and aren't reliable," Zev said.

"They're reliable when you have a satellite that can be homed in on them at will. As for where we got it, well, let's just say we have connections," Bull said this as he looked at Demon. It hadn't started out that way, but his wife's uncle Tommy was the man behind Smoke getting access to this years ago. Smoke's years of service with the government had made it possible.

"Jesus Christ, who the fuck are you guys? The military doesn't even have that shit," Zev asked in awe.

"We could tell ya, but then we'd have to kill ya," Rebel said with a grin.

"Just know that when it's needed, we have resources you can't imagine," Bull added.

After that, there was very little to plan. We were in a holding pattern until they found someone or something. I wasn't sure how I'd keep from going insane waiting. The only thing that kept me from screaming and running out half-cocked was knowing I had to keep Byron calm. When I got Raina and Belle back, they'd kill me if anything had happened to him. When Bull dismissed us, I slowly lumbered off to find him. We could at least keep each other company while we wallowed in misery.

Raina: Chapter 18

Three days. We'd been locked up in this musty old basement for three days. It seemed like three months. The men who were our jailers didn't say much. Three times a day they'd bring us something to eat then leave. At the same time, we were unchained so we could use the bathroom. If we needed to go in between, there was a bucket left close to us. They made us empty it on our next bathroom break if we used it.

When I wasn't trying to keep Belle's spirits up or planning what we would do when we got out of here and home, I thought of Joker and Granddaddy. They had to be losing their minds. If I wasn't thinking of them, I was trying to figure out who these men were and why they took us.

The night the truck rammed into us on our way home had been a blur. I was knocked unconscious. When I woke up, it was to find us in this basement. Belle had been hysterical. She thought I was never going to wake up. From what I got out of her, after we were rammed, two men got out of the truck and took us out of the car. They tied our hands and feet and threw us in the back of a panel truck. I knew it was one of those from the description Belle gave me.

They transported us here and took us to the

basement, where they chained one of our ankles to rings bolted into the floor. No matter how much we heaved on them, they wouldn't budge. There wasn't much of anything down here except for two rickety cots that had thin foam mattresses on them. Thankfully, it was summer, so we didn't need to worry about freezing. There were a few boxes stacked in the far corner, I had no idea what was in them. We couldn't reach them.

By the smell and the number of cobwebs, I knew no one had been using this place for a long time. There was a tiny window on the far wall as well. It was too small for me to get out, but if I could find a way to get Belle free, she just might fit.

Whenever the men came, it wasn't always the same ones. In total, I'd seen six different guys. As much as I tried to get them to talk, they would only snap orders and leave. To me, they seemed to be waiting for something, but I didn't know what. If they kidnapped us expecting to be paid a ransom, no one we knew had that kind of money. They were out of luck. If it was for some other reason, I wanted to know what it was. Deep down, I wondered if this had anything to do with Parker.

For the main part, they gave us bland looks. Those were better than sexual ones, except there was one guy who gave me the willies. He would leer at me and then at Belle. I prayed he'd never be left alone with us, because if he was, I could see him trying something. If he touched my daughter, I swore to myself I'd find a way to kill him with my bare hands. So far, they always came in pairs so we'd been lucky.

It was hard to sleep more than an hour at a time since we were always afraid to sleep and they'd come for us. When I wasn't thinking and worrying, I was praying that somehow, some way, Joker and the club would find us. I didn't know how it would be possible, but I still prayed for it to happen.

It was almost dark according to the dimly lit basement. That meant they'd be bringing us something to eat and taking us to use the bathroom. The bathroom was down here on the other side of the basement. It wasn't much, just a toilet and sink.

"Mommy, what if they never let us go? I don't want to die down here," Belle whimpered. She was curled up on my cot with me. I petted her hair.

"Honey, we're not going to die. Remember what I said, if no one can find us."

"If no one comes and we get a chance, I'll climb out the window and go for help. But I don't want to leave you here. They might hurt you," she said fearfully.

"Belle, it might be our only chance. If the time comes and I can get you free, don't argue, don't wait, you get out and you run. You run and hide if you have to. Stick to the woods until you find a road. Stay in the trees until you find someone you can trust to reveal yourself to. When you do, you tell them to call the Archangel's Warriors in Hunters Creek, or the police in Hunters Creek. Promise me you'll do this and not argue."

"Okay, I will. I promise." She sniffed as more tears ran down her cheeks. It seemed like she'd shed at least a tub of tears since we'd been taken. She tried to be brave, but she was just a child. Hell, I wanted to cry all the time too, but I had to be strong for her.

We laid there not saying anything for a while until we heard the basement door open and heavy footsteps coming down the rickety stairs. There were two of them as usual. I noticed one was a new guy. He looked younger than the others. He nervously glanced around. The other one, we knew. He was the grumpiest one. They were carrying two bags. I knew from our prior meals it would likely be a sandwich, maybe a bag of chips and an apple. It could've been a lot worse. The fact they fed us made me hopeful they were concerned about our health. If they planned to kill us, surely they wouldn't feed us. They sat the bags down on Belle's bed.

Without saying a word, Mr. Grumpy came over and unlocked my manacle then Belle's. He pointed toward the bathroom and grunted. We didn't have to be told what to do. We shuffled over there as fast as we could. It had a door on it, so I could shut it so we had privacy. Taking care of business as fast as we could, we washed our hands and faces then brushed our teeth with our fingers. I felt so gross and disgusting. My hair looked like a greasy rat's nest and so did hers. Our clothes were wrinkled, dirty and smelly. What I wouldn't give for a shower, clean clothes, a hairbrush and a toothbrush and paste.

A loud bang on the door made us jump. "Hurry the fuck up. I don't have all night," Mr. Grumpy snarled.

Opening the door, we hurried back to the cots and sat down. Again, Mr. Grumpy shackled my ankle, then handed the key to the other guy to shackle Belle's.

"Let's go. I can't wait until the others get here. I'm ready to be off this babysitting duty for the day" he grumbled as he pointed to the stairs. The young guy followed him, but he kept glancing back at us. I wondered if they hadn't prepared him for what or who he might find in the basement.

When they were gone, I opened the sack. We dug into our sandwich and chips. It was dry, but I couldn't complain. They fed us. In the bags were a bottle of water for each of us. We tried not to gulp it down. When we were done, we crumpled the bags and put them in an empty box at the foot of the cots. Lying down, since there was nothing else to do, we cuddled together, and I told her an elaborate fairytale to take her mind off our situation. I hoped it might lull her to sleep.

We must've both nodded off because a sound jarred us awake. It was pitch black in the basement, except for the weak moonlight coming in through the window. I could hear someone breathing in the room with us. I sat up in fright. A shadow moved. I opened my mouth to scream but stopped when a voice hissed softly. A flashlight came on. It was the young guy from earlier. He looked terrified.

"Shh, don't scream. If you do, then we're all dead. We don't have much time, so listen. Edgar is taking a shit. You need to get out of here. I didn't sign up to hurt women and kids. I can't let you up the stairs or he'll know I helped you and he'll catch you, then he'll kill me. You've got to find help before they move you. I can let your daughter go and she can climb out the window over there. At the back of the house is the woods. Stick to it and a couple of miles east, that's right when you're looking at the woods, you'll find a road. About a half mile down it, there are a few houses. Go to one of them and ask for help. Whatever you do, don't let them catch you."

"What's your name?" I whispered.

"Diego," he whispered back as he unlocked the manacle on Belle's leg.

She was shaking in fear. Knowing we didn't have much time, and he'd have to help her to get up to the window despite the boxes underneath it, I grabbed her chin, so she would focus on me. "Belle, you go the way he said. You don't stop until you find someone. Remember what I told you earlier."

She nodded. She was crying again. Giving her a kiss, I pushed her toward Diego. Lifting her up he carried her to the window and shoved it open. He pushed her through it. It was a tight fit. He handed her something then he came back to me. I couldn't see her in the dark.

"What did you give her?"

"A flashlight. She'll need it when she gets into the deeper woods. The moonlight won't reach there." He started for the stairs.

"What will you do when he finds out she's gone?"

"I'll swear I locked the manacle. Hopefully, by the time they figure out she's gone, I'll be away from here and on the run. No way I'm staying with them."

"If you get out, please go to the Archangel's Warriors MC in Hunters Creek and tell them who you are and where I am," I begged.

His eyes widened. "You're part of an MC?"

"Yes, my man's name is Joker."

"You're an old lady?" he asked incredulously, when I nodded yes, he swore. "Fuck." Like a rabbit he was across the room, up the stairs and gone. As I laid there in the dark, I prayed no one would come and figure out she was gone until morning. It was all up to Belle and possibly Diego now.

The hours dragged by as I sat awake listening to every creak and sound from above. From time to time, I could hear footsteps on the floor above or muffled voices. None were ever raised very high, so I took that to mean Edgar had no idea Belle had escaped. Or whoever was now up there. By now, the guards should've changed.

As the sky grew lighter and more light began to enter the small window, I heard the pound of feet then the door open. I held my breath as they thundered down the stairs. I laid there waiting to see what they would do when they saw she was gone. I recognized them. They were the two who had crashed into my car. Belle had told me which ones they were. The look of astonishment on their faces made me want to smile.

One of them ran to the bathroom, then back to me. He was gasping for air like he'd run ten miles. His expression looked half-crazy mixed with half scared.

"Where the fuck is she?" he shouted.

"She's not here," was all I said.

"I can fucking see that, bitch. Where is she? How did she get out?" he screamed. His buddy went to the window. He pushed on it and it easily lifted open.

"She went out the window. See, it's unlocked," the other one said.

"When? How?" Guy One said.

"You'll never catch her now. Her chain wasn't latched I guess. It fell off and she got away. I told her to run and not look back. She climbed on the boxes and was able to reach it." I explained, hoping they'd believe me and not go looking for Diego.

"Sonofabitch! We're dead. Make sure she's secure and then let's go call this in. He'll have to talk to Edgar and Diego and see who the dumbass was who didn't make sure she was locked," Guy Two said.

He seemed to be the one in charge. Guy one checked my manacle then they left. They didn't bother to take me to the bathroom or to leave the bag they had with them, but that was fine by me. All I cared about was Belle making it to safety. Even if the club couldn't find me, as long as she was okay, I'd be content.

There was a lot of running around and loud voices coming from upstairs. I don't know how long passed before I heard the sound of motors. They stopped outside. Until then, no one had driven right up to the house. I assumed it was because they were parking a distance away. Suddenly, I heard a loud bang upstairs and then a herd of feet coming, They were down in the basement in no time. There were the two men from earlier and five others. Edgar was one of them. I didn't see Diego. Three others were ones who'd been guarding us as well. The one I didn't recognize came over to stare at me hard. He was an older guy, maybe in his early forties. He had long hair and a scraggly, filthy beard.

"You think she's gonna bring back help, but even if she does, all they'll find is an empty house. You're coming with us. You're the one he wants anyway," he sneered.

I screamed and fought as they came at me, but I was no match for that many men. They unlocked my ankle then tied my hands together and put a gag over my mouth. They marched me toward the stairs. I tried to sit down and not go, but they just hauled me up over a shoulder and carried me out. Upstairs, I got a glimpse of an old house. It looked as bad as the basement. Next thing I knew, I was outside, and being thrown in the back of a black panel van.

What shocked me was there were bikes sitting by it. Oh my God, were they bikers? Was this a rival club who had it out for the Warriors? They didn't have on cuts. Who wanted me? All these questions and more ran through my head as they started their bikes and the van. In no time we were zooming away from my chance at a rescue. I cried.

Joker:

It was official. I was going to lose my mind, and they'd have to commit me to the loony bin. It had been three-and-a-half days since Raina and Belle were taken. There had been no leads. Payne's visit to Parker in prison hadn't given us any leads. No matter what he threatened or did, Parker kept saying he didn't know anything about them being taken. That he hadn't asked anyone to snatch them. With him having his hearing yesterday, Payne hadn't been able to torture him like he wanted. He did beat the hell out of him and kept the marks to those you couldn't see unless he was naked.

Payne said he wasn't one hundred percent sure Parker was telling the truth, but he'd taken the beating he got without breaking and there weren't many men who could say that. Our plan was to scoop him up as soon as he made it outside the prison today and bring him back here to interrogate more thoroughly. I almost felt bad for Parker. Payne took it personally that he hadn't broke and was devising even more gruesome ways to torture the truth out of him.

At dawn, Bull sent him, Loki, Ace and Vex to go pick Parker up. If he thought someone else was coming, boy was he in for a nasty surprise. The rest of us stayed here to await their return. The way I was feeling, I didn't think Payne would get a chance to touch him. I'd be the one to torture it out of him.

I'd barely slept or eaten these past three days. I couldn't stop going over in my head what could be happening to them. I knew there were sick bastards out there. The thought of them being tortured or sexually assaulted wouldn't go away. If I was in bad shape, Byron was in worse shape. He was concerning me with how pale and gray-tinged his skin seemed to be. I tried to have him taken to see his doctor, but he refused to go.

It was barely eight in the morning and we were all gathered at the clubhouse. No one had been spending much time at their houses. We all wanted to be close at hand if there was any news. The old ladies had fixed breakfast for us. I tried to eat, but it just kept getting stuck in my throat. I got up to take my plate to the kitchen. As I did, the door to the clubhouse came slamming open and in ran Walker. In his arms was Belle. She was sobbing. I dropped my plate and ran to them. He handed her over.

"Shh. you're alright. I've got you," I told her. "Where's Raina?" I asked Walker. He shrugged.

"You mean she's not with her? How did she get here?" I half yelled at him.

"It means I don't know. Some car pulled up and an older man was driving it. He said Belle told him to call us, but he thought it would be better if he brought her to us. As soon as she said she knew me, he let her out of the car and he took off. I tried to stop him, but he kept going and I thought it would be better to bring her to you than chase after him. I got his license plate number though, in case we need to go talk to him," he said with a satisfied look.

"Mommy's still there. We have to go back and get her," Belle said as she raised her head out of my chest.

"Honey, we'll go get Mommy. Just tell us where she is," I said.

"She's at the house in the basement. Diego let me out. He said to go for help. I asked the man to call you but he wouldn't listen. He said we had to come here."

"Which house? Whose Diego?" I asked her.

"I don't know. They took us there and chained us in the basement. Diego was the new guy. He came back and helped me escape. He couldn't get Mommy out. He told me to go through the woods and when I got to the road to keep walking until I found the houses. I did. Only the man wouldn't call like Diego told me to tell him to do."

My head was spinning trying to figure out what she meant. The biggest worry was finding out where the house was. The only way I could think to do that was to find the man who brought her here and go from there. I looked at Walker.

"Give that license number to Outlaw so he can run it. We've got someone to go see."

He nodded then went over to Outlaw. They talked for about ten seconds then Outlaw was running to his office. I saw Byron trying to get to Belle, so I took her over to sit at one of the tables so he could sit with her. We took turns trying to console her while she cried and begged us to find her mom. I was about to cry myself when Outlaw came back waving a piece of paper.

"I've got it. Let's go."

Taking a moment, I crouched down beside her chair. She was still slightly sobbing in her great-grandfather's chest. "Sweetheart, I'm going to go find your mom and bring her home. You stay here with Granddaddy and keep him company. He's been so lonely since you've been gone. Will you do that for me?"

She rubbed the tears out of her eyes and nodded. "I can do that. Just find her. The house through the woods. It's an ugly green color. Diego said it was a couple miles through the woods and then another half mile to the houses."

"Thank you, Love Bug, that'll help us a lot. Love you." I gave her a kiss on the cheek.

She threw her arms around my neck and hugged me close so she could kiss me and mumbled, "love you too." I handed her back to Byron and gently squeezed his shoulder as he nodded to me. Then I was out the door with several of my brothers right behind me. We had work to do.

Before we tore off, I checked the address and put it in my phone. It was a Sparta address, but that covered a lot of outlying areas too. When it was plotted, I was relieved to see it wasn't more than ten miles away. Armed with that, we took off. The ride seemed to take eternity to me, although it wasn't far. When we came up to the house, I saw a car sitting out front. We parked our bikes so we were surrounding the car then shut down and got off our bikes.

As we walked to the door, it opened and an older man came out. He looked terrified. "I didn't hurt her. I brought her straight home to you."

"Mr. Harrison, we never said you hurt her. We want to know where she came from and why you didn't just call us to come get her?" I asked, trying not to lose my patience.

"She came knocking on the door at first light. She was crying and not making a lot of sense. The one thing she was clear on was she belonged to your club. I thought it better to drop her off rather than have her call you and wait. I shouldn't have just left her at the gate, but when I saw those walls and that gate, it scared the hell out of me. She said she knew the guy who came to open the gate. He was a friend to her dad, so I thought it was safe to leave her," he explained in a rush. I could see we were making him nervous as hell. As much as I wanted to chew him out for it, I needed information, so I smiled at him.

"Hey, I get it. It can be a bit intimidating when you're not used to it. I'm her dad. The name is Joker. Here's the issue. She and her mom were taken almost four days ago. They never made it home. We found their car smashed along a road. We've been frantically trying to find them and who took them. This man here, he's a police officer. He's been helping us too. Belle said she came through the woods for a couple of miles and then it was maybe a half mile to your house. The house she was in was painted green. Would you happen to know of a place like that nearby?"

"Actually, I do. If you go through the woods, maybe two and a half miles or three, there's a lone house that sits out there. I have no idea who owns it. It's been empty as far as I know for a while. It has an ugly green siding on it. It's weathered and needs work. I've seen it a few times when I go squirrel hunting in those woods. That's the only one I imagine she's referring to. If you stay on the main road, you might miss the turn off. It's overgrown. I can show you how to get there through the woods if you want. You won't be able to take your bikes that way though."

Zev came closer. I was glad he'd been at the compound when Belle came back, Having him here made the visit seem more legitimate. Mr. Harrison would be much less likely to call the cops if he saw one with us. Zev took out his badge and showed it to him.

"Just so you know, I really am a police officer. I work with his girlfriend, the girl's mom. We'd appreciate any help you can give us, although I'd prefer if you didn't go with us to the actual house. We have no idea how dangerous it might be. The men who took them have a score to settle, we think. We don't want to get anyone hurt. If we show you a map, can you give us the directions?"

"Sure, I know this area like the back of my hand." He was relaxing and becoming even more helpful.

Zev brought a map up on his cell phone and I joined them to see the route he indicated. It didn't take Harrison long to show us. When we had it, we were ready to go. I shook his hand.

"Thank you so much for bringing her home. I can't tell you how relieved we are. If you ever need anything, please stop by the compound," I told him as we parted ways. He was smiling when we took off down the road. I hoped that meant he wouldn't call the law. That was the last thing we needed.

We were able to ride our bikes the half mile or so to where the trail he indicated began in the woods then we left them there. Although he wasn't excited about it, Predator volunteered to stay with the bikes. After we had her, we'd get back to the bikes, so I could take her home. If she was unable to ride, then we'd figure it out. I had been in such a rush to go, I didn't think to bring my Bronco.

We made decent time. Of course to me, it seemed like it was taking forever, but it was in reality about forty minutes. The terrain was uneven and that slowed it down. We ran at a slight jog pace when we could. As we approached the spot Mr. Harrison said was about a quarter of a mile away from the house, we slowed down and split up. We'd come up to the house from different directions. We had no idea if they had sentries or an alarm system to alert them of someone coming. I thought it was unlikely that Belle was able to get away without getting caught. They likely had guards, especially knowing she got away.

It was eerily quiet when we finally converged on it. There was a back and a front door. There were no vehicles in sight. Creeping up on the front porch, I had Maverick, Ajax, Bear, and Iceman at the back door. Zev, Renegade, and Stalker were with me. Using my phone, we counted down and kicked in the doors simultaneously. We all had our guns drawn and ready. Quickly moving through the upstairs, we found it empty.

There were signs that people had been here recently, but they were gone. Dirty dishes filled the sink. Finding a door to the basement, we swept down the stairs like a wave. My heart sank when I saw it was empty too. There were two heavy chains bolted to the floor with manacles on the other end. Those were close to two small cots that showed signs of being used. A tiny window was on one wall. That was how Belle escaped and I could see why Raina hadn't been able to go with her. However, there was no Raina.

I wanted to scream and cry at the same time. Jesus Christ, they moved her. They got scared when Belle got away and they ran. Why the fuck didn't we think of that? How would we find her now? I sank down on one of the cots and held my head. A hand on my shoulder shaking me was what made me look up. It was Bear.

"Joker, I know it looks hopeless, but don't give up. We'll find her. I feel it in my gut. I don't know how, but we will. I think we need to call Bull and let him know what we found and then leave a couple of guys here, just in case one of them comes back. The rest of us will head home and see what we find out. Remember, Parker is going to be with us sometime today. You can take some of your frustration out on him," he said that last bit with an evil grin on his face.

Most people saw Bear and thought despite

his size, that he was a teddy bear. And in some circumstances he was. However, piss him off and he'd show you how he got the name Bear. It was gruesome.

"Okay, let's go. Stalker, I want you to stay here. We'll send Predator to keep watch with you. If anything suspicious happens or someone comes back, detain them, and call us. We'll send reinforcements."

"You got it, Joker," he said.

It was a pretty discouraged group who trekked back through those woods then rode their bikes back to the compound. I hated having to face Byron and Belle and tell them we hadn't rescued Raina.

Joker: Chapter 19

We'd been back at the compound for about an hour when Gavin came running into the common room again. He was still on gate duty. I jumped to my feet. Maybe he was here to tell us Raina was back! The likelihood was almost zilch, but a man could wish. Seeing me standing by the table where Belle and Byron were sitting, he came right to us.

"There's a man at the gate. He says he was told to come here by Raina. He says his name is Diego. Do you know anyone by that name?"

I was about to say no when Belle cried out and came out of her chair. "I do. He's the one who helped me get away. He wanted to help Mommy to get away too, but she wouldn't fit out the window and if we tried to go upstairs, Edgar would see us. He told me what to do and gave me the flashlight," she explained excitedly.

"Bring him here, now. Is anyone watching him?" I was suddenly terrified he'd disappear before I could talk to him.

"Walker has him. I'll go get him." He ran back out. I paced as we waited. We were all on pins and needles. Without a lead, we were simply waiting for Parker to get here. We got the call from Payne telling us he'd been picked up and would be here in a couple of hours.

A minute or so later, the door opened again and in came Gavin pushing a man ahead of him. The man was young, I'd say in his mid to late twenties. He was Hispanic by the looks of him. He was looking around. He was doing a good job of hiding his fear, but I could tell by the way his eyes were constantly scanning that he was terrified. Gavin shoved him right up to me. Before I could say anything, Belle ran up and greeted him.

"Hi, Diego. This is my new dad, Joker. And this is my granddaddy. I told them you helped me get away. Are you here to help them find my mom?"

"Hi, little one. What do you mean? Haven't you gone to the house to get her?" he asked me with a look of worry on his face.

"Jocelyn, would you take Belle to play with the other kids? I need to talk to Diego." I didn't want her to see me get ugly or hurt him.

"He helped me, Dad," Belle said urgently. It melted my heart to hear her call me dad. This was the first time she'd done that. Byron grinned at me and nodded.

"Love Bug, I know he did and I appreciate that so much, but I need to talk to him and there might be things you shouldn't hear."

"You mean you don't want me to hear you swear or see you beat him up. I get it. Fine, I'll go but you better not hurt him. He's my new friend," she told me a tad snippily before she followed Jocelyn outside. The guys chuckled. I couldn't help the tiny smile she put on my face, but it was soon wiped away when I looked at him again.

"We did go to the ugly green house and there was no one there. So, Diego, why don't you tell us who you are and why the hell you would show your face here? Sure, you helped Belle escape and I want to know why. Also, what in the world made you come here? You told Gavin that Raina told you to. Spill."

"Raina did tell me to come if I ever got away from the others. Listen, I had no idea they kidnapped anyone, let alone a woman and a kid. Yesterday was the first time they sent me to that house. They said they needed my help with guard duty. When Edgar took me to the basement and I saw them, I knew I had to get out. I've been regretting my decision to join them for a while and I didn't know how to get free of them. However, I knew I wasn't going to let them go through with whatever plan they had for them."

"Why help Belle and not Raina?"

"Because I had to wait until Edgar was in the bathroom taking a shit to go back down. I knew I didn't have long and if I snuck them upstairs, he'd hear us. The only chance was to go out the basement window. If you've been there, then you saw how small it was. Belle could hardly fit through it. I told her to run and where to go and how to find a house to call for help. As soon as she was out, I went upstairs and said nothing."

"When did they discover you helped her escape and how did you get away from them?"

"As far as I know, they don't know for sure I

did help. We were relieved of guard duty this morning. Edgar and I never went downstairs again. They had to discover she was gone after we left. If she wasn't there, then they moved her. I went back to my place, grabbed a few of my things and left the rest then decided to come here. I'm hoping I didn't make a mistake."

"That's yet to be seen. Tell us who the men you were with are? You said you joined them. What do you mean by joining?"

Looking at him and the way he was dressed, I'd guess he was a rider. His left boot had the typical scuff mark across it that riders got from shifting the gears. The rest of his attire was jeans and a t-shirt with a motorcycle logo on it.

"I mean I asked to prospect for their club. I've been with them for six months and I knew two months in, they weren't the kind of club I was looking for. Only problem is, if you try to get out, they give you a beat down and most people don't survive it, I heard. Of course, I found that out after I joined. When your old lady told me who she was, I almost died. I know this means war."

"What is the name of your club?" I asked urgently. Although there were lots of other clubs around, there were none that I was aware of who had a beef with us. This was news to us and would have to be investigated.

"They're called the Devil's Cannibals."

I looked at Bull and Bear. They had been around the longest and knew almost every club who had been in our area over the last thirty-plus years. I'd never heard of them. Bear swore as he looked at Bull.

"Jesus Christ, they disbanded years ago. They were rotten, and no one wanted anything to do with them. Finally, after so many of them went to prison or got killed and they couldn't replace them, the few remaining ones disbanded and then disappeared. I always figured they moved on and found other rotten outlaw clubs to join. I had no idea anyone had restarted the club," Bear muttered darkly.

"Maybe they didn't disband like we thought and they've been lying low and secretly building back up. How many men are in this club and where is it located?" Bull asked Diego.

"They're out by Mawbray Mountain in Soddy Daisy, down by Chattanooga. I don't know how long they've been there. I heard of them for the first time about two years ago, but some guys seem to know each other and are older. I wouldn't be surprised if they had been elsewhere and moved there. There's fifteen patched members and four prospects if you count me."

"What's your last name Diego and where are you from?" Outlaw asked out of the blue. He was sitting at one of the tables with his laptop. I knew he was going to start digging into him.

"It's Medina. I grew up in Ooltewah, but I've lived all over Tennessee and even parts of Georgia. Why?"

"We like to make sure people are who they say they are. Assuming they moved her because Belle escaped, where would they take her? Do they have any other safe houses or hidey-holes?"

"If they do, I never heard of them. If I had to guess, they took her back to the clubhouse. It sits out in the country and no one would easily stumble upon 'em. Also, they'd be able to lock her up better. They keep cells in the basement." His unease over the thought of those cells were obvious.

I exchanged glances with Outlaw, then Bull. Could we trust him? Whether we could or not was to be determined, but I knew one thing. I'd be going to check out this supposed clubhouse. And once I found her, I'd be asking some men a lot of questions. The biggest ones being, why did they take them and what did they hope to achieve by doing it? They hadn't sent us any demands. What were they waiting for? Why come after us in the first place? There were plenty of MCs around they could have gone after if they wanted territory or to take over their illegal businesses and routes.

"Diego, come here and show us on this map where their clubhouse is," Outlaw ordered him.

We all couldn't gather around to see, but as Diego took a seat next to Outlaw, myself, Bull, and Tank stood behind them. After we had it laid out, I knew Outlaw would work with it and send the detailed map to the phones of the men going with me. There was no way I was going to wait until after Parker got here. If I could rescue her before, all the better. No matter if she was back safe, he was going to be answering my questions. It looked like it was going to be a busy remainder of the day and night. We'd have more than one man to torture.

Diego pinpointed the spot on the enhanced map,

which allowed us to see roads and streets. He was right, it did sit out in the country and no one would stumble upon them accidentally, not unless it was in the fall and hunters were out and about. I didn't know how much land they had, but it was likely posted for no trespassing or hunting.

"Do you know how much property they have at this clubhouse? Are there more buildings? Any houses?" I asked him. Outlaw was busy messing with pulling up aerial views or something.

"They don't have anything like you do. Maybe three acres max. It's not fenced in and other than a rather old clubhouse, which is really an old house they converted to one, there are no other structures other than a garage where they keep the bikes in winter," he was quick to supply.

"Do they post guards or have cameras or anything like that set up around them?" Bull asked as he stared at the screen.

"They never did before, but maybe if they took her there, they might post guards. As for cameras, they're not that sophisticated. They like to brag about how badass they are, but I've discovered they're mainly a bunch of overgrown kids who like to bully those weaker or different from them. I was a fool to join them. I know that. Even if they find me and kill me for leaving and helping her escape, it's better than staying with them. They're toxic."

He sounded very sincere. I hoped he was. There was a chance he had been a man who got into a situation before he knew what they were really like and regretted it. There were clubs that wouldn't easily let anyone leave, even if they weren't patched in. Killing someone wasn't unheard of so they wouldn't tell anyone your secrets. However, if he was tricking us into an ambush, he'd die a very hard, painful death.

"What kind of weapons do they have? Is it mainly handguns and rifles? Anything bigger, like assault rifles, grenades, or RPGs?" Tank asked. The way Diego's eyes widened, I knew that had shocked him.

"No, nothing like that. All of them have handguns and there are shotguns, regular rifles and a few AR-15s. I never saw anything else or heard them talk about them. They'd brag if they had those."

"Okay, I've got it. I can send it to your phones. Who's going with Joker? I know there's no way in hell he's waiting," Outlaw said.

After a few minutes of back-and-forth debating, with every single guy offering to go, it was settled. Bull, Bear, Ajax, Slash, Demon, Iceman, and Walker were going with me. This left Tank, Player, Rebel, Maverick, Outlaw, Renegade, and Gavin here to protect the compound, in case this was a trick. Zev was still with us and he offered to go too, but I thought it best if he stayed here. He was still unknown. He didn't need to witness firsthand us killing men. Payne, Loki, Vex and Ace would be back soon to add to that protection. We made the decision to pull Predator and Stalker off guarding the house to join me. We would still be outnumbered, but I'd put us up against a ragtag bunch of men any day.

"Diego, you'll stay here. You won't have a free run of the place. You'll stay where you're told and do as you're told, Understood?" I told him sternly.

"Understood. I can't tell you enough how sorry I am this happened. They didn't deserve that."

Nodding my head to acknowledge what he said, me and the guys going with me left to gather our supplies. We'd be going in loaded down with weapons. Ten to eighteen odds would be pared down to even or better with our firepower. Walker would drive one of the vans and he'd haul the majority of our firepower. Although we were all efficient and didn't waste time, I wanted to yell at them all to hurry the fuck up. The more time we wasted, the bigger chance she'd be hurt or moved, assuming she was even there.

When we were ready to go, I gave Belle a kiss and tried to reassure her and Byron that we'd be back soon with Raina. I hoped I wouldn't turn out to be a liar again. Hitting the road, we went as fast as possible without wrecking or attracting the attention of a cop. It was an hour and a half ride. I was going to do my damndest to make it closer to an hour. We had sent a message telling Stalker and Predator where to meet us along the way. I sent up another prayer asking God to please let me find her and for her to be alive. Anything else we could recover from.

Raina:

I'd gone from a bad situation to a worse one. I thought the musty old basement had been bad, but this place was a nightmare. When they stopped driving and took me out of their van, I saw we were out in the country still, but in a whole new location. We'd driven for a while, over an hour I'd guess. The only things I saw around were a big garage and a somewhat battered two-story house. There were bikes parked all around the front on the trampled and dying grass. A gravel road led up to it.

I was shoved toward the steps to the porch, where several men stood watching us. It was then that I noticed they were all wearing leather cuts. The guy walking in front of me had the name *Devil's Cannibals* on the back of his. Who in the world were these guys?

"Move, bitch, you're turning out to be more trouble than you're worth," one hissed as he shoved me from behind again.

I tried to walk faster. I'd go along with what they said as long as I thought it might protect me. However, when it became clear that wasn't the case anymore, then I'd resist. If I was going to die, I'd rather go out fighting and not as a scared mouse. As I walked, I scanned the area. Anything might be helpful in an escape.

When we reached the porch, they stopped me in front of an older guy. I saw on his cut he was the *President* and his road name was *Bastard*. Fitting name, I thought sarcastically. He stared at me coldly. I refused to look away or cower. Eventually, he nodded.

"Well, at least she's not a total sissy, not that it'll help you here. Do you know who we are or why you're here?"

I raised my brows. How did he expect me to talk with a gag over my mouth? Noting the problem he looked at one of the men behind me. "Well, take off the fucking gag. It's not like anyone out here can hear her scream for help."

One of them undid it. My mouth was so dry, it felt like the desert, but I cleared my throat and answered. "I have no idea who you are or why you took me, but I know you'll regret it."

Like a flash, his hand came up and he backhanded me. Pain exploded along my cheek. My eyes prickled with tears, but I held them back. He wasn't going to make me cry.

"Mouthy bitches don't fare well around here. And I'm not afraid of the Warriors. They've thought they're kings of Tennessee for too long. It was time they learned they're not. The Devil's Cannibals are far superior to them and this has been a long time coming. I can't wait to see their faces when they learn that truth. We intend to take them out and you were just a way to do it. Plus, you're a secondary insurance policy for us.

Get her inside and make sure this time, she can't get away like the kid did. Has anyone seen Diego? I want to know why he didn't double check he locked the damn thing," he growled crossly.

"No, he left earlier after he got off guard duty," one of them answered. I saw his name was *Ox*. He was built like one. His cut said he was their *Enforcer*.

"Well, send his ass to me when he gets back. It's a fucking pain that our safe house is blown because of him," Bastard grumbled.

I breathed an internal sigh of relief. At least it didn't sound like they thought he helped Belle to escape. It sucked that even if Belle could lead Joker and the others back to the house, I'd be gone. There was no way they'd find me here. They had no idea who took me, I bet. That meant, my only hope of getting out of here was to escape on my own.

Again, I was shoved from behind then forced into the house. Inside, it was a pigsty. The air was filled with smoke, the smell of body odor and stale alcohol. I gagged. I couldn't imagine how long it had been since they gave it a good cleaning. By the looks of it, never. One of them marched me to a door then down in a basement. This one was worse than the last one. It was like upstairs and it had the added horror of cells. I was pushed into one and the door was slammed and locked behind me. The guy, this one was *Gravel* according to his cut, shook the door to make sure it was locked. He gave me a leer then walked off leaving me to worry.

Checking out my new home, it was depressing.

The cot was worse than the ones we had at the safe house. I was afraid to lie down on it. The stains and odor coming off it made me sick to my stomach. There was a bucket in one corner. I knew what that was for. With this set up, I had to wonder if I'd ever be taken to an actual toilet or if they'd remember to feed me. I could imagine they threw people down here and forgot about them often. Only when the stink got worse than the usual stink, would they come to investigate.

Come on, buck up, Raina. You can't let them get you down or to give up hope. You'll find a way out of here. And if you don't, then Joker and the Warriors will find you. They could be on their way right now. I told myself.

I paced the cell and listened to the muffled, loud footsteps and voices above my head. I scanned the area outside my cell to see if there was anything I could use as a weapon or something to get away if they ever took me out of here to the bathroom. This one was filled with shelves of jumbled stuff. Like it was their storage for odds and ends. There were more boxes stacked willy-nilly around too. Like the other house, the window was small, but there were two instead of one.

I lost track of how long I paced and studied the area before I heard the door open and then light steps coming down the stairs. I wondered which one it was and what they wanted. Imagine my shock when it wasn't one of them, but a young woman. She came limping toward me. I estimated her to be a bit younger than me. She had pale blond hair caught up in a messy bun on her head. Even at a distance, I could see she was very pretty. Was this one of their old ladies or a bunny? She was carrying something in a bag.

She stopped a foot away from my cell. She was studying me. I thought I saw sorrow on her face.

"Who're you?" I asked when she didn't say anything.

"I'm Aria. I brought you something to eat and some water. I wish it was more, but it was all I could sneak." She held out the bag to me. I slowly reached out and took it. She went to turn away, but I stopped her.

"Thank you, Aria. I'm Raina. Are you one of their old ladies or one of the bunnies? I don't want you to get in trouble for doing this."

"I'm neither. I'm sorry you're here. It's a terrible place to be."

Excitement started to bubble up. If she wasn't an old lady or a bunny and she felt sorry, maybe she'd help me escape. "Please, if you help me escape, I can take you with me. You don't look like you want to be here anymore than I do," I pleaded.

She shook her head and looked even sadder. "There's no escaping them. If you try, they'll only hurt you and make you regret it. Believe me, if they're not doing it now, you don't want to cause them to do it. You'd better hope they either ransom you or you die, otherwise your life will be hell here." She moved again toward the stairs.

"Aria, wait! Are you here because you want to be?"

She shook her head no.

"My man is an Archangel Warrior in Hunters

Creek. If you can't get me out, can you get a message to him and tell him where we are? He'll come for us and I promise, I'll take you with me."

A spark of hope flickered in her eyes then died. "They would never let that happen. If they did, he'd kill them. I used to think I could escape, but they proved me wrong. I wish I could help you, but I can't."

As she limped up the stairs, I tried once more.

"I have a daughter. She's eleven and her name is Belle. They captured her too, but she got away. There is hope, Aria. Just think about it."

She paused and listened. That was something. Maybe she'd think about it and help me. That was my hope anyway. She slowly climbed the stairs. Taking a seat on the floor since it was cleaner than the cot, I opened the bag. Inside was a sandwich, but it looked to be a homemade one, not like the store-bought ones they'd been giving us. There was an apple and a bottle of water. Hating to trust the food, but starving, I took a bite and moaned. It tasted so good. I quickly ate it and kept the apple for later.

A little bit later, I heard several of the bikes start up and ride off. I wondered where they were going. A while later, maybe a half hour or so, I was surprised by Aria returning. She ran over to my cell. She had a key. Her hands shook as she unlocked it. Opening the door, she whispered frantically.

"Hurry, a bunch of them left. This is your chance. They're going to pick someone up. It'll take them a few hours, it sounds like. I'm going to sneak you out over here. Once you get out, stick to the trees and head west. You'll eventually come out on a road. Watch for them. You should be able to wave down someone and they can call and get you help."

Stepping out of the cell, I followed her to where a tall pile of boxes were. To my surprise, there was a short set of stairs behind them leading up to doors above them that looked like storm cellar doors. They had a chain and lock on it. She held up another key and went to work on the lock. When it was undone, she slowly lifted a door and peeked out. It must've been clear, because she opened it wider, but not fully. She looked back at me.

"Good luck. I hope you get back to your daughter. Warn the Warriors that the Cannibals are coming for them soon."

I grabbed her hand. "Come with me. We can both be free."

She shook her head. "I can't. I'll only slow you down. You need to run and run fast." She pointed to her leg. I wondered what happened to it.

"I can help you."

"No, you can't. Now go." She pushed me toward the opening. Knowing I couldn't waste this chance and hating I was leaving her behind, I stepped out. As a final thought, I told her. "I'll have them come back for you. I promise."

"Don't. It'll be too late anyway." She shut the door before I could ask her why.

Shutting her haunted face out of my mind, I crouched low and ran for the woods. Fortunately, I knew how to tell directions based on the position of the sun. Something Granddaddy had taught me when I was a kid. Entering the woods. I found the sun and headed west. I ran as fast as I could without falling and hurting myself. That wouldn't do me any good.

I ran until I had a stitch in my side and could barely breathe, then I ran more. I was scared I'd hear them coming for me, but it was quiet. I don't know how long I ran before I came out on a road like she had said I would. It was deserted. Sticking to the edge, so I could dart into the woods if I had to, I kept walking. It wasn't long until I heard the roar of what could only be motorcycles. Scrambling, I ducked back in the trees and crouched down. Hopefully, they'd ride right past me. It had to be them either coming for me or the others returning. As the bikes came into view and got closer, I felt like my heart was going to explode in my chest. It wasn't from fear. It was from excitement.

For one thing, they were coming from the opposite direction of where I thought the house was and the other was when they got closer, I could recognize them. It was Joker and at least half his club. Riding behind them was a van. I ran out into the road and waved them down. How had they found me?

Joker: Chapter 20

I couldn't believe my eyes. Running out in the middle of the road, waving her arms like mad was Raina. Rolling up to her, I parked my bike then bailed off it to grab her. I didn't bother to shut off the engine. Hugging her tight, I wept. I didn't care if it made me look unmanly to some, I was so fucking relieved to have her in my arms and safe, that I couldn't help it. She was sobbing against my chest. Finally, as the others stopped and surrounded us, I pushed her away so I could see her face.

Before saying a word, I had to give her a kiss. It was one I hoped told her everything I was feeling at that moment. Hers was just as desperate as mine. When we parted, Bull was the one to say something. I was still speechless.

"Raina, it's so damn good to see you, darlin'."

"Not as good as it is to see you," she said with a smile.

"As much as I'd love to stand here and chat, we have some business down the road. You can tell us all about what happened later. Right now, we need to exterminate some Cannibals," Bear growled.

"He's right. We don't want to lose the element

of surprise. I want you to stay here with Walker. I'll leave my bike with him and drive the van. If something happens, you get her the hell out of here," I told him. He nodded.

"No, I'm not staying behind. The rest of them could come back and we could get caught. I want to stay close to you. Plus, I can take you through the way I snuck out. You'd have to hide the bikes here, but it would give you a better chance," she pleaded.

"What do you mean, the rest might come back? How many left and when? Do you know where they went?" Bull asked.

"I don't know how many or why. All I know is I heard several bikes leave at least an hour ago, maybe more. It's hard to keep track of time. I was locked in the basement, so I couldn't see them, only hear them." She sounded upset that she couldn't tell us more.

Tugging her tighter to me, I kissed her briefly. "Babe, you have nothing to apologize for. Knowing some are gone is good to know. Bull, what do you want to do? Wait and see if the others come back or take out who we can and worry about getting the others later?"

I would prefer to get them all, so we knew we had no enemies out there who could come at us at any time. It was hard to stay alert for weeks on end, let alone months. However, if we didn't take the ones who were there out now, they could move, and we'd have no idea where they were. Better half than none.

Bull thought about it for a minute while the rest all chimed in with their opinions. In the end, he listed the exact same things as I did. He put it up for a vote with the ones here. It was close, down to one vote difference but in the end, the decision was to deal with the ones there and then we'd work on finding the rest and eliminating them.

As for Raina and leaving her behind, that was part of the debate too. They left it up to me, even though Bull and Bear both thought sneaking through the woods was a better way to approach. I wanted her to be as far away as she could be, but with some of them on the loose, it was a risk she could be caught by surprise and captured. I knew I didn't have long to agonize over it, so I sent up a prayer that I was doing the right thing and gave them my decision.

"Okay, if we take you with us, you will hang back with Walker. We'll load up with as many weapons as we can carry, since the van will need to stay behind too. We'll get it and the bikes back in the woods so they're not visible from the road. Thank God it's summer and there are plenty of leaves on everything. If Walker gets a text to take you and leave, you will go with him and not fight him, understood? If you can't promise me that, then you'll stay here or I'll just send him back with you now," I warned her.

"I promise. I do think with my help, you have a better chance to sneak up on them. Are you ready?"

It took a good ten minutes or so to get the bikes and van maneuvered into the woods far enough and to get as much firepower as we could carry. When that was done, I took the lead with Raina, Bull, Bear and Demon.

She impressed us by continually checking the position of the sun. That along with the map Outlaw had given us, kept us on course. When the trees started to thin out, she stopped.

"The house and garage are just another quarter of a mile or so straight ahead. I have no clue how many stayed. Good luck and be careful, all of you."

I couldn't leave her without one more kiss, though I kept it short. When I was done, I handed her a handgun from my waistband. She knew how to use it. "Stay safe and I love you."

"I love you too, Aaron," she whispered so the others couldn't hear her using my name. I didn't give a shit if they did.

"She's my life. Protect her with yours," I told Walker.

"I will, Joker," he promised.

Walking away from her was the hardest thing I think I'd ever done. All I wanted to do was stay there and make sure she was safe. As we got closer to the house, I shut my mind to thoughts of her and put them all on the mission. We were going slower now and constantly scanning for sentries. It would suck to blow it when we were this close.

When the house and garage came into view, it was overall quiet. We could hear faint sounds of voices coming from the house. I had no idea if any of them were in the garage. We stopped to regroup.

"Ajax and Slash, I want you to go check out the garage, just in case there's any of them in there. If at all possible, take them out quietly. The rest of us will take the house. Stay alert and if possible, we take one alive. If it is down to you or them, kill them. We can live without a prisoner to question. We can't live without any of you. Good luck and stay frosty," Bull ordered.

All nodded then we made our move. The worst part was making it to the house without being seen, since there was no real cover between us and it now. Slash and Ajax could still use the trees to get to the garage. Surprisingly, the house didn't seem to have a backdoor, which I thought was odd. It did have cellar doors, but a tug on those showed me they were locked. No way in that way. It would have to be the front door and windows. We made sure our watches were synced. We'd go when the clock hit eleven, which was only a couple of minutes away.

Me, Bear, and Bull took the door. Predator and Stalker took the two windows on the left side of the house and Iceman and Demon took the windows on the right side. They were those oddly extra-long ones, which would make it easier to get through them. If we all tried to come through the front door, even fanning out, we'd be bottlenecked and easier to shoot. Even though we did have Kevlar vests on, head shots would stop us. Hopefully, the guys inside weren't the best shots.

When my watch hit eleven, I kicked in the door. I went straight while Bull went down and left and Bear did the same on the right. The door opened into the living room rather than a hallway, which was a bit of luck. We were able to scan the room and find our targets. At the same time we kicked in the door, the others busted through the windows and poured inside with us.

There were startled yells and men went scrambling. For a minute or so it was mayhem. Shots were fired, screams and yells rang out, bodies dropped and people dove for cover. As soon as the Cannibals were down and not getting back up, we split again and half of us checked the remainder of the bottom floor which were a few rooms, while the rest of us went upstairs. I was part of the ones going upstairs. We found two more up there. Unfortunately, they put up a fight, so they were killed. It didn't look like we were going to have anyone to question after all.

We were taking pictures of the ones we had killed, knowing the ones downstairs would be doing the same. It would allow us to look at them later and see if anyone recognized them. Also, we took their IDs out of their wallets. Anything to help us identify and possibly trace these men. We wanted to know where they'd come from. We were about to rejoin the others when we heard a loud shout.

"Get out, the goddamn house is on fire. Run," Demon's voice boomed up to us.

I could smell the smoke as we reached the first floor. It was filling up the air really fast. We didn't have time to worry about what caused it, although it seemed to be coming from the basement. Damn it! Had anyone gotten a chance to see if there was anyone hiding down there? If not, whoever was would be dead soon. Racing outside, we gathered on the lawn.

"Is everyone alright?" Bull asked. I was relieved to see we were all here, including Ajax and Slash.

"I got winged in the arm," Demon said dismissively.

"Same for me but it's on the thigh for me," Iceman said.

They were both tying bandanas around them. We'd have them looked at when we got home. Zara would patch them up. She would likely give Demon hell for getting hurt.

"Did you find anyone in the garage?" Bear asked Slash and Ajax.

"Nope, just their bikes," Ajax answered.

"Well, we'd better get the hell out of here before that smoke attracts unwanted attention. Everyone took pictures and grabbed IDs?" Bull asked.

We all said yes. We were about to head back in the woods, when my phone dinged, alerting me I had a text. Taking it out in case it was Walker warning us the others were on their way. It was him, only he wasn't warning us. He was giving me a message.

Walker: Raina said there's a woman, Aria, there. If you find her, please bring her with you. She helped her escape. She's not there because she wants to be. Raina is freaking out that she didn't tell you.

"Shit! Raina said there was a woman here. She

helped her escape and isn't here because she wants to be. Did anyone see a woman?"

They all said no.

"She had to either have left or be in the basement," Stalker said.

"If she's in the basement, she's probably dead already," Predator stated.

I didn't want to go back to Raina and tell her that we didn't know what happened to Aria, but no one was going to go in that basement not knowing if she was there or even alive. Just as I opened my mouth to tell them let's go, we heard someone screaming. It was a woman's voice, and it sounded like it was coming from the basement. We were close to the cellar doors or we would've never heard her.

Before any of us could think, Slash took off running back into the house. We yelled at him to come back, but he didn't listen. In a panic, I ran to the cellar doors and tried them again. They were still locked.

"Stand back, I'll see if I can shoot whatever is holding it closed loose," I told the others.

Anxiety over my brother made me willing to try anything. Taking out my handgun, I aimed it for where I thought a lock would be and fired six shots all around that area. When I was through, Ajax and I grabbed the doors and yanked on them as hard as we could. They gave some, but not all the way. The others grabbed where they could and we heaved again and again. I was about to give up when they came flying open and landed us on our asses.

Smoke billowed out. We coughed and hacked as we inhaled it. I started down the steps with tears in my eyes from the smoke only to back up because someone was pushing against me and coughing up a storm. I reached out and grabbed who I hoped was Slash and yanked his dumbass out into the fresh air.

It was him but he wasn't alone. Lying in his arms, not moving was a woman. She was covered in soot like he was. I took her away from him as he stumbled. Good thing I did because he landed on his knees and was coughing his head off. I placed Aria, I presumed, on the ground and checked her breathing. She wasn't breathing.

"She's not breathing," I hastily told the others before starting to give her mouth-to-mouth. Demon joined me and we ended up working on her together. It was a few tense minutes before she inhaled then started to cough. We rolled her on her side and let her recover. Slash was only coughing a tiny bit now.

"You're a fucking dumbass," Ajax told him. Slash just grinned and gave him a thumbs up.

"We need to get her out of here. Someone text Walker and let him know I got his message and we have her."

"I'll do it," Predator offered. I looked at Bull.

"She's tiny. We can take turns carrying her through the woods to the van and bikes. We've got to go," he ordered.

Slash staggered to his feet. "I've got her."

"No, you don't. You inhaled too much smoke. Your lungs won't appreciate you hefting her out. I've got her and I'll let you know when she starts getting too heavy and one of the others can take a turn," Stalker told him gruffly.

Slash tried to argue, but no one paid attention to him. Stalker picked her up and we took off. She was still mostly out of it. I hoped she wouldn't wake fully until we got to Raina, so she could reassure her. We didn't make as good a time as going, since we had her and no one wanted to leave Stalker lagging behind. I was happy when we got back to Walker and Raina. She saw us and came running over. She fluttered around Stalker, who was still carrying Aria.

"Oh my God, is she alright? What happened? We saw smoke."

"The house caught on fire somehow. We almost didn't hear her screaming. Not sure why she wasn't doing it at first," I explained as we kept walking. Eventually, we made it to the bikes and the van so we could lay Aria in the backseat of the van.

"Why isn't she awake? Do we need to take her to a hospital?" Raina asked anxiously.

"Baby, she inhaled a lot of smoke and so did Slash, since he went in to find her. In her case, she wasn't breathing when he first got her out. Yeah, she probably should go to the hospital, but we can't chance it, at least not down here. Let's head toward home. If she gets worse, we'll find a hospital, but if we do that, we can't stay with her. We'll drop her at the ER and leave. We can't raise any suspicions or answer questions about where we found her or why we were there."

She didn't look happy, but she nodded. She turned around and rushed over to throw her arms around Slash. He made a grunting sound in surprise.

"Thank you, thank you for going after her. She saved me and she knew they'd kill her if they figured it out. They've been cruel to her, I think. She's not there because she wanted to be. She denied being an old lady or bunny for them."

He patted her on the back then let go. "You're welcome. Now, I don't know about all of you, but I'm ready to get the hell out of here."

Taking our cues from that, we got situated. Raina in the van with Walker and Aria and the rest of us got on our bikes. We cautiously made our way back to the road then toward home. We stayed alert since we didn't have any idea which direction the rest of the Cannibals took when they left. Fortunately, or maybe it was unfortunately, depending on how you looked at it, we didn't meet them. It took us close to an hour and a half to make it back home. I kept thinking how we had so much to do and the day was already half over. However, before any of that, I had to make sure Raina was really fine and settle her with Belle and Byron.

When we stopped at the clubhouse, the door opened and a wave of people came spilling out. In the lead was Byron and Belle, no surprise there. I noticed

Payne, Loki, Ace, and Vex were back. Which meant Parker was out in the crematorium. In the back of the bunch was Diego and Zev.

Helping Raina out of the van, I noticed that Aria was awake. She looked scared stiff and was looking around with wide eyes at all the people and the noise. I saw Demon talking to Zara. She was trying to fuss over his arm, but he was pushing her toward the van. It was pandemonium for several minutes, as greetings were made, conditions checked out, injuries cataloged and such. Finally, Bull had to call everyone to attention and issued orders.

"Demon, Iceman, Slash, Raina, and Aria to the clinic room, so Zara can check you out. The rest of you, check in your weapons and equipment. After we know everyone is okay, we'll be paying a visit to our guest, then we'll have church. It's gonna be a long day and evening, so let's get started."

Raina tried to say she didn't need to be checked out, but I wouldn't listen and neither would Zara. She was marched to the clinic room we had set up for this kind of thing in the clubhouse. Zara treated us from there when she could, rather than going into town to the main clinic. There were fewer questions from nosy people.

Zev slithered up next to me as we walked to the clinic room. "How did it go?"

"We only found part of them. We'll know more after church. Right now, I'm glad Raina and Belle are home and we'll get our information."

"Let me know if you need any help. I can see how your method comes in handy sometimes."

"Thanks, appreciate it. Let me go in here so I can see what Zara has to say. I'll be back out in a bit." He waved me off, so I could go in with my woman. I had to be sure there wasn't anything she hadn't told us about her captivity.

We were finally getting down to business. I was relieved to find out that Raina was perfectly fine. They hadn't done anything to her or Belle. Overall, they ignored them except when it was time to feed them or take them to the bathroom. She shared what little Aria had said to her. As for Aria, she was still in shock and not saying much. Zara didn't think at the moment she needed to go to the hospital, which was good. We'd give her some time to recover, but not too long. We couldn't afford to wait. We needed to know everything we could about the Cannibals and their plans. We were hoping what Diego couldn't provide us she could.

Demon and Iceman's bullet grazes were cleaned and patched up by Zara. Slash was bouncing back fast. He hadn't had as much smoke inhaled as Aria. We tried to get him to rest, but he wanted to be in on the questioning of Parker and Diego. On top of wanting that, he seemed to be very concerned about Aria and that she would be made comfortable while she recovered. Raina promised she'd stay with her while we went to see Parker. He was chosen to be our first conversation.

Walking into our special place, I met my cousin's angry gaze with a smirking one of my own. I had never once gone to see him in prison. Looking at him, he'd definitely aged and not in a good way. He looked way older than me. His hair had started to thin on top. He was sporting a small pot belly. I guess they ate better in prison than I thought. His skin looked dry, and he had deep lines all over his face. Hell, Bull and Bear were in their fifties and they didn't look nearly as old as he did and he was only thirty.

"I should've known you were still a part of them. What's the matter? Can't let me have even a moment outside of prison without you ruining it?" he asked with a sneer on his face.

"Don't play stupid with us, Parker. You know exactly why you're here. You sent a letter not long ago to Raina and in it you swore revenge on us and her. All because of your own stupidity. We wanted to talk to you when you got out to make sure you weren't actually dumb enough to go through with it. Surely, you realize there's no way you can harm us or her without it coming back on you?"

"Ah, so you and my whore of an ex-wife have been talking, have you? Did she show you the letter? What proof do you have other than her word? And let's face it, her words aren't good for shit. She gave her word to honor, love and obey me no matter what and at the first sign of trouble, she divorced me and took my kid away from her grandparents. Mom and Dad haven't seen Belle in ten years."

"Jesus Christ, you are delusional, aren't you? She didn't leave you at the first sign of trouble. You got in it more than once. She stayed. When you went to prison, she had enough. You weren't going to change and let's face it, you cheated on her more than once. Why should she stay with you? And I didn't need to see the letter. Raina isn't a liar like you are."

"I would've never gotten into that mess if it wasn't for her and this club, you especially. If you hadn't gone behind my back and convinced the club to kick me out, then I wouldn't have had to find other ways to make money. If she hadn't gotten knocked up, I wouldn't have had to make money anyway I could to support her and Belle. You were all jealous of me," he partially yelled.

Hearing him talk showed me he truly was far from in touch with reality. The way he looked and sounded told me he actually believed the nonsense coming out of his mouth. I exchanged amazed looks with my brothers. They shook their heads and rolled their eyes at me. He saw them.

"Why did you kick me out? I was doing my job as a prospect," he said angrily.

"No, you weren't. And it wasn't Joker who suggested we kick you out. In fact, we kept you around longer than we would've someone else, because you're his cousin. You complained all the time. We'd go looking for you and couldn't find you. You'd tell us when we asked that you were home with Belle and Raina, but we found out that was a lie. You didn't like to take direction or criticism. You argued with us. However, the one that really pisses us off is you were cheating on your wife!" Bull snarled at him.

"That pisses you off the most, why? You're bikers. I know none of you had old ladies then, but since, I bet you have them now. Don't lie and tell me you're faithful. Fucking whoever you want is one of the best things about being a biker. The pussy just flocks to you," he said with a grin.

As much as I wanted to punch him, it wasn't me who did it. It was Bear, although all the married guys moved toward him. "You little worthless cocksucker, you don't know shit about being a biker! Our families, including our brotherhood family, means the world to us. I have a wife, kids, and a grandkid now and I'd never think of cheating on Ilara. Neither would any of us in this room who've claimed someone. You make me sick. I knew you were a weasel ten years ago, but I had no idea how much of a lowlife you were."

Parker spit on the floor a spat of blood. He wasn't smiling now. He scanned the room and didn't find a single friendly face.

"Before we get into the big talk, I want to know something. Why the fuck did you have your parents lie and say they didn't know where Raina went and they had no way to reach her when she left Hunters Creek? Why lie to her parents and tell them they'd get a cut of some supposed big stash of money you have from the things you stole? You didn't get much of anything from those thefts. What you did have, you spent. Even if you were mad at her for divorcing you, Belle is your daughter. She deserved to have family around her.

Maybe not your parents or Raina's, but the rest of us and Raina's grandparents."

"Who said I was the one who told them to lie? Dad and Mom decided they didn't want anyone here having contact with Raina. Why should she keep her family when I couldn't? As for Rudy and Gwen, well they believed what they wanted to believe. I never told them there was any money. As for Belle, I'm not even sure now that she's my kid. Raina could've lied and been sleeping with someone else for all I know."

I didn't hold back the roar that welled up inside me as I lunged at him. I drove my fists as hard as I could into his stomach then both sides of his ribs. The air rushed out of him and he vomited on the floor.

"Motherfucker, that's for daring to say she would lie or cheat. You know damn well, she only ever slept with you. You took her goddamn virginity, asshole. As for not telling her parents that, then you had your parents do it."

He gagged a couple of times before he could answer me. Our intent was to question him, put the fear of God into him, along with a severe beating, so he'd know not to bother any of us. However, the more he talked the more I wanted his head.

"Screw you, Joker. You're just jealous she was mine. I saw the way you looked at her. You wanted her, although she's probably screwed so many men by now, even you wouldn't want her," he said hoarsely. Leaning close, I saw him flinch, which filled me with satisfaction. The next part made it immense.

"You're right. When I met her I was pissed that you met her first. She was always too damn good for you, but unlike you, I would never try and take a woman away from her husband. She wasn't then nor now is she a whore. Well, you might've cost me ten years that we could've been together, but not anymore. She's mine. Belle is mine. And I'll kill any fucker who tries to hurt them in any way. All I can say is she seems very thankful she has a man who loves her, won't cheat and is adventurous and ensures her pleasure in bed not just his. There haven't been any men except for me. I thought you had skill and moves even at your age, but I was so wrong. You didn't even know the basics, boy."

The guys all burst out laughing and jeering at him when I lobbed that verbal grenade at him. I knew attacking his masculinity would not only infuriate him, but it would also maybe loosen his tongue. Parker had always been someone who when you got him angry enough, he'd tell stuff he shouldn't.

He tried to kick me, but I was too far away for him to reach. I laughed hard and smirked at him as I did. He was tied to the chair, so there was no way he could take a swing at me. He was so mad he could only make growling noises and sputter. I let him do that for about a minute then I pushed again.

"I bet he didn't even have a plan when he got out. That letter was just him mouthing off, acting like he was a big bad someone. He wouldn't dare to try and get revenge on us. Guys, we don't need to worry about him. I bet he'll tuck his tail between his legs and scurry home to Mommy and Daddy and cry to them about how mean we are. If we're lucky, they'll be so ashamed of him, they'll all leave town."

"You wish. You wait until you see what I have in store for you," he yelled.

"Why don't you wow us with your great plans, oh mighty one?" I said with a laugh.

He sat there mute. I guess we'd have to do this the hard way after all, perfect. I nodded to Payne. When he approached him, I saw Parker flinch then he tried to pull away. I guess he was still feeling the "talk" they had. Grinning evilly, Payne untied his arms from the back of the chair and jerked him to his feet. He shoved him into Tank's hands. Tank dragged him to the table in front of the crematory doors. When he was a prospect, he wasn't ever here. He eyed it but had no idea what it was. Tank threw him down on the table and secured him tightly to it.

My phone rang, interrupting my next taunt. Taking out my phone, I saw it was Raina. Answering it, I hoped nothing was wrong. "Baby, what's wrong?"

"I know you're busy and I wouldn't call but I thought you would want to know this," she said rapidly.

"Go ahead. What do I need to know?"

"Aria has started to talk. She overheard Diego mention you guys going to talk to Parker. She got agitated and asked if he was the guy getting out of jail soon. I said yes. According to her, he had some kind of deal going on with the Cannibals. They were going to help him get his revenge."

"How does she know that?"

"She overheard them talking and there's a tie between him and her. You have to come back here and talk to her. She's scared."

Fury at this news and the possibility he was what got Raina and Belle kidnapped began to rise up. "I'll be right there. Don't let her go anywhere."

As I hung up, I faced my brothers. "It seems Aria has something to tell us. About how Parker and the Cannibals were working together to get revenge. It seems Parker was the one who had them kidnap Belle and Raina."

They swore. Parker gave me a startled look. "Kidnapping? I don't know what you're talking about. I didn't have anyone kidnapped."

"I see you don't deny knowing the Cannibals," I shot back.

"I-I don't know them. Who are they?"

This I knew he was lying about. He had a tell when he lied. His right eye would twitch ever so slightly. If you weren't looking for it, you'd miss it. His eye was twitching, although it didn't when he said he had nothing to do with the kidnapping. Interesting. As much as I wanted to finish with him then send him off, this news changed our plan. I needed to speak to Aria and Diego first then finish with him.

"I need someone to stay here with him. I need to go talk to Aria and find out what she knows."

"Iceman and I will stay with him. Go find out what the woman knows then we can finish with this piece of shit," Renegade stated.

"Thanks, I'll be back as soon as I can. The rest of you, you can either hang here, go home, or come with me."

As expected they wanted to go see what we didn't know, so we left our volunteers to listen to Parker whining and bitching. I didn't envy them as we hurried back to the clubhouse. I had the feeling Aria would shed a lot of light on things. Maybe even more than Diego and Parker could.

Raina: Chapter 21

As we waited for Joker and maybe the others to get back to the clubhouse, I watched Aria. She was so upset, she could barely sit still. She had been upset the whole time they had been gone. I knew she was afraid, and I tried my best to reassure her she was safe with us. I don't think she could bring herself to believe it. It wasn't until she overheard Diego that she said something and insisted she be allowed to speak to Joker. Finding out Parker and the Cannibals weren't strangers, and he was the cause of the kidnapping, made me want to go beat the hell out of him myself. When Joker and the others came through the clubhouse door, I swear she shrank in on herself. She went pale and backed away from them. I caught her arm.

"Not one of them will hurt you, Aria. Just tell them what you know. Anything is helpful. That's all they want to do is help. They'll help you."

"Why would they do that? They don't know me. What will they want in exchange for help? I fell for that once and I'm not going to do it again. I'll tell them what I know then I'm out of here."

"They won't ask anything in exchange. What do you mean, you fell for it once? Where will you go? Do you have any family you can go to, who will help you?

Keep you safe?"

She snorted. "Family is what got me into this hell. I don't know where I'll go, but as long as it's far away from the Cannibals, it'll be fine. Hopefully, I can disappear and none of them ever find me. If they do, I'm dead. Maybe it would've been better to leave me in that house and let the fire have me."

"Like hell it was! What kind of talk is that? I don't want to hear you say that again," came a very gruff and angry reply. I jumped. She jumped and cowered. I gave Slash a stunned look. I'd never seen him close to angry. His face was scowling something fierce.

"Slash, you're scaring her," I admonished him. I saw that he was trying to tone it down, but she wasn't relaxing. She moved even further away from him.

"Darlin', I didn't mean to scare you. I'm sorry. Please don't look at me like that. I just hate the idea you think it's better to be dead. Why don't you sit down and tell us your story? Joker said you have something to tell us about Parker and the Cannibals," he said sweetly.

"I'll tell him my story. Once I'm done, I want to leave here. Can I do that?"

"Aria, my name is Bull. I'm the president of this club. I can promise you none of my people will harm you. Raina said you weren't with the Cannibals of your free will. Is that true?"

She jerkily nodded her head yes.

"Okay, then let's sit down here and talk. I'd like all my guys to hear it, so we don't have to waste precious time repeating it. We still have Parker to deal with and the Cannibals who got away. Can you start by telling us first what you overheard about Parker and them?"

She cautiously took a seat, which Bull pulled out for her. As she sat down, he took the seat next to her. I thought Joker would sit on the other side of her, but it was Slash who went to sit down there. When she edged away from him, he sighed then moved over a seat, so Joker could sit next to her. She wasn't totally relaxed with any of them. I stayed nearby, hoping I might give her some reassurance. I gave her an encouraging smile and nod when she glanced at me. That got her talking.

"The Cannibals started talking a while back about something big happening in a few months. There was a guy who was coming up for his parole hearing and they thought for sure he was going to get out. When he did, they were to work with him on getting revenge on another club. A club that did him and others wrong."

"Is that when you heard the name Parker? Did they say what that revenge was going to be or why they were willing to help him? How did they know him?" Bull asked her.

"No, at first, they never said a name. It wasn't until a couple weeks ago I heard them say the name Parker for the first time. What the revenge was going to be, no one said either. However, it seems that they weren't supposed to make a move on the woman, Raina, until after Parker got out."

"Then why did they kidnap her and Belle before he did?" Joker asked.

"Bastard, the Cannibals' president, had information from inside that Parker might not be trustworthy and in order to make sure he didn't welch on the agreement, they wanted insurance, so they decided to take her early. None of them said anything about taking the little girl, so I think that was just bad luck."

"Information from the inside? Who? You didn't say how they know Parker," Bull prompted.

"His cellmate for the past several years is how they know Parker and he was the one to tell them not to trust him."

"What's the name of this cellmate? Do you know?" Joker asked.

She glanced down at her hands, which were clenched on the table, then back up as she nodded yes. "His name is Josiah Canedo. He's a member of the Devil's Cannibals."

I jumped and so did she, as Bull, Bear and several others swore and exchanged looks of disbelief.

"Who is Josiah Canedo?" I asked.

"Josiah was a goddamn prospect with us about fifteen or so years ago. He was worse than Parker and we soon kicked his ass out of the club. The last I heard was he left town, and no one knew where he went or what happened to him. Good riddance, I thought. How long has he been a Cannibal and how long has he been in prison? For what?" Bear asked swiftly.

"I-I don't know how long he's been with them. I got the impression it's been a long time. He's been in prison thirteen years. He was found guilty of second-degree murder while distributing cocaine. He killed one of the dealers and it happened to be that the police were doing a sting operation on the dealer at the time. He got twenty years for it."

"How do you know all this, Aria? About Josiah and the rest? Raina said you claimed not to be an old lady or bunny. Why the hell would they talk freely around you? Why did you help her escape?" Joker asked. He sounded suspicious. The others were giving her dubious looks, like they didn't know if they should trust her or not. Instantly, I felt the tension in the room grow, and she looked sick.

"I'm not an old lady or bunny. I'd never go near them if I had a choice. I helped her because no one deserved to be held at their mercy. I knew whatever they had planned would be awful. When she told me she had a daughter, I knew I had to help her, even if it did sign my death warrant. They talked freely because they didn't see me as a threat. I wasn't gonna go tell anyone."

"Why didn't they worry you'd take off and tell someone? Maybe go to the police?" Slash asked her out of the blue.

She didn't answer him. As she sat there staring off at the wall, Payne slammed his fist on the table. "Answer us, damnit!" he said.

He didn't raise his voice much, but the effect

along with his fist electrified her. She came up out of her chair and ran for the door. I heard someone swear. They came to their feet and were after her. Slash was the one to catch her. She fought him, kicking and clawing, as he brought her back and sat her down in the chair. She tried to get back up, but he held her down by the shoulders.

"Calm the hell down. Just answer the questions," he murmured to her.

"Fuck you. Do you think you can hurt me more or do anything to me they haven't done already? Do your worst? I knew you were just like them. All clubs are murdering, raping, lying goddamn animals. You need to get your daughter and run," she hissed at me.

"Aria, we're not at all like them. I'm sorry Payne scared you. He won't do that again. He's our enforcer. He only wants to protect the club and our families. Were you there because they took you as insurance against someone else? How long have you been with them?" Bull asked her softly.

"I was taken for my supposed protection. What a crock of shit. I've been anything but protected, so excuse me if I don't believe in MC protection. It's an excuse to hold you against your will and do whatever the hell you want to a person, to make someone's life not worth living."

"Did they make your life not worth living? Did they rape you?" Slash asked out of the blue. I know I wanted to know if they had, but I didn't expect anyone to bluntly ask her.

"What they did is none of your business," was all she said back.

Slash opened his mouth to ask more but Joker stopped him. "Do you know where the others went today? The ones who left before you helped Raina escape. Thank you by the way."

"Six of them and two prospects left to go pick up Parker. He was released today. That's what I heard them talking about right before they left. Bastard went with them. You should've waited and hit the clubhouse when they were all there. Now, you have to worry about them coming for you when they see what happened."

"Do they have another safe house? How long have they been in Soddy Daisy? Diego said he heard of them two years ago. Were you with them before that?" Bear asked.

"I have no idea where they were before now. The club existed is all I know. I've been with them for a year and a half. I can't help you with the rest. I never heard of or met any of them before eighteen months ago."

"It's okay. You've given us enough to get started on. We appreciate it. A few more questions, then you can rest. Who asked them to protect you? And where is that person now? We can get a hold of him or her if you want," Bull offered kindly. Which made her ugly laugh worse.

"You think giving me to the person who asked for their help is helping me? God, that's rich. The person who asked them to protect me is the same one who told them to keep me at their clubhouse, no matter what they had to do. That as long as I kept breathing, that's all he cared about. And you can't give me to him because he's still serving twenty years in prison."

"Are you telling us Josiah is behind your imprisonment?" Demon asked, incredulously.

"Ding ding, give the man a prize. Yes. Josiah is the one who sent them to take me from my home in the middle of the night and to hold me in their godforsaken clubhouse in the woods. He said it was for my protection. I don't need protection other than from him and his evil club."

"Why? You're what twenty-three? twenty-four?" Demon asked. She nodded. "If he's been in prison for thirteen years, you'd have been ten. That doesn't make sense."

"I never heard of him until a year and a half ago after they took me. It seems that my mama forgot to tell me some things about my dad. I knew he was worthless and a manwhore. She spent a week with him when she was young and then he left town. A biker on his way through the state. He left something behind when he did. She raised me as a single mom. She didn't know where he was."

"Well, Josiah isn't old enough to be your dad, sweetheart. He's only thirty-five or so. If they told you he was, that's a lie," Bull told her.

"But he's old enough to be my older half-brother. Apparently, when our daddy died, he made a deathbed confession. It was all sweet and shit, I bet. His son was at his bedside. I guess being in the same prison comes in handy. He told Josiah that he had a half-sister and where to find me. According to what I've been told, he made Josiah swear he'd look out for me. Josiah's solution was to get his club to kidnap me and hold me prisoner until he gets out, which isn't for at least the full twenty years."

"You're his damn sister and he let them do whatever they wanted to you?" Slash almost yelled as he came to his feet.

"You think I'm weak, don't you? That I should've fought and found a way to escape like Raina did. Well, I tried. And each time I did, they caught me, brought me back, and I was punished. The last time, they decided to slow me down, so I couldn't run or at least not as fast."

"Oh no, your leg," I whispered.

She nodded then pulled up her pants. I thought it was weird to be dressed in long pants in the humid summer. Now I saw why she was. Her left lower leg was badly scarred. It looked like something had ripped it open. The guys all growled in outrage.

"What the hell did they do?" Slash asked. I thought it was weird he kept asking so many questions and getting more upset than the others. They were angry, I could tell, but not like him.

"When I ran, they caught me and brought me back. Ox decided, as enforcer, he had a good way to reinforce the idea of me not running while inflicting pain. He had the prospects tie me down on the ground using stakes and then he ran over my leg a couple of times with his bike. I don't really know how many times since I ended up passing out from the excruciating pain. When I woke up, my leg was crushed. They sure didn't take me to have it fixed, so it healed like this. He got his wish. The pain and the inability to run kept me from trying anymore. After I helped Raina escape, I knew what my fate was, but I decided I'd steal their pleasure in killing me."

"You're the one who started the fire in the basement. You did it so you'd die," Bull said softly. The look of compassion on his face was heartwarming and heartbreaking at the same time.

"I did. I hoped when I heard the fight upstairs, that someone was finally taking them out, but I couldn't be sure. It was my dream that whoever wasn't shot and killed would somehow burn up with me. Now, you've put me in the spot of not knowing where to go to find safety. As long as any of them and Josiah are alive, I'll never be safe. I don't want to live like that. You should've left me to die."

Slash yelled, "fuck," as he kicked over a chair. He barged out the door slamming it shut behind him. She watched him go with a stunned look on her face. The men looked upset. I felt sick. I could only imagine how she'd suffered. I had no doubt they must've raped her more than a few times plus beatings, then to cripple her on top of it. I wanted to vomit.

"Sweetheart, you don't know how much we wish we had known about you and could've saved you sooner. However, I swear to God that you won't be left to them. You will be protected. I hate to leave you like this, but I need to talk to my men and Parker. I want you to stay with Raina. If you need anything, let her or Walker and Gavin, our prospects, know. They'll be here for your protection," Bull told her.

"You mean my jailers."

"I hope you won't think like that, but they won't let you leave. It won't be safe until we deal with the rest of the Cannibals and your brother. While we're gone, write down the names of the men who got away and everything you know about them. We'll need it to find them, since they have no clubhouse to go back to. We'll be back as soon as we can," he added.

She didn't say anything else. They spent a few minutes talking to the prospects. Before they left again, Joker came over and gave me a tender kiss. I saw her watching it with a puzzled look on her face. Maybe while they were gone, I could work on her and change her mind about the Warriors. They were nothing like the Cannibals and they would keep her safe.

Joker:

I know we all felt sick when we rode back to the crematorium. Slash had been outside pacing when we came out. He didn't say a word as we got on our bikes to ride back to see Parker again. Before going inside, I stopped them.

"I know the original plan was to put the fear of God into him then let him know what would happen to him if he made a move on any of us. That's not going to be enough. To be with men like the Cannibals, he's rotten and I have no doubt that not only will he not stay away, but he'd do just as awful things as they did to Aria to Raina or any of the women. My vote is we finish questioning him and then Parker just doesn't ever show up after getting out of prison. I assume no one saw you pick him up?"

"No, we made sure of it. He was walking to meet them somewhere. All we knew was he was going to meet someone who had to be his ride out of the area. There's not much of anything around the prison, mostly farmland. It's about twelve miles outside the main town where the prison is," Payne told us with a smile.

"Good. That makes it safer for us. As far as anyone knows, he took off and is in the wind. He'll be seen as violating his parole and a fugitive. Do you agree?"

"I agree. I didn't think we'd have to go to this point with it, but after hearing what Aria said and knowing he had a deal with the Cannibals, I can't see another way. However, first, we need to know what he was using as collateral to get them to help him. I doubt it was friendship alone or that they both have reasons to hate us," Bull added.

"Agreed. Okay, let's get this done and then when it's time, I'll do the deed. Joker, he's your kin, even if he doesn't act like it. You leave that part up to us," Payne said.

"I appreciate the offer, but I'd like to see it done. He stopped being kin to me a long time ago. Any residual feelings I might've had are long gone," I assured them.

With that settled, we entered. We found him as we left him. Iceman and Renegade were sitting over against the wall on a couple of chairs. They were talking when we came in. Seeing us, they got up and came over.

"He's been whining and trying to bribe us to let him go, but that's it. Glad you're back. I was about to stick my foot in his mouth to shut him up," Renegade said in disgust.

"Thanks for staying with him. We'll fill you in on the rest later, but for now, we need to finish this up," Bull informed them.

We gathered around him. He saw our grim expressions. "What? What happened?"

"Tell us about your cellmate, Josiah, and why he agreed to help you get revenge on us and Raina? What did you have that he wanted, Parker? And don't lie or play stupid. We know for a fact you have been cellmates for years and his club, the Devil's Cannibals, were going to help you. We also know that he didn't trust you and had his guys kidnap Raina and Belle before you got out," I told him.

"I don't—"

"Don't lie," I said. "Payne, the next time he doesn't answer me truthfully, I want you to take a hunk of flesh off him with your favorite knife," I told Payne.

He got a satisfied grin on his face and pulled out his knife. It was huge and put the fear of pain in more than one person over the years. Jayla and their son Storm might have mellowed him in some ways, but not in this. He was still very invested in his love of pain when it came to torturing enemies. I heard Parker whimper.

"He and I started talking after we became cell mates five years ago. He found out why I was in there and I told him how you all screwed me over. He told me you guys did the same to him about several years earlier, but he left and found a club that wasn't full of pussies. His words not mine," he quickly said, when Payne started toward him.

"Go on," Bull prompted.

"Anyway, over the years I've helped him and he helped me. When we found out it was looking good that I would get parole, he said we could get revenge on all of you and his club would help. I agreed. They were supposed to wait until I was out then, we were to plan the kidnapping and how to take you all out. Josiah assured me that you didn't know the Cannibals exist anymore. Something about disbanding but in reality they only left Tennessee. I had no idea they took her or Belle early."

"What did you promise him in exchange for helping you?" I asked.

"Nothing."

Payne's hand snaked out and in two quick slices, he cut a small chunk out of Parker's arm. He howled in pain. "Stop! Stop, I'll tell you. I made him think that I had money hidden from the heists I did before going to prison. I promised him half of it."

"You lied to him. There's no money. What were you going to do when he asked for his share?" Bear asked him.

"I was gonna figure that out later. If nothing else, my parents would get me the money. I just needed the Cannibals help and he wouldn't do it for nothing. He would've gone after you but not her."

"What was your plan for Raina and Belle? To kill them?" I snarled.

"No, not kill them. I was going to send them somewhere else. Where they had no family or friends."

"You mean you were going to sell them, isn't that what you mean?" Payne hissed.

Parker shook his head no, but the guilt was written on his face. I let out a roar, then wrapped my hands around his throat. He gagged and fought for air as I choked the hell out of him. It took Payne, Bear, and Player to get me off him before I killed him. I was panting in rage.

"Finish it. Tell us the rest before I kill you."

"That's it. I didn't have plans after that. I thought with you guys gone, the Cannibals would let me join them. I have no idea what they had planned other than to destroy the club for kicking Josiah out."

"What about his sister, Aria? What were his plans for her? He had his club hold her hostage. Why?" Slash snarled.

"He didn't say. All he kept on about was she would pay off big when he got out. Something about his dad. He told them to keep her there no matter what."

"And beating, raping and crippling her was fine by him," Slash added.

"I don't know. I wasn't there for his conversations with them when they came. He never told me that part. When I asked, he said it wasn't my concern."

"Do you know where they went when they left Tennessee years ago? When did they come back here?" Bull asked.

"It was somewhere in Kansas around Topeka, I think. They moved back a couple of years ago."

From there, we asked a few more questions, but

they were insignificant and he had no new information. For good measure, Payne got to torture him a bit, just to make sure. Growing tired of this and knowing he was merely a pawn in a much bigger game, I signaled to the others it was time to finish it. As much as I might want to torture him more, he wasn't really worth it. We had work to do and wasting time on him wasn't something we wanted to do.

I was the one who did it in the end, much to Payne's regret, I know. I could've slit my dear cousin's throat, or shot him, and called it a day. However, I needed to know he suffered at least a bit more before he died, and to have him see his life flash before his eyes and maybe realize how wasted and worthless it was. In order to do that, I finished what I started earlier. I wrapped my hands around his neck and slowly choked him to death. It was strangely satisfying to watch him turn colors and the blood vessels in his eyes burst, as he tried to fight for air. I felt the hyoid bone give not long before he breathed his last gasp.

Washing my hands afterward, to get the feel of his skin off mine, the guys got the crematory fire going. As soon as it was hot enough, he'd be tossed in and burned to ash. Those ashes would then be taken and scattered all over the county. No one would be able to piece his body back together.

On the ride back to the clubhouse, all I could think about was the upcoming fight with the remainder of the Cannibals, and the next steps in my relationship with Raina. I know she said to wait a while before bringing up marriage again, but I couldn't. Not after almost losing her and Belle. The worst she could say was no. If she did, I'd work on convincing her to say yes the next time I asked. A once-a-month proposal would wear her down, eventually.

Raina: Epilogue - Six Months Later

Today was a bittersweet day for all of us but especially for me. It was the end of a very crazy six months for me, the club, and our loved ones. There had been lots of ups and downs during them. On the positive side, two more babies were added to the Hunters Creek family. Maverick and Rylan welcomed baby Autumn in September, just a couple of weeks after my rescue from the Cannibals. Tank and Brynlee's son, Ethan, was born two months later, in November.

Belle and I became fully accustomed to our new family and loved living at the compound. We had to stay on lockdown for a while, as the club worked to locate and take down the remainder of the Cannibals and deal with Josiah. As part of that, Aria was freed and her life had taken some unexpected turns as a result. She was finally free to have a life. Over the months we'd grown very close and became the best of friends. Another person's life took a turn for the better too. Diego was granted prospect status with the club for helping me and Belle so much. He was like a new man.

During this time, Joker asked me three times to marry him before I said yes. I couldn't say no to a man who did everything in his power to make me and my daughter happy. He promised he'd keep asking me monthly until I saw the light. I'll admit, I pushed it to three times before agreeing just to see if he'd ask more than twice. When he did, I couldn't say no. As soon as I did, wedding preparations began. We set the wedding for the following June.

However, the best plans often don't go as we expect. In January, Granddaddy became very sick and was admitted to the hospital. The doctors said his time was near, and they didn't know how much longer he'd be with us. That's when Joker made me love him even more. He knew how much it meant to me for Granddaddy to be at our wedding, even if he couldn't walk me down the aisle, so he brought everyone together who were crucial to the actual ceremony and surprised me with a wedding at Granddaddy's bedside.

Some might not think that was romantic, but it was to me. It was a wonderful and beautiful day for us. The smile on Granddaddy's face as we watched us exchange vows was the best picture of all. When he got out of the hospital a few weeks later, he came home on hospice. We held our reception, at his insistence after that. He even came and spent a couple of hours, then went back to the house with his caregiver. The hospice staff were amazing and made sure his every need was taken care of.

It was painful to watch him get weaker and struggle more and more to breathe. There were many nights I'd go to bed and cry in Joker's arms. He was my rock and I wouldn't have made it through without him. Just like I wasn't able to make it through today without him or our extended family.

Watching them lower the casket into the ground made me cry, but they weren't all tears of sadness. There were some mixed in there that were tears of happiness. For one, I was happy Granddaddy was no longer suffering. Another reason for my happiness was that he was now reunited with my MeMe, Mabel. She was the love of his life and he had never recovered fully from her death. He was laid to rest beside her. The club had gone and ordered a brand-new headstone. It was much fancier than the old one and proudly displayed their names and *Beloved Mother and Father* and *Beloved Grandmother and Grandfather* on it.

The one thing I could've done without today was my parents. They hadn't bothered to try and see him or even visit him in the hospital, but they thought it was appropriate to show up at the funeral. I knew it was just to make people around town think they were decent, loving people. I ignored them during the viewing, and during the minister's graveside speech. I would've gone on ignoring them until the end, but they couldn't leave it alone. Which is how I was now facing them over the freshly dug grave. They were standing in front of me staring hard at me and Joker.

"Well, aren't you going to say anything, Raina? Don't you think ignoring us is petty? We're your parents. You're the one who kept us from my father the last several years of his life," my dad said snidely. I felt Joker tense. I knew he was a second away from annihilating my dad. Any other time, I'd say go for it, but not here, not today.

"What would you like me to say? And I never kept you from seeing him or MeMe. It was their choice not to associate with you after I left. It was your choice not to bother coming to see him when he was in the hospital. I know you knew he was in there, because a message was left on your answering machine informing you. Joker left it himself. So why bother coming here today and acting like the grieving son and daughter-in-law?"

"You've always been an ungrateful child. We never did anything to you. You're the one who left and stayed away for years," my mom said back with a frown on her face.

"I never came back because you hounded me to marry Parker, then you hounded me not to divorce him. You chose to tell people I moved without a forwarding address or number, which was a damn lie. Let's just leave well enough alone. I'm heading home. Feel free to stay or not. My husband and daughter are ready to go, along with my real family." I pointed to the club.

"Yeah, I heard you embarrassed yourself, and married Parker's cousin. People are talking about it all over town. They ask us why you would ever do something like that. Speaking of Parker, have you heard from him since he got out of prison? I would've thought he'd want to see his daughter. Or are you stopping him?" Dad asked coolly.

"No, I haven't seen him. Have PJ and Bernie? After all, they're his parents. They would know where he is, not me. Why? Are you worried that he's not going to give you your cut of the fictitious money he didn't have that he promised you? Sorry, but you're not coming into any money," I said bitchily.

"I wouldn't count on that," Mom said with a smile.

That's when Joker said something. "If you're hoping Byron left you his house or any of his money, think again. He made sure years ago to cut you two out completely. Everything goes to Raina. We're still deciding what to do with it all. The lawyer already spoke to us. I had no idea Byron was such an investor all these years. The money he left will come in very handy for Belle and our other children."

They both gasped and gave us disbelieving looks. "There's no way he did that. I'm his only child, his son. No matter how angry he might be, he would've never left me with nothing. What did you do? Bribe his lawyer to lie?" Dad asked Joker angrily.

"I didn't need to do that. I'm not like you. It's all legal and the dates show he did it years ago. I had nothing to do with it. I hope you weren't counting on that money from him or Parker. Babe, it's time to go. You've been out in this cold long enough and so has Belle. Rudy, Gwen, please stay away from my family. I won't be as nice or tolerant as Byron was." His glare told them he wasn't kidding. We left them standing there looking panicked.

It was a quiet ride back to the clubhouse, where the club was holding the wake. In honor of Granddaddy's wishes, we were making it a celebration. He told us he didn't want a bunch of sad faces. He wanted music, drinks, and dancing, so that's what we did. Dad and Mom didn't show, thank God. It was hours before the last person left and we could relax. Several of the Warriors' friends' clubs had been here as well along with Dublin Falls. It has been wonderful to get to meet all of them over the past six months as well.

We were shooed away and told to leave the clean up to the others. I kissed and hugged and thanked so many people it was a blur. When we got back to the house, Belle was out so hard, she never opened her eyes as I undressed her and put her in her pajamas. After a long hot shower with my husband, I crawled into bed with him. I snuggled into his arms. He gave me a tender kiss.

"How're you feeling, my Queen? I hope you didn't tire yourself too much. You should've taken that nap earlier," he said as he rubbed his hand back and forth across my stomach. I smiled at him.

This was the one final thing we gave Granddaddy before he died. The news that I was pregnant. I was only about six weeks along and the baby wasn't due until November, but he'd known, and had been so happy. He cried when we told him and told us that if we had a boy, not to name him Byron. Apparently, he'd never liked his name. I didn't make any promises.

"I'm fine, Aaron. You worry too much."

"It's not too much when you, this baby and Belle are my world. I love the club, but they're not the ones I need to be able to breathe every day. I'm sorry today was made harder by your parents, baby. If they wouldn't have caused a huge stink, I'd have kicked them out at the funeral home."

"They're the least of my worries. Besides, the look on my dad's face when you told him he wasn't inheriting anything made up for it."

He laughed which made me giggle. I couldn't stop myself from giving him a kiss. Which as it always did with us, caused us both to become hot and bothered. I slid my hand underneath the covers and cupped his hard cock.

He groaned. "I'm trying to be good, Raina. You need sleep, not me pouncing on you.

"No, what I need is my husband to pounce on me and show me again how much he loves me and to be able to show you how much I love you. A lovemaking session will be the perfect thing to send me off to sleep. If you do that, I promise to stay in bed all day tomorrow."

I knew I had him by the smirk and sexy smile he gave me right before he growled and pounced on me. I laughed, but it soon turned into a moan as he began to push me toward a tremendous orgasm. My life really had turned around in ways I never imagined. There was nothing better than being Joker's Queen.

The End Until Slash's Dove HCAW Book 11

Made in the USA
Columbia, SC
21 October 2023